Kokopelli's Thunder

Fall of the Anasazi

Sean M. Cordry

iUniverse LLC
Bloomington

KOKOPELLI'S THUNDER
Fall of the Anasazi

iUniverse books may be ordered through booksellers or by contacting:

iUniverse LLC
1663 Liberty Drive
Bloomington, IN 47403
www.iuniverse.com
1-800-Authors (1-800-288-4677)

Because of the dynamic nature of the Internet, any web addresses or links contained in this book may have changed since publication and may no longer be valid. The views expressed in this work are solely those of the author and do not necessarily reflect the views of the publisher, and the publisher hereby disclaims any responsibility for them.

Any people depicted in stock imagery provided by Thinkstock are models, and such images are being used for illustrative purposes only. Certain stock imagery © Thinkstock.

ISBN: 978-1-4917-1981-7 (sc)
ISBN: 978-1-4917-1983-1 (hc)
ISBN: 978-1-4917-1982-4 (e)

Printed in the United States of America.

iUniverse rev. date: 02/07/2014

Look on my works, ye Mighty, and despair!
—Percy Bysshe Shelley, *Ozymandias*

Acknowledgments

So many to thank for support and encouragement. My sounding boards: Duncan, Jeff, Becky, Dave, and John and Amber. My readers: Dave, Jeff, and Becky. Big shout-out to the coffee shops in my little town and the folks there: John and Amber (again), April and Elisha, and Ellie and Jim. For editing help and input: Duncan, Dave, and Kathi. And huge gratitude to my wife for giving me space and time to complete this dream.

The High Road

1910, CHACO CANYON, NORTHWEST NEW MEXICO TERRITORY

Spirits and gods watched from above while the instrument of fate sliced air with crimson wings of leather, eyeing the two unsuspecting riders far below. Up and down. It glided, climbed, descended in freefall. Utterly skillful. Entirely silent. If it could be seen, one might have been mindful of a falcon's agility. But at those altitudes, invisibility was virtually certain—a mere stitch across the fabric of the sky itself.

Somnolence descended on the world below while bright, clear sky imperceptibly eased into twilight.

The instrument waited.

* * *

Jehu Weatherby affectionately patted his horse, Ginger, and stroked her mane. From a distance, the pair blended smoothly into the sepia-toned landscape surrounding them: her ginger color and his typical rancher attire of leather chaps and gloves, wide-brimmed and worn hat, revolver, rifle, penetrating eyes, and well-weathered exterior. Great sandstone cliffs rose up behind them and before them as they crossed the width of the large canyon from the east side to the west.

The shallow river that snaked through the canyon floor was easy to ford, being more mud and sand than water.

They headed toward an ancient structure now known as *Casa Rinconada*, following a trail that would take them out the west canyon entrance between two mesas. Then they would leave this well-worn trail, break to the left, and head up to the broad, flat plateau of the South Mesa. Like all the structures around this haunted canyon, the "Casa" held its share of mysteries, including its shape: a great circle dug out of the ground with elaborate entrances on opposite sides. The walls were made of cut stone and mortared together with eight-hundred-year-old masonry so exquisite and elegant that it instantly charmed the observer. Here and there, patches of stucco and plaster still clung to stone, hinting at some original beauty. In typical Anasazi fashion, the entrances of the Casa were perfectly opposite each other but not aligned with any compass points.

The rancher pondered this mystery briefly as they passed near it. "Damn strange—these Ancient Ones," he said, shaking his head.

He had long given up trying to understand the people that had lived and vanished so long ago here. Even the direct descendants of the ancient canyon dwellers held conflicting views of their forefathers. Some revered them as having created a *Shangri La* of peace and prosperity, while others demonized them with accusations of having built their great structures on the backs of slaves who languished beneath harsh beating rods and a merciless desert sun. The majority of locals, however, didn't have an opinion; they were interested only in the pragmatic aspects of the present canyon: its spiritual power.

Every year, winter and summer solstices saw great multitudes of pilgrims converge at various *kivas*, dancing and singing their way to some kind of better tomorrow. Weatherby had watched a few of the ceremonies, amused by the elaborate masked costumes and rituals. "Can't do any damn thing till we sing and dance about it," he was fond of saying, simultaneously flapping chicken-wing elbows and hopping around. Their strange customs even extended to simple directions: not only did they have physical directions like north and south, but they had spiritual directions that were associated with the solstice positions of the sun. Weatherby had another saying: "If you get directions from one of 'em to Texas, your ass'll end up in California."

2

The very way they viewed the universe was fundamentally at odds with whites and the opening of the new century.

He glanced at his traveling companion and sometimes business partner, an ancient-looking Navajo riding an equally ancient white mare of mixed breed. Born and raised in the area and having never even ventured the few miles north into Colorado, the cocoa-skinned man seemed generally content with his small, strange, and isolated universe, but his wardrobe betrayed a brewing conflict: traditional, thick, white cotton shirt and tan pants, silver-spurred leather boots, scarlet bandana wound around his head, dark green-and-black plaid waistcoat complete with silver pocket watch, and a Colt "forty-five." The new century, it seemed, intended to have its way with the old people.

As they neared the Casa, the white man said, "Let's go up the old way."

The Navajo turned in his saddle to face him, asking quietly, "Why you want work so hard, Weatherby?" The cadence of his words carried the distinct rhythms and chops of a southwestern native. He spoke not only English and Navajo but also Zuni and Hopi and several other dialects and languages.

The various Native tongues blurred together for most whites. After all these years, Weatherby himself still couldn't distinguish one from the other, thinking they all sounded like the same mumbled gibberish. Someone suggested that he ought to at least learn some Navajo. "Turns my stomach," had been his response. "They make sounds with those dirty mouths that ain't natural."

Weatherby pushed his hat back from his forehead slightly with a thumb and then let his wrists sit crossed on the horn of his saddle. "Well, you should know by now, Alta old boy."

"Know what?" asked Alta'halne'.

"That in this business, you never do exactly what the other guy wants." He paused to clumsily spit saliva and tobacco juice and then wipe his chin where some had dribbled. The large, dark stain on his left jacket sleeve betrayed years of incompetent spitting.

"Ah." Alta reached under his collar and pulled out a small silver pendant tied around his neck with a thin leather cord, revealing an icon of Kokopelli, the hunchbacked, wild-haired flute player. He

3

rubbed the shiny figure between the finger and thumb of his left hand and then rubbed his right elbow for luck.

"You all are the most damned superstitious people that I've ever known—and that includes my ignoramus-bitch mother-in-law back east." Weatherby spat again, less because of fresh spittle, more for punctuation.

"I want him to know I honor him."

"Bah . . ."

"You should be kind to mother of your children's mother," Alta said.

"Why the hell should I do that?"

"Harmony, Weatherby. You need harmony, pale friend."

"Harmony ain't worth dick." Incompetent spitting followed.

"Harmony is the only way . . ."

"Yeah, yeah. And if I'd just dance and sing, the universe would line up and smile on me. I don't want to hear it, Alta. I don't believe in your ways. You know that." His face flushed as the intensity of his voice rose. "The universe I live in don't know how to smile. It only knows how to crap." He spat again, abused his sleeve again.

Weatherby huffed and motioned toward one of the ancient stairways cut into the rock, just south and west of the Casa. "We'll go up that way. On foot. Leadin' the horses by the reigns. That way, if he's got any surprises, we at least show up quietly from an unexpected angle."

"Okay, Boss," said the Navajo, returning to his characteristically agreeable tone. "A good plan."

Weatherby looked at his companion askance, eyes narrowed slightly.

*　　*　　*

The descending darkness was of little concern for the instrument of fate. With eyes the size of melons, its daytime visual acuity was beyond that of an eagle's, and its night vision beyond an owl's. Even in the fading light and at a distance of a mile, it could discern which way the riders' eyes were cast. Besides flying, watching was what it did best. As it did so, blood pulsed through its veins: stronger, harder, faster, racing, anticipating the rider who bore deliverance ever closer.

4

It watched the two riders skirt around and south of *Zatu Quetz'ki'va*, the ancient Birthing Chamber, now in disuse for centuries. The structure itself, barely recognizable by the large circular pit where so many of its kind had hatched, was a metaphor for its own memories—crumbling and faded after centuries of idleness and decay.

The two humans dismounted their rides and led the horses up the ancient, steep stairway cut into the sandstone. Twice, they stumbled and slipped—nearly falling. The instrument almost acted prematurely. But it stayed itself.

Wait, it sang to itself. *Master has a plan. Follow the plan.*

* * *

At the top of the mesa, they paused to catch their breath. The two men and their horses were hardly as spry and agile as they used to be. Only a few years ago, Ginger would have willingly and eagerly followed him up the ancient staircase, but now she resisted.

Panting, Weatherby said, "Damn, Ginger. You tryin' to put my agin' ass in a pine box?"

Alta laughed quietly.

"What's so funny, lead ass? I didn't see you and that walking bottle of glue exactly sprintin' up the steps."

"Two old men," the Navajo said. "Two old men who don't know when to quit. How dignified we are." He laughed again.

Weatherby chuckled, too. "You might be right. Maybe time to consider retiring." Standing beside Ginger and stroking her as she caught her breath, he turned east to look down into the broad canyon that had been his home for several years now. The Casa lay directly below them, and across the muddy little river, the remains of several other so-called Great Houses could be seen, *Pueblo Bonito* being the most prominent. Not far from that massive ruin was his simple homestead, where his new, pregnant, sixteen-year-old bride would be waiting for him.

As both men looked over the canyon, watching the shadow of the rim creep across the canyon floor with the setting sun, the white man asked, "Navajo?"

"Yes, Weatherby."

"What happened here?"

"Beats me, Boss."

"I mean, where'd they go?"

"They're still around: Hopi, Zuni, Tewah. All children of the Ancient Ones."

"And you?"

"No. Not Navajo," he replied, indignant.

"Where do your people come from?"

"The Great Spirit made us from the wind, the rain, and a whirlwind of fire."

"Right." They both laughed at this familiar line given to tourists, migrants, and travelers heading for California. Usually, this answer preceded relieving someone of their hard-earned cash.

"Really. Where from?" Weatherby asked again.

"Oh. Beats me, Boss."

As a young man, Weatherby had "discovered" the Anasazi ruins of Mesa Verde in Colorado while running down cattle. Climbing and mapping the stone structures, he initially tried hard to understand the lost peoples who had abruptly abandoned centuries of settlement and history, but after a traveler from back east offered him three dollars for a piece of pottery, his interests took a turn for the less academic. Callously, he looted the Colorado ruins, ransacking and pillaging wherever and whenever he could. Pottery became his staple, each attached with a sappy story designed to enhance its value. It became a lucrative business, and in less than a year, he began running out of artifacts, but not the need for prostitutes and whiskey. For a while, he "created" more history by hiring some Arapaho to produce fakes—dream catchers, bits of fabric, shards of pottery, and the like. Eventually, the "craftsmen" wanted a bigger cut, and the jig was up.

South into New Mexico Weatherby went, where opportunities multiplied in Chaco Canyon. He diversified, adding ranching and rustling to his lucrative looting business. Ranching had been an easy cash cow since there were plenty of Apache or Hopi he could hire for dirt. Plus, he found that it was a simple matter to make covert excursions up north for herd "enhancement." As his fortunes grew, he became a virtual king in the county. In fact, looting took a backseat, becoming more hobby than job, freeing him up to explore and exploit the ruins of the canyon at his leisure.

The Mesa Verde settlement back in Colorado was a large and elaborate structure nestled into the side of a cliff—an impressive structure by any account. However, the Chacoans had built thirty or more comparable structures, called "Great Houses," that were spread over several square miles. Some of these wonders rivaled and exceeded both the sheer size and architectural prowess of their Colorado cousins' single construction. Clusters of the Great Houses even seemed to be connected by arrow-straight roads—some of which went right over the top of mesas. These mysterious ancients had thrived, lived, laughed, loved, died, and vanished long before any white men set foot in North America. Precious few clues remained to tell their stories, and time and sky conspired to keep their secrets safe.

Weatherby's most profitable finds in Chaco Canyon were always the unique pots of elaborate black-and-white pottery, found in hidden chambers deep within the structures. For his own purposes, he started to make intricate maps of the canyon and its structures. By now, he had quite a library.

Unfortunately, the boom-bust cycle of his life had edged into quite a deep bust, looking grimmer by the day: once again the legitimate artifacts were drying up, and now there was talk in the wind of the state or feds or someone declaring the whole canyon to be a historic preserve. Roosevelt and his Antiquities Act had already caused trouble for some of Weatherby's "colleagues" elsewhere in New Mexico, as well as Arizona. Looting was about to become very risky. He had confided in Alta one day: "It's one thing to piss off 'injuns' or marks or competitors, but it's entirely different to piss off the gov'ment."

Patting a pouch on his saddle, the rancher said, "If this goes well, I just might retire after all."

Removing his left-hand glove, he unbuckled a leather strap and took out a four-inch-by-ten-inch piece of stone slab, the only Anasazi artifact ever discovered with writing carved into it. The writing resembled a cross between Egyptian hieroglyphics and Chinese characters. Such a find would shake up the anthropological world and fetch a retirement-worthy purse.

"That'd be nice, Boss."

"Sure would. I hope this guy we're meetin's the real McCoy."

"Boss?"

"Yes."

7

Pointing, the Navajo said, "Your hand. Get stung?"

"Oh, that," he said. An enormous red and puffy welt covered the back of his left hand. A blood-red dot was in the center. "Don't remember," he lied. "Do you . . ."

"What, Boss?"

The rancher passed the stone back and forth between his hands, considering something. "Do you believe in the stories about the desert nymphs?"

"Huh?"

"You know," he said with annoyance. "Nymphs lying around to seduce and kill men."

"Oh, those desert nymphs. No. Why?"

"Nothin'. Me either," he said, but that was a lie, too.

Only two nights ago, an annoyingly bright, full moon chased away Weatherby's sleep, so he wandered out into the canyon and traveled south on foot, past the strange outcrop known as Rain God Rock, all the way down to the Great House known as "Crooked Nose." He stepped over the crumbled outer wall, crossed its once-lush garden spaces, and entered an apartment. With no roof to block the lunar brilliance, he quickly found the small, square opening in an interior wall that he had spotted a week before. Such secret chambers were best checked discreetly, where the cloak of night made it harder for greedy, spying eyes.

The hidden opening was a couple of feet off the dirt floor and just big enough for him to squeeze his shoulders through. The short, narrow passage then opened into a circular room with a domed ceiling. The little chamber was about ten feet in diameter and five feet high in the center. The light from the moon couldn't penetrate this far into the structure. "Should've brought a lantern," he mumbled to himself, but he pressed on, gingerly feeling his way around the room to avoid scorpions, tarantulas, and other creatures with dangerous, pointy bits.

Suddenly a warm, rosy glow filled the chamber. He reached for his holster, spun back toward the corridor, and looked for an uninvited guest wielding a torch and bad intentions, but no one was there. Light just seemed to fill the chamber, barely allowing sight and giving the room a surreal, dreamlike quality.

Then to his left, a woman's soft voice asked, "What are you seeking?"

Startled, he turned back around and sat clumsily on his butt, gun trained on a beautiful woman sitting naked on the other side of the room. Her exact appearance defied description: white or Native, tall or small, hair color, hairstyle—all questions he couldn't have answered now. Except for her voice, his only real recollection of her was the impression of raw beauty, sexuality, and sensuality, which had filled him so completely that he would never forget it. Even now, two days later, the thought of her made him flush and tremble.

"What are you seeking?"

The question had been clear enough, but it was lost on deaf ears as glazed eyes stared at the rounded flesh of her breasts. Weatherby's mouth opened and closed, smacking dryly.

"What are you seeking?" The smile and lips dripped desire, mixing question with invitation.

After swallowing hard, he replied as coolly and manly as possible through a trembling voice, "Anything you're givin' away, sweetheart."

"You can have me," she started, letting a hand slide down her body, caressing her bosom and thighs. "Or . . ." She reached around her back, pulled out a small slab of stone, and placed it in her lap between her legs. "This," she finished.

Ripples of desire, excitement, and anticipation shook him, and he began to shiver. "I . . ." His eyes shifted nervously from breasts to stone and back.

After a few minutes of enduring his indecision, the woman sighed impatiently and tilted her head to the side.

"I have to choose?" he asked.

"Come now," she said slowly. "Choose." She leaned back, slightly spreading her legs and licking her lips, one hand cupped to a breast. Her eyes gently closed.

He edged toward her, delicious-looking, full lips drawing him in. His heartbeat boomed in the chamber, pulsing and pounding harder and louder in his chest as he neared her. Leaning over her body now, he slowly closed the distance to her expectant face.

Inching closer on hands and knees to reach promising ecstasy, he suddenly jerked his left arm back. Blood erupted from the meaty part of his hand between his index finger and thumb. He held the wounded hand with his right, watching a scorpion skitter away in the dim light.

Balance failed as he half-swooned and tumbled face-first into the woman. She opened her eyes wide and smiled broadly, ready to welcome her lover, but then she cried out in a desperate, aching moan as his right hand, which shot out to steady himself, landed on the little piece of stone.

"You have chosen," she said, countenance falling, sorrow lacing her words. Her form began dissolving before him like a mist, and in the few seconds of dim light that remained, it was possible to see an army of scorpions pouring out of a hole in the wall where her head had just been.

"Mother of God!" he exclaimed.

He grabbed the stone, spun around, and wriggled out of the tiny chamber and back through the tunnel. Emerging into the brightly moonlit apartment, he shook and brushed himself off over and over again, as if a thousand tiny legs crawled up his body. After one final brush and shake, he fled the apartment, ran across the courtyard, leaped over the crumbled outer wall, and jogged home.

Each time he stopped to catch his breath, the rosy, erotic chamber drew his gaze back. The bleeding scorpion sting, however, pushed him homeward.

He had handled the stone as little as possible. In fact, the first he'd touched it since that night was when he tucked it into his saddle earlier today.

Shaking off the memory of the phantom nymph, Weatherby placed the stone back in the saddle pouch and scanned the area warily as he mounted the old horse.

*   *   *

The instrument of fate made a low, angry rumbling sound as it watched the two riders talking quietly and handling the sacred stone. Muttering, it sang, *Humans. So much trouble. So ignorant. So weak. So delicious.*

The two figures rode toward *Zatu Shdishdaoh*, old home of the *quetz'al* trainers. It was a smaller apartment complex that overlooked the *quetz'al* pen centuries ago. Now just a few walls and covered with scrub, the structure guarded the lonely mesa in near isolation. Without shade or water, it was only habitable to snakes and scorpions.

As the riders neared the small ruin, they warily approached the crumbling remnants. The white man only scrutinized the layout of the walls, but the Navajo scrutinized the environment, casting his eyes across the desert and into the sky. Catching a glimpse of the watcher above, the Navajo's jaw went slack, and he grabbed his silver Kokopelli pendant, wheeled his horse around toward the south, and spurred it hard in the flanks. The dark man and his pale horse rode hard and fast while the white man yelled something, waving fists in the air.

Soon, now, the instrument sang.

* * *

"It is him!" yelled Alta as his horse began to run. "He is here. Death has come for us."

The rancher twisted left and right in his saddle. "Who? What?" he asked.

Snatching his hat from his head and beating it against his saddle, Weatherby yelled, "Goddammit! You chicken-livered bastard." Watching the Native ride away and breathing heavily, he said to himself, "Damned buyer managed to scare the bejesus out of you with that damned Kokopelli notion." Raising his voice, he called out, "Well, you'll get yours for this, you weak, superstitious bastard!" A string of expletives followed a wad of spit and tobacco after the Native.

The rancher was just on the north side of a small decrepit structure called *Tsin Kletzin*. He started backing his horse away from it while pulling out his Winchester. After chambering a round, he drew the rifle to his shoulder and tossed his aim rapidly from wall to wall, hiding place to hiding place.

"And there you are," he said to himself, taking a bead on the small man who appeared from behind one of the walls. Clearly a Native, not only was the man's skin dark, but he wore a ceremonial outfit: a cape with a big lump in the back, a long flute, and feathers woven into braids that wrapped around his head, giving the look of wild, flaming hair.

"Very clever," he complimented under his breath. Then he yelled, "I ain't fallin' for that Kokopelli crap."

The man didn't respond, but only adjusted his grip on the flute.

Weatherby adjust his grip on the rifle. "You get on outta here," he said, panic rising in his voice. When the strange arrival still didn't acknowledge him, he added, "I mean it," and fired a shot over the man's head to emphasize his point. "If I ever see you again, I'll kill ya where you stand, bastard. Go on now, goddammit!"

Still unfazed, the man calmly lifted the wooden flute to his mouth, and long, low tones emerged to fill the air.

"What the *hell* is wrong with you?" Weatherby screamed. "Get outta here." Reluctantly, he fired another warning shot. Though a crooked thief and a liar, he had never murdered—or killed—anyone. "I'm starting to think I'm gonna have to kill you." The rancher lowered his aim: the next shot would be fatal.

*   *   *

His master had called. Fate would answer.

At last. His eyes went wide, and every fiber of his sinewy body stretched taut in anticipation of battle. The pale horse and its dark rider still ran south. The white rider and his horse had fired at his master.

Insolent, pale one first, he sang to himself. *A surprise!*

He pounded his wings, filling the air with the voom-whoosh of his might. Air rushed past him, feeding a nascent adrenaline rush. After gaining more altitude, he folded himself sleek and dropped in vertical freefall, gaining speed every second. When he was almost level with the plateau of the South Mesa, he opened his wings, membranes shaking violently and booming out his thunderous prowess.

He shrieked, *I am Tuhj! And my thunder comes with the rain of blood.*

Cutting horizontal sharply, he flew only feet off the ground, the target just now aware of the attack.

*   *   *

Weatherby startled at the bone-crushingly loud sound behind him—part thunder, part cannon fire. Turning to look at the sight of the source, air left his lungs, and strength left his body. The sight of the enormous dragon-like thing flying at him from the other side of the plateau paralyzed him body and soul. His jaw went slack, and he dropped the rifle.

Where Weatherby's body failed, Ginger's did not. She instinctively turned and ran at full speed away from the monster bearing down on them. The bucking motion snapped her rider back to awareness.

Grabbing the reigns, he steered Ginger toward the ruins where they would at least have some protection from a flying attacker. Not even a fresh, young horse could outrun the flying terror, and Ginger was neither young nor fresh. "When this is over, I'm going to have to reconsider some of my notions about Native superstitions," he said to no one.

While the monster was still fifty yards away, something wet and sticky struck him and the horse across the backside with considerable force, momentarily knocking his newly recovered wind back out. Several strides later, another wet, sticky shot hit them, and flames began to spread across his back and Ginger's rump.

As the panic-stricken horse ran aimlessly, Weatherby twisted out of the flaming jacket and used it to try to beat down the flames that were covering her hindquarters. With her flesh burning and boiling, her eyes went wild with agony, and she screamed, as his efforts only spread the flammable mixture.

Abandoning his efforts and pitching away the jacket, he looked up just in time to see talons the size of his forearms closing on him, and he reflexively bailed off the horse. Upon impact with the hard desert ground, his right collarbone snapped, and the accompanying shoulder dislocated. He staggered to his feet and headed again for the ruins— unaware of the large chunk of prickly pear embedded in his left thigh.

After scanning the sky for the monster, he looked around for Ginger. Her burning rear half lay twisted on the ground, blood and entrails spilling out from beneath the still firmly attached saddle. The animal's front half was missing.

Hiding behind a disintegrating section of stone wall, he caught sight of the flute player running toward the body of his horse. "What the hell?"

The mysterious Native knelt down and removed the small piece of Anasazi stone from the saddle pouch.

"Oh no you don't, you rat-bastard." Launching himself with a guttural scream, he charged the small man. When he had mostly crossed the distance to Ginger's half-corpse, something fell out of the sky, blocking his path. Weatherby stumbled, tripped, and fell.

He came up face-to-face with the bloody carcass of his Navajo companion, Kokopelli pendant firmly gripped in the left hand.

* * *

Tuhj circled around, scrutinizing his work. The white man was down on the ground, screaming in frustration and terror.

Glorious, the *quetz'al* sang.

His master signaled for Tuhj to burn the man, and so he obediently performed an impressive double-spit from an altitude of over five hundred feet. His targeting was flawless. The flailing and screaming man ran off the top of the mesa and plummeted to the ground, a flaming, parabolic arc that lit up the evening sky.

Tuhj sighed. *Pity. Would have been delicious.*

Coasting about and doing aerial acrobatics, the cool air refreshed and exhilarated.

Ah, Master, that was the most fun I've had in years.

▼△▼△▼△▼△▼△▼△▼△▼△▼△▼

Demon in the Serpent

DECEMBER 21, 1177, FAJADA BUTTE, CHACO CANYON

Spirits and gods watched from above as the lone elder climbed. Foot followed hand, followed foot, making the scramble up the steep side of the butte look casual.

His last time? the spirits asked.

Yes, the gods answered.

He seems to enjoy it.

Yes.

He will be sad.

Yes.

Does he expect a Word?

Yes. No.

Usually they had no Word to give him. Silence was generally best: human hope peaked when operating in the dark. Perhaps the season would be good. Perhaps bad. Joy. Sadness. Surprise. Fear. Uncertainty and necessity pushed The People forward through ingenuity.

But this time they would not push forward. Grave news must be delivered, and a heavy dew of dread coated the spiritual realms.

* * *

The fresh layer of snow blanketing the canyon testified to Mother Earth's deep slumber. *Ton'ah Tashteh* (Fajada Butte) rose up from the desert floor like a great trophy, proclaiming the rock's defiance against the elements. Dirt, debris, and pulverized rock formed the broad cone of its base while solid rock rose from the center of the cone. The butte stood as sentinel before the southern entrance to Chaco Canyon, home of The People.

Quaatsa Mukaama's feet were cougar-sure as he ascended *Ton'ah Tashteh,* and they knew the path up to the Telling Place well: up the slope, around the cliff face to the southern side, and behind the three great stone slabs known as *Tjok, B'jok,* and *Nakath.* Behind them, uncountable winters ago, his forefathers carved the two Sun Serpents. Light from the sun passed between the slabs and fell onto spiral carvings, forming two sun daggers striking at Earth—the Greater Serpent, and Moon—the Lesser Serpent. The positions of these slices of light changed with the seasons, sometimes striking both Serpents, sometimes just one. This solar calendar helped The People mark time, plan for harvests and plantings, rains, and drought. On this first day of winter, the two daggers of light should frame the Greater Serpent.

At the top of the slope, he slid sideways along a narrow ledge that took him around to the south side of the butte. The constant wind was brutal at this height, blowing the powdery snow from his path and diving under his robes, icy breath stinging his fifty-winters-old skin.

Usually Quaatsa found no Word at the Telling Place, just the regular marks of time for him to announce to his people, who would then prepare for the coming season. On a few occasions, a subtle— or not-so-subtle—message from the gods greeted him. One Word he experienced warned of a terrible winter ahead, enabling them to prepare. Another time, at the beginning of spring, a scorpion was killing a white rock spider as he arrived. A road runner suddenly ran from between *Tjok* and *B'jok,* grabbed the scorpion, killed it, and ate it, allowing the spider to escape with most of its legs intact. He relayed the Word to the other two *Shat'kuhat,* and they had the people prepare for war. A moon later, an emissary from the Snow Cliff People, their distant kin to the north, arrived and begged for help against plains people raiding from the east. The People sent sixty strong warriors, twelve priests, and half a dozen war-trained *quetz'al.* With the help, their kin beat back the invaders, who were forced to make peace offerings of bison meat and skins.

At last, he reached the three slabs. Holding four eagle feathers to his face, he smelled the sage and other sacred spices used to bless the spiritual tools. Then he turned to the Heavenly Corners of the Earth and recited a prayer to each in turn, ending with the rising position of this morning's solstice sun. On *Tjok*, he sprinkled maize kernels dipped in the blood of a freshly killed rabbit, to thank the gods for Life from Life, the blessing of meat and meal. Before *B'jok*, he stacked a tiny teepee of twigs surrounded by small stones, to thank the gods for the gifts of fire and shelter. Finally, on the face of *Nakath*, he smeared two handfuls of fresh *quetz'al* dung in the shape of arched wings, to thank the spirits for gifts of wisdom and the *quetz'al* themselves.

* * *

No joy, the gods said.
No joy, the spirits replied.
Send the Word. The gods turned their backs, unable to watch.
So be it, the spirits answered, whirling and spinning as ethereal mist. Bright colors intertwined, gradually becoming golden flecks mixed with bright green dots. Their misty transparency faded as they compacted and took shape: eyes, four legs, twin tails.
The shape descended to Mother Earth below.

* * *

Quaatsa turned away from the slabs, snow crunching under his feet in this wind-sheltered spot. Fur-lined leggings covered his legs from knee to toes, and a thick sole of leather strapped around each foot protected his feet from sharp rocks and the occasional cactus. Layers of long wool shirts, a bison pelt robe, and a rabbit skin hood did their best to keep the cold at bay.

He removed his hood and turned to step around *Nakath*. As he squatted down to enter the Telling Place, a set of tiny animal tracks heading into the natural chamber caught his eye. Only a moment before, there had been nothing there. He froze momentarily and then bent down to look at the tracks more closely.

"A sun-loving, heat-craving craggy creature with the icy smoothness of the fresh snow?" he said to the three slabs. "Is there more?"

Squatting down to enter the small natural chamber, he waddled in and looked at the Sun Serpents. There, as usual, vertical shafts of sunlight cast from the two spaces between the three rocks framed the Greater Serpent. But as he studied the two bright sun daggers, they warped and bent toward the center like two bows shooting arrows at each other. He turned to look at the three slabs, but they were just as before. The curved light beams gradually bent more sharply, becoming angled and touching to form a large, bright X across the Greater Serpent.

At the moment the bent sun daggers touched, a broken-twig-like cracking sound filled the chamber, and a tiny lizard-like creature, no bigger than the palm of his hand, appeared in the center of the spiral carving.

Quaatsa sank to the ground on his knees. "What terrible vision is this?" he asked.

He closed his eyes, shook his head, and rubbed his elbows for luck. When he opened his eyes, the omen was still there, in the middle of the Greater Serpent, brightly lit by the supernatural sunbeams. When he reached a trembling hand up toward it, the creature leaped from the stone face to his finger, tiny claws digging into his leathery, old skin for purchase. It crawled up to the back of his hand, and he brought the demon nearer to his face for inspection: golden, shiny skin, blue-green striping that looked like it was made of actual tiny turquoise stones, eyes of carved black onyx. Twin tails ruined the creature's surreal beauty: one being wrinkled, leathery, and gnarled, the other so pale that he could see bones and blood pulsing through veins beneath its skin.

As he studied it, it turned to look at him and spoke: "Lonely Mother."

"What?"

"Lonely Mother."

"I do not understand."

The creature repeated the words every few seconds, and Quaatsa repeated them also, memorizing them. Then the lizard abruptly turned into a fine, powdery charcoal figurine, and a tiny gust of wind disintegrated it. His eyes darted to the Greater Serpent just in time to see the two sun daggers snap back to their ordinary positions, as if it had been a perfectly normal winter solstice day.

"Lonely Mother?" Placing his hand on the Greater Serpent, he said, "I do not understand."

On the back of his hand, a series of tiny red welts rose across his index finger and hand where the golden creature had dug in its claws.

The Word had become flesh.

* * *

Well?
We gave the Word, the spirits answered.
Will he call on us?
Most assuredly. We left many questions. And reminders.
Excellent. We shall wait for him.

* * *

Quaatsa donned his hood and began his descent. Over and over, he recited the words of the demon. Aloud. Silently. Slowly. Quickly. Loudly. Softly. Even backward. The harder he tried to understand, the more frustrated he became.

He possessed Human Spirit, which had indwelled him since he came of age. It gave him powerful gifts of song, art, and tongues. Languages were his plaything; travelers from the distant corners were amazed to converse with him as though he shared their same mother tongue. Through his gift of song, he became the keeper of songs—and therefore the history—of his People. He often composed for seasons and rites, and he even taught others to do the same. With his gift of art, he protected the People from evil spirits, using powerful sand paintings and rock images.

The other two *Shat'kuhat* also had spirit gifts. Sheweh Du'hat possessed the Eagle Spirit and used her gift to teach the People the ways of fighting, courage and honor; training young warriors in the arts of war and protecting The People were her primary duties. Coyote Spirit indwelled Gohm Thlahk; he was wise and knew how to build things, how to grow crops, and how to heal. Sheweh could win through war, Gohm through peace.

Waiting to greet him at the base of the butte were Sheweh, Gohm, his wife and three children, and a few other ministers. His face was blank, and he covered the glowing scars on his right hand with his left.

"Well?" asked his wife, Kwi Dreh, cocking one eyebrow. She juggled their infant from one hip to the other. "What was the Word?"

About thirty summers, but still as spring in her beauty, he was always glad to see her face again. He smiled at her and then turned serious and said to the group, "Yes. There was a Word. The gods sent the spirits with an omen—a lizard demon."

The small audience exploded with questions: "What was the sign? Did it mean good or ill? What should we do? Shall we prepare for a season of prayer?"

He raised his hands, silencing them. "The omen was strange and left marks on me." He rotated his wrists around, letting them see the glowing footprints on the back of his hand. They all gasped, while some stepped closer, craning necks, and others stepped away.

"We need to prepare the Birthing Chamber so the *Shat'kuhat* can perform the Smoke and Rising ceremony tomorrow night. After that, the meaning of the Word will be plain."

Quaatsa stepped to his wife's side and took their tiny daughter from her arms. He breathed her infant smell deeply into his lungs. Exhaling and hugging the girl tightly, he said, "I must go into a season of prayer and preparation for the Smoke and Rising now."

The small group dispersed, quietly lost in their individual anxiety.

"Father?"

"Yes, Totahmaa?"

His twelve-winters-old son looked him in the eyes and took hold of his right hand. The boy studied the mysterious marks there. "Father, will you tell us?"

He smiled. "Some. Yes. Have you ever seen a lizard with two tails?"

The boy's eyes widened. "No."

◩ ■ ◩ ■ ◩ ■ ◩ ■ ◩ ■ ◩

Restoration

JUNE 19, 1938, CHACO CANYON

Franklin Yellowtail sat on a small rock outcrop known as Rain God Rock, watching clouds and dreaming. The coming day's agenda would be the same as usual: nothing. Suddenly, the skinny nineteen-year-old sat up straight, pointed an index finger skyward, and announced: "Turq, I have a-an idea."

His audience of one didn't respond.

"Ah-hmm," he said, clearing his throat loudly. "I *have* an idea."

The twelve-year-old Native American, Turquoise Moonhawk, turned his coffee-colored face and espresso eyes toward him and said, "What? Oh?"

Brushing thick, black hair from his face, he said, "I said, I have an idea."

"Right, Frankie. I am all ears."

"Wh-why . . . don't we h-hop a ride on the Tin Lizzie and b-bug-on down to Weatherby's to peep the new workin' stiff pip."

The younger boy smiled, clasped a hand on the teen's shoulder, and said, "Franklin, my good man. I have no idea what you just said."

"I said, 'Wh-why don't we h-hop a ride on the new Tin Lizzie and b-bug-on down to Weatherby's to peep the new workin' stiff pip.'"

"I heard your words. I do not understand them," said Turq. "Have you been eavesdropping on the new CCC guys?"

"Yes. H-how'd you know?"

"Because every time we get some new Corpsmen, you start talking in ways that make no sense. Do you even know what you said?"

"Yes. Do you w-want to know?"

"Of course."

"There's a n-new g-girl working the trading p-post. I heard she's *very* pretty."

"Well, why did you not say so?"

"I did," responded Frankie proudly. What Turq had said was true: Frankie liked listening to the men of the Civilian Conservation Corps that came to this lonely stretch of desert from all over the country. A few months ago, a group that came from across the south had Frankie sprinkling his sentences with hefty doses of "y'all," "fixins," and "okreeh." (The fourth time he came home and said, "Hey, y'all. I'm fixin' to get me some okreeh," his mother put an immediate stop to it.)

Turq had been Frankie's best friend and protector since the teen and his mother had arrived in the canyon two years earlier. Frankie had physical problems: weak, often sick, poor coordination and balance, one leg longer than the other, and his left hand curled up unnaturally. Being slow, bad at games, and having a stutter often made him the target of bullies, but with Turq around, no one ever bullied him twice. Ever.

"Pretty girl, you say?"

"Yeah. A 'pip.'"

"So, we should go down to see the pretty girl?"

"We'll 'p-peep' the 'pip.'"

Turq put hands on his knees and stood up. "Okay. Let us go 'peep' a 'pip.'"

They laughed, amused by their plan. Each tossed a pebble at the feet of a lizard, who scurried quickly away. Just when they hopped down, a rock landed near their feet and skidded past them, scattering dirt all over Frankie's shoes and startling him. "What?" he said.

They looked up. Some of the new CCC men in the distance were pointing and laughing. One of them bent down, picked up something, threw, and within moments, another rock landed at their feet.

"Oh dear," said Frankie, nibbling on a fingernail.

"Relax, Frankie."

"That m-must be B-buddy Womack."

"Who is he?"

"One of the n-new Corps men. I heard some of the older Corps m-men call him a 'm-mean sumb itch' drunk who w-washed out of the Yankees. I don't kn-know what 'sumb itch' is."

"What are Yankees?"

"Baseball, T. Don't you know b-baseball? Murderer's Row? B-babe Ruth? Lou Gehrig? Joltin' Joe D-d-diMaggio?"

"No. Do you hear baseball on your radio?"

"Yup. B-but you don't 'hear' baseball, you 'l-listen' to a game." He pointed a finger up in the air for emphasis. "Sheesh, T, you really n-need to get a r-radio. It's how e-everyone knows what's g-going on."

"My father says radio will rot people's brains. That one day everyone will just sit around paying attention to little boxes in their hands, forgetting how to talk and be human."

"That's silly. How c-could you forget to be human?"

"I do not know, Frankie. Does it use electricity?"

"Of course," he said, rolling his eyes.

"Well then, we would have to get electricity fir—"

Another rock hit. It skipped up to hit Frankie in the shin.

Frankie bent over to nurse the spot, rubbing it with slightly trembling hands. "I d-don't like this, T."

"Me neither, Frankie," Turq said, putting a reassuring hand on Frankie's back.

"Those g-guys are being mean. He's a b-bully."

"Yes, he is, Frankie."

"L-let's get o-out of here," Frankie said, standing upright.

"Good plan," said Turq. "Which way to the new truck?"

"I think it's o-o-over there n-near the Kettle."

"Then let us head that way."

As they started walking toward one of the Great Houses known as Chetro Kettle, another missile struck Frankie. He grabbed at the red welt on his right arm with his weak left hand, squeezing it and turning his body away from the baseball player. "L-let's run, T."

"No: you go around behind the Rain God." Turq's voice was calm, authoritative.

"B-but we've got to run."

"No. You go around the rock. There," Turq said, pointing, voice more adamant.

"Okay, b-boss," said Frankie, giving a little army salute.

"And crouch down."

Another rock struck Frankie. "Ouch. Okay, okay. I'm g-going." Frankie obediently scurried away, hobbling around to the far side of the outcrop, and then hunkered down in the dirt just as the assault escalated. The sound of larger stones shattering on impact with the outcrop made him cringe. The bullies' laughter was cold, harsh.

"Turq!" Frankie yelled. "T! Come on b-back here. It's safe." He poked his head out to see what was keeping his friend.

Turq casually scanned the ground while deftly dodging incoming missiles. He eventually picked up two stones: one cantaloupe-sized and one silver-dollar sized. Frankie watched his friend lob the larger stone in a great, high arc toward the bullies—so high it was difficult to see. The young men on the receiving end paused to watch, mesmerized and laughing nervously. They shielded their eyes from the sun to try to spot the incoming threat. At this precise moment, Turq threw the smaller rock low and fast. The bullies never saw it coming, and the missile pegged one of them right in the middle of the chest, folding him like a piece of paper.

The man fell to the ground clutching his chest, kicking his legs, and yelling. The other three watched their comrade go down and forgot about the first, larger stone. When it landed in their midst, dust and dirt splattered everywhere, startling them all.

Frankie didn't understand the words that the men were saying. "I d-don't think M-mother would approve," he said. Then he added, "I w-wish you could p-pitch for the Yankees, T."

After a brief pause, two of the men rushed the outcrop.

"Oh no," cried Frankie. "T, we have t-to get out of h-here."

In seconds, the two men had crossed the fifty-yard distance and were at the outcrop. One of them lunged at Turq, but the boy skipped out of the way quickly. The man lunged again, committing more effort, and Turq evaded with a hand-spring. The man stumbled, recovered, and turned to face Turq, but the boy jumped forward and hopped onto the man, legs wrapped around ribs in a crushing vice grip. Stunned by the counterattack, the man tried to peal the boy off, but Turq head-butted him and brought down powerful elbow strikes against the man's collarbones. Frankie heard a couple of pops, and the man screamed, collapsing to the ground.

The protector broke free and turned to face the other attacker, who had pulled a knife.

The knife wielder twirled and twisted the five-inch blade menacingly, but the intimidation tactic failed. Turq wasted no time: he feigned right and then dove left while the attacker sliced air, just missing him. Rolling and then hopping up on his feet, the boy jumped up and mule-kicked the man in the butt, sending him face-first into the dirt. The kick sent Turq to the ground too, but a quick, kip maneuver brought him to his feet. The man was on hands and knees, trying to get up when Turq jumped on his back, knees first, sending him sprawling into the dirt once again. Grabbing a handful of hair, Turq pounded the man's face into the dirt several times. Then he shifted his weight so that both his knees were on the back of the man's right arm, pinning him to the ground. The attacker released the knife. Turq bent forward, grabbed the knife, and hopped to his feet.

"Now, you tell that baseball player that my friend is off limits. If he wants to pick a fight with a small person, tell him that I await his pitiful efforts."

The two men struggled to get to their feet and stumbled quickly back to their leader. Then the gang of four sauntered off, frequently looking back over their shoulder.

"Wow, T." Frankie grabbed Turq's hand and pumped it up and down, vigorously shaking hands. "You're a g-great fighter. You k-kicked their butts."

"Well, technically, I only kicked one of them in the butt."

"With b-both feet."

"True," said Turq, dusting off his dungarees. "Well, do we have a Tin Lizzie to catch?"

*   *   *

The late morning air was still cool. Eleven new Corpsmen sat nervously on a low wall that ran across a small open area in one of the ruins where they would be taught the basics and finer points of masonry—Anasazi style.

Vince Nesci, recent Italian immigrant, surveyed the new crew and seemed to make up his mind about something. Frowning, he rubbed calloused hands together and addressed the men with a booming, harsh tenor voice.

"And I 'mind you again this morning. Two things!" said the stocky Italian, half-preaching, half-yelling angrily. "*Primo*, this place is no yours to be 'eh-splore.' These 'runes' are sacred to *Americano Nativo* and to be respected. And *secundo*, they are *molto* dangerous *di notte*. Even though she's a *luna piena*—a full moon—last night, Krenshaw, he fall from retaining wall and die."

"Which wall?" asked one of the young men.

"That wall. Under your *posterior*."

The eleven looked down at their two-foot-high perch, confused.

Another Corpsman started to ask what everyone was thinking, but the small, silver-headed Native American standing beside the Italian intercepted. "Not the fall. The scorpions," he said tersely, voice quiet and deep.

Simultaneously, the young men, in identical dungarees and white shirt sleeves, lifted their feet to inspect the ground.

"Whole body swell up like the *rancido salame*," added the Italian. "Seems he fall into swarming bunch of *scorpiones*. Bad *fortuna*. *Fortissimo tormentoso*." He bowed his head, making the sign of the cross and mumbling a Latin prayer. Several Corpsmen followed his example.

He pointed a thick finger at them and wagged it violently up and down. "So, no go out at dark! *Capisci?*"

They looked at him blankly.

"You no understand?"

They all nodded vigorously.

"Okay, then. Say '*capisci*,' so I know I not teach *imbecille*."

Eventually, they all managed to say it. The Native American smiled, leaned over to him, and said—in perfect Italian, "Vince Nesci, you like the look of these men?"

Vince replied back, also in Italian, "Yes. I think they will do fine work. They paid attention so far, and they have strong-looking hands."

"I agree. Are there not supposed to be sixteen?"

The Italian recounted the workers. "There should be," he noted, returning to English. To the men, he asked, "So where are the others?"

The Corpsmen looked around, at each other, at the sky, at the ground, at anything but their loud Italian supervisor.

Mumbling curses in Italian, the stocky mason swiveled his head, scanning the area. A worn leather journal suddenly appeared in the Native's hand. Vince took it, noting the strange scars that ran across the back of the man's hand like tiny footprints. He mumbled his thanks to the middle-aged Native, opened to a ledger, and returned his attention to the men.

"I should no have to call names!" he said. "This is desert. Where you go for a good time? It eighty miles to train station. Yesterday Sunday—no liquor for sale anywhere."

As he angrily read the names from his roster, Corpsmen answered, "Here," in turn. Krenshaw's absence was accounted for, but four others were not: Stanislov, Miller, Hughes, and Womack.

"Womack. He looked like trouble. Probably Polish." The Italian scanned the men for a reaction; there was none. "He will spend day making small rocks for us to use." In Italian, he quietly said to the Native: "Please, take your horse and go find the missing bastards."

"*Si*." The Native quickly walked away, mounted his horse, and galloped off purposefully.

"You can see," Vince said to the men who had showed up on time, "I no care for you be late. *Capisci?*"

Again, they looked back blankly.

"I said, '*Capisci?*'"

Almost immediately, the fear-struck men answered back, "*Capisci.*"

"Now," he began, with a twinkle in his eye, "let us talk of the *magnifico* work of *arte muraria*. Masonry!" Casting a prepare-to-be-amazed look, he said, "The wall upon which you *posterior* sit? She is over one thousand years old."

Amazement ensued. Jaws dropped. Some hopped up from the ancient architecture to kneel beside it—partly in admiration, partly in reverence. The suddenly tangible gravity of their restoration work here sweetened the morning air like incense.

For the first time that day, Vince smiled.

* * *

The "Tin Lizzie" that Frankie had referred to earlier was a 1924 Ford Model TT—the heavy-duty version of the Model T truck. It ferried people and supplies up and down the canyon for the Service.

Frankie and Turq rode in the back, happily bouncing along with legs dangling off the end of the flatbed. The driver's dog, Bobo, sat between them, eagerly absorbing their attention. The rush of the twelve-mile-an-hour wind in their hair intoxicated all three.

When they pulled in front of Weatherby's Mercantile, the driver suddenly slammed on the brakes, bringing the Model TT to a dust-kicking, sliding stop. The boys and Bobo tumbled arse-over-head backward into empty crates at the front of the flatbed, laughing excitedly.

Frankie said, "That was the m-most hilarious thing—ever."

The horses tied up in front of the store looked down their long noses at the peace-wrecking arrivals. One of them defecated.

"Hmm. The horses do not share your opinion," said Turq.

Frankie laughed. "I think you're right, T."

The two friends collected themselves and raced the dog into the store, passing two Navajo putting the finishing touches on a porch repair. The workers greeted Frankie in English, and Turq in Navajo.

In moments, they were inside. The long, narrow store with its rich, dark wood was cave-like compared to the bright sunshine outside. Huge banks of shelves lined the walls on either side. Long counters with glass cases in front of them allowed customers to see even more merchandise. One wall displayed food and market items, and the other had clothes, linens, and other necessities. At the very opposite end of the store was a small soda fountain, which sometimes actually had soda—and on rare occasions, ice cream.

An assortment of hard candy stored in glass jars adorned the soda fountain's counter. Frankie hurried to the back of the store, hopped on a stool, and started scheming.

"Do you think sh-she'll l-let us w-work for a candy stick?" Frankie thought aloud.

"I do not know," said Turq. "The last woman did, but if there is a new lady, who knows? We will just have to ask."

Eyeing the new goodies on the wall behind the counter, Turq asked, "Are you sure that you want a peppermint?"

"Oh, yes, T. It's my f-favorite."

"Who is your favorite baseball player ever?"

"The B-babe. The Great Bambino, of course." Frankie rolled his eyes. "D-dumb question, T."

"Well, you might want to think about a new favorite candy," said Turq, taking a seat on the stool beside him.

He poked his lower lip out and shook his head. "Nah." His gaze hadn't left the jar of peppermint sticks. Licking his lips and rubbing the palms of his hands together conspiratorially, he said, "I can't wait."

"Look at those."

Frankie's eyes followed Turq's finger to see what could possibly be more interesting than peppermint sticks. He saw it and gasped.

"B-baby R-ruth?" Frankie took a moment to get his mind wrapped around it. "First a b-baseball player—the greatest ever. And n-now a candy bar? Surely it m-must be the greatest candy b-bar ever." His excitement bubbled over into jiggling and twitching in his seat. "I w-wonder if it tastes like p-peppermint."

"We can find out if she lets us work for it. All I have is lint in my pockets."

"Ooh, Mr. M-moneyba . . ."

From a back room, an angel emerged, gliding behind the soda fountain counter. Her platinum-blonde hair was cut short and parted on the side like a man's, but with waves and curls around her ears in the modern fashion. She had golden skin and piercing, bright green, luminescent eyes. Though tiny, she carried herself tall and elegant. Her dress was simple, but she filled it out in wonderfully complex ways.

"Turq," he squeaked. "D-do you s-see her? I d-don't think her feet touch the g-ground."

Turq switched his gaze from the candy bars to the new arrival. For a couple of seconds, he and the woman locked eyes, in one of those don't-I-know-you moments.

Then the screaming started.

Turq shoved Frankie off the stool and shouted angrily in some unknown language. The angel engaged the verbal assault with equally vile intensity.

Frankie hit his head on the floor after falling. "Hey!" he yelled. "This r-really hasn't been m-my day." He rubbed his head, confused by the strange words and sudden fury behind them. "T? T! Hey, T-Turq."

But Turq didn't respond; he was busy picking up stools and throwing them at the tiny woman, who seemed to have an uncanny knack for dodging flying furniture. The yelling and cursing continued, and when the stool arsenal ran dry, jars of peppermint sticks and candy became the missiles of choice. Objects flew around the store with deadly intent.

Frankie covered his head and curled up in a ball on the floor as glass, polished brass, and stained oak crashed around him. "This isn't a g-good d-day," he said, shutting his eyes tightly.

Finally, the lady retreated into the back room. Turq scooped up Frankie, cradled him, and then carried him out the front door, saying, "Bad, bad, bad, bad." Once outside, the Native threw the bigger boy across both shoulders—fireman style—and ran him back north through the canyon.

For three miles.

Faster than any Model TT.

▼△▼△▼△▼△▼△▼△▼△▼△▼△▼

Smoke and Rising

DECEMBER 22, 1177, NEAR CASA RINCONADA, CHACO CANYON

Tuhj Eh Naht landed quietly on the roof of the Birthing Chamber *kiva* beside two other *quetz'al.*

Like them, his skin quickly adjusted its pigment to a pattern of mottled tans and browns—perfect camouflage against the terra cotta and thatch structure. With their wings folded loosely against their sides, their poised bodies hunched low, with long necks stretched forward, heads and beaks pressed flat against the thatch surface, absorbing the stored heat from the rooftop. They scoured the sky with their large golden eyes, appearing harmless.

As for harmless, that was pure illusion. Sharp edges on powerful beaks could easily snap the thick pine timbers of the Chaco Canyon structures. Short, springy legs tucked beneath them ended in massive talons evolved to crush and impale smaller, land-bound creatures for a fresh meal. The short, whip-like tail sported razor-sharp scales protruding along its spine, which were useful for shredding the wings of rivals.

The three flyers watched a handful of other *quetz'al* circling far above, on patrol for this important event. Two masters, Quaatsa and Sheweh, stood before the door of the Birthing Chamber, wearing ceremonial robes. The third master, Gohm, was down inside the *kiva's* large circular room, preparing and purifying it with incense and chants with several lesser officials.

So much gibberish, sang Tuhj, shaking his head. *Who knows what humans say to each other?*

At least, started Luahti, sitting next to Tuhj, *the masters can speak proper Song and not just . . . whatever it is: punchy, choppy pops, clicks, and squirts.*

Our masters are up to something, sang Naskiteh.

Clearly, sang Tuhj. *I will not fly now. This smoke makes me . . . wobbly.*

Me too, sang Luahti.

And me, agreed Naskiteh. *Not so wobbly as they will be, though.* He nodded toward the masters, and the flyers laughed quietly, having seen their masters under the influence of the hallucinogenic smoke in the past.

Tuhj frowned with his eyes and said, *Entertaining but not dignified. Who knows why masters do what they do?*

*   *   *

The sun was setting behind the mesa, long shadows stretching across the canyon. Quaatsa stood beside Sheweh and watched the *quetz'al* on the roof making their low singsong calls to one another in the day's fading winter light.

"Beautiful. I never tire of watching them," said Sheweh.

"Indeed," said Quaatsa.

"Sometimes, it almost seems like they are talking to each other."

"Yes. But what would they have to talk about?"

Sheweh shrugged, turned to face him, and said, "You look exhausted. Must have been some 'season of prayer and preparation.'"

"Let me only say that while I may be old, *Ton'ah Tashteh* (Fajada Butte) was not the only thing towering in the night."

She laughed loudly. "Good for you, Old Man. Old mesas do not always reach the sky, I'm told."

"My wife can assure you that the mighty mesa yet reaches the sky," he retorted flatly, renewing her laughter.

Quaatsa studied his fellow *Shat'kuhat*. She was around twenty-five summers—half Quaatsa's age—and frequently reminded him of this fact with glee. The painful irony was that while she teased him about losing virility, she herself was barren: her *Shat'kuh-hateh* (spirit gift) would not allow it. All, male or female, who had been possessed by Eagle Spirit over the generations had no descendants. Sheweh seemed to accept this—at least, she had never complained to him about it. In a way, barrenness seemed to have its advantages for her: the intense physical training she demanded of herself and her warriors required an enormous commitment of time and energy. Also, it was thought—not by a few—that Eagle Spirit had a way of driving its indwelt slightly insane. Occasionally, Sheweh would disappear without explanation for days, only to return bruised and bloodied.

The two *Shat'kuhat* stood in front of *Zatu Quetz'ki'ma* (Casa Rinconada), the birthing chamber, with a large crowd behind them. The stone methods used for all the Chacoan structures throughout the valley were also employed for this enormous *kiva*: carefully stacked flat stones that only needed a miniscule layer of mortar to hold them together, perfectly vertical walls, round log beams for cross members and tie-ins, and a thatch-earthen roof laid over a woven stick support frame. Its doorways resembled short, thick cut-outs of the letter T in order to accommodate the removal of young *quetz'al* after they hatched. (The hatchlings had trouble controlling their wings and were unable to fold them compactly against their bodies.) The door before them faced the direction of Summer Rising Sun—the direction of sunrise on the day of summer solstice.

The sixty-foot-diameter *kiva* was only about ten feet tall on the outside, but a dugout floor inside made the ceiling height twenty-five feet toward the center. In the middle of the roof, a large square hole had been framed in, through which a pregnant *quetz'al* could be lowered to lay her single egg. (It was believed that the *kiva* looked like a nest to the flyers.) The three *quetz'al* belonging to the *Shat'kuhat* sat on the roof and peered through this large opening, watching the ritual cleansing going on down inside.

Quaatsa watched Gohm Thlahk, Klanl Hivaht, and several Lesser Shamans exit the Chamber through the T-shaped door, incense wafting behind them as they emerged. Quaatsa locked eyes with Gohm, the third *Shat'kuhat*, who walked over to join him and Sheweh. The Lesser Shamans dispersed to drums and other duties, while Klanl, the High Shaman, raised his arms above his head, holding eagle feathers tightly in each fist, looking triumphant. Mystery symbols, painted white on the High Shaman's near-black skin, could be seen beneath his robe.

After Quaatsa gave the signal to start, soft drumming began, and Klanl shuffled his feet in time with their rhythm. At this, the people watching knelt on one knee and bowed their heads.

The High Shaman sang:

Gods above, we are your children.
Spirits between, you guide and protect us.
Mother Earth below, you provide for us.

Klanl recited this Incantation of Recognition to each of the Four Sacred Directions. The crowd turned with him: first northeast, then southeast, then southwest, and finally northwest. With each recitation, they rubbed their elbows, then hid their faces in their palms with thumbs touching, and finally gently swept the back of their fingers along their thighs. The gesticulations held deep symbolism: the first action brought luck and blessings, covering the face acknowledged human feebleness before the World, and the final gesture signified respect for all the lower things that were then feeble to humans. In unison, they cried out, *"G'nah-weh wito"*—that is, "It is surely so."

Next, the High Shaman faced south, looked straight up into the sky, and held his arms straight out horizontally in the shape of a cross. Clenching eagle feathers tightly in each hand, he began shaking violently, and blood dribbled out from inside of each fist. The red droplets fell, soaked in, and formed tiny black splotches in the pale, powdery earth. All the people—except the three *Shat'kuhat*—sunk to both knees and lifted hands high.

The High Shaman cried out:

Gods above, we ask for council.
Grant us some small part of your wisdom
That we may know the way forward.
Spirits between, we ask for safety.
Guide these Elders and Servants heavenward.
Protect them from those who would snatch them into the underworld.
Mother Earth, do not reject them when they return to us.
Go now, Shat'kuhat. *Descend to Ascend.*

The People said, *"G'nah-weh wito."*

Quaatsa noted that he had goose pimples; the power of the unified mind of The People penetrated deep within him. Taking a deep but stealthy breath, he led Sheweh and Gohm down into the Birthing Chamber.

* * *

Tuhj sniffed the air curiously and turned his attention to the chanting High Shaman who had blood dripping from clenched fists. *How could he have the blood of rabbits in his veins?* he sang rhetorically.

The flyers watched the three masters descend into the great Birthing Chamber after the ceremonial rituals finished. Thick incense smoke obscured their view through the roof opening, but the masters could still be seen down inside the enormous *kiva*, sitting on the ground before a small, incense-burning fire. Sheweh, Luahti's master, pulled a pipestone from beneath her robes. Gohm, Naskiteh's master, pulled out a wooden pipe stem. These two handed the pieces to Tuhj's master, Quaatsa, who then assembled the pipe and crammed a small wad of dried and crushed herbs and mushrooms into the pipestone chamber.

Quaatsa passed the readied instrument back to Gohm, who lit the pipe from the little fragrant fire and handed it to Sheweh.

Klanl descended into the *kiva*, discreetly discarded the rabbit livers, and wiped away most of the rodent blood from his palms with a rag. From under his robe, he pulled the sacred stone tablet: the *Shat'kuh Mongehweh*, which was about as long as the man's forearm and half as wide. Muttering secret words, he gave the tablet to Quaatsa, who then started softly chanting in the language of the gods. The other masters joined in on the quiet but intense incantation, and Klanl left the *kiva*. The rhythmic sounds from the masters grew slowly louder, and the stone tablet began to hum softly and levitate.

Tuhj stuck his head through the roof opening in order to see better, holding his breath to avoid the hallucinogenic incense. A gold-and-green, metallic mist poured from the tablet, like bees emerging from a hive. At first, the strange swarm flew chaotically throughout the *kiva*, but eventually it formed a ring encircling the three Ascenders. These mists were the *Ahteh Shat'kuh*: the Spirits-In-Between—powerful entities used by the gods to do their bidding on earth. Generations ago, the gods had given the sacred tablet to the masters, so that they too could call upon the power of the *Ahteh Shat'kuh* when needed.

As the circling dance of the spirits slowed, Sheweh put the pipe stem to her lips and drew in a long, slow breath. Holding the drug deeply within her lungs, she quickly passed it to Gohm, who repeated the draw. He then quickly passed it to Quaatsa, who also took a long draw off the pipe. When they exhaled the smoke simultaneously, their eyes rolled backward in their sockets, eyelids slowly rising and falling.

Watching intensely, Tuhj sang to himself, *Wait for it . . .*

Then, as if rehearsed, all three masters cried, "*G'nah-weh wito,*" and keeled over backward.

Unconscious, their spirit bodies emerged as little tendrils of smoke curling out from their noses. The *Ahteh Shat'kuh* spun themselves into a colorful "dust devil," surrounding the disembodied entities and escorting them as they flew out of the opening in the top of the *kiva*. Tuhj jerked his head back to avoid getting hit.

Off you go then, sang Luahti.

* * *

The spirits formed a protective shield around the three *Shat'kuhat* as they Ascended, greens and golds whirling around them in a phantasmal bubble. The trio of spirit bodies glided rapidly higher and higher in tight, helical path. *Kiva* shrank. Village shrank. Canyon shrank.

Gohm became conscious first, startling immediately at the sight of Mother Earth retreating. Just as his breathing returned to near normal, he spotted a dark, arrow-shaped object hurtling toward them from the distant south.

"Quaatsa! Quaatsa!" Gohm called, but he didn't stir. "Sheweh! Awake! Sheweh!"

The warrior woman stirred, slightly at first, and then abruptly awoke, going into full battle mode. Her eyes quickly locked on to the incoming danger, and she positioned herself defensively between the black missile and the other two *Shat'kuhat*. With her flint dagger drawn and held forward in her right hand, her left hand went to a guard position near her throat. Eyes narrowed and icy, body poised to spring, she could have been a cougar with threatened cubs.

"You do not really do 'defense,' do you?" Gohm said.

She gave a subtle sideways smile and said, "Defense? Never heard of it."

A shrieking sound grew out of the quiet to an intensity that interrupted all thought. It pulsed and ground at their ears, making them rattle. The penetrating sound came from the black arrow, which looked like it was made from a thousand tiny vipers, all of whom directed screams at Quaatsa. Sheweh seemed unfazed by the sonic assault, but Gohm grimaced, covered his ears, and started shaking.

When the black arrow reached the swirling, green-and-gold mist around them, it was shredded—scattered to the four winds without a sound. The abrupt silence was physically jarring.

Gohm looked at Sheweh, who trembled ever so slightly, asking, "Okay?"

She simply raised one eyebrow and shot him a look. Pointing to Quaatsa, she said, "We must wake sleepyhead here. This whole Ascending was his idea. Pity for him to sleep through it all." She grabbed his foot as it floated near her. "Hey! Quaatsa! You are going to miss it, Old Man. Hey!"

Gohm joined in the prodding and hollering, but only the hollow whump sound of their arrival in heaven woke Quaatsa.

The three Shat'kuhat lay in the middle of a bright meadow with spring flowers and scents that promised hope to one's soul. The sunless sky glowed bright blue. Green-and-gold mists occasionally swirled past them purposefully, on their way to fulfilling some mission.

You are well? came a voice.

Their heads swung around, searching for the voice's owner.

"Where . . ." started Sheweh.

Quaatsa looked at the clouds, then the ground, touching the vegetation. He turned to Sheweh, who had never been to heaven, and explained, "Human eyes cannot see the gods. Human ears cannot hear them." Sweeping an open hand around, he continued, "The spirits provide this so that we will not be driven insane."

You appear well, spoke another voice.

The eldest *Shat'kuhat* addressed the gods. "The Telling Place," he said. "We beseech your council on the Word you gave."

Ah yes: The Word. Still a different voice. Green and gold shimmered past them.

Sadness comes. Each time the gods spoke, the voice was different.

Heavenly spirits wound around each other, descended between the trio of mortal spirits, and assumed the shape of the two-tailed creature that had appeared to Quaatsa at the Telling Place.

"That is it," Quaatsa said, unconsciously rubbing the marks on the back of his right hand. "The Word that came to me at *Ton'ah Tashteh.*"

Our languages and yours are not the same. Our realities and yours are not the same. Our times and yours are not the same.

Quaatsa reached to touch the "lizard," which, in heaven, was the size of a small dog. Almost in a trance, his fingers traced the metallic marking down its back while a voice spoke: *The gold zigzag symbolizes the far south. The Sadness comes from the ancient lands of a dying people.* Then Quaatsa's hand ran the length of the shriveled and black tail: *One tail is for the Sadness that is old and shriveled—unnaturally ancient, beaten by sun, wind, and its own pain.* His hand went to the other tail: *The second Sadness, pale and without sun; its loneliness drives their quest.* Back to the head: *Black eyes mean it will arrive during the longest night.* Then—just as before—the lizard turned to black ash and blew away.

"That is tonight," said Gohm.

The End.

"End?" Sheweh asked.

"The end of the Telling," Gohm explained.

"No." Quaatsa's face was white. "The End of The People."

"What?" Frustration wrinkled Sheweh's face as she swatted at green-and-gold "gnats" whistling past her face.

"The End of The People?" Gohm asked. "How is this possible? How can such a thing happen?"

Sheweh turned her head upward toward the unseen gods. "Explain!" she demanded. Pumping her fist in the air, she shouted defiantly, "The People shall know no End. Our lineage will stretch from the dawn of the world to its dusk."

"Is it the end of the World?" Gohm asked.

No. The People will End. They will be no more.

Distress rose in Gohm's voice. "But why? Surely there must be some way to save them."

"We are guiltless," Sheweh pleaded. "If we have offended you, we shall atone tenfold."

"Can this thing not be unwritten?" asked Quaatsa. "Why would such a thing come upon us?"

Why?

The three waited for what seemed several minutes.

Why does a raindrop fall here but not there? Why does the hawk prey upon the rabbit one day and the sparrow the next? Why do some infants take The Journey before they leave their mother's womb?

"Hard questions," Quaatsa said. "With difficult answers."

Answers do not always exist. Answers do not always comfort.

Sheweh pointed her index finger at the puffy "clouds," noting, "But solutions always exist."

Often true. Not always true.

"Then we shall fight to the last warrior. Our blood will be shed in glory," Sheweh said.

No battle.

Sheweh burned livid, but there was fear behind her angry eyes, and she became withdrawn.

"What are we to do if we face destruction?" Gohm asked.

The People will be no more, but the people will carry on.

Rubbing his forehead, Quaatsa said, "Scattered, like the ashes of the golden lizard."

Yes.

"And what of us?" Gohm asked.

You will all sacrifice. Two will take The Journey soon. One will endure many lonely summers. The Shat'kuh Mongeweh will be broken— the pieces hidden in time and space.

Quaatsa's knees buckled, and he stumbled. "How can this be? The *Shat'kuh Mongeweh* is eternal."

Sheweh reached out to stabilize the older man.

Gohm suddenly began fidgeting, pain etched deeply into his face. Beads of sweat popped up across his forehead as an alarming crimson glow began emanating from his feet.

"How do we find the pieces?"

"Who will be alone?"

Look now: your spirit bodies cannot remain here in heaven so long while you have not yet taken The Journey. You know this. You must now return to Mother Earth.

"But we still need your wisdom," Gohm said. "We need guidance."

We have not told you everything. What we have told you is the most important. Go now. Take heart: the tribulation will be short, your courage long.

"I feel like a pot being fired," said Quaatsa, sweating profusely. "The gods are right; we must go."

Flames burst to life and crawled up from the fingers of Sheweh's right hand, past her elbow, and toward her shoulder. She stoically endured the pain, betrayed only by a thin sheen of sweat across the back of her neck.

Quaatsa screamed as smoke emerged from beneath his robes. He beat furiously at the flames with his hands, arching his back, face twisted. He tried to run.

Just then, the heavens around them disappeared, and they began a rapid descent. The air rushing past them cooled their spirit bodies and brought some relief, but Quaatsa continued writhing and crying out.

Suddenly, everything went silent. Quaatsa's pulse roared in his ears. Underneath the drumbeat of his existence, a whisper like a distant coyote howl began to emerge: "Lonely Mother."

* * *

A sudden, loud pop caught Tuhj's attention as a quick whirling gust of wind blew down into the *kiva*—like a miniature tornado dropping from the heavens. *The masters have returned*, he sang.

Luahti and the other *quetz'al* awoke from their nap. Tuhj nodded toward the square hole. Peeking down into the opening, they saw the three *Shat'kuhat* curled up on the dirt floor, shivering in pain. Tears streamed from the corners of their eyes, yet they did not cry out. Smoke wafted from their bodies.

They smell of heaven and burnt flesh, sang Luahti.

Look! Tuhj announced as the masters began to stir.

I see it, sang Luahti.

This never happened before, said Naskiteh. *They live. Barely.*

Why must masters do this? asked Luahti.

They were gone much longer than normal. Much danger, sang Tuhj. *Perhaps they had much to do this time?*

The other two flyers agreed that it was a reasonable suggestion.

Some humans come, sang Luahti, not hiding her distaste and annoyance.

The entourage, led by Klanl, poured through the *kiva* door and descended on the three *Shat'kuhat.* The new arrivals covered the masters with blankets and tried to get them to sip fermented cactus juice. The leader spoke something to one of the other humans, who briefly disappeared and then returned with a pot of aloe-based ointment. They tried to apply the ointment to Quaatsa's burnt back, waking him, but he resisted.

Leave Master alone, sang Tuhj in a low, angry tone. *You cannot help. You cannot help, imbecile humans. Mortal balm cannot soothe spirit wounds.*

Luahti suggested they leave, and Tuhj approved this idea by springing straight up into the air with powerful legs, wings extended in front of him. He reached a height of over forty feet before he unfurled his wings and gave a mighty wing stroke. The single thrust took him another thirty feet up. Just a few more thrusts took him to nearly 150 feet above the *kiva.* Then he angled slightly and spiraled upward. Within seconds, he had disappeared into the clouds.

* * *

Quaatsa regained consciousness and tried to wave away the balm, but despite his intentions, Klanl and the assistants insisted, painfully peeling him out of his robe and tunic. As they gently rubbed the mixture onto his sensitive skin, he winced and groaned.

A snap-cracking sound exploded within the circular stone room. Clumps of plaster, clay, and dirt rained around them. Everyone froze.

"What was . . ." Sheweh said.

Hearing the characteristic rumbling of *quetz'al* wings taking flight, Quaatsa said, "Someone is angry." He quickly scanned the ceiling and found a split in the roof cover that was letting in the last of the light from the evening sky. A pile of debris had collected beneath it. "There," he said, pointing. "Tuhj has cracked that beam and torn the ceiling."

"That will take weeks to repair," said Klanl.

"Maybe it will not matter this time," said Quaatsa distantly.

▼△▼△▼△▼△▼△▼△▼△▼△▼△▼

Demon Child

DECEMBER 22, 1177, TWO MILES
SOUTH OF FAJADA BUTTE

Rooshth Va Manahken eyed the broad expanse of desert floor before
them. The next village could just be seen in the evening sun from her
vantage, tucked into a little canyon.

"All the beauty of a scab," she said quietly. Putting fists on hips
and smirking sideways, she continued her analysis: "Undoubtedly
primitive—like all the others—and like all the others, undoubtedly no
powerful magic."

Her stomach growled, a loud reminder that supplies were low
and hunger had dogged her for two weeks now. She grew weak and
weary these days—sometimes to the point of despair, doubting that
her decades-long journey this far north might ever pay off. She missed
the lush green mountains of her homeland, the songs of her people, the
bountiful food.

Cuddled with their large pack dog under blankets, her sole
companion in life still slept, only a couple of spots of his snow-white
flesh exposed to the air. He generally covered himself completely; his
sensitive albino skin couldn't handle even the pale, cold, northern
winter sun without burning. This was her son, Chur Keleh, and
though she loved him dearly, he was most pitiful to her.

He was conceived under a Blood Moon, an act to be avoided
at all costs, but she was "in love" and under the influence of strong
herbs and fermented juice. The boy's father, a newly minted warrior

43

named Tha'n, had golden skin, rippling muscles, and gorgeous eyes. He wanted her, and she him. As they made love, she dreamed of giving him equally beautiful sons—six or more if the gods would have it.

When she later told him of the child growing in her belly, her lover was pleased. They had a simple wedding, with friends and family lavishing them with gifts for starting a family together. Life looked promising as her belly swelled. After the usual time, she began to labor. The midwives of the village came to do their work. Shooing her lover out into the night, they talked with her, imparting collective wisdom about child rearing and keeping husbands happy. All of them wished and prayed for her that her firstborn would be a man-child.

"*Nah-thlata ti-eh thla-nahta*," said an old lady. ("Man-child for the child-man.") They all laughed.

Her labor proceeded well at first but turned harder than usual. Naturally, the midwives wanted to get to the bottom of the problem.

"Have you been eating monkey?" Everyone knew that monkeys were crazy; eating their flesh while pregnant could pass the craziness to one's child.

"Have you slept naked under a full moon?" The Moon God could slip inside and maliciously tie a child in knots just for laughs.

"Did you find a snake in your home?" The fright could cause a stillbirth.

"Spider bite?"

"Struck by lightning?"

"No, no, no, no, no," she replied. "No more questions. You honorable ladies are making my head hurt as much as my back."

But there was one more question, asked almost in a whisper: "Did you mate your husband under a Blood Moon?"

The dark red lunar eclipses were rare—and easy to avoid. Her people had calendars carved into giant stone structures predicting them for hundreds of seasons into the future. The highly visible calendars dictated every aspect of their lives: rituals, plantings, harvestings, times of good luck, times of bad luck; everyone knew which dates were important and why. And nobody—nobody dared to mate under a Blood Moon. The resulting child would be a disfigured demon, bringing blood-lust rage and a life of destruction.

"No," she lied.

Kali, a midwife apprentice and her longtime friend, brought her a drugged drink. It stunted the pain, slowed the process, and helped her relax for a short time, but soon the agony returned, greater than before. The ladies chanted to the Rainbow Gods for a speedy birth as contractions peaked and strained her body, locking it into giant spasms. Neck veins bulged. Corneal capillaries ruptured. Consciousness threatened to slip away more than once.

No one spoke it, but everyone knew she would die a slow and painful death if the child didn't come correctly.

She groaned and cried aloud, "Give me poison that I may call upon Ixtab to escort my soul to heaven!"

Then the baby crowned.

Screams and pandemonium erupted around her. Midwives were pointing between her legs and fleeing.

"Liar, liar!"

"Demon child."

"Evil and torments have come to us."

Kali alone remained to deftly and calmly bring the child into the world.

"Let me see it, Kali," Rooshth pleaded, tears forming at the corners of her eyes.

"Not yet, my Satchah."

"Let me see it. Is it a man-child?"

"It is."

"Does the child have his father's golden skin?"

"No," came the measured reply.

With some trepidation in her voice, Rooshth asked, "Does he have hair? Is it thick and dark?"

"No, but he is so young."

"Will my husband be pleased?"

"You have done well," Kali said cryptically.

"What? Kali, please let me see the child."

"Soon," came the response. With a small, rare obsidian knife, the young midwife cut the umbilical cord. "I must clean him and say a blessing."

The newborn cried, and Rooshth stopped weeping and frowned at her friend. Pushing up onto her elbows, she brushed sweat-soaked hair from her eyes and asked pointedly, "Is there something wrong with the child?"

"Satchah, my friend, my lovely one, the child is not right."

"What do you mean, 'not right'?" she asked, her voice growing intense.

"You and I both know that you conceived this child under a Blood Moon. Such things cannot be hidden from close friends."

"We were intoxicated with each other . . ."

Kali sighed.

Rooshth looked away and then back to her friend, saying, "But those are just old women's tales and nonsense. The gods would never allow such a thing. We used to laugh at such notions."

"We did. But we were wrong." Kali paused and then added, "And they have allowed it."

The new mother began trembling.

Responding to the pandemonium, Tha'n appeared at the doorway.

"My love," said Rooshth.

He couldn't look at the child but kept shielding his vision from it, as if even seeing it might infect him with evil. "What is this? What have you done?"

"Tha'n," she pleaded. "Our child . . ."

"No child. That is a demon." He spat on the child and then spat on Rooshth. "That thing must be given over to The Jaguar or we will all perish. Prostrate yourself to him, and perhaps we can redeem you for your evil."

"No, Tha'n. How could you—"

But he had vanished out the door.

"Your husband is right. The village will drive you away. The child must be given over."

"No."

"Yes. You know it is so."

"No." Sobs and grief overwhelmed Rooshth.

"It is the only way. I can do it for you."

"No!"

"Who knows what evil this child will bring to the village. He must be given over."

With her jaw quivering, Rooshth struggled to get to her feet, protesting, "You do not know that!"

"I will do it."

"But . . . no!"

Kali held the crying bundle in her arms and ducked out the door, calling behind her, "It is for the best. I will leave her for Ixtab."

"Kali! Please!" Her friend had disappeared into the night. "Tha'n! Tha'n," she called out desperately, but her husband was gone, too. Stepping forward to follow, Rooshth passed out.

The sounds of the wakening jungle filled the hut when she awoke, though the sky was not yet brightening. The scene was surreal—dreamlike: dried blood and birth fluid spread across the floor and pallet, their acrid smell permeating the air. Her bleeding had dried up, and she cleaned herself with a rag and some leftover water. Aloud, she wondered, "Did it really happen?" She probed her deflated, squishy belly.

Breathing heavily, her face going red, a white-hot rage exploded from within her, spraying the little hut with curses that sprang from a deep internal hell. Rooshth screamed at everything, cursing her home, the ground, the bounty of the jungle, the stars of the sky, her family, her husband, her own life. She even dared to curse the gods themselves—except Ixtab and Xibalba, whose help she would soon need.

Her rage temporarily spent, she caught her breath, donned a fresh tunic, and grabbed supplies: a large satchel filled with as much food as it would hold, small pouches of herbs for healing and cooking, and the rare obsidian knife that had cut her child's umbilical cord. The midwife's sharp, black tool felt good in her hand, empowering and liberating.

"It can bring life," she said. "It can bring death, too."

Rage, sorrow, and drugs clouded the next memory. She remembered inhaling a pinch of dried, ground coca leaves and invoking the spirit of Xibalba, the Jaguar God who had avenged his father against the lords of the underworld. Her madness, fury, and sense of justice had opened her to his spirit, and he filled her with superhuman power, cunning, and speed.

"They will all pay," she whispered to the dark from her psychotic darkness.

With blood lust in her eyes, Xibalba's heartbeat pounding in her ears, and cocaine racing through her veins, she effortlessly and quickly stole into hut after hut, slaughtering the occupants as they slept. Throats were cut, and blood flowed in torrents through the village. None could resist her. None could escape. She killed them all: friends, family, and even her husband.

Her best friend was the last to die, and by the time she got to Kali, dawn was just breaking. Swiftly, and now with an experienced hand, she pressed a bloody wad of fabric against Kali's face, bracing her against the bed pad. The razor-sharp stone knife flashed across her neck left-to-right as Rooshth pulled Kali's head right-to-left. Crimson life began pulsing out and spraying Kali's already-dead husband. Unlike the others, Kali did not struggle as she bled out.

Satchah-now-Rooshth pulled the fabric back from her friend's face, already visibly ashen even in the pale morning light. The girl had only moments left. Their eyes locked. Tears ran down Kali's face, and for the last time ever, Rooshth's face softened.

In barely a whisper, Kali said, "*Tanahg Tuleh-oh.*"

The avenger's face hardened, the razor intensity returning to her eyes. She said, "Just stupid wives' tales."

"Are they?" came a gagging response. "*Tanahg Tul . . .*" Kali's words dropped out as she slipped into the permanent night.

"You should have listened to me," Rooshth said, slipping out of the hut.

The smell of blood and death hung in the air, a sickening morning dew. Rooshth staggered, stumbled, and vomited. After spitting to clear her mouth, she said, "Maybe you were right, Kali. The child has indeed brought evil and bloodlust, but it is your doing."

Standing up and breathing deeply brought color back to her face. Then she ran hard and savagely down a well-worn jungle path toward the ancient shrine, *Tanahg Tuleh-oh.*

After a while, she paused, listening. Fortunately, only "safe" sounds filled the air. The small birds, monkeys, and rodents high in the trees were undisturbed by her frantic racing. A tarantula rippled across the path before her, and she smashed it with the heel of her bare foot. The crunching sound of its exoskeleton made her smile.

Having climbed high into the sky, the sun beat down hard now, rays stabbing through the jungle canopy, god-like spears impaling the ground from the heavens. Sunshine played across her face, alternating light and shadow as she ran down the trail. She slowed, turned off onto an overgrown side path, and climbed up to the base of an ancient, miniature pyramid. It was nearly invisible in the thick growth— even though the gray stone structure rose thirty feet above the jungle floor. Half-covered in roots, vines, and assorted greenery, the jungle's tentacles had already reached up from below to devour most of the stone shrine.

She trod carefully up the steps, avoiding entangling foliage and loose stone. Carved serpents and jaguars watched her from the face of the pyramid with stone eyes that mixed sympathy, judgment, and shame. Calendar symbols and hieroglyphics mocked her.

A twig snapped under her feet, and the jungle went silent, sensing the importance of the next moment. A tiny, beautiful voice descended from the top of the structure.

Caution forsaken, she sprinted to the top. There, on the altar, a bloody bundle of rags wiggled and cried. Her stony fortitude collapsed under the winds of an emotional hurricane, switching from rage and despair to something between relief and ecstasy—and back again. On her knees, holding her child, she wept openly.

"Stop it," came a commanding and annoyed voice from the jungle.

Rooshth startled and turned toward the source of the command. There, walking out from dense undergrowth, was a naked, eight-foot-tall, beautiful woman: Ixtab herself.

Awkwardly, Rooshth prostrated herself while still holding the boy. "Ixtab, oh Great One," she acknowledged through a jagged voice. Tales of such encounters with gods and goddesses abounded, of course, but nobody actually knew anyone who had really experienced it. Her whole body shook with fear and excitement.

"The child is mine," said Ixtab. "Offered to me here. Given to me here."

"My friend, she . . ."

"I should care?" asked the goddess.

"Please," Rooshth said. The new mother had not yet actually seen her child. She looked at the bundle, slowly pulling back the swaddling. The child had nearly transparent white skin, with pink eyes squinting at the filtered sunlight. For some time, Rooshth simply stared at her offspring. A tear formed in her eye as she said, "He is hideous. Unfit for your greatness."

"How do you know what is fit for me? You do not know what will come of this boy."

Rooshth studied the tiny bundle.

The goddess continued, "I might make something great of him." She paused and then added, "We know what you've done. Nothing is hiding from us."

The young mother held her baby tightly, possessively, ready to fight or flee.

"Xibalba is furious with you," Ixtab said. "You have brought shame to him, and he seeks to devour you." The goddess raised a finger and wiggled it slightly at Rooshth. "Lucky for you, I'm quite angry with The Jaguar right now—for reasons beyond you. It pleases me for you to escape him. Go north," she said with a conspiratorial smile. "Perhaps you will find some magic or a sympathetic god to fix your son."

"My son?" Rooshth held the bundle more gently and then turned her head toward the north, imagining something.

"Rooshth," said the goddess firmly, jerking the shocked mother from her thoughts. "Do not be in this valley when the sun goes down. The gods burn with anger against you, and they search this area. You are lucky I found you and have chosen to offer you compassion."

"Yes, Goddess."

"I like you, Satcha-now-Rooshth, and I will watch you with amusement. But you have done much evil here today, and the gods are overwhelmed with the souls of the angry dead flooding heaven."

"Yes, Goddess. Thank you, Goddess."

"Go quickly from here. Xibalba is nearby," Ixtab said, stepping back into the undergrowth. "I am merciful," she called back. "He is not."

Some unknown amount of time passed as Rooshth clung to the small bundle of life. Once the child slept, she ate some maize cakes. Shortly though, the child stirred with hunger and began to cry again. Her milk let down.

She gently unswaddled her child from the blood-stained bundle and wiped him down, massaging and cleaning his fragile body as she went. Bringing his face up to her breast, the child latched on quickly and easily. She trembled, and tears flowed freely as the baby started suckling. Alabaster face pressed into her cocoa breast, he calmed down and cooed gently.

The child tested his eyes, opening and closing briefly as he nursed: his first glimpse of his mother—the one who had killed in his name.

"I guess," she said softly, "we are both monsters. But every child should be loved by its mother. No matter what. Even if it has white skin. Or no hair at all. Or if its eyes are pink." Shifting him to the other breast, she added, "We cannot fix me. But we will fix you."

*   *   *

The terrible memories of their survival in the jungle and endless wanderings from village to village faded, and Rooshth's awareness returned to the present moment and the desert before her. They had gone north—as Ixtab had commanded. They had pursued magic—as Ixtab had commanded. Yet nothing they found had ever been able to help the boy. "Well, a curse on her," she mumbled to herself. "This is it. I go no further north. This weather is harsh, unpredictable, and cold."

Her companion began to rouse from sleep again. Pulling the blankets further around her son's head, she said, "Sleep some more." Since they traveled at night and slept during the day, they would soon trek across the open plain in the dark. Then in the morning, they would set camp just outside the village.

She looked up at the sky abruptly. Spirit winds blew toward the village, gathering and swirling high in the air. "So there is powerful magic there," she said. "Good."

"What, Mother?"

"Nothing. Keep sleeping, child. I will return in a moment."

Rooshth left him under their primitive tent and scrambled up a small mound to get a better view of their destination while there was still light.

The spirit winds increased, making a rustling sound like blowing dried leaves. Quickly, she dug a downy feather from a pouch. The desert hawk's feather had dried blood on the quill end and a brown powder dusting the fluff end. She swept the fluff end across her eyes, wincing. Then she quickly stuck the sharpened quill end into the bridge of her nose, blood trickling down.

Real magic worked. It was ugly. It was costly. But it worked.

The hawk sight came upon her almost as soon as she jabbed herself. Buildings and structures could be seen as if she were right next to them. The magical viewing also let her see the spirit winds, which converged and ascended into the heavens over the village.

As she watched, three human figures rose up and out of the canyon, carried by a spiraling spirit wind. Green-and-gold protector spirits swirled about them.

"On some important mission to see the gods, are we?" she asked.

She chewed off the end of a long fingernail, retrieved a pinch of black viper powder from a hidden pouch, and sprinkled it on the fingernail shard now lying in her open palm.

"Let us see how important."

Rooshth cast her gaze hard upon one of the rising figures and blew the fingernail/powder mixture in his direction. At first the particles drifted out into the air, unnaturally, slowly twirling and coasting toward their destination—apparently immune to gravity. Then she spat at the floating black cloud. The blob of saliva passed through the black powder, hitting the fingernail shard. Powder and saliva coalesced on the shard, which then began accelerating toward its target. It grew in size to a great, deadly arrow made of thousands of tiny black vipers.

Subconsciously, her left hand pinched her chin, and a smile curled to the right side of her face. Shaking her head and sighing, she said, "I love magic. Too bad my pitiful son can do none."

The magic arrow flew on target, getting closer and closer. Two of the people were aware of it now, and a woman prepared to defend against it. Rooshth chuckled. "This should be entertaining."

"Oh?" The green-and-gold spirits swirled against her black magic, slicing and shredding the arrow like a thousand sharp knives.

"Indeed. We are on a very important mission," she said to the distant trio.

She removed the hawk feather from her face, clasped her fingers around the sleeve of her tunic, and used it to wipe the blood from between her eyes. A little pressure applied to the wound stopped the bleeding. Then she had to pinch the tip of one of her fingers; in her haste to attack with the magic arrow, she had torn the nail into the quick.

Real magic was costly—but always worth it.

"We are finally here."

Secrets

JUNE 19, 1938, CHACO CANYON

"Fine! Who needs you, anyway?" He glared angrily as the other three men headed quickly toward the masonry class at Chetro Ketl.

One of them rubbed his chest and hollered back, "C'mon, Buddy. We're late. We'll be in trouble."

"Oh, boo-hoo. You go on ahead and be a good little inmate. Make some nice little rocks out of big ones for me. I'll be thinking about you while I'm putting away the last of the hooch." Drinking at ten o'clock in the morning was nothing new to Buddy Womack.

Returning to the bunk house, he made his way to his foot locker and his quarry within: a three-quarters-full bottle of bourbon. "Sad. A party somewhere got cut short. Shan't make that mistake again," he promised the bottle.

Lying next to the bottle of empty dreams, wrapped in a worthless-in-this-heat flannel shirt was his prize from the night before.

The past twelve hours had been quite eventful. This morning, he had conned the three other Corpsmen into harassing two local kids. The younger boy's fighting talent was legendary around the camp, and Buddy smiled, remembering the performance. He pantomimed pitching and said to no one, "God! I miss baseball."

Events even earlier—in the dark of night—had involved that very bottle of bourbon and a Native woman. When he first arrived at the CCC camp, he bonded immediately with Isaac Krenshaw, a Minnesota kid. Except for being reluctant masonry participants, the only thing they had in common was their mutual admiration of all things alcohol.

The two quickly fell into a nightly habit of venturing into the ruins with a bottle of whatever Weatherby's stocked, which generally meant something strong and cheap. However, they had stumbled across a bottle of expensive bourbon and enthusiastically embraced the chance to compare its hangover to that of the cheaper whiskey that had been their custom. A bright, full moon lit their way out into Chetro Ketl, where they planned to share both the bottle and dead dreams.

Plans changed when they saw a beautiful, young Native woman frolicking in the ruins, flirting with them.

The drinking buddies first spotted her peeking out from one of the rooms in the ruin. Immediately, her charms seized them both. The moonlight revealed that her charms were naked, though long hair and shadows conspired to hide her more interesting bits as she darted back and forth. They watched for several minutes as she teased, smiled, waved, and wiggled. Accepting her invitation, they moved in for a closer look—expecting more than just a look, of course.

Inside the little room, she backed herself seductively into a corner, flashing a sensuous smile between full lips, and said, "Well, boys, are you looking for something?" Her English was perfect.

Krenshaw blurted out, "Oh, any adventure we can find." His slurred English was not.

"Adventure?"

"Yeah. Do you know where we can get some adventure?" The Minnesotan tilted his head to the side and laid a finger alongside his nose.

"Why yes."

"Great!" replied Krenshaw, starting to unbutton his shirt.

"But what kind of adventure?" She sounded almost childlike.

Krenshaw, shirt half-off, paused. "What do you mean?"

"You must choose," she answered.

"Choose what? Looks like things are pretty obvious to me." He quickly finished pulling off his shirt.

"You can have this . . ." She let her hands drape around her body, parting and combing her hair alternately to hide and reveal tempting flesh. "Or . . ."

"Or what?" Krenshaw had a bit of saliva at one corner of his mouth. He fidgeted incompetently with his belt buckle.

Womack, with a higher tolerance for alcohol, felt wary and scanned the ruins suspiciously, eyebrows furrowed.

"Or you could have this," the woman finished, pulling a small square bit of stone from behind her back—as if she had a secret pocket.

She offered the stone to the men, waving it, like flashing a diamond ring.

"What is it?" asked Womack.

Smiling, she just wagged a finger as if to say, "You naughty boy. You know what it is."

"Futz no!" cried Krenshaw adamantly. "I don't want a stupid rock. Let's go." He had his pants unbuckled, fly undone. "I want some adventures on Titty Mountains. I want to go cave diving in Crotch Caverns." Moments later, his pants were down to midthigh, and he clumsily advanced on the woman.

"Hey," Womack said. "We don't know who this is. It's too easy. Could be a setup."

"Ah, shut up, pansy. Go handle yourself in the corner while I handle her like a real man."

The playful nude slipped past Krenshaw when he stumbled for her with an awkward reach. She turned toward Womack and said, "His choice bulges within his pants. How about you, Buddy Womack? Which do you desire?"

His eyes blinked rapidly as they darted suspiciously around the ruins again. Frowning, he stared hard at her and said, "That." He snatched the stone from her, evading her attempt to brush against him.

She flashed him a pouty, disappointed smile and blew him a kiss. Then, waving her fingers at him, she deftly fled out the door, calling, "Come get your prize, Isaac Krenshaw."

Krenshaw ran after her, running awkwardly as he held up his pants.

"Krenshaw. Don't . . ."

Womack started to follow but felt suddenly exhausted and left the ruins to return to the bunkhouse for the night. After packing the bottle and the stone safely away in his locker, he fell down on his cot and passed out.

Now in the daylight, a good breakfast in him and a good laugh behind him, he eyed the bourbon and the stone prize lying there. Without taking his eye off the flannel-wrapped stone, he grabbed the bottle, opened it, and took two quick swigs. Closing his eyes, he visibly relaxed.

Then, he abruptly spun toward Krenshaw's bunk.

He raised his bottle in the direction of his companion's empty bed, saying, "Didn't see you at breakfast, lucky bastard. Here's to you and your beautiful conquest." After a long draw off the bottle, he sighed and set the bottle down.

Unwrapping the stone from the flannel, he examined it carefully. It had carvings on both sides, but they were nothing like the petroglyphs around the canyon. The "front" side of the stone was divided into squares, and inside each square was an image. Some of them were abstract while other images had the likeness of an animal or a person—like a different version of Egyptian hieroglyphics. On the "back" side, the marks were shallow, hard to discern. Some of the shapes were obviously people, one of which had a hunched back, wild hair, and was holding a flute—like the Kokopelli character known throughout the Southwest. There were also images of winged creatures.

Congratulating himself, he said, "Not bad, Buddy. This should bring a pretty penny from someone. Whenever you get out of this godforsaken desert prison." He raised the bottle over his head and said, "To me."

In the middle of swallowing his own toast, something in his mind clicked. His eyes went wide with panic as choking and violent coughing seized him. He finally cleared his burning lungs and returned both stone and bottle to his foot locker. After closing the lid, locking it, and double-checking, he scanned the bunkhouse quickly, carefully, warily.

"Oh, God," he said. "How did she know my name?"

* * *

Turq Moonhawk didn't tire of carrying Frankie Yellowtail, but Frankie tired of being carried. "T?" he squeaked between bounces. "Y-you're much b-boun-ouncier I think than the Tin Lizzie-ie."

"Sorry."

"P-please p-put me dow-own now."

"Okay." The protector put him down, adding, "But we must keep running."

"I need to stop and catch my breath."

"No. Come on, Frankie. We have to keep going."

"Why? Are you scared of the pretty lady?"

"Not scared. Worried. She is dangerous." Turq looked back toward Weatherby's Mercantile, apparently watching for something.

"She was so p-pretty," Frankie proclaimed dreamily. Then giggling, he rubbed his hands together conspiratorially. "I w-want to m-marry her."

The younger boy turned to him, reached up to grab his shoulders, and looked straight into his eyes. "No. Frankie. She is pretty on the outside but ugly on the inside. Ugly, ugly, ugly." He shook Frankie with strong hands, making the older boy's eyeglasses bounce around. "Do you understand, Frankie?"

"Yes."

The shaking continued. "You must stay away from her. She is *evil.*"

"Okay, T," Frankie said, a little louder.

Turq stopped shaking Frankie, but his grip tightened as a troubled and distant expression came across his face.

"T! That h-hurts me," he said.

There was no response.

"That hurts."

Turq's face came back to the present moment. His gaze fell to his grip on Frankie, and then he released him immediately. "Sorry, Frankie."

Crossing his arms to rub both aching shoulders simultaneously, Frankie said, "It's okay. I'm all right. You s-cared me. Don't d-do that again, okay?"

"I will not. I apologize." Turq gave the older boy a sideways hug.

They walked along in silence, each lost in his own thoughts. After a while, Frankie asked, "D-do you know her?"

"Yes, Frankie, but I don't want to talk about it."

"But how c-could you know her?"

"From a long time back."

"B-but she just got here."

"She has been here before, Frankie."

"But I w-would have remembered." Frankie sighed and gazed longingly toward the south. "I would remember her. So p-pretty."

Under his breath, Turq said, "She has always been here. Waiting. Watching. That evil . . ."

"What?"

"Nothing. Frankie, I *do not* want to talk about it, okay? It was before you were born—I mean before you came back to the canyon."

"What? B-but how could you know her? I'm o-older than you."

"Frankie!"

"It's j-just a question," he said innocently, pushing his glasses back up on his nose.

His friend stared at him.

"How c-could you?"

"Frankie, go ahead: ask me one more time. I will throw you over my shoulder and run up and down the whole length of this canyon."

Frankie's eyebrows shot up. "Oh my. Okay, Turq." After a few minutes, he said, "I'll a-ask you t-tomorrow."

*   *   *

Kenneth McKinney, a tall, white man with loud boots and a tall, white Stetson casually entered his store, Weatherby's Mercantile. Broken glass, broken cases, and smashed displays brought him up short. He pushed his hat back off his forehead, saying, "What the hell?" The cigarette in his mouth went slack as he surveyed the destruction.

"Mr. Mah-kin-hey!" The voice came from the back room, wrapped in a heavy accent. The owner of the voice appeared in the doorway, broom and dustpan in hand. Her pretty face dissolved, water works beginning.

"What the hell, Ruth?" Kenneth's voice mixed accusation with sympathy.

"These two boys," she started, wilting further as she recalled the ordeal. "They come in your store. Suddenly start throwing chairs. No warning. Hurt me—they tried. I do nothing! They smash candy jars. Smash wall display. Smash shelves. I do nothing!" She sniffed back tears, dabbing at her eyes with a small, white linen.

"Oh, dear. Rough second day on the job," he said. Ruth Van Manekk had appeared two days ago, armed with a letter of reference from a merchant he knew in Taos. She was a recent immigrant from Holland and seemed to know her way around a mercantile and soda shop. Like many European immigrants, she was probably running from something—maybe wasn't even Dutch, but Kenneth believed in letting private matters stay that way.

"This normal? More nasty people here? I no stay."

"No, Ruth, this ain't normal. What did these rascals look like?" He took a draw off his cigarette and then frowned, concentrating.

"What is rascals?"

"The boys."

"Oh. One tall, skinny. He dark hair. Glasses." She delicately tapped the side of her head. "Slow of thought. He no cause trouble. Other one, he cause attack me."

"And the troublemaker?"

"Small, nasty boy. Very mean. I want whip him."

"Was he Native?"

"Native? I no . . ."

"Was his skin white like yours and mine? Or dark? Straight, black hair? Headband?" He circled his head with an index finger.

"Yes. Red, I think. Long, black hair. Single braid."

Kenneth took his hat off and rubbed his head. "Only one pair of boys matches that description to a T."

"You know them?"

"Yes. Yes, I do." He walked to the door. The finished cigarette butt was flicked out into the desert, and then he gingerly walked to the back of the store, trying to avoid crushing more broken glass.

"The skinny one's Franklin Yellowtail." Stopping momentarily, he picked up a toppled stool, set it at the soda bar, and dropped his weight onto its small seat. "You noticed he ain't quite right in the head—stutters a lot, ain't too bright. Clumsy kid but ain't got a mean bone in his skinny-ass body. Oh, pardon my French, Miss Ruth." Pulling a flask from inside a jacket pocket, he motioned to Ruth to fetch him a glass. "And throw some ice in, please."

Pouring his whiskey on rocks, Kenneth continued: "Frankie's maw—that's what we call him, 'Frankie'—is Natasha Yellowtail. She's raised the boy herself. Got raped by some white man in the canyon

59

looking for artifacts. Probably seventeen, eighteen years ago. Can't remember now. He didn't have no respect for people or the canyon. Some of these bastards can't keep their pants on around the young ladies—Native or Mexican or white. Raped two more, too. Well, we found him, and he got his. He won't find anyone to bother down there in hell."

He took a swig and swished it around his mouth, physically washing away a painful memory, anesthetizing emotions and taste buds. "She went to live with some relatives near Farmington. 'Bout three years ago, she moved back here looking for work with the CCC as a translator and English teacher. We all help her out. Boy's got folks looking out for him all up and down the canyon.

"The other kid's his best buddy: Turq. Turquoise Moonhawk. He and his father been around forever. Something wrong with that kid, too. He ain't grown a lick in all this time. Damn peculiar. Pardon me."

"His father, you know?" asked Ruth.

"Yeah. His name's a bitch. Oh, pardon me again, miss. Gawd-awful Indian name. Let me think . . ." He paused, looking to the ceiling for help. "Oh right. Z-teh-something." He looked at the floor, concentrated, took a slow sip. Then snapping his fingers, he blurted out: "Right! Z'teh-nohk . . . uhm . . . damn."

"Z'teh-nohktesheh," Ruth said, rubbing her chin. Through a crooked smile that looked like she just got a subtle joke, she mumbled, "Mr. No-Change."

"Yeah. Z'teh-nohktesheh Moonhawk. How'd you know that?"

Her eyes went wide for a moment, and she froze. "One of the boys must have said it. I good at the language. You know, I speak also French, German, and Russian."

"Sure you are. Yes, you told me. Spanish and Navajo would be more useful around here though." He looked at her askance, thinking something over, but then let it pass and continued his earlier train of thought. "Everybody knows the boy's father as Zed."

"I learn the Spanish and Navajo if you want. You know where I find Zed? I wish speak him about boy. Give whipping."

"You let me talk to him. It's my store, my duty. Besides, I've known him for years." He swished the rest of his whiskey around the bottom of his glass before tossing it back. Then he continued, "Usually he's up in the middle of the canyon. He helps train the CCC guys on masonry work for restoration. The man's a damn genius at the stuff. A real artiste."

Stepping off the stool and placing his large hat back on his head, Kenneth tilted the glass up to his lips and let a chunk of ice slide into his mouth. He slid his empty glass across the counter to Ruth and said through crunching ice, "Almost like he built the damn things himself. Pardon my French."

▼△▼△▼△▼△▼△▼△▼△▼△▼△▼

Pitiful Boy

DECEMBER 22, 1177, TWO MILES
SOUTH OF FAJADA BUTTE

Churl Keleh stretched and tossed back his blankets, edged out from under the canopy, and peeked up to the sky, disappointed that his twinkling friends were hidden tonight behind a thin veil of clouds.

He called into the darkness, "Sqatweh. Sqatweh?"

There was no response. Apparently, the dog was on a scout about. Sighing, he said, "Pity," puckered his lips, and blew "smoke" from his warm breath into the cold night air.

The albino muttered to himself, "Mother had said something . . . Maybe something about the fire?" He scanned the immediate area and found a little rock corral stacked with dried scrub brush and leaf litter. "What is she thinking? Can she not just light the damn thing herself?"

With a huff, he grabbed a small satchel and rifled through it until he found the right pouch. Using a pinch of the gray-brown powder from inside it, he sprinkled the brush and kindling. Leaning over the pile, he said, "*Queh pwey.*" Then he scanned the rocks ringing the campfire and punched one of the flatter ones.

Holding hurt knuckles, he rocked back and forth, face scrunched up. As usual, there was no blood. Self-inflicted wounds were beyond him.

Quietly, he said, "Well, you should be used to disappointment by now, Mother." Shaking his head, he cupped a hand around an ear, saying, "What's that? Right. I know: 'Real magic costs.' But costs what, Mother? Your life? Your sanity?"

He started rifling through his satchel again, muttering, "My life? My sanity?" The flat flint stone and chunk of granite deep in the hidden space at the bottom wouldn't fail to produce a nice, warm fire in mere minutes. "And Mother will never know," he added.

Minutes later, Sqatweh came trotting up to the steady fire, having returned from his canine patrol. He dropped a limp rabbit next to the fire and sat back on his rump.

"Good." Churl smiled and petted the large dog's head vigorously. "You brought us some breakfast."

Sqatweh's tail pumped up and down, beating the ground.

Churl held his mother's old obsidian knife firmly in his left hand, held the rabbit down with his right, and stabbed into the rodent's chest.

Screaming, the rabbit jumped up.

Startled, Churl jumped up.

Annoyed, the dog jumped up—and shot a look of disappointment at his master.

Breakfast fled, with Sqatweh in hot pursuit.

Wincing suddenly, Churl's eyes watered, and he grabbed his right hand. Blood oozed out from underneath his left hand. He had accidentally drawn the knife edge across the back of his thumb. Slumping over onto his side, tears streamed down his face, and a wailing cry started in the back of his throat.

"No," he said angrily. Sitting up, he squeezed the thumb hard, breathing in shallow, rapid gulps. The ordinary sorts of scrapes and scratches that most people shrugged off were excruciating to his fragile, pale skin. "Gods be cursed! Why did you do this to me? Why?" He kicked his feet, stamping the ground with his heels.

After calming down, he lay on his belly, face to the fire. A dusting of magic powder still covered one of the rocks ringing the fire. He let a tiny drop of blood land in the powder, and a fire ball the size of a large pumpkin inflated within the campfire and floated up into the dark sky. If he had had eyebrows, they would have been singed.

Sobbing, he said, "There you go, Mother." He stared into the fire, holding his wound tightly until Sqatweh returned.

In its mouth, the dog had the breakfast—its head crushed in. Dropping the definitely dead rabbit at Churl's feet, he looked up and away from his master and sniffed.

"Sorry. How was I to know it was still alive?"

In the manner of large dogs, Sqatweh flopped onto his side clumsily and exhaled deeply.

"Fine. I see how it is."

The dog rested while Churl flayed the rodent and roasted it on a spit. He picked open the skull, scooped out the remaining bit of brains, wrapped them along with the entrails in some green leaves, and roasted them on a small rock set into the hot coals. The skin he stretched across a flat rock after scraping away the meager bits of fat and connective tissue that clung; it would make a nice patch or pouch.

After eating the bulk of the meat and organs (he saved the brain for his mother), he started packing for their nightly travels, pulling out satchels, pouches, and bedrolls from beneath the canopy.

The residual warmth of the thick fur blankets brought to mind the dream he'd had: he was lying, talking, laughing with a beautiful girl. Her jet-black hair was wispy around her heart-shaped face, with eyes a deep, penetrating brown. Their fingers were interlaced as they spoke softly, breathing each other's breath. She threw a dark, golden thigh across his pale legs, stroked his white chest, and spoke fondly of his alabaster tenderness. Then, like they do, the dream memory washed away like footprints in the sand.

This wasn't the first time he had been with this dream lover. She first started visiting him months ago—rarely at first, but now several times a week. In some ways, it was like he knew her very well. He had even given her a name: Ten-aht. He sighed. "Are you real, Ten-aht? Can you take me away? Escape from Mother?"

He rolled up the dream with blankets, binding everything into tight bundles with grass-cord straps. "I know," he said. "That's asking too much of a dream."

The shelter was something like a lean-to, with two walking sticks that propped up one side about four feet above the ground. The top sloped down to the ground a few feet away and tucked under like a sideways V so that it also formed the floor. The canopy of the shelter was a massive grass weave with patches of fur sewn on to one side to provide a waterproof layer. He removed the walking sticks from the slits in the canopy where they attached, and the "top" collapsed, virtually folding the shelter in half.

Behind the shelter were two long poles, the rails of the travois, which Sqatweh would tow. From one of the pouches, Churl pulled a bundle of leather straps. "Sqatweh, come," he said.

The dog sat up, noticed the harness in Churl's hands, and obediently came to be harnessed but pouted.

"Okay. We won't load you up until Mother arrives."

As they waited, Churl softly sang, studying the embers as they died in the darkening night. "I wonder what disaster awaits us in the next town," he said, digging fingers deep into Sqatweh's thick mane.

The dog didn't seem to know.

* * *

Sqatweh beat his tail against the ground, content with Churl's touch. *Rest now,* he thought. *Travel soon.*

He grew tired of these strange lands far from home. Always his master, Churl, and mistress, Rooshth, traveled. The lush mountains of his youth: gone. The ample hunting through forest and field: gone. The thrill of the pack closing in on a boar: gone. The sweet meat of large fresh game: gone. The scrawny things he'd chased down the last few years were hardly worth the effort. *But,* he thought, *a dog's got to eat.*

And the weather here was miserable: too hot, too cold, too dry. And always windy. People had no idea how that crippled a dog's olfactory sense. Imagine ten people talking all at once—and some of them talking backward. It was a real nightmare.

And the water. Not that he was a big swimmer like some dogs, but he enjoyed the occasional trounce in a stream or river. Here, there was barely enough water to stay alive. Once, Sqatweh even went two days without any food or water—and all the while pulling the sled.

He knew it wasn't his place to question Churl, but he had serious reservations about his master's mother. She was forever on the hunt, dragging the three of them to the corners of the earth. Even scarier than her possible madness was the darkness within her. He never showed weakness because he was afraid she might beat him—like she did the first dog, Nochtu.

The old female had served Churl and Rooshth as faithfully as any. Yet one day, when they had been staying in a city built on a lake, Nochtu somehow displeased the woman. Their mistress cornered her and beat her with a reed whip. The first dog cowed in humiliation, surrendering all honor, but the beating was relentless, forcing Nochtu to try to flee. The mistress cornered her again and used a short stick to beat her senseless. Then the woman cut her throat and skinned her.

As if this unprovoked violence alone wasn't strange enough, the woman then stripped and danced around a campfire, singing bizarre songs. Then she rubbed oil and powder all over herself and did it again, using Nochtu's hide as a ceremonial robe. Covered in magic potions and dog blood, she tried to get the boy to do the same, but he refused. He became distraught, angry, and confused. The two screamed at each other awhile. At some point, Rooshth grabbed the reed whip and beat Churl until he nearly passed out. Then she slumped to the ground and wailed loudly.

Barely an adult at that time, Sqatweh curled up in a corner, shaking and crying. His whimpering caught the woman's attention, and she shot him a look of contempt. The look froze him, and he never showed fear again. No matter what.

The next day, Rooshth's skin was loose and sagging on her bones, like it was three sizes too large. Over time, it shriveled up, giving her the complexion of something between dried fruit and cracked, worn leather. For several days, the boy and the woman went about their usual routines as if nothing had happened—though in total silence. They didn't even bury Nochtu.

It was the darkest, most miserable time of Sqatweh's life.

A slight *woosh* sound in the night air swept away the dog's awful memory. Both he and the boy looked around for the mistress, who would have just appeared from nowhere. Sqatweh spotted her walking from the direction of where the shelter had been.

Churl offered her the fresh rabbit meat and brains, but his mother frowned and shrugged away the offer. Then, with some glee, she snatched it out of Churl's hand and threw it to Sqatweh.

Thanks? the dog thought, giving a courtesy wag. The scrap was basically a lump of charcoal now but passed the sniff test. His tail started wagging vigorously as he crunched on the morsel. *A dog's got to eat.*

* * *

67

Churl stared at his mother's skin as she walked up to him and Sqatweh but looked away quickly when she noticed. "How was the spirit world?" he asked.

She had been Spirit Walking again—a way of traveling great distances in the physical world by taking a shortcut through the spirit world known as the In-Between. While there, the spirits would sometimes tell her things—sometimes secret, dark things. Her knowledge and powers increased greatly once she learned to Spirit Walk.

She contemplated for a moment and then said, "Quiet. But whispers of something afoot."

"Something? Or someone?" He looked pointedly at her.

She made a knowing smile.

"Do we travel to the little canyon tonight?"

"Yes."

"Did you Skin Walk there?"

"No. You know I can only walk where I have walked previously."

"Have you tried it before?" he pushed.

"Yes." She pointed to a scar on her left calf. "I stepped out of the In Between and fell off a cliff. I nearly died."

"What is it like?"

"The spirit world? Or nearly dying?"

"The In-Between. The spirit world."

"Words fail. Shapes, images, colors, smells, and sounds—all different. They do not have mountains or grass or sky or anything you would recognize."

He knew all of this, of course. It was a conversation they'd had many times. The light in her eyes was what he craved: to experience vicariously a world beyond this one. He longed for—yet feared—the freedom that she had. The more she Skin Walked, the more at home she was there, as if a little piece of her stayed behind each time. He wondered how many more times she could do it before she simply wouldn't return.

"Can the spirits cross over to us?"

"Yes, but they prefer not to."

"Why not?"

"They say this: for them to give up their spirit body and assume a flesh body would be like you or me giving up ten fingers for only two."

Churl looked at his hands. "Oh. Strange."

"Yes."

"Do you get more fingers when you are a spirit there?"

She laughed. "No. Just a way of thinking about it. I am normally flesh, and so I cannot fill a spirit body completely."

"So, you are a two-fingered spirit?"

"Something like that."

She pinched a small bit of dirt and spread it between her palms, rubbing them together like one might do to sift chaff from wheat. Giving the earth a small sniff and a small taste, she said, "Finish packing. We must make it to the canyon village tonight."

Churl hopped up and snapped his fingers at the dog, who immediately came to be saddled. As he worked, Churl tried engaging her again: "I am surprised that it is not storming."

"Oh?"

"Well, when you left, I briefly woke to the sound of a great rushing wind."

She turned to him, eyes beaming. "Could you tell its direction?"

"Yes." He pointed toward the canyon, saying, "Actually, it was blowing in the direction of the canyon village."

She seized his arms excitedly. "Son, that wind had nothing to do with weather."

He was confused.

"You heard the spirit wind blowing." A tear welled up in one of her eyes. "Son, there is powerful magic there. I think it is already working on you. We will finally fix you."

He smiled weakly, having never actually felt broken.

When she wandered off, muttering excitedly to herself, he bent down, close to Sqatweh's face. Rubbing his fingers through the dog's plush mane, he whispered to it, "What? Oh sure, who wouldn't love to have thick, black hair, golden, tanned skin, and sinewy muscles. I know: real magic costs, but the price is too high."

Sqatweh licked the side of Churl's face with his enormous tongue and wagged his tail.

"Thanks, my friend. I agree." He scratched the dog's mane vigorously. "Who is a crazy lady? Who is a crazy lady? I know who is a crazy lady."

□ ■ □ ■ □ ■ □ ■ □ ■ □

T57

June 20, 1938, Outside Weatherby's Mercantile, Chaco Canyon

C. J. Blackwood's drive from Santa Fe had been uneventful. He had seen seven herds of antelope, twenty-three hawks, two eagles, eighteen armadillos, twelve men riding horses in the middle of the road, two cars, and one broken-down Indian motorcycle. (The proud biker declined the offer of a ride, sure of his own mechanical prowess.) Finally arriving at the canyon, he pulled off the narrow road that ran its length and stopped in front of a little cluster of businesses: a telegraph office, a bank, a saloon, a diner, a gas station, and a mercantile. The latter had the moniker "Weatherby's."

"Mr. Weatherby must be important," he noted aloud, taking his car out of gear and engaging the hand brake.

A flatbed Ford pulled out of a nearby space. The driver, who had a large, white cowboy hat, gunned his engine and spun tires, showering the area with dust and gravel.

Blackwood glared at the sight of a million tiny specks of dust accumulating on the hood of his car, each minute scratch in the finish a tiny paper cut across his pride. The layer of dust covering the passenger's seat to his left caught his attention and was bestowed an equally disdainful glare. He pulled his driving gloves off, one finger at a time, calmly folded the fingers over the palms, and then stacked them together and laid them in their reserved spot in the glove box. Using a soft cloth to wipe most of the offensive earth away, he mumbled to the elements, "Leather trim. Not terracotta. New Mexico clearly has boundary issues."

As he opened his door and stepped out, he surveyed the area more closely: he was at the south end of a large valley set between two mesas, known as Chaco Canyon. The region's only apparent draw had been as a hotspot for archaeology for several decades now. The scenery of sandstone bluffs, desert scrub, and dirt possessed a certain beauty with limited appeal—a ruggedness that tugged at one's inner soul, calling for adventure and challenge. However, it was clear that this same desert charm could turn wild in an instant, devouring souls and bodies without warning, without remorse.

"Must be a hearty breed of people out here," he said to himself.

Two Natives walked out of the telegraph office, personifying the juxtaposition of disparate times and cultures: one wearing traditional pants with a silk suit jacket and no shirt while the other had the suit pants belonging to the jacket and wore a leather vest with no shirt. Each had a necklace with turquoise and silver pendants and beads, the colors a bright contrast against their espresso-colored, leathery skin. Their horses stood at the hitching post, enduring yet another long wait under the hot sun. One animal had a barely-holding-it-together saddle while the other didn't even have a blanket.

Blackwood's assignment had him bound for Casa Grande, an ancient ruin in Arizona, located halfway between Phoenix and Tucson. Word of a crooked antiquities dealer allegedly specializing in stolen *kachina* dolls and other Hopi sacred objects had come to the Foundation. His mission was to investigate the veracity of the rumor, bringing resolution to the situation as needed.

This pit-stop in Chaco Canyon was a mini-vacation for him. Anthropology and psychology were his hobbies, and the upcoming solstice ceremonies here would provide ample opportunities to study a variety of different cultures. Participants would come from all over the region, from different nations and tribes, all making appeals to their gods and showing off their unique rituals. Physics and relativity had unraveled the basic ideas of the origin of the universe; Darwin and company had done the same for biological descent and diversity. Blackwood awaited the next genius to ascend humanity's last intellectual peak: understanding human nature. (His money was on Carl Jung.)

The next day's events would involve dancers with elaborate outfits performing in *kivas*—circular sacred structures scattered throughout the ruins. Some of the costumes would resemble authentic *kachina* dolls, and a nascent familiarity with their style would help him ascertain whether or not the Arizona *kachinas* in question were genuine. If they were fakes, then the Foundation would have no interest in taking action. On the other hand, if legitimate stolen heritage items were being sold, then they would want him to take care of it discreetly, employing his specialty: arranging certain "accidents."

Though this was his first foray into the Southwest, his employers had sent him all over the rest of North America in the last few years. In Washington State, certain sacred robes had been returned to the rightful owners; the wrongful possessor's car went off the road into a steep ravine, ending in a spectacular explosion. In Florida, there had been Seminole lands where developers were poisoning people to get them to leave; the lead developer managed to suffer a severe cramp while swimming off his yacht and drowned. Blackwood's furthest mission so far had been in the Alaska territory, where Inuit ivory carvings were making their way onto the black market; somehow, the perpetrators managed to get mauled by a four-thousand-pound male walrus.

Working for the Foundation had both emotional and financial rewards. The investigations and their challenges were intellectually stimulating, and he always met interesting people. Plus, he was able to exercise his imaginative side when various problems required a creative "solution." Financially, the Foundation provided modest but adequate compensation, but they allowed him to engage in the odd "recovery" or "elimination" job on the side—as long as it didn't interfere with Foundation business or land him in prison. As to his work-related expenses, they never failed to provide for his needs, nor did they question them—even when "needs" included the procurement of a brand-new, bright yellow, specially outfitted Bugatti T57 Grand Raid Roadster.

Despite his art-deco transport and generous expense account, all the solo travel left him lonely occasionally, a hole filled with female company as needed. Attracting women presented no problem for him; "tall and handsome," "well-bred," and "of means" were terms commonly used to describe him. Generally, his woman troubles consisted of being the target of unwanted advances; more than a few had flung themselves at him over the years.

Presently, he needed to find a place where he could tent-camp, since there were no nearby hotels.

Scanning the storefronts, he fetched his cigarette case from his jacket pocket and opened it. He stared for a moment at his last Wills' Gold Flake cigarette and then removed it with a sigh. After glancing around covertly, he flipped the silver case over and reopened it, exposing the contents of a hidden compartment. Everything was there: garrote, poison tablets, knock-out drops in a tiny glass syringe, and two reefers. (The latter was strictly for professional use—brandy or cognac being his preferred recreational drug.)

Lighting up with his silver, monogrammed Zippo, he muttered, "Probably only have Camels or those detestable Philip-Morris." Stepping through the tall door of Weatherby's Mercantile, he scanned the place: soda fountain in the back, clothes and sundries on one side, groceries on the other. Several glass cases and shelves were broken, and shards of glass had been swept into piles.

A tiny woman emerged from the back of the store, responding to the jangling bell hanging from the door frame. "Hello," said Ruth, smiling. "Sorry for the mess. I still cleaning after . . . some trouble with 'rascals.' Nice day. How you are? What I get you?"

He took a long drag off his smoke, held it for a moment, and then answered her as he exhaled: "*Bonjour, jeune femme. Très bien. Merci.*"

She returned him a blank stare.

"Ah . . . *Sto bene. Grazie!*" he tried, smiling.

Blank again.

He raised an eyebrow and tried, "*Ich bin gut. Danke.*"

Once again, blank.

"Sorry. I'm doing well. Thank you so much for asking." He looked around for a place to flick his cigarette ash and found a suitable brass spittoon. "I spent time in Europe during the Great War and thought I might recognize your accent."

"What I get you?" she asked, not taking the bait.

"First, I need to know where you're from." Blackwood dialed up the charm. "I'll not be able to concentrate until you solve this mystery for me." He leaned against the bar and looked at her with intense—but smiling—eyes and drew another breath from his last Gold Flake.

"Well . . ." She glanced quickly away in a shy manner. "I Dutch. Nederlander."

"Oh, the Lowlands. Which province was your home?"

She went pale and then flushed. "It so tiny. You never hear of."

"Oh, don't be so sure. I lived in Belgium and Switzerland for several years and had many Dutch friends and acquaintances."

"So tiny. I sure you never."

He smiled and said flatly, "Very well. If you say so."

They exchanged a knowing look, and an unspoken agreement passed between them: they both knew she was lying, but they would both proceed with the fiction.

Pulling the cigarette out of his mouth and holding it toward her between two fingers, he said, "I require more smokes."

"What your pleasure?"

"It's a long shot, but do you have Wills' Gold Flake?"

"Is what?"

He sighed. "Imported. From Britain."

"I . . . no, we not have."

"What brands do you carry?" He looked up and away from her, tapping his fingers on the counter.

"The Camels."

"What? No Philip-Morris?"

"I check." Walking around the counter to the grocery side, she searched low on the shelves and came up beaming. "Here," she said. "You lucky. It last one." A pack of Philip-Morris was proudly displayed in her hand.

"I was just curious," he informed her. "Sorry."

She looked disappointed. "Most around here, they roll their own," she offered.

"I'll take that."

"Take what?"

"Smokes that I roll myself."

"Oh. What paper?"

"Paper?" He paused. "Right. Show me what you have." He selected the most expensive brand.

"And leaf?"

"What have you?" Again, he picked the most expensive of three options.

She carefully wrapped his purchase in a brown paper bundle and tied it with some string. "Okay, sir." As she deftly operated the bright brass cash register, digits popped and pinged up and down.

He shook his head and paid her, asking, "Do you know where I can camp here in the canyon? Can I camp anywhere?"

"I not know. Go up canyon road. Find station. Ask there."

"Thank you. I shall."

Back in his car, Blackwood opened the bundle and studied the papers and the pouch of tobacco carefully. He set them in the passenger seat—after wiping it off again—and started the car. It roared to life, and he revved the engine. Patting the dashboard lovingly, he said, "The perfect marriage of science and art."

The noon sun burned brightly down on him as he sat in the T57 convertible. He quickly retrieved his driving gloves, made all the usual—and redundant—adjustments to mirrors and such, and dropped the transmission into reverse, pulling out of his spot gently. Then he put it in first gear, revved the engine slightly, and popped the clutch, spraying a shower of rocks and dirt. "When in Rome . . ." he said.

In moments, he was heading north again through the canyon. Along the way, he passed both white men and Natives on horseback—he even passed a prairie schooner driven by a "miner-forty-niner" old man with a potbelly, suspenders, enormous white beard, and beat-up leather hat. The sight made him shake his head and wonder aloud, "This is like an *Amazing Stories* episode. I've been transported backwards in time fifty years."

About halfway up the canyon, two boys were walking northward. Blackwood honked, slowed down, and pulled along beside them. Turq Moonhawk gave a slight bow respectfully while Frankie Yellowtail pointed at the convertible T57 with his mouth alternately opening and closing.

"Perfect," Blackwood said under his breath. "Hi, boys," he said warmly, flashing his don't-you-think-I'm-cool smile.

"Hello, sir," said Turq.

"H-he-hello. Nice wh-wheels," said Frankie.

"Beautiful day for a walk," said Blackwood.

"Yes, b-but it's h-hot," said Frankie, wiping his brow dramatically.

"Maybe we could help each other out," Blackwood said.

"How so?" asked Turq, skeptically.

"I need instructions and directions, and you need a ride in the coolest automobile ever."

"Y-yes. We certainly d-do."

Blackwood stepped out of the car, bundle of cigarette materials in hand, and asked, "You boys smoke?"

"Of course," they both answered, as if the man were asking if they breathed or liked girls.

"Have you ever rolled smokes? I'm embarrassed to say I don't know how."

"Y-yes. We c-can roll smokes," said Frankie confidently.

"Great. I usually buy them pre-rolled, but someone told me that I hadn't smoked until I'd rolled my own." He unbundled his Weatherby's purchase and presented it to the boys. "How do I get started?"

Frankie started laughing, holding his stomach, and guffawing.

"Bad, bad, bad, bad. First, you must get your money back." Turq grabbed the tobacco pouch, opened it, and pulled out a large twisted braid of chewing tobacco. "Sir, someone sold you chaw. This cannot be rolled in a smoke." He rubbed it between his fingers, which quickly stained brownish-green. "See: too much moisture, and it is not cut fine. This stuff is hard to burn even in a fire. You need fine-cut, dry loose-leaf, sir."

Blackwood huffed, lifted an eyebrow, and said, "Well, you boys have just saved me a long, embarrassing frustration. Thank you. I need to go pay someone a visit." He turned to the car, released the catch for the rumble seat, lifted it into position, and indicated for the boys to hop in.

Turq thrust the tobacco back into Blackwood's hands and leaped into the rear seat in a single bound. Then he helped Frankie climb in, who struggled with the effort.

"W-we're ready!" said Frankie, turning around and sitting gingerly.

"Okay," Blackwood said, sliding into the driver's seat. "By the way, before we set out, we need to have introductions. You can call me Mr. Blackwood."

"Okay, Mr. B-Blackwood," said Frankie. "My name's Frankie—
Frankie Yellowtail. And this here's T, for Turq M-M-Moonhawk.
Ouch!"

Frankie glared at Turq and rubbed his ribs, saying, "That h-hurt."

Turq glared back.

"What?" said Frankie.

Turq turned away from the older boy and folded his arms across
his chest, saying, "Never mind."

"Okay. Now, l-let's go!"

"I need to find a good place to pitch my tent and camp for the
solstice ceremonies. And I bet you boys know all the best places in the
canyon."

"S-sure! Sure we d-do."

"We can show you several good, safe places, Mr. Blackwood,"
added Turq.

"Great. But first, I need to zip back to Weatherby's and get the
right cut leaf."

Turq went stiff and said, "No, Mr. Blackwood, sir." He started
climbing out of the rumble seat. "We will wait here for your return,
then show you around."

Frankie disagreed. "No, T. We can s-see that pretty l-lady again."

The Native boy gave his friend a don't-you-remember-what-we-
talked-about look.

Frankie said, "Oh. Right. We'll w-wait, Mr. Blackwood."

"That's okay. I'll just go back later. But what's wrong, boy? I
wouldn't mind another look at that dame. She was easy on the eyes."
Blackwood smiled broadly.

Looking off into the distance, Turq said, "She's no dame, Mr.
Blackwood. She's a witch."

▼△▼△▼△▼△▼△▼△▼△▼△▼△▼

Arrival

DECEMBER 23, 1177, OUTSIDE CHACO VILLAGE

Three *quetz'al* glided peacefully through the golds and mauves of the cold morning clouds. The sun eased over the horizon, its meager rays warming their skin as they approached Chaco Canyon.

Needing some adventure after the *Shat'kuhat* ascended to heaven, Tuhj, Luahti, and a young adult named Tyleh left the canyon during the night. They had flown far to the north and east to prey upon a bison herd that had been spotted several days before. There had been plucking, chasing, and games. The picking had been easy and the eating good. In the end, they ate five complete bison—bones and all—and partially ate four more, leaving the rest for the coyotes.

That was great, sang Tyleh dreamily. He had only been an adult for a couple of years, and this had been the first time any important adults had allowed him to tag along on a hunt.

Look, sang Luahti, in their singsong language. She was close to Tuhj in age and had mated with him several times. Few *quetz'al* became a Life Pair, but they had.

Where? the older male asked.

Village boundary. Near Zatu Nashtehweh Tza Bu'vah. (The Great House, *Hungo Pavi*)

Oh . . . yes.

Like so many of them, the Great House at the southeast corner of the canyon was a large D-shaped *pueblo*, with the majority of apartments forming a long, multistory complex on the straight side. The curved wall surrounding a courtyard had a single level of recently added apartments. A ceremonial *kiva* was more or less centered in the courtyard, surrounded by sleeping garden beds.

Midway between the Great House and the canyon wall, two travelers and their dog were finishing erecting a small shelter. An old woman was in charge, and her body language suggested impatience with her male companion. The enormous pack dog was a safe distance away, looking concerned.

I need dessert, sang Tyleh.

Ooh, Luahti approved. *You?* she asked Tuhj.

This gave the alpha male pause, but then he sang, *Good sport. True. But the empty shelter would generate questions.*

We could take it beyond canyon, sang Luahti.

An easy solution, sang Tyleh.

Indeed, admitted Tuhj.

Shall we? asked Tyleh.

Let us, agreed Tuhj.

I am anxious to taste their tangy-sweet flesh, sang Tyleh, a little too enthusiastically.

A few power strokes took them higher above the canyon floor and out of human sight. Then collapsing their wings, they dove, peregrine-falcon-like, reaching tremendous speed until the air itself tore at their skin. When a mere hundred feet off the ground, they opened wings behind the small shelter and cruised over it. The popping of their flight membranes sent a thunderous boom throughout the canyon. Dust, dirt, and debris flew everywhere. Then, like Harris hawks, they skimmed the surface of the earth in flight, tails nearly touching the ground.

The man hit the deck at the sound of the boom, and the dog scurried away sideways, tail tucked in. The woman squatted slightly for stability, long, silver-blonde hair billowing out chaotically in the *quetz'al*'s turbulence. She pushed tangles back from her face with a leathery forearm and grimaced.

Her look of fury caught Tuhj's attention. *Strange,* he sang, *she is not afraid.*

She should be, sang the youngest flyer.

The trio of *quetz'al*, in a triangular attack formation, banked and rose up over the Great House, flew south out of the canyon, and circled back. They silently glided across the top of the mesa and descended its canyon-side cliff to make their second strike. Visions of forbidden fruit danced in their heads, driving them on.

By now Churl was on his feet, running full speed toward the Great House, spurred by terror and fueled by adrenaline. Sqatweh ran beside him. Rooshth, however, was making large circling and sweeping motions with her arms, screaming something in a tongue that was part human and part spirit talk.

No, commanded Tuhj.

What? asked Luahti.

Danger. Break off.

From wrinkle-woman? asked Tyleh. *You joke.*

No.

Tuhj and Luahti split off from the line of attack, one banking left, the other right. But Tyleh, possessed by attack fever, accelerated.

A "crack-foom" sound filled the air, rattling their ears. Tuhj looked back and saw a swirling ball of ice and snow strike Tyleh with full force in the head.

The impact sent Tyleh tumbling end-over, backward through the air, eventually slamming into one of the canyon walls. His unconscious, limp form slid/tumbled/bounced down the wall, leaving a crimson trail. Eventually, he formed a crumpled, morbid heap at the bottom of the cliff, dust quickly settling around. The unnatural position of Tyleh's body suggested death: wings torn and smashed, tail dislocated, broken leg and wing bones protruding, bright red blood pooling. Blood and foam oozed from the gaping skull injury where his right eye and cheek used to be.

Tuhj said to Luahti, *Let us break away, hide, and then try another sneak.* However, she wasn't listening.

Luahti was circling back on the woman, rage in her eyes.

No. Wait, Tuhj sang, his voice angry, yet pleading. *No!*

Her battle scream drowned out his pleas as she bore down to attack. He cut his turn short, but there was no way to intercept her in time; she would be upon the woman before he completed his turn.

Rooshth waved her arms again and spoke more strange words, making snow and ice swirl about her, an icy dust-devil in the desert.

Luahti, no!

In moments, the swirl had compacted into a ball the size of a pumpkin and flew toward its mark—an icy projectile with a destiny.

Luahti swerved. The projectile missed her head but struck her right shoulder, glanced off, and punched a hole through the taut skin of the same wing. She screamed.

* * *

A few minutes earlier, when the thunderous sound of the three attacking *quetz'al* plowed through the canyon and practically jolted everyone from their beds, twelve-year-old Totahmaa Kwi Mukaama actually jolted from his bed. The oldest child of Quaatsa Mukaama had stayed the night at *Zatu Nashtehweh Tza Bu'vah* (*Hungo Pavi*). (His family's home was at the south end of the canyon, quite some distance away near *Ton'ah Tashteh* (Fajada Butte), but his mother sent him to stay with another family after his father and the other *Shat'kuhat* had ascended to the gods.)

"Bad, bad, bad, bad," he said as he laced up winter sandals and bounded leggings. He rubbed his elbows and bolted out the door, across a roof, down several ladders, and had made it halfway across the courtyard before getting his shirt and cap on properly. A few strides later, he pushed aside the courtyard barricade and sprinted through the gate. Outside, he nearly collided with an albino and a dog running hell-bent toward the gate.

He stopped them and directed, "Go inside. It is safe there. *Quetz'al* will not attack inside the courtyard." (As hatchlings, the flyers were trained to avoid the Great Houses, so the adult creatures never came inside.)

Angry and frightened, Churl jabbered words unintelligible to Totahmaa.

Totahmaa said, "I will bring Father soon. He can translate for you." Then he motioned for the albino to enter the Great House.

"Father is not going to like this," Totahmaa said, running back through the gate.

An unauthorized *quetz'al* attack hadn't happened in years, and the *Shat'kuhat* wanted to keep it that way. The People had little interest in and less tolerance for the *quetz'al* lately. With the dwindling crops over the past few years, disturbing talk of slaughtering the creatures for food even arose from time to time. In the old days, the *quetzal* were a source of power and pride for The People, but now most of them thought that the flyers just seemed to be a lot of effort. As instruments of war and sacred animals, they were very valuable, but they were also very dangerous: anyone who thought otherwise was a walking snack.

Totahmaa was scanning the sky for trouble when Luahti's piercing battle cry rocked the canyon. She tore through the air with savage ferocity toward an old woman, who merely stood there, waving her arms.

"She going to just shoo her away?" the boy wondered aloud. "This is bad. Bad, bad, bad, bad. Father will kill her—maybe both of them."

Though he had forgotten his scarlet vest in his effort to race out here, the boy had managed to grab his bright yellow, turquois-studded, conical hat, symbols to help the *quetzal* recognize the trainers. As he ran full speed toward the old woman, his hat kept alternately flopping down over his eyebrows and falling off the back of his head. "Probably the cap alone will be enough. Probably," he said.

A strange "crack-foom" sound stopped him in his tracks. Pushing the cap up out of his eyes, he looked up. The giant flyer was tumbling out of the sky, wing destroyed, fluttering like a grotesque flag. She hit the ground on her back and was sliding across the gravelly dirt and snow, tail-first, directly at Totahmaa.

He back-pedaled, turned, and ran in the opposite direction. His hat slid off his head and rattled against his back. Feet pounding, heart pounding, eyes wide, he dove to the right, avoiding being crushed, but a wing caught him up, sending him tumbling with the creature. Folded inside a leathery wing, his body alternately spun and slammed into the ground. He wrapped his arms around his head, protecting his skull from getting crushed, but one of his elbows broke and dislocated.

When the motion stopped, pain and bruising began. He was not unconscious, but not entirely conscious either. Within seconds, the *quetzal* began stirring, and so did the boy, scrambling on knees and his good hand to get out from under the creature.

Once on his feet, he scanned the area and got his bearings. Except for the ringing in his ears and a broken arm, he was fine. "Could have been worse," he consoled himself. He reached back to put his hat on, but it was gone—crushed and disintegrated during the crash. "Bad, bad, bad, bad," he said.

Slowly, he backed away from the downed flyer, saying, "Do you see my pretty yellow pants? I am here to help. You need not eat me."

Tuhj suddenly touched down near Luahti and slid to a stop. The large male turned toward the woman, beating his wings furiously and screaming. Dust and debris scattered everywhere.

Carefully and quickly, Totahmaa gave the two flyers a wide berth, circling around to see the object of wrath. "What?" His mouth gaped.

The tiny old woman, with an equally tiny knife, ran full speed at Tuhj and Luahti. Her silver hair and ragged, blue tunic splayed out behind her, while her apparent death wish trumpeted before her. Screaming unintelligible words, she was a blue-white flame tearing across the desert.

"Obviously out of your mind," Totahmaa said. "But you get credit for courage." Sighing, he shook his head and ran toward her, waving his good hand in the air. "Stop, stop, stop!"

The woman saw him and stopped. Hunched over to catch her breath, she pushed silver-white hair out of her face and looked up at Tuhj, wagging her small knife at the flyer as if to say, "This isn't over." After a few seconds, she stood upright and turned to face the boy. Her left hand was on her hip, and her right arm extended, pointing accusingly at the two *quetz'al*. Anger flowed from every pore. Ugly speech punched the air, ricocheting from canyon walls.

Tuhj paused his threatening display and looked at Totahmaa, who had started singing a calming song to the creatures. The large male visibly relaxed but remained on guard. Luahti was struggling unsuccessfully to get to her feet. Shredded flight skin barely clung to the framing bones of her devastated wing; large segments of the thin skin were altogether missing. Such damage was beyond repair, making her permanently lame. If she survived, the other *quetz'al* would cast her out, leaving her to die alone in the desert.

The woman walked angrily toward Totahmaa, who stopped singing and stepped farther away from the male *quetz'al*, while motioning for her to also give it a wide berth. Oblivious to the danger, the tiny fury ignored his signals at first, but his persistence persuaded her. That the *quetz'al* were large was obvious. Less so were their lightning-like reflexes and ability to instantaneously spring forward several body lengths. Those who thought they were safe just because they were farther than a neck-length soon found a snug new spot inside a belly.

In addition to hideous, shriveled, and wrinkled skin, the woman had a piercing, high-pitched voice that simultaneously cut like a knife and crushed like a stone. She was speaking rapidly and getting nowhere with Totahmaa. She switched languages several times, finally falling into bits and pieces of the language of people toward *Tza Sheh*, the direction of sunset at winter solstice.

"Boy. Boy. You hear me? Hear me?" It was choppy, with overlapping accents.

"Yes," he answered, much more fluently.

She raised an eyebrow, lifted her chin, and huffed, obviously unimpressed at his command of the language.

"You have traveled? Studied many tongues?"

"No. My father taught me. He has the gift of . . ." He paused, looking away for a moment, and then continued, "He is well-traveled and wise."

"Father is important leader?"

"Yes."

"Who he is? I speak him."

"He is resting now. I will tell him of your request."

"Request?" Fists on hips, back arched, and chin tilted up, she wore indignation with pride. "I repeat: I must speak him."

He folded his arms and tilted his head sideways, looking down on her tiny frame.

The woman backed down. "I request humbly. Audience with your father," she said, bowing her head ever so slightly.

Other *quetz'al* herders and handlers now poured out of the *Zatu Nashtehweh*, running toward the two flyers. Bright yellow pants and turquoise hats flashed brightly in the yellow-orange morning light. The first ones out were mostly Totahmaa's age.

A couple of adults, similarly clad in bright yellow, followed. One of them ran to Totahmaa and the woman, saying, "I see Tuhj and Luahti. Tyleh is missing."

"I have not seen him," Totahmaa answered.

"Who is this woman? Is she okay?"

To the woman, Totahmaa asked in their shared tongue, "Are you injured?"

"No," came the offended reply.

"Ask her name."

So Totahmaa asked.

"I have many."

Totahmaa bit his lower lip and waited.

"My people call me Rooshth Va Manahken. It means Lonely Mother."

He turned to the older herder. "Foolish Old Yelling Wrinkles says—"

The adult herder put his hands on his hips and gave the boy a sharp look of disapproval.

"I mean, Old Woman says her name is Lonely Mother."

"Take her into the courtyard. Her companion is there." Then the man turned away to go help with the inspection of the *quetz'al*.

Totahmaa reluctantly held out his open palm. "Come inside *Zatu Nashtehweh*. Your companion is there."

He grimaced slightly when she grasped his hand.

"My *glauchas* . . ." she said.

He looked at her, confused.

She turned away, looking into the sky, brow furrowed. "Son. My son. My little boy."

"Oh. Your companion? He is your son?"

"Yes. My good little boy." For the slightest moment, her face relaxed, softened, and glowed faintly, but then just as quickly her face returned to its distant and piercing demeanor.

"Do you mean the albino with the dog?"

"Of course. Who else?" she asked, genuinely puzzled.

"But he is so old."

She gave him a smile that was half-smirk. Taking his hand with both of hers, she patted and rubbed the back of it.

His vision blurred slightly. The world sounded hollow and seemed to flow in slow motion as the transdermal drug she applied took effect.

□ ■ □ ■ □ ■ □ ■ □ ■ □

Frankie's Find

JUNE 20, 1938, OUTSIDE CHETRO KETTLE, CHACO CANYON

Buddy Womack tucked the small, ancient square stone under his shirt, just in the small of his back underneath his waistband. Glancing around nervously, he said to unseen forces, "You ain't going to get me."

Krenshaw's excruciating death by scorpion had the whole camp buzzing, and most attributed the tragedy to the man's recklessness. Womack knew better. He had spent most of the previous day hiding and had avoided any contact with the stone until now.

Eyes squinting as he left the bunkhouse, the sinking evening sun still shone brightly as he looked around, warily surveying the landscape. Keenly avoiding any spot suitable for an ambush, he cautiously made his way down to Chetro Ketl. After finding the little room where the nude nymph had been, he pulled the artifact from behind his back and scanned the room for a place to stash it.

"Hello, Buddy."

Dropping the stone, he wheeled around to see the nymph standing before him, just as nude, just as alluring as before.

"How do you know my name?"

She waved a hand dismissively. "It doesn't matter. What are you doing, Buddy?" Her voice was smooth, sensual.

"Who are you? Did you kill Krenshaw?"

"Your friend got what he deserved," she said, shrugging her shoulders. "He made a poor choice."

"So you did kill him."

"The desert is filled with danger."

He took a step backward. "But who are you?"

"Ixtab," she answered, as if this were common knowledge.

Trying to repeat it, he said, "Ish-tab?" Her body rippled and grew more sensuous at the sound of her name. "Ixtab," he repeated, her body rippling again.

"Say it again."

"Ixtab."

"Do you like it?" She stepped closer to him.

"Yes," he croaked.

"Say it again."

He obeyed, and her eroticism increased, drawing him in. His vision blurred, and he started whispering her name over and over as it filled his mind. "How strange. How beautiful. Ixtab!"

She advanced a step, and he retreated a step, stumbling slightly on a rock. The imbalance cleared his head from the quickly deepening trance. She looked disappointed and pursed full, pouty lips.

"Say my name again," she pleaded, thrusting her shoulders forward to push her breasts together. "I like it when you say my name."

He looked around the room in alarm, eyeing the door longingly. "Who *are* you?" He fought the urge to stare, and tried to look anywhere but at her, but his eyes betrayed him, alternately fixing on her breasts, stomach, and hips.

"I am a goddess. Within me your deepest desires come true."

"Goddess? Goddess of what?"

Suddenly, the nymph huffed angrily, grew two feet taller, and loomed over him. With eyes now burning like white-hot coals, she said, "I am the Mayan Goddess of Suicide and Lust: Ixtab, the Seductress, She Who Strews White Flowers Along the Path to Heaven, She Who Drowns Men in Their Desire, She Who Induces Madness. And I, Ixtab of the Rainbow Gods, now grow tired of you. You must choose."

Her terrifying voice and imposing size drove him backward. Sweat erupted across his face, and he started hyperventilating. Suddenly, his face cinched up as he went stiff and grabbed his left arm. His eyes went wide with panic. "I . . . I'm dying . . ."

The goddess tilted her head sideways, seeming to look through him. With a curious smile on her face, she said, "Yes. You are."

"Now, you . . ."—she started, growing even taller—". . . must . . ."—her voice dropped into a deep and utterly inhuman vocal range that was more felt than heard—". . . choose." Loose dirt and plaster sprung from ancient brickwork.

He stumbled backward and fell, hitting his head against a stone wall. Unaware of the blood pouring from the back of his skull, he stood on his knees, wobbly and clutching his chest. His paralyzed left arm burned and throbbed. After a moment, he fell over. His eyes blinked hard, locking onto the stone artifact lying in the dirt a few feet away. It seemed to call to him like a distant, unreachable savior.

"Choose, mortal." The sultry voice returned, as did her previous diminutive and alluring form. She sat in the dirt in front of him and next to the stone, hugging her knees coyly. "Me or this," she said, patting the artifact.

He reached for the stone with his right arm, but it seemed to weigh two hundred pounds, and he collapsed, his arm falling across her lap. At the moment of contact with her, his body began to convulse. Smoke curled out from his nostrils, up around his face, and he screamed. It felt as if Ixtab were dragging razor blades through his body.

Over the sound of his agony, she said, "Ah, your soul! Your beautiful, corrupt soul." She inhaled sharply, sighed, and as if in the start of an orgasm, threw her head back and moaned. Then, licking her lips, she uttered the last words he would ever hear: "Delicious."

Ixtab dissolved, replaced by a four-inch-diameter rattlesnake utterly without appreciation for human contact.

His exhausted, pain-wracked eyes simply closed in acceptance as lightning-quick strikes landed huge fangs over and over again, deep into face, arms, and throat. Coagulants in the toxins quickly thickened his blood. His breathing went shallow and labored, each pounding heartbeat threatening to burst delicate capillaries as his blood pressure reached a fatal level.

After a terrific "wump" deep within his chest, the former baseball player stole home to eternity.

* * *

Frankie Yellowtail, Natasha Yellowtail, and Turq Moonhawk sat around a table in the Yellowtails' tiny kitchen. It wasn't so much a real kitchen as it was a corner in a forty-year-old cabin with a twenty-year-old stove and wash basin of unknown antiquity. A crucifix on a wall, a statue of the Immaculate Virgin, a couple of *kachinas* sitting on a shelf, and a bundle of maize hanging from a ceiling rafter watched over the cabin's occupants.

Natasha threw her long, black hair over her shoulder with a toss of her head. As she scraped the last of the *frijoles* from the pot, the metal spoon clanked pleasantly against both the cookware and Turq's tin plate.

"Don't eh-eat too m-many beans, T. You're f-farty enough already! Whew!" Frankie held his nose and fanned his face with his other hand. "G-good thing it's windy t-tonight." His jest brought hearty laughter from his audience.

Smiling broadly, Natasha said, "Oh, Big Man is a comedian. You should get a vaudeville show. Call it Big Man's Big Show."

"G-good idea, Mother. I c-can dance, too. See?" He stood bow-legged, wiggling his knees left and right while waving his hands across them. "That's the Charleston."

Turq looked skeptical. He said, "I think you will need more practice."

"Okay. I'll p-practice. You eat. Then w-we can listen to the r-radio."

In no time, Turq was done, and Frankie went to sit by the radio. "I h-hope you get t-to hear some b-baseball tonight."

"Me too—" started Turq, but he abruptly sat erect in his chair, looking out of the window with serious intensity. Wiping his mouth with his napkin, he said, "Miss Yellowtail?"

"Yes, Turq."

"I just want you to know that I caused some trouble yesterday in the mercantile."

Frankie swallowed nervously as his mother's head flipped back and forth between the two boys. She looked confused. "One of your pranks go badly?" she asked.

"No. I only wish," Turq answered, looking distant.

"What happened?"

"Frankie can tell you." The Native boy folded the towel and placed it next to his spoon, then stood up from the table. "I have to go now. I just wanted you to hear it from me. Know that Frankie had nothing to do with it."

Turq started for the door, but Frankie intercepted, saying, "But, T, we were g-going to listen to the r-radio."

"Sorry, Frankie. I need to go now. Miss Yellowtail, please apologize to Mr. McKinney on my behalf and let him know that I will pay for everything." Stepping out into the night, he added, "Oh, and thanks for the *frijoles* and *tortillas*. They were delicious as always."

Frankie's face flushed as his mother squared up her chair to face him. She said, "So, you want to tell me what happened?"

"N-no."

"At least you are honest. Now tell me."

He did, recounting the previous day's events, from the bullies throwing rocks to Turq throwing candy jars and chairs. He even added how they had spent most of today hiding from Mr. McKinney, and about touring around with Mr. Blackwood in his fast, yellow car.

"I t-told him that h-he should g-give the car to m-me."

"And why would he do that, Big Man?"

"B-because . . ." He steepled his fingers together across his chest. "B-because my name is Yellowtail, and the c-car has a yellow t-tail." He wiggled his eyebrows up and down, expertly imitating Groucho Marx in *Ducksoup*. "He s-said I was nuts, but I s-said it was j-just the k-kind of thing a s-squirrel like him should g-go for." Two fingers of his right hand held an imaginary cigar while eyebrows still waved.

"L-listen. That's a F-ford pick-up," he said, going to the window to look. Kenneth McKinney's truck was rolling up the Yellowtails' bumpy little lane. Vince Nesci bounced in the passenger's seat.

Together, the mother and son went to the screen door to greet the guests.

"T kn-knew that Mr. M-McKinney was coming."

"Yes, he did, Big Man."

"He's g-got really good ears." Frankie pointed to his own for clarity.

"Apparently he does." She greeted the two men as they came up to the porch. "Hello, Mr. McKinney. Mr. Nesci."

"Hello, Miss Yellowtail," said Kenneth, somberly.

"*Signorina.*"

"Hello, Mr. M-McKinney. Hello, Vince." His mother's reminder to the back of his head caught him by surprise. "I m-mean Mr. Nesci."

"Could we speak to you out here, Natasha?" Kenneth asked. He had removed his large hat, holding it politely against his chest.

"Itz about da boyz," Vince said.

"Of course. Frankie, my Big Man, you get started on the dishes, and I will be there in a few minutes, okay?"

"Okay." He pranced back to the table, practicing wiggling his eyebrows and using spoons as cigars while he collected and sorted the few items for washing.

Natasha stepped out onto the porch, which wasn't out of earshot for Frankie. He heard her say, "Frankie told me what happened."

"Uh-oh," he muttered to himself. "Now I'm r-really going to get it."

Natasha continued, "Turq wanted me to apologize on his behalf and said that he would pay for everything. He left a few minutes ago. He will pay you back."

Kenneth cleared his throat. "I know. I'm not worried about him paying back, ma'am."

Frankie's strained to listen.

The three adults compared Frankie's story to Ruth's version as she'd told it to Kenneth. On most points, the two versions lined up, but in the Dutch woman's story, Turq had shouted death threats and cursed. They agreed that the woman seemed to have told her version specifically to make Kenneth angry at the twelve-year-old.

Natasha said, "Well, do you know how much the damages cost?"

"Probably around thirty dollars," said Kenneth.

Frankie startled and almost dropped a tin plate.

His mother whistled. "That will be tough."

Kenneth rubbed the top of his head. "He'll have to work it off, I'm sure. He'll make it good. He's a damn good kid—pardon my French—and his father's as straight up as they come."

Fidgeting, the Italian said, "But . . . that no the real *problema.*"

Frankie picked up a dish and slowly dipped it into the basin of soapy water, gently and quietly wiping it in circles with a rag.

Kenneth said, "Right. Tell her."

Vince continued, "I was at Kenneth's store this morning, and I tried to talk to the pretty, *giovane signora*. She seemed definitely like she might need some company. I mean . . . you know . . . I make sure that she no in need. *Specialmente* if she need a man's company. After all, things can get lonely out here in the desert . . ."

"Okay, Vince. Stay on topic, lonely man," said Kenneth.

"Ah, *scusa*. So I talk to her. Seem nice, until I ask about her job. Then she very angry. Talk about Zed's son, Turq. Oh, she *molto arrabbiato*—very angry. Then she say she actually glad to see boy again. That she wait long time to get him."

Kenneth clarified: "She wants to kill him."

"*Si. Assassinare* the boy."

"What did she mean that she had waited a long time?" Natasha asked.

"I not know," said Vince.

Frankie, who had been working at a snail's pace, but listening at a rabbit's, started shaking. He dropped the dish in the basin, and it broke into several large fragments. When he reached in to get the pieces out, something sliced the back of his hand along his thumb.

"Ouch," he cried quietly, pulling his hand out of the water. A thin red line started bleeding. Crimson trickled out, partially smeared by water and suds, and ran down across the back of his wrist. His eyes went wide as he watched his life oozing out and dribbling. Quickly, he grabbed the bleeding wound with his left hand. With his eyes watering, he rocked back and forth. A cry tried to escape his lips, but he stifled it, covering his mouth with a forearm.

Rocking led to bouncing, which in turn led to hopping up and down while again tightly holding his wound. His eyes darted longingly from front door to window to window, seeking escape.

"N-no," he said aloud.

"Everything all right?" Natasha called from the porch.

"Y-yes, Mother. Everything's f-fine."

He dashed to an open window in the bedroom, unaware of the bloody handprints on the door knob and windowsill he left behind. Clumsily, he climbed through the window and fell. The rough siding scratched his arms, and some rocks tore a hole in his new dungarees. Beneath the tear, a nasty, bleeding gash showed through.

"Oh no," he said. "First Mother's d-dish. And n-now this. What's next?"

Adrenaline grabbed him, shook him, and whipped him forward. Down the canyon he fled, staying out of sight. Faster and faster, until everything hurt: hands, knees, lungs, feet. Then he stopped to get his bearings, hunched over and panting. The crumbling walls of Chetro Ketl Great House were just a short distance away.

"There," he said, "I c-can hide and r-rest."

Once he stepped across the threshold of the ancient structure, the night went suddenly quiet: no chirping insects, no slithering reptiles, no squeaking bats, and not even the gentlest wind. "Strange," he said, eyeing the ruins suspiciously.

After crossing the courtyard quietly, he retreated into a nearby small room. The cozy, little space suggested security and solitude. Light from the full moon poured into the roofless space, making it easy to see. He looked around for a place to sit. In a corner, in the dirt, something small glowed with a soft, rose-colored light.

Shuffling over to investigate, he wiggled his eyebrows up and down, saying, "W-well, w-well. A secret p-prize inside."

As he reached down, a puff of wind filled the room, and a woman's voice said, "Wait."

Turning with a fright to see who it was, his virgin eyes fell upon a beautiful, naked woman.

"Hello, Frankie. What are you looking for?"

▼△▼△▼△▼△▼△▼△▼△▼△▼△▼

Novel Magic

DECEMBER 23, 1177, INSIDE CROOKED NOSE GREAT HOUSE (HUNGO PAVI)

Like most of the village, Klanl Hivaht, High Shaman, woke to the thunderous *quetz'al* sound rumbling through the canyon.

"Oh, good. Rain. No need to get up right away." He rolled over in bed and spooned with his young wife, Jooh Niteh, smelling her hair, caressing her shoulders, and kissing the back of her neck.

She rolled over to face him. "I am glad you did not have to Ascend to heaven yesterday."

"Me too."

They began exploring each other and kissing, but a sudden commotion in the courtyard below interrupted their passion.

Klanl paused, listening. "Whatever it is, it can wait," he said, resuming their intimacy.

"Good." Jooh laid a hand against his face and kissed him long and hard.

"Klanl Hivaht! Klanl, Klanl." The voice's owner stood just outside the apartment. "I think the *quetz'al* have killed someone." A thick lisp muddled some of the words.

Pulling away from his wife, Klanl sighed and said, "Tenateh."

Romantic intentions ran for their lives like a grasshopper in the summertime as Klanl untangled himself from Jooh. Reluctantly, he jumped into a tunic, sandals, and a cold-weather robe. Starting for the door, he said, "I will make this fast."

"Hey," called his wife.

He turned back.

"You forgot something." His eagle-feather cap sat temptingly between her exposed breasts.

"Unforgettable." He grabbed the cap. She grabbed him and gave him a lingering kiss, stroking the inside of his thigh.

"Do settle the matter quickly," she whispered in his ear. "I need a baby in my belly."

"You do know how to motivate me."

Klanl rushed out the door. His personal assistant, a young woman named Tenateh, stood there, flushed and panting from the hasty sprint to Klanl's apartment on the second level of the Great House.

"Sorry to disturb you, High Shaman." She had a cleft lip, and the deformity affected her speech—and her chances of marrying.

"Someone killed, you said?"

"I think so," she said as they turned to descend the ladder to the courtyard of the Great House. "There is a great deal of confusion right now."

In the courtyard, people gathered around two new arrivals: an albino and a large dog. As Klanl and Tenateh reached the circle of bystanders, a space opened for the VIPs, allowing them full access to the strangers.

Klanl spread his arms out, palms up, and bowed slightly. "Are you well? We wish to help you and apologize for the *quetzal* if necessary."

The man looked at him blankly.

"Do you understand me?" After no response, Klanl said quietly, "Obviously not."

Klanl looked at the man's outfit: simple tunic, hooded robe, sandals with coverings. Everything was nondistinct—no telltale signs of origin. Physically, however, he was very distinct: pink eyes, no hair—not even eyelashes—and daisy-white skin so fragile and thin that you could see the man's blood pulsing in the veins of his forehead.

The dog was a male beast equal in size to his master. His jaws looked powerful enough to snap a man's arm in half. The thick tail might accidentally beat someone senseless with its constant wagging.

With long legs and a thick, muscled chest and back, it was bred for war or work. A leather harness wrapped around its brindle fur.

"I hope that thing is well-trained," Klanl said.

Tenateh asked, "High Shaman, why would anyone be traveling during this treacherous season of cold and shadows?"

"I do not know. We must find out, but we will need Shat'kuhat Quaatsa to interpret."

"Shall I ask for him?"

Klanl gestured to the man and then to the *kiva* in the middle of the courtyard. "First, take him into the *kiva* and away from these gawkers. Then go fetch Quaatsa."

"Yes, High Shaman."

After a bashful and silly smile, his assistant motioned to the bystanders to make room and then made motions for the White Man to follow her, which he did, with a strange smile on his face. The two crossed the courtyard to the *kiva*, dog trotting along behind, tail vertical and nose scanning the air in all directions. A few onlookers followed at a polite distance and then hovered outside the *kiva* once Tenateh and her charges descended inside it.

Klanl stared at the *kiva* for some time, deep in thought. Finally, looking back up at his apartment, he saw Jooh standing in the doorway, blanket barely hiding her voluptuous body. He waved and sighed. She waved back. Reluctantly, he turned away and made his way to the Great House gate.

*   *   *

Chur Keleh scanned the blue sky warily. "I hope we do not see any more of those flying monsters, Sqatweh," he said, stroking the dog's head.

As they followed the canyon girl, he shamelessly admired her assets: maybe twenty-or-so winters, beautiful, dark eyes that would swallow a man's soul, heart-shaped face framed by wisps of thick, black hair spilling from under her hat, a goddess-like body that layers of winter robes failed to hide, and golden honey-tinted skin. Like a puppy following someone with a juicy chunk of meat, his every sense was trained on the prize.

"What, Sqatweh?" he said.

The dog looked up.

"You are right. There is something about her. A haunting, illusive thrill that I cannot quite place."

Sqatweh went back to looking, sniffing, and listening to the new environment.

"Ah . . ." Churl said. "Just like the girl from my dreams, Ten-aht."

She turned to face him just as he tripped over a rock. Pointing at the offending stone, she smiled and said something, laughing off his embarrassment.

When their eyes met, neither turned away. They smiled awkwardly.

The dog bumped into him, breaking their gaze and nearly knocking him over. "Right," Churl said, "I need to pull it together, or she will think me stupid."

The woman called out to some children playing, tossing around the hairball from a buffalo. She instructed them to do something in lovely but firm tones. They obeyed immediately, scurrying dutifully to their mission.

"Good with kids," Churl pointed out to Sqatweh.

They reached the *kiva* in a few seconds. Touching the lintel of the door, he studied the structure's construction. Clearly the work of expert masons, the small stones were cut with precision and only required the finest line of mortar to be secured. The round structure was half-buried, with tree-trunk-sized posts in the center that held up thick beams of timber to support the roof.

He scratched the dog's head, wondering aloud, "Where did they get that wood? We have seen no forests out in this desert."

Poking his head inside the doorway for just a moment, he said to the dog, "Strange." He poked his head back inside for a second look. "No carved stones. No murals. Surely they must have images of their gods somewhere. Or record their conquests somewhere. Why would they not carve their history into stone, preserving it forever?"

Sqatweh didn't have an answer, and Tenateh didn't know there had been a question.

"Life here must be very harsh," he said to Tenateh, who just smiled politely back. "All about just trying to stay alive, is it?"

The woman entered the building first, extending a hand to help him on the descending stairs ahead. He took it readily, but overreached and almost lost his balance. She noticed his wobble and steadied him by the shoulder with her free hand, their faces coming close.

Her facial expressions asked if he was all right.

He smiled back, saying, "You smell like wildflowers and sweet spices."

She released his hand at the bottom of the stairs, and he sighed.

The interior floor was several feet below ground level, and despite no fire, it was noticeably warmer. He wrapped his arms around himself, patting opposite shoulders, and said, "Good to get out of that wind."

She smiled and nodded, wrapping her arms around herself, too.

Light came in through a square hole in the dome-shaped roof. A ladder was set so that people could climb out onto the thick rooftop. "Maybe they go up there to worship their gods?" he asked Sqatweh.

Tenateh was pointing toward a large hearth and making motions with her hands, talking rapidly. She invited him to sit beside her on a thick, wool pallet that lay across a stone bench. He joined her on the seat, tapping his fingers on his knees excitedly.

Suddenly, she giggled, covered her mouth, and pointed back toward the door.

Sqatweh stood at the top of the stairs, looking very unsure about the steep steps. He looked to Churl and then back at the stairs, clearly not pleased.

The canyon woman stood, leaned over, and patted her thighs, trying to appeal to Sqatweh with high-pitched, soothing coos. She removed her bonnet, and long, jet-black hair cascaded down, covering her face. A practiced hand delicately tossed locks over her shoulder, and she turned to smile at him.

"You do know, do you not?" Churl said to her. "That the sun would rise or set if only you asked."

She nodded, giggled, and pointed at the dog.

"Sqatweh. Get down here. You embarrass me." His tone was sharper than needed.

The dog seemed hopeful that perhaps his master would reconsider, given the circumstances.

"Now!"

The dog's head bobbed up and down, the animal hesitating in one last-ditch effort of procrastination. Apparently seeing no viable alternative, he leaped down the stairs in two great bounds.

The girl sat down again, and the huge animal padded over to her and covered her entire lap with his head.

"Good boy. Can we trade places?"

Sqatweh's eyebrows skewed back and forth as he tossed his attention from her to him and back.

"It is okay. I would not trade either."

Tenateh laughed.

Churl put his hand on his chest and said, "Churl."

She nodded and placed her hand on her own chest. "Tenateh."

His eyes went wide for a moment, and he sat up a little straighter. "Ten-aht. It is you. You are real," he said.

She cocked her head sideways at his surprise and said, "Tenah-teh. Tenateh."

"Right. Tenateh."

She nodded approval and returned the gesture: "Chur-leh."

"Close enough."

They sat, smiling at each other, mutually pleased with the connection, unsure how to continue.

The moment evaporated when a commotion suddenly blocked the light coming from the doorway; the children she had spoken to earlier were descending the stairs with armloads of wood and kindling. She pointed to the hearth, and they deposited their load. Asking them about something, they jabbered back to her, all speaking at once and pointing to the top of the stairs. There, the largest of the children, a boy of about ten, was descending the stairs with a clay pot in his hands. A bit of smoke trickled out of the container, and the child hurried to get rid of his load.

The boy dumped a few hot embers out of the pot and into the hearth. He pushed kindling around them and blew gently on the meager heat source while fanning it with wagging fingers. He pushed kindling closer. Blew again. Fanned again. Rearranged again. Blew again. Fanned again. This went on for several minutes.

Tenateh screwed up her face and spoke to the boy. He shrugged and pointed to the fading coals.

Churl walked over and gently nudged the boy aside, smiling. He raised an eyebrow in a knowing fashion, reached down, and grabbed the coal by two fingers. The boy's eyes went wide with amazement, Tenateh gasped, and the other children chattered excitedly. Deftly, he passed the coal back and forth from hand to hand.

They hadn't seen him lick his fingers and coat them with ash before touching the ember, which was the perfect temperature for this slight-of-hand trick: hot enough to look dangerous, cool enough to quickly pass between cool, damp fingers. For starting a fire, it would never do.

Churl smiled, gave the boys a wink, and returned the lukewarm ember to the hearth with more pomp and circumstance than necessary.

While they watched one hand fiddle with the ember, the other hand discreetly reached into his satchel for a pinch of fire-starting powder, which he then sprinkled on the wood with one quick, smooth motion of his hand. Then he bit his lower lip and smashed his injured thumb against a stone, bringing fresh blood from the previous evening's knife wound. With a great flair, he squeezed the wound, and a few drops of blood fell into the wood pile. A large fireball—several feet across—sprang up from the hearth and drifted slowly through the roof opening and into the morning sky. Intense heat radiated from it, filling the structure with light and warmth.

The children gleefully jumped up and down, dancing around the new fire now blazing and crackling. They spontaneously broke out in song.

Churl laughed and clapped along with the boys, smiling through the excruciating pain. Blood drained from his face, and he blinked repeatedly, willing himself to stay conscious.

After a moment, his lightheadedness passed, and Churl turned back to Tenateh expectantly, but she was ducking out of the doorway at the top of the stairs. She briefly glanced back at him before departing, a suspicious look in her eyes.

"Damn."

* * *

As Quaatsa Mukaama stirred awake, he heard his wife, Kwi Dreh, say, "I did, but the *quetz'al* thunder did not wake him."

A different voice said, "It must have been quite an ordeal this time."

Kwi sounded exhausted. "He was in pain most of the night. What balm? What herb do you use for the burn on a spirit body?"

Quaatsa felt guilty.

"How many times has he gone to heaven?" asked the other voice, which he then recognized as belonging to Tenateh.

"I do not know. He speaks not of it."

"Has it ever distressed him this much before?"

There was a pause, and then Kwi said, "Not this much."

"Did he say . . ."

"No," she lied.

Quaatsa and Kwi had talked of the Ascending extensively into the night. They had sent their children to be with other families, and he had told her everything: of the rapid ascent, the attack from the strange black arrow, the Word about the End of The People, and the agony of spirit burns.

Eventually, he either passed out or fell asleep. Apparently, she had not.

Tenateh said, "Do you think he can attend to this new matter?"

Quaatsa sat up in bed, leaning on an elbow, and said, "I will come. It will be important."

Kwi mouthed to him, "No," and gave him a scolding look. For a long moment, they looked intently at each other in a silent battle. She surrendered with a sigh and turned to get his clothes.

In a few minutes, he was out the door, Tenateh struggling to keep up with his long, quick strides. As they rushed, she apprised him of the situation.

"Shat'kuhat Quaatsa?"

"Yes?"

"One more thing."

"Speak."

"It is urgent."

"So, speak now," he said with, a slight rise in vocal intensity.

"I cannot while we walk. It is a thing which I feel requires discretion."

He stopped, wheeled around, and faced his young assistant, giving her his whole attention. Calmly, he asked, "What is it?"

"I told you of the White Man, Churl, and his dog."

"Yes."

"He can work magic."

"Oh?" He gave her a condescending smile, which made her bristle. "Sorry," he said, face going solemn. "Please tell me."

She relaxed and said, "He held a fire coal in his hands and passed it back and forth. It did not harm him."

Quaatsa looked into her eyes, gently laying a hand on her one of her shoulders. "Young woman, that is a trick I will show you someday. It is not magic. Come on now." He turned to continue, but she hesitated, looking half-relieved and half-annoyed, unsure where to take the emotion next. Her face tilted way over toward "annoyed" but then quickly donned "amused."

"Very good," she said, seeming to have made up her mind about something. "Thank you."

"Of course. Now let us go while there is time."

"Time?"

"Just old man ramblings."

"Okay." She smiled, looking relieved.

They continued their rush toward the *kiva*, and she added, "And the fire trick, too."

"A fire trick?"

"You must, please, tell me the secret of his fire trick." She started explaining the trick, but when she described the blood and the fireball, he stopped cold.

He glanced around. They were just yards away from the *kiva*'s entrance and alone for the moment. "Here is a thing you must know, child."

"Yes?" She stiffened at the seriousness of his voice.

"The first stunt was not real—just *ni'tewan* (a trick). Tossing a fire coal around is harmless and painless and only requires some practice. *Mongeh'tewan* (real magic) costs you something. It is painful and requires sacrifice."

"But the fire trick . . . ?"

"That was *mongeh'tewan*. Some bit of *him* went into making the fireball. He will never get that back—a small part of him died."

"Died?" She looked down at the ground, apparently confused. "Yes."

"Without taking The Journey?" she asked, distress in her voice.

"That is right."

"What does that mean?"

"He can never be whole when he is born again to his ancestors. They will not embrace him in the heavens. He will never depart with them to live under Eternal Sun. Slowly, piece by piece, he trades away his Sacred Self for simple tricks and games."

"Why would—"

"Who knows." He turned and braced her by her shoulders, admonishing her, "You must not speak of this. This new magic must be a secret."

Children and adults surrounded the *kiva*, hopeful to glimpse something exciting.

"The large fireball must have attracted attention," she said. "What about the children who saw his magic?"

"Worry not about them. We will talk to them later."

"Yes, but there is one more thing."

"Go on," he said impatiently.

"The white man, Churl? He has visited me in my dreams many times during the past few months. I recognized him at once." She cast her gaze down and added, "He is my spirit lover."

Quaatsa sighed. Both his spiritual and his physical body ached, but neither was going to get a chance to rest anytime soon.

▼△▼△▼△▼△▼△▼△▼△▼△▼△▼

Mother Tongue

DECEMBER 23, 1177, INSIDE CROOKED NOSE GREAT HOUSE (HUNGO PAVI)

Lonely Mother was beaming like a full moon on a clear night when they reached the *kiva*. She turned to her escort, the canyon boy named Totahmaa, let go of his hand, and said, "The winds of fortune are blowing my direction: gods and spirits alike are smiling on me."

The blank expression on the twelve-year-old's face started to fade, and he looked, confused.

"Thank you," Rooshth said, in the tongue they shared.

"For . . . ?"

"Saving me from those awful creatures. I would have certainly been killed had you not come along."

The boy seemed skeptical, blinking and shaking his head, like he'd been in a fog. A few minutes earlier, she had applied a contact drug to his hand. The potent paste made him easy to manipulate; she could rearrange his memories, make hypnotic-type suggestions, and dig deeply for information. As usual, it had proved fruitful: this boy was the son of an important village elder, privy to secrets and power unknown to his peers or the other villagers.

She asked him about the elders; he answered in great detail about the *Shat'kuhat* with their spirit gifts. She asked about their gods; he told her of gods mediating and guiding through the spirits and of their transcendence to the physical world. She asked about their sacred rites; he talked of the Smoke and Rising ceremony, with the three *Shat'kuhat* visiting the realm of the gods and how difficult the previous night's ceremony had been for his father. She asked of how they were able to rise to the gods; he spoke of the *Shat'kuh Mongehweh* and the sacred tablet's ability to stir and command the spirits. She asked about their ability to control the flying beasts; he spoke of the tablet's ability to allow a master to impress a hatchling, bonding master and flyer for life. She asked where this special source of power was kept; he told her that it was hidden in the apartment of Klanl Hivaht, High Shaman.

"I must go and check on my boy. You go help your friends bring our tent and supplies," she said.

"Okay." Totahmaa walked away toward the entrance of the Great House, still shaking his head occasionally, apparently still occluded by the chemical-induced mental haze.

She practically skipped down the stairs into the round underground space. "Hello," she said brightly.

Down in the darkness of the *kiva,* Churl and Sqatweh stood to greet her. He said, "Hello." The dog just stared, seeming skeptical that any of this fuss would benefit him.

"You look well. Those monsters did not hurt you?"

She laughed. "Silly, Pitiful Boy. You should ask, 'Did you hurt the monsters?'"

"Did you?"

"No more than they deserved. Foul demons of the sky. Fools for trying to make a meal of us."

Rooshth mentally disappeared into her own world, randomly walking around the floor for several minutes in silence.

"Mother . . . ?" came her son's voice.

She paced for another minute, stopped, and smiled to herself. "I'm very good at guile."

"Mother."

"Yes?"

"You have good news?"

"Indeed I do, Pitiful Boy. We are finally going to fix you."

Churl rolled his eyes and sighed. "Again?"

Her face flushed. "We will fix you. These people possess powerful magic. You will be healed. You will live a normal life." She reached for him, but he pulled away.

"Mother? How can I live a normal life?"

Seizing him by the shoulders, she said, "Beautiful, golden skin. Long, dark hair. Strong, sinewy muscles—like your father. Life will be yours for the taking!"

Unconvinced, he asked, "You want me to be like my father?"

"Yes, of course."

"The man who abandoned us?"

She let the provocative jab pass. (He didn't know that she had slit the man's throat.) Smiling pleasantly, she explained enthusiastically, "We can return to our people in the south. You can be a chief. A village leader. Marry the finest of the women—as many as you would like. You can be a god!"

"Please!" He huffed, shook his head, and wiggled free of her grasp. "Mother. How many winters have I walked this earth?"

It was her turn to roll her eyes and sigh.

"How many, Mother?"

"You are long-lived."

"Forty-seven, Mother. And you are sixty-three." The intensity in his voice was rising rapidly. "We have traveled hard, sleeping in the day, traveling at night. Sometimes starving, sometimes thirsty. Almost fifty winters. Further north. Further north. On and on and on. No friends. No family. No offspring. We are at the end of us. Driven to death by your relentless quest."

"But I can heal you, boy," she said dreamily, but her tone quickly turned. "Why do you fight me? Why now stand up for something?" She stretched her arm toward him, palm up, and declared, "Now, Churl, the Pitiful Boy, is going to stand up for something. Should I feel pride? Or anger?"

"Look at me, Mother!" he said, towering over her. "I am an old man now—not your little boy. Besides, your plan will not matter—if it even works. We have failed . . . No, *you* have failed so many times. People have died. Pets have died. All in the name of your precious and futile quest."

Anger shoved pride out of the way, and Rooshth said, "You will not speak to me in the manner of an ungrateful slab of dog meat." Spit flew from her mouth as staccato words pelted him. "Dog meat! Pitiful Boy. The wild dogs and cats of the jungle would have long ago devoured your delicate flesh, pulling you apart, and fighting over your liver."

Her words struck him brutally, making him grimace and cow.

"Your very life is mine," she continued. "I own you, and you owe me. From my belly you came. Between my legs you crossed into the mortal plane to crawl miserably across Mother Earth. The gods cursed you, but by the gods themselves, I will break this curse."

Her wrath partially spent, she stopped and panted.

Churl sat on a bench, looking away from her. The dog had disappeared.

Turning away from the conflict herself, the unnatural dancing of the orange-yellow flames in the hearth and the acrid smell of the fire-starting powder caught her attention. Kneeling before the blaze, she swiped a finger along one of the stones, looking closely at the residue left on her fingertip. She smelled it, tasted it. Turning on her heels while still squatted, she reached a hand out, touching Churl's chin, and then stroking his cheek with the back of her unnaturally wrinkled hand. "You did this?"

Slowly, he turned to face her. "Yes."

She smiled at him. Pride pushed back on anger—and won. "Let me see."

He obediently held out his hand with the cut thumb. The bandages were loose and saturated in fresh blood.

Gently, she unwound the cloth, squeezed it, and wrung out the blood and ooze that had accumulated. From a hidden satchel, she applied a paste made of chilies and cactus to the re-opened wound, her old leathery hands still nimble and gentle. After waving the cloth over the top of the fire until it was dry, she tightly rewrapped his thumb and hand, neatly tucking it into itself so that it wouldn't flap about and slide off.

"Better?"

He nodded his head like a small child, and she smiled.

Sqatweh appeared from somewhere and rolled over onto his back in front of the pair. A truce between mother and son took form as they both petted the dog's belly while he playfully nipped at their hands.

"Sqatweh seems to have weathered the attack well," Churl said.

"Yes. He is tough and fast, is he not?"

"Indeed. He did wait for me, though." Churl scratched the dog's belly vigorously, his small hand disappearing into the animal's large chest full of thick fur. "No, he did not abandon me, did he? Did he? Who was a good dog? Who was a good dog?"

Basking in the affection, Sqatweh clearly knew that it was he who had been the good dog in question.

Rooshth smiled weakly, feeling tired. "He is a good dog." She gave Sqatweh an equally hearty scratch. A silly smile spread across her face as she rubbed the dog.

"Mother?" came Churl's voice distantly.

She was lost in thought again, pondering the alignment of favor the gods seemed to be bestowing her at last.

"Mother?"

She looked up.

"There is this girl in the village."

She rolled her eyes. "My son . . ."

"It is she from my dreams."

"How do you know this?"

"What? How do you know your right arm?"

Her left eye squinted up, and she studied him intently through her right eye. "Well, you speak truth. At least, you believe it to be truth."

"It is true. She is the one." He paused and then added, "She spoke to me and was not afraid."

At this, she started laughing—almost uncontrollably. "You . . ." trying to catch her breath, "you do not even speak the same language."

"We talked without words." As soon as the words came out of his mouth, he looked down, embarrassed, and covered his face with his hands. "Idiot," he said to the palms of his hands.

She let his ridiculous statement go.

"Is she pretty?"

"Like moonlight on a still lake. Pink-drop flowers blooming in the forest. Sunshine through the canopy of the jungle after a hard rain."

"Like a dart frog?" (She referred to the brightly beautiful jungle frogs that were deadly to touch.)

"No. She is nice—at least, as far as I can tell."

"Okay."

"What?"

"Nothing . . ." She turned away.

"Tell me."

Looking back to him, one eyebrow lifted skeptically, accusingly. "You want to take her back home?"

He faced away from her and said, "The people here . . ."

"Yes?"

Turning back, he said, "They seem nice. What if—"

Her sudden indignation roasted him. "We are not staying here. We will break the curse. We will return home. We will find you a proper woman, unless this local hussy will come with us. And then we shall still find you a proper wife."

"Hussy?" He took a deep breath, exhaled slowly, and said, "The sunlight does not hurt my skin here."

"The seasons will change. The summer sun will hurt. You will pop and fry like a worm cast into fire."

"You might be right, but it could still work. I could hide during the day if I needed to. And other times I could walk in the day— among other people. Talking. Laughing. Part of the village."

She stared hard at him. "Have you been chewing the Peyote?"

"No." He stomped his foot and stood. "Listen to me. I want to be part of the people. One of them. Not outside. Not always afraid. Live like you said: normal."

Also standing, her anger morphed. "This local girl could be a fine mistress for you when the curse is broken. You can have all that and more."

"I want to *live* for the rest of my days—not waste them on endless, worthless quests. What if the curse cannot be broken? What if you cannot overcome the magic of the gods?"

"Stop! I will."

"But—"

"I will." Fists emphatically punched into the air, punctuating her point.

He stepped back from her, slumping, and said, "Okay." He sighed. "Could we try to persuade Tenateh to go with us?"

"Who?"

"The girl, Tenateh."

"You did not tell me she had a name, Pitiful Boy."

Churl's hand went to the top of his head as it shook. "Of course she has a name." The hand came down, palm up. "It is Tenateh."

"Ten-aht-eh?"

"Close enough."

"Of course. But how did you come to know her name?" She raised an eyebrow again.

"Not as dumb as you thought." He looked pleased. "I told you that we had a conversation. I put my hand here and said my name." He modeled the gesture. "And she returned the same."

Rooshth was intrigued—almost to the point of being impressed. However, she still simmered at a dangerous level. "Good," she said after some reflection. "Do you know *anything* else about her?"

"Not yet."

"Yet you are ready to steal her away from everything she knows and loves."

"Mother!"

"Well? You would deny her a home and family here."

"You should know something about denying someone a home and family." He turned away, avoiding the fiery gaze that was returned.

Instead of yelling again, she only retorted with a muffled "hrmph" sound. Then she said, "She could be promised already. She could have a husband and family already."

"Of course, Mother."

"Or worse: she could be an outcast adulteress, seeking to trick some young man into caring for another man's bastards."

"Too far, Mother."

"Well . . . I only point out the obvious: you know nothing about this woman."

"I can learn."

She shot him a puzzled look. "How? You cannot even talk to her."

"There must be some shared tongue. Or we can learn each other's language."

"No. These people share no languages with us," she lied. "It is hopeless."

"You are hopeless," he muttered.

"What?"

"I said, nothing is hopeless. I can learn her language. She, mine. People do that all of the time. Of course, it will take some time. But . . ."

"But what?"

"We have . . ." he started.

An idea stirred in her head. Her face changed as it began to simmer, stony anger melting into a deep, thoughtful look. Her eyes looked up and away as her mind raced somewhere. She stood and paced. The idea reached its boiling point, and she stopped to rifle through a satchel. Out came a pouch, a roll of herbs, and a clay mixing urn. Spinning toward him, she announced her idea. "We can give her our tongue."

Sounding skeptical yet hopeful, Churl asked, "How?"

"Oh, Pitiful Boy. It is what I do," she said, giving a slight bow.

She unrolled the herbs, selected a few dried specimens, and put them in the jar. Then she added a pinch of reddish-brown paste from the pouch. The intense acrid smell brought tears to Churl's eyes. Sqatweh sneezed, moved out of range of the stench, and flopped down.

"Is that something dead?"

"Ask not, boy. This magic comes special from the flying-snake worshipers." She tilted her head sideways. "Strange, we never saw any actual flying serpents when we were there."

"No, we did not."

"I wonder if the people here worship the flying lizards?"

Churl shrugged.

"We need to see her again. To get her alone."

"Then what?" he asked, reluctance in his voice.

"Well . . ." she said, flashing a chilling smile. "We will cut your tongue, mix your blood, and spit in this jar." She presented the mixing urn. "And then we will make her drink it."

His eyebrows jumped up, and he swallowed hard. "Okay."

The light inside the *kiva* dimmed, and they turned to see people at the doorway.

The canyon girl, Tenateh, was descending the stairs, followed by important-looking men.

Rooshth caught Churl smiling broadly and hit him hard in the belly. She whispered sideways, "Stop it. You look like an idiot. Or guilty. Probably both."

Suddenly, a *quetz'al* shriek pierced the air, forcing her to cover her ears and bend over. Then thunder exploded outside the *kiva*. Debris fell from the ceiling, crashing around them.

▼△▼△▼△▼△▼△▼△▼△▼△▼

The Mark

DECEMBER 23, 1177, NEAR CROOKED NOSE GREAT HOUSE (HUNGO PAVI)

Tuhj climbed and dove, crying and screaming a mixture of despair, anger, and pain. Tyleh was dead, and Luahti lay near death.

The world below him shrank away as updrafts carried him far into the upper atmosphere; the canyon became a mere sliver, the Great Houses mere dots, the people nearly imperceptible to even him. Pounding his wings against ever thinner atmosphere, it was cold, and he gasped for air. A slight smile spread across his eyes just as he passed twenty thousand feet and felt himself blacking out.

Unconscious, he dreamed of the rich hunting grounds to the northeast that he'd just visited. Large herd animals roamed and covered the plains, ebbing and flowing across the lush, open expanse in great rivers of fur and dust. In his dream, the living was easy: swoop, munch, repeat.

He startled awake to the violent tumbling of his fall, oxygen-rich air satisfying his starving lungs. Regaining control of his flight, he rolled over backward and screamed, diving with wings folded against his side. He accelerated at a staggering rate.

Wind pulled rivers of tears from his eyes. Everything below got bigger as he descended: canyon, Great Houses, people milling about. Wrinkled Old Woman was entering the *kiva* below him.

Evil woman, he sang. *I will destroy you. I could do it now . . . just "forget" to pull out. Smash into the* kiva.

A motion south of the Great House caught his eye. Luahti, his mate, lay there gasping for breath, her wings flapping as she tried to get to her feet.

She needs me, he sang wearily.

Screaming again, he spread his wings, power-braked, and sharply cut a horizontal flight path, missing the *kiva* by feet. The thundering of his wings and the vortices behind him blew off half the thatching, exposing the timbers and packed earth of the *kiva's* roof.

Oops, he sang sarcastically as he glided toward the southern end of the canyon.

Luahti had given up trying to stand. She was curled up in a ball, being attended by trainers, and could barely manage to raise her head to look at him.

Okay. I'm coming, he called.

He finished his canyon run and swung around to the southwest, re-entering the canyon by swooping low over a canyon wall. Silently, he landed next to her, the trainers fleeing like startled rabbits.

A mixture of blood and dirt caked to his feet as he scooted closer to her and put his head beside hers. Bruises and lacerations covered her body. Both wings were horribly torn and mangled, bent and broken in directions not intended by Nature. She whimpered as tears flowed freely down her face and mingled in the massive pool of her own blood. A bit of bright red foam collected at a corner of her mouth.

Tuhj maneuvered around to lie beside her, folding one of his great wings over the top of her in an embrace. They cried together.

The attendant trainers wept and mourned loudly.

Luahti coughed up blood, gurgling and gagging, unable to catch her breath. As Tuhj held her warmly, her breathing became more and more labored, more and more shallow. Gasping, trying to gulp the air, she attempted to stand again, eyes wide with fear, but it was impossible; she was weak, struggling for breath, body beat to hell.

Tuhj pulled her closer, caressed her. They locked eyes. Her breath came in worthless sputters now. Slowly her eyes closed. Slowly her head went down into the blood and dirt. Slowly her whole body went limp. Finally, a long, low foaming sound emerged from her mouth as the last of the air in her lungs pressed free under the weight of relaxing organs.

Farewell on your Journey, Tuhj sang. *Wrinkle Woman will pay for this.*

The trainers discreetly backed away even farther, giving the grieving alpha male a wide birth.

Tuhj bellowed, lifting his head to the sky slowly as the pitch of his voice rose from infrasonic to a shrill screech. Again and again he cried out, sometimes shaking his head side to side and slamming his wings against the ground. Standing, he stretched his wings and flapped them forcefully, blasting wind and debris everywhere. He clawed at the ground and threw chunks of rock and dirt.

One of the trainers approached him, arms raised, singing a calming song.

A primal darkness took the light from Tuhj's eyes. Instead of holding his head up high, he leaned forward with wings slightly spread and curled menacingly downward. Drooling with First Spit, he became the image of Lucifer himself; medieval dragons would have fled in terror.

He folded his wings back and spat on the singing trainer. The large mucosal blob knocked the boy backward. When the trainer got to his feet, shaking in terror, Tuhj nailed him with Second Spit. The poor soul burst into flames and simply fell forward, dead before he hit dirt.

The other trainers bolted in a panic.

Tuhj ran them down easily, knocking them over with his wings. He swung his tail, striking several in a cluster. They rolled and tumbled across the canyon floor like so many tossed pebbles. He laughed and did it again. And again. And again. Only a few escaped to make it into the safety of the Great House.

Luahti, what a great game this is! he called. *You've got to try . . . Luahti?* After he turned back to see her, he sang, *Oh, right,* and growled ferociously.

He turned around to face one of the trainers who was lying on the ground, holding a leg and wailing. Quickly, Tuhj picked up the boy by the broken leg and tossed him high into the air, letting him strike the ground with a loud crunch. Tossing several other trainers similarly, he laughed gleefully.

Then another lone trainer ran at him, trying to sing and holding only one hand in the air.

Not so quickly this time, he said.

Holding one arm, the boy fearlessly ran right up to Tuhj.

Fool. You want *to die today? Okay. No need to wait.*

Then Tuhj froze. A spark of sanity glimmered in his eyes as he sang, *Totahmaa?*

But the spark vanished quickly, and Tuhj lurched forward and then skidded to a stop, spraying the boy with debris. Then he struck Totahmaa with the lead edge of a wing, sending the boy sliding ten feet or more across the dirt. Tuhj walked to the child, stood over him, and stared down menacingly.

He slowly placed a foot on top of the terrified boy, singing, *This day you will not see the sunset. Tomorrow will not be another day for you. I break now my oath and duty as I break your body.*

Totahmaa's eyes went wide with shock.

Yes, sang Tuhj. *You know Song. I know you understand.*

The gigantic flyer slowly pressed down, watching the boy strain against his foot, face turning red, eyes slightly bulging. A loud popping sound indicated ribs giving out under the weight. The young trainer squeaked and passed out.

The smell of Luahti caught Tuhj's attention and gave him pause. It lingered on the boy, and Tuhj remembered how Totahmaa had stood up to the witch.

Suddenly, the darkness fled from his soul, and Tuhj froze.

Like a madman returning to his senses, Tuhj saw the carnage with sane eyes: scores of young humans lay dead or dying, lying in pools of their own blood, broken bodies twisted, and his master's oldest offspring lay near lifeless under his heel. Withdrawing his foot from the boy, he ground his feet into the dirt and threw debris in his own face.

What . . . how could I have . . .

His memory of the last few minutes evaporated like water spilled on a hot rock.

Murderer, he said. *I have killed all these . . . They will execute me, and I deserve it.*

Tuhj lifted his head at the sound of a mass of humans running. Armed warriors and mature *quetz'al* handlers were already running in his direction. In no time, other *quetz'al* would be marshaled to hunt him.

An arrow struck the ground at his feet, nearly impaling Totahmaa. The next one struck the flyer in the leg, about midthigh.

Damn!

Quickly and gently, he scooped the boy up against his belly and started bounding on one leg across the desert floor, wings flapping. Arrows rained around him, several striking his back. Finally, he became airborne, leaving the pursuers far behind. In moments, he and the boy were above the canyon, out of arrow's reach and heading south.

* * *

A few minutes earlier back in the *kiva*, Churl was bracing himself against the bone-shaking *quetz'al* thunder that filled the structure. As the whole building shook, dirt and debris filled the air. Tenateh, who had just arrived, dove at him from the stairs, and they landed together on the floor, her body covering his. Churl looked up at the ceiling. Sunlight poured in through places that it shouldn't.

"What was that?" he asked, standing.

Tenateh sprang to her feet, face flushed with embarrassment. She started talking, pointing up in the air and making flapping motions with her hands. Churl nodded and pantomimed a long beak. The girl smiled, nodding vigorously.

The important-looking men who had come down with Tenateh ran back up the stairs, out of the *kiva*. People outside shouted in fear and anger, scrambling after some emergency. The girl looked up at the doorway, indecisively.

He touched her arm and said, "Do not go."

She didn't.

Churl stood and wiped away chunks of dirt and bits of thatching. Neither he nor Tenateh were injured. Sqatweh found something under a stone and was sniffing and scratching at it eagerly. His mother stood, brushed debris from her hair, annoyed. The fire had gone out. Except for the roof damage, everything appeared to be intact.

He smiled at Tenateh, and she returned it, something passing between them. Unconsciously, he slid his hand around hers.

She didn't pull away.

He saw his mother cock her head to one side with a curious expression on her face. Then she cast her glance down at the intertwined hands.

"This is her?" she asked.

"Yes. Her name is Tenateh."

"You told me." Her tone was flat with hints of irritation.

At the sound of her name, Tenateh turned and approached Rooshth. She held out her hands, palm up. His mother grabbed them, and Tenateh lifted her arms out, drawing their bodies together in a cross formation. Smiling, she spoke in respectful tones to his mother. When she had finished, she crossed back to Churl and slipped her hand back inside his.

Rooshth smiled opportunistically, and Churl frowned.

"We are alone now, Pitiful Boy."

"Yes?"

"We have the girl."

"And?"

"Do you not want to speak to your new love?" Her tone mixed sincerity and mockery.

"Of course."

"So, let us do it now, while no one is around."

"Right now?"

The sounds of chaos outside the *kiva* cascaded erratically down through the door.

He looked at Tenateh, who seemed to sense the brewing conflict between mother and son.

She said something, but unable to understand her, he turned back to his mother, who seemed to know that he had just made up his mind.

"Okay," he said, lacking enthusiasm.

Rooshth produced a small urn from beneath her robes and wiggled it back and forth, holding it between her thumb and index finger. "We will need something."

Churl reluctantly took the jar. "I know," he said, blood draining from his face.

Tenateh looked at him, concern scrunching her face.

He waved a hand and smiled reassuringly.

His mother called to the Tenateh and motioned to a place on the stone bench beside where she herself had just sat. Tenateh turned and sat delicately in the indicated place.

"Okay," Rooshth said.

She pointed toward the door, and Tenateh's gaze followed. Then, like a bolt of lightning, Rooshth slid behind her and grabbed a handful of hair, snapping Tenateh's face to the roof. When the girl instinctively brought her hands up to tug at his mother's grip, she bound up Tenateh's up-reached arms in something like a Full Nelson. She then immobilized Tenateh against her chest by wrapping one leg around the girl's waist and the other around one of the girl's legs. Finally, Rooshth slid her right hand around under the Tenateh's chin, clamping her mouth shut.

Churl retrieved the dagger, and the girl's eyes went wild. She struggled, tried to scream, tried to fight Rooshth, but the old woman was too strong.

The stone tool trembled violently as he brought it to his mouth. He gagged and choked back some vomit. After a long moment of heavy breathing, he stuck his tongue out, placed the knife's edge on top of it, and bit down rapidly. His teeth thrust the sharp edge into the smooth muscle of his tongue.

He cried out, partly from pain, partly from horror.

After dropping the knife, he leaned over the little jar and tried to collect blood as it ran off his tongue.

"Spit!" his mother said. "You must spit."

"Easier said than done," he tried to say, but his words just came out jumbled and slurred. After several failed attempts, he finally managed to produce and spit several globs of crimson foam into the jar.

When the little jar was half-full, his mother said, "Enough. Now mix it with your finger."

He turned away from his mother and the girl, gagging and heaving.

"Come on, boy! She is strong."

Wiping his mouth, he stuck his finger into the small jar and stirred the paste, making a slurry that brought him to the verge of retching again.

"Bring it. Quickly!"

With her pupils dilated and her skin covered in a sheen of sweat, the horrified girl shook and hyperventilated.

"Put the jar to her lips."

He obeyed.

"Pour it slowly."

Churl obeyed again. When the concoction touched Tenateh's lips, she pressed them closed tightly, causing overflow to dribble down her cheeks and chin. Rooshth moved a hand around to pinch Tenateh's nose, holding her head back tight. The girl opened her mouth, gasping and choking, and he quickly poured in the red-brown slurry. After a minute of struggling, the girl passed out, the nasty elixir half inside her, half all over Churl and his mother.

"Okay," Rooshth said, panting. "Stop."

He vomited.

When he finished, he stood over the unconscious girl. The scene was surreal: a blood-covered hand, an empty jar of poison, a lifeless-looking virgin covered in blood, an evil hag strangely satisfied with the treachery, and the stench of sweat and adrenaline filling the space. Dust and particulates illuminated by sunbeams hung ominously in the air, floating like lost spirits. The atmosphere was darkly quiet, hung-over from violence and guilt.

Churl turned away from his mother, stomped at the dirt, and pounded his head with his fists. Facing her again, he railed, "How could I have let you talk me into this?"

"Lay her here on this bench," she commanded.

He threw the potion jar, breaking it into pieces against a stone pier.

"You stupid fool," she said.

"You, your potions, jars, and stupid magic can all go to hell," he said, cradling Tenateh's limp body. He gently stretched her out on the bench while his mother fumed and ranted over the broken jar.

When he turned to face his mother, she shoved a moist rag in his face. "Suck on this. It will stop your tongue's bleeding."

He tried to resist, but she held the back of his head and pressed the rag forcefully against his lips.

"Suck on it," she insisted. "It will help."

Reluctantly, he took it, jerking his head free.

Churl was turned away, sobbing and sucking on the rag. When he turned back, his mother was applying a paste to Tenateh's forehead.

He turned back and caught her by the arm, saying, "Hey! What are you—"

"So she will not remember," she said.

He could almost feel her burning a hole in his hand with her stare, and he quickly released her. "Oh," he said. "I could use some of that."

"Clean yourself up," she said, disgust lacing her words. "There is water in that stone basin there. Probably some ritual holy water. I will clean up the girl."

After tidying up and hiding the evidence of their crime, they sat together in silence, staring into the dying fire.

Sqatweh appeared from somewhere, coming up to Churl, seeming to know exactly when his affections provided maximum emotional tonic. Churl embraced the large animal, hugging its head and scratching its rib cage vigorously. Tears flowed, and he sobbed silently into the thick, warm fur of Sqatweh's neck.

Rooshth sneered something, but after a few more minutes of silence, she put a hand on his shoulder, shaking it gently. "Yes, it is rough now, but it will be worth it. Remember, real magic costs something. You have paid the price for your heart's desire. Magic will reward you."

"Ith iz bether." His words were distorted by an aching and swelling tongue. He pulled away from her touch, wiping sorrow from his face with his sleeves.

"This is what you wanted. Do not whine."

"What? What I wanted?" He marched away from her, Sqatweh's gaze following him to the other side of the *kiva*. He squatted sullenly on the dirt floor, facing away from his mother.

Time passed slowly, but finally Tenateh stirred, blinked her eyes, and looked around the *kiva*. Her gaze fell first upon Rooshth, and she looked confused. Then she saw Churl and smiled but abruptly frowned, asking, "Oh, Churl. What happened to your mouth?"

"Oh, I fell. Tried to catch myself with my face." Smiling feebly, he gestured to the stone moorings of one of the large support timbers.

A sly smile spread across Rooshth's face. "Impressive," she said quietly. "There is hope for you yet."

Before Churl could respond to his mother's backhanded compliment about his lie, Tenateh said, "I apologize. I must have had my own problems. Did I fall ill?" The drowsy girl pushed up on her elbows and then sat upright on the bench.

Churl started to speak, but his mother cut him off. "You must be very tired. After you sat down next to me, you simply slumped over, fast asleep and dreaming."

"Dreaming?"

"Yes. You were moving around quite a bit and making strange noises. Do you remember what you were dreaming?"

Tenateh looked up at the roof thoughtfully, pursing her lips. Then, as if she were suddenly remembering some horrible memory, her face cringed. "I dreamt of blood." She looked horrified. "I was drinking blood."

"Oh dear. Dreams can be so strange and awful sometimes. Especially when they are so realistic. Even friends can seem like enemies."

Suddenly, Tenateh blurted out, "I can understand you. And you me!" She looked back and forth to each of them. "How is it that we can have the same tongue now?"

"You are right," Rooshth said with surprise. "We can freely talk now." She looked at her son.

"Yes," he said, providing reinforcement. "That is amazing."

Suspicion and deep thought lined Tenateh's face. "But how?"

Churl looked at his mother, silently asking, "Well?"

His mother looked back, silently answering, "Like this." Then she spoke to the girl: "Perhaps what you dreamed . . ."

"Yes?"

". . . was somehow the gods making your destiny possible." She smiled at the girl and then at him.

In his head, Churl rolled his eyes.

Tenateh paused and then said, "Perhaps." Then she quickly stood and started for the doorway. "I must tell others what has happened. I should tell Klanl."

Rooshth stood. "Oh, wait. No need to hurry to tell everyone."

"But . . ."

"Let us visit. Tell us of your people. Your land. Your customs." His mother offered a hand and gestured to the bench.

Tenateh hesitated, smiled at Churl, and then took the hand and sat. Starting with the legends of how her people were brought from the south by the gods, she spoke of their farming, the *quetz'al*, the seasons, the beauty of the desert, and the power of the *Shat'kuh Mongehweh*.

His mother sat forward, taking a warm and inviting posture. "Tell me more of this sacred tablet."

The girl's voice took a distant, monotone quality as she continued and told of the times they had used its power to call the spirits for rain, and of times when spirits intervened against plagues. She spoke of the ferocity of the *quetz'al* in battle and their prowess when hunting. Finally, she spoke of the spirit gifts given to the three *Shat'kuhat*: Human Spirit, Eagle Spirit, and Coyote Spirit.

Suddenly, the girl stopped, puzzled.

"Go on, girl. Your people—The People—are fascinating."

"I think I should not. I am rambling. Besides, already I have spoken out of my place."

"Really, go on."

"What of your people?" Tenateh asked eagerly.

Rooshth didn't answer but instead touched the back of Tenateh's hand, covertly reapplying the mind-control agent. Tenateh's face went blank, and her eyes stared straight ahead. "Please go on," she said.

"Mother!" Churl said, scolding. "What are you doing? That is too much."

"We need her to do a job for us."

"What job?" Alarmed, he was ready to do battle again.

"Just something small, and then we can leave."

"Oh, Mother." He was exasperated.

"It is nothing." She waved her hand dismissively and turned back to Tenateh, saying, "Girl!"

"Yes?" came the slow and vacuous response.

"We need you to get something for us."

"Okay." Her voice was lifeless and hollow sounding.

"I would like to see the *Shat'kuh Mongehweh*. Can you take us to it?"

"Yes, but I do not think that it is wise."

"Why not?"

"It is special. Very few ever see it." The girl's speech was slurred.

"I can keep it a secret," his mother said, raising eyebrows conspiratorially.

"Oh. That is a good idea. We should definitely keep it a secret." The girl nodded her head and raised her eyebrows, too. Then she turned to Churl, pointed, and squinted one eye. "What about you?"

"Me?"

"Yes. Can you keep a secret?"

"Oh, yes."

"Okay then." Tenateh beamed.

Rooshth stood. "Is it nearby?"

"Oh, yes. Klanl, the High Shaman has it in his apartment. I am his assistant." She looked proud. "It is there." Tenateh swung around on her perch and stretched out an arm, her index finger pointing straight out a small window and across the grounds to a set of apartments that were set into the tall, straight wall of the Great House.

"There?" Rooshth pointed in the same direction. "Just out there?"

"Yes. Just up that ladder on the second level," she said, seeming satisfied with her ability to provide a succinct answer. Then blinking and slightly wobbly, she added cheerfully, "His wife, my sister, is there. She is nice. You will like her."

□ ■ □ ■ □ ■ □ ■ □ ■ □

Taken

JUNE 20, 1938, OUTSIDE CHETRO KETTLE, CHACO CANYON

The immortal Goddess of Suicide waited in the In-Between, eagerly watching the young mortal, Frankie Yellowtail, as he crept anxiously into the little room in Chetro Ketl. Naïve-looking and weak, she muttered to herself, "Not too impressive, Ixtab." Then she "read" his insides: healthy, disease-free, virgin. She squinted and looked more carefully. "Something's wrong . . . Oh, a child inside a man's body." She frowned, disappointed. "Let's look at your soul." So she did.

And grinned broadly.

Materializing in a puff of air, she called to him just as he reached to grab the *Shat'kuh Mongehweh* fragment. "Wait!" she said.

He turned around.

"Hello, Frankie. What are you looking for?" She stretched out her arms toward him in a motherly way.

Even in the moonlight, different shades of red could be seen crossing the young man's face as he realized her "natural" state.

"Y-you're naked!" Somehow, he blushed even more and turned his face away.

"Don't you like me?"

"Y-you're naked," he repeated, as if the problem of her nudity was obvious.

"It's okay, Frankie." She stepped closer to him. "I want you to look at me."

125

"I sh-shouldn't."

"Please, Frankie?"

"M-mother wouldn't l-like it."

"She's not here, Frankie. It's just the two of us. Don't you want to look at me?" She gingerly took another step.

"Y-yes."

"Then why don't you?"

"I'm n-not supposed to l-look at girls like that."

She smiled. "Like what?"

"Without c-clothes on." He clamped one hand over his eyes. "Are you g-getting ready to t-take a bath?"

"Yes. Of course. I'm going to take a bath. Nobody takes a bath with clothes on. Or goes swimming."

The boy squeaked.

"Have you had a bath today?"

He shook his head.

"I could give you a bath. Would you like that?" She smiled at his giggling. "Yes. I think you would like that." Stepping even closer, she continued the seduction: "The water would be warm. I could scrub your back. It would feel really nice."

More child-like giggling shook his body, while man-like peeks from under his hand stoked his interest. After a few moments, he asked, "Wh-where's your b-bathtub?"

"Oh, it's in a magical place. I'll have to take you there."

"Magic?"

"Do you like magic?"

"Of course. C-can you do tricks?"

She licked her lips and smiled coyly. "How about this?"

Lifting her hands toward him and over her head, her arms pushed her breasts forward through long hair draped down her torso. When her fingertips touched together over her head, a beautiful, rosy-red glow filled the space between her hands and cast light around the small room.

The boy's amazement swept from her breasts up to the faint light. "Wow," he said slowly.

"You like it?"

"Th-that is some r-real magic."

"Yes it is. It's a special light I use to guide people to heaven. I shine it, and they follow me. I make sure they don't get lost."

"How c-can you get lost on the way to h-heaven?"

"Many ways, but don't worry about that. I'm very good at keeping them safe. Haven't lost one, yet."

The light mesmerized, entranced him. "That's good." His stutter had vanished.

"And I'll keep you safe when we go to the magic place for your bath. You can touch the light if you want to."

"Really?"

"Of course, Frankie." Lowering her hands, she brought them down to rest between her breasts. "Come closer, Frankie."

He stepped forward hesitantly and slowly reached a trembling hand toward the light but suddenly stopped, frozen in midreach.

"Go on, Frankie."

His eyes were locked onto her left breast, breaths coming in shallow puffs. He shook slightly and started to sweat.

"Would you like to touch something else?"

"Yes," he whispered dreamily. Eyes glazed over, tears streamed down his cheeks. "So beautiful. So soft. So round. So pointy."

Ixtab looked down and smiled proudly, admiring her erect nipples, which were bathed in the rosy glow of her guiding light. Laughing quietly, she asked, "Do you want to see how they feel, Frankie?"

"Sure." The boy's fragile body now shook with each pounding heartbeat, and he began to hyperventilate.

"Go on, Frankie." Concern and impatience crept into her voice.

Still, he froze there, immobilized by the conflict between manly desire and childhood inhibitions.

"Did I tell you my name, Frankie? It's a beautiful name, and I'd like to hear you say it." She studied his face for signs of understanding. "If I tell you my name, will you say it?"

"Oh, yes."

Pleased, she said, "Ask me what my name is."

With eyes still locked on the peaked flesh before him, he obeyed. "What is your name?" His voice was monotone, barely audible.

She carefully said, "My name is Ixtab, and I am a goddess." Then her voice pleaded, "Say my name, Frankie."

"Ixtab."

A small spark of her divine fire jumped into his soul, linking the two as if with an ethereal spider thread. "Ooh, Frankie. Say it again. I like it."

"Ixtab." Another spark. Another link.

"Ixtab. Ixtab. Ixtab!" His voice grew in intensity with each repetition.

She opened her mouth, face toward the stars. Breathing heavily, her eyes rolled back into her head.

"Ixtab. Ixtab! I love you, Ixtab."

Ixtab began to writhe in ecstasy. "Show me, Frankie. Show me. Touch me. Touch me." Her voiced pleaded and begged. She bounced ever so slightly and smiled in anticipation, anxious for the coming orgasm that would overtake her body when his tiny, boy-like fingers touched her nipple.

*   *   *

Walking through the spirit world of the In-Between was still a surreal experience, even though Ruth had done it thousands of times. Both spiritual and physical realities were visible to her—something like having one's face half in and half out of the water: one eye below the surface and the other above.

A drama unfolded before her in the ruin's little room: Ixtab was up to her usual tricks. This was the first time Ruth had actually seen the goddess at work, and it was truly one of life's finer performances. Caution suggested staying well out of the way, since Ixtab was dangerous—even the greater gods and goddesses gave her a wide berth.

The young man who was about to lose his soul had been at Weatherby's yesterday with the runt son of her mortal enemy. She knew sooner or later that she would run into either Totahmaa or Quaatsa himself, only wishing for more time to scope around for the poor soul who had discovered the final piece of *Shat'kuh Mongehweh*.

Her thoughts turned briefly to her son, Churl. "I am so sorry, son," she whispered. "I hope that you can hear me and forgive me. But I have finally figured it out. I will be able to fix you."

Ruth's life's quest had been to restore the sacred tablet, but such a task had proven to be a frustrating failure so far. She tried wandering the spirit world looking for the pieces, but that had been utter folly, since it was even larger than Earth; a million lifetimes would be required to find such a small fragment there. Under the light of the full moon, the pieces migrated into the mortal world. If she happened to be in the right place at the right time, then the piece should be easy to grab. At least, easy for her. A mortal had to get past Ixtab, and that had only happened successfully twice before.

The first time had been one of those Spanish Conquistadores who combed the region looking for a mythical city of gold. (Somewhere back in the seventeenth century, someone was laughing his little, brown, Peyote-smoking ass off, having sent those steal-wearing hoarders on a wild chase.) Ixtab had been thrown for a loop that time: turned out, that particular gold-hunter liked men—her charms were a complete failure. The second time—only two decades ago—a white man had somehow gotten past the goddess.

In both cases, Quaatsa and Totahmaa had somehow come away with a stone fragment. She fought them hard over the first one, but there were two of them—and they had a *quetz'al* with them. The battle had been epic, but ultimately Ruth had been near fatally wounded, and the Chaco canyon dwellers seized the fragment. In the case of the white man, Weatherby, they had simply found him quicker than she had.

As Ruth watched Ixtab and the young victim, a still-bleeding cut on the back of the boy's hand caught her attention. Her face softened. Churl, her son, had also had such a cut the day he died. Images of the two boys' wounded hands merged, memory blurring reality.

"Let it go," she told herself, blinking back tears. "He is of no use to you." She began to walk away but paused, furrowing eyebrows deep in thought.

"Or is he?"

*   *   *

Ixtab stood naked before Frankie, smiling.

"Go on," he whispered to himself, but he was moving in slow motion, something within holding him back. He bargained with his conscience: "Just one touch. A once-in-a-lifetime opportunity. Then I will go back home to Mother."

Just then, a whirlwind filled the room. Dust, dirt, and pebbles swirled everywhere. Frankie pulled away from Ixtab to shield his eyes.

With her hair flailing savagely in the wind, the goddess quietly uttered a curse in some strange language. Something changed behind her eyes; an ominous glow penetrated the outside world from within her troubled inner fire. "Say my name, Frankie," she said in a commanding voice.

He barely heard her.

More loudly, she said, "Say my name!" No longer pleading or enticing, her voice was unpleasant, deep, and harsh. She stared angrily, stepping closer to him.

He glanced around the room, hands still protecting his eyes. "N-no," he said, weakly, stutter returning.

"What is my name, Frankie?" She became tall, towering over him—a dangerous giantess, smearing together terror and desire.

"I-I don't w-want to . . ."

"Say it, Frankie!" she barked.

His eyes went wide as the force of her words blew back his hair. Turning away from her, the still-glowing stone caught his eye.

"Frankie?"

Her suddenly soft voice soothed and intrigued him. He turned to face her.

She had returned to her former diminutive size. "Is that what you want?" she asked, her eyes pouty, disappointed. "I thought we could be friends. Can't we go have a bath?"

Frankie was speechless and frozen again, his mind racing yet numb.

"Don't you want me to scrub your back?"

He nodded, still shielding his face from the whirlwind's random missiles.

"I know you do." She extended her hand and pleaded, "Please take my hand. I'll take you to the magic place. Show you more tricks. Scrub your back."

He reached out to take her fingers.

* * *

At that moment, Ruth materialized out of the dissipating whirlwind, lunged at the Frankie, and shoved him out of Ixtab's reach.

The boy fell to the ground, surprised to see her. "Pretty lady?" he asked, confusion in his eyes.

"You!" said Ixtab, fire flaring behind her eyes. "I let you have a man-child of mine once."

"Grab stone, boy!" Ruth commanded.

His gaze tossed randomly from her to Ixtab to the stone.

"Witch! You . . ." The goddess hunched slightly, prepared to fight. "Do not interfere here."

"Demon," she taunted.

At this insult, tongues of fire leaped from the goddess's eyes and spread along her body. "I will devour your pitiful and corrupt soul next, tiny woman." She stepped toward Frankie, growing in stature until she was eight feet tall.

As Ixtab reached for the boy, Ruth stepped defiantly in between the two. "You no want my soul," she said, laughing. "Boy, grab stone. I cannot save from evil demon, but stone can. It sacred, give protection."

Still largely unresponsive, he began to look around the little room. Ruth pointed at it. "There, boy!"

A large fist landed across the back of Ruth's neck. The crushing blow cracked and dislodged vertebrae, sending tingles down her limbs, and her body to the ground. Getting to hands and knees, she shook her head gently, trying to regain equilibrium.

Again the goddess tried to grab the boy, and again Ruth intervened by placing her tiny frame in the way. The boy backed away, moving in the wrong direction.

"Boy!" Ruth said. "There!"

Ixtab suddenly grabbed her by the ankles, picking her up like a floppy doll.

She screamed as the goddess's touch drew out her soul. However, time and magic had taken its toll: her soul was a mere shadow-thing now, spread thin and ragged throughout the spirit realm and diced to pieces in the physical one. Powerful magic was costly, and she had paid the price a thousand times.

The goddess coughed and made a gagging sound. "Your soul is even worse than I thought. Like trying to eat the charred carcass of a field mouse." Then rejecting Ruth's soul, the goddess violently flung her across the room.

Ruth barely raised her hands in time to prevent her head from being crushed against the ancient masonry. "Stone, boy! Get stone!" Getting to her hands and knees proved challenging. She stood on wobbly feet, holding her neck with one hand and bracing ribs with the other.

A look of awareness finally clicked into place in the boy's face, and he crawled toward the stone on the other side of the room. Ixtab glared at him, grabbed a handful of pebbles, and tossed them toward the stone. When the tiny rocks hit the ground, they quickly grew into dozens of scorpions randomly poised around the stone. Frankie screamed and retreated from the arachnid patrol.

Ruth staggered toward the stone. "Frankie!" she yelled furiously. "Come stone now!"

Standing in the middle of the scorpions, she picked them up one by one to fling them back at the goddess. Each menace stung her multiple times, and her hand started to swell. Stings covered her red and swelling feet, too. Thanks to her strange immortality, the experience was excruciating but not fatal. (She could hunger, but not starve; thirst, but not dehydrate; choke, but not asphyxiate; experience death a thousand times, but never die.) Some of the stinging threats hit Ixtab and changed back into pebbles.

Frankie moved again, making a direct line toward the fragment.

Furious, Ixtab dove on top of Frankie as he reached for the stone, the length of her giant body smothering him. Moaning in ecstasy, she started absorbing his soul while he screamed in terror and agony.

In an animalistic rage, Ruth jumped on top of the goddess's legs and bit deeply into divine flesh. Instead of getting a mouthful of blood when her teeth gnashed together, a thick, orange fluid flowed copiously from the wound.

Despite being immortal, the bite was painful and forced Ixtab to relinquish her hold on the boy.

Freed from the goddess's soul extraction, the boy wheezed and slowly dragged his body to the stone fragment. In only seconds more, the deity would have completely devoured his soul, merging it with hers and leaving him a near-lifeless husk.

With her spirit vision, Ruth saw the bulk of the boy's soul return to its skinny, whimpering shell. His soul had a slightly different color and texture. "Strange."

Ruth took a ferocious kick to the face as Ixtab wheeled around, yelling, "No, Frankie! No!"

At the sound of the goddess's voice, the boy grabbed the stone and clutched it to his chest. Curled up in a fetal position, he sobbed and cried for his mother.

Now that he clung to the fragment of sacred tablet, the boy was off-limits to the goddess—but not Ruth.

Ruth knew this.

And she knew that Ixtab would take this loss very personally.

Spitting ancient curses as she scooted backward across the dirt, Ruth watched angry tongues of fire re-erupt along Ixtab's body. Unbridled fury rippled across the goddess's face, and divine, white-hot eyes threatened to burn holes through her. With flaming hair standing on end, Ixtab lunged at her with glowing hands of fire.

Ruth's flesh burned as the deity seized her by the neck, picked her up, and slammed her against the wall. Her feet dangled and kicked hopelessly, six feet off the ground. As the goddess's enormous hands and super-human grip closed around her tiny neck and pressed her into the wall, her breath came in chokes and coughs, then in raspy honks, and then not at all.

She beat feebly against the goddess's oak-like arms, face turning from red to purple. Blood vessels in her eyes burst while spit foamed at the corners of her mouth, and she tried to speak.

"What's that?" asked Ixtab. "No swift retort from that sharp tongue? No magic incantations?"

Ruth's eyes started rolling back in her head as her head flopped sideways.

Suddenly, the goddess dropped her.

Ruth landed hard and clumsily on the ground. Air rushed in to fill starving lungs, wheezing and scraping through a half-crushed windpipe. Clumsily, she rolled to her back, arching and panting and gasping for air; breathing and swallowing were excruciating but necessary. Her hands went to touch her throat, but Ixtab's clutch had left it painfully blistered, charred, and bruised.

"Frankie!" the goddess was calling. "Frankie!" There was pleading in her voice.

Ruth lifted her head to look. The skinny, young man was beating the goddess mercilessly with the sacred fragment. Landing blow after blow, he struck her in the knees, in the legs, in the arms, in the body—anywhere he could, over and over and over. Ixtab retreated from his onslaught.

"You . . . s-stay . . . away . . . from the . . . p-pretty . . . lady." The boy punctuated each word with a strike.

The turn of events and the return of oxygen allowed Ruth to summon the strength needed to pass into the spirit world. In a few minutes, she found her weapon of choice and quickly returned to the tiny room, where events had turned again: the boy now retreated from the goddess to cower in a corner, holding the sacred fragment like a shield before him.

"Hey! You ugly demon!"

Ixtab whirled around to meet the taunt, which is when Ruth swung the Ax of the Rain God with all her might.

Lightning and thunder exploded as the blow struck the goddess, nearly cleaving her in half. Ixtab fell to the ground screaming, her body unnaturally folded at the site of the deep cut like a broken twig. An orange, creamy, glowing pool of light oozed from her wounded divine body. Picasso would have been inspired.

Ixtab literally pulled herself together and then stood, glared menacingly at Ruth, and released a deep-throated, animal-like howl that shook the room. Then a numbing silence dropped into the space as she turned some invisible corner and disappeared into the spirit world.

The boy hunched down in the corner, crying and openly sobbing while he held tightly to the fragment.

Ruth shook. Dropping the axe, she fell to her knees and brought both hands to her face. Distress, agony, and exhaustion leaked out in a series of guttural sounds and sighs.

After a few minutes, she had emotionally recovered. "Finally," she said, "I have the advantage." Looking at Frankie, she continued, "I have the last piece of the *Shat'kuh Mongehweh* and the only friend of Totahmaa Mukaama."

Standing up and picking up the axe, she spoke to Frankie, "Your friend's softhearted father will trade his two pieces for you." Then smiling sideways and pushing silver-white hair out of her face, she said, "Of course, only one of us will be trading fairly."

She allowed herself a brief celebration of joy, dancing and holding the ax aloft to shoot lightning bolts high up into the night sky. "Look, boy," she said. "The stars themselves twinkle in admiration and delight for me."

Just as she had finished, the boy spoke something softly.

"Boy? What?"

"Mr. Blackwood." Frankie was pointing at a tall figure running through the doorway directly at him.

"Oh no, you not!" she yelled, sprinting for the boy.

Arriving first, she grabbed one of Frankie's arms, just above the elbow, spun around toward the new arrival, and held the ax fiercely before her.

Then she stepped into the spirit world, taking Frankie with her.

The Edge of Chaos

DECEMBER 23, 1177, CROOKED NOSE GREAT HOUSE (HUNGO PAVI)

In the courtyard of the Great House, thatching and roof debris was settling to the ground after Tuhj's violent flyover.

Leaving Tenateh below with the two strangers, Quaatsa Mukaama dashed outside the *kiva*. "We will talk to her and her son later." Watching Tuhj up in the air, circling around to land just south of the Great House, he turned to the three ministers with him and said, "Go see if Tuhj is guarding the downed flyer."

The men quickly ran across the courtyard and disappeared through the gate.

Walking slowly and breathing deeply, he also made his way to the gate. Once outside the Great House, he looked north and saw Sheweh Du'hat sprinting his way. She was leading a single-filed battalion of Elite warriors, all outfitted with spears, bows, and daggers. Klanl Hivaht, who had gone to *Zatu Nashtehweh Kana'steh* (Pueblo Bonito) to retrieve her, trailed some distance behind the warriors.

When Sheweh and Klanl arrived, Quaatsa relayed what Tenateh had told him about the boy, the woman, the *quetz'al* attack, and the strange magic.

"So only one *quetz'al* is down?" Sheweh asked.

"One for sure. Possibly two."

"Did the strangers provoke them?"

He shook his head. "Not as far as we know. I was just going to talk to them in the *kiva* when Tuhj flew past, rattling the timbers." He gestured to the scattered roofing material. "He must be very disturbed about something. It is uncharacteristic of him."

He heard a commotion to the south, on the other side of the Great House. He looked but couldn't see anything. "I saw Tuhj land over there," he said, pointing.

Just then, one of the three ministers he'd sent out a moment earlier came running up from the direction of the commotion.

The man bowed, fingers laced together and held near his chest. "*Shat'kuat* Quaatsa," he said in a low voice while still bent over, "Tuhj has gone rogue. He is attacking and killing trainers."

"Tuhj?" Quaatsa asked, shocked. He shook his head as the minister stood upright.

Sheweh sent her Elites to investigate. Klanl went with them.

"No," Quaatsa said to the minister reassuringly. "Must be some other *quetz'al.*"

The bond between master and *quetz'al* was lifelong and deep—almost spiritual. The image of Tuhj's emergence from his egg still stood clear in Quaatsa's mind: tiny, slimy, eyes peering curiously—and hungrily—at the world. As a juvenile, his larger-than-usual size and quick reflexes made him a powerful ally and a horrific foe; he became the alpha male of the herd at a very young age. Twice, Quaatsa had taken him into battle. The first time, the marauders from the east simply turned and ran at the sight of Tuhj and the other *quetz'al.*

The second time, things went much differently.

A Word from the gods had sent warriors north to aid some kin-people who were defending their pueblos against relentless invaders. Sheweh led her Elites directly into the heart of the danger, placing themselves between the pueblos and the invaders. Quaatsa and a few handlers waited on a bluff some distance away, but close enough to see the fighting. The half dozen *quetz'al* they had taken with them circled in the sky, far above and out of sight.

At the right time, Sheweh signaled on her *tzetoh quetz'iteh*—a long, low-frequency flute with a bagpipe attachment slung across the back. Quaatsa heard the low, rumbling sound resonate in the valley and responded with a series of descending tones on his own *tzetoh*. Wing-borne death, waiting above, heard the attack signal and dove in formation, with Tuhj in the lead. Like lethal hailstones, they descended on the invaders from the rear, bringing blood and destruction on a massive scale. The unfolding of their wings as they pulled out of their dives created an explosive cacophony that any storm spirit would envy. The terrifying noise loosed men's bowels and drove some to madness.

During the first pass, the *quetz'al* swooped over the heads of their enemies, spitting their liquid fire and sending scores of men into agony, writhing on the ground. (Some who dared to stand their ground lost their heads and any future need to duck.) They then flew vertically up the side of the pueblo's cliff, turned, and descended again for a second pass. While most of the invaders ran in blind panic, some turned and threw spears or shot arrows—something *quetz'al* took quite personally, being sensitive about their wings. Such fools were snatched up, taken high into the clouds and dropped, or simply flung into the side of the cliff.

It was merciless.

In the end, man and beast alike chased the beaten invaders far from the cliff house. The lucky ones died at the end of a flint dagger or arrowhead. As for the unlucky ones, when people asked, he explained it this way: "Well, eventually the *quetz'al* got full and just flew away to digest."

Quaatsa's mind came back to the present. He turned to Sheweh and said, "Whoever the rogue is will have to be put down."

She sighed deeply. "I know."

When Quaatsa and Sheweh rounded the Great House, a guttural noise escaped his lips as the extent of the carnage hit him: a horribly mangled flyer lay dead in a pool of blood and mud, injured and dying young people were strewn across the area like shards from a shattered pot, and Tuhj prepared to crush a trainer under his foot.

The senior's mouth dropped open, and his shoulders slouched. "Tuhj. Why?"

The Elites started volleying arrows at the giant flyer.

Tuhj glanced at the warriors, scooped up the trainer, and flew away, heading south.

Sheweh came back and stood beside him. "How many down?"

"What?"

"How many down?" Sheweh repeated. "I thought you were counting."

"Oh. No. I do not yet know." He looked at her, face pale, and said, "Tuhj."

"That downed flyer looks like it died in a crash-landing," said Sheweh. "I cannot tell who it is from here." Pointing at the speck in the sky that was the retreating *quetz'al*, she asked, "Who was that?"

His voice cracked. "I said it was Tuhj."

"Oh. You are certain?" She put a hand on his shoulder.

He glanced down, to the right, to the sky, his eyes going moist. "Yes."

"Who was the boy?"

"I do not know."

Elites gathered around the two *Shat'kuhat*, some a little too close for their own good. "Go count the dead and tend to the wounded," commanded Sheweh sharply. "We will track the rogue later." The warriors scattered, duly chastised. Then she called one of them back to send word to Gohm Thlahk about the tragedy. "Tell him we will need *much* medicine and many attendants." The young woman sprinted back to the north.

Sheweh shook her head. "This is strange."

"I know," Quaatsa said.

"I can see Na'atsu or Ski'atseh pulling such a stunt. They are emotionally unstable. Prone to violence. Not very obedient." She scanned the skies and sighed. "I am sure we must put them down one day soon."

"We may have to put all of them down soon."

"What do you mean?"

He hung his head, inhaled and exhaled deeply, almost mournfully. "The People . . . The People are tired of them. I do not understand why."

She looked thoughtful. "Yes. I sense that sometimes."

"They are a part of us. A gift from the gods."

"Of course. I love my own Luahti dearly. I cannot imagine being without her. We are joined souls. But some would say that the *quetz'al* have become a curse from the gods."

"I have also heard such foolish talk," he said.

The People were stressed: summers had been brutal, crops less productive, wild game scarce, and supplies of wood were getting farther and farther away. Even the sky seemed to be turning against them: clouds seldom appeared, and when they did, they hoarded their rain. (The little river that ran through the canyon had been drying up for a few weeks at a time during the summer.)

Many were calling upon the *Shat'kuhat* to use the *Shat'ku Mongeweh* to bring rain and game, but the three Elders refused, wary of tampering with the natural rhythms of the desert. They replied: "Mother Earth, dependent upon us to know when to send rain? Nonsense. Foolishness. We will wait; she will provide." And Mother Earth did provide—only it wasn't enough. There would be hunger come spring.

A young trainer ran up to Sheweh and fell to one knee. "Masters and Elders, please." The young girl was trembling.

Quaatsa took a breath and exhaled slowly. "Speak."

"I must give you terrible news. Please forgive me."

"News is not your fault, young one. Speak."

"Luahti is . . ."

He saw Sheweh stiffen.

"Is what, child?" Quaatsa put his hands on the girl's shoulders.

"She is . . ." Sobs came. "She has taken The Journey. Her body lies there." She extended a shaky arm, pointing at the downed, lifeless flyer.

Sheweh immediately ran to her *quetz'al*, and Quaatsa started to follow, but the girl caught the hem of his garment. Startled and in no mood to deal with such a breach of social protocol, he looked down with a scowl and barked, "Stop it, fool."

Releasing him, she fell on her face and burst out with, "Your *quetz'al*, the thunderous Tuhj, has flown away with Totahmaa." Wails and sobs exploded from her, threatening to shake her small body apart.

"My son?"

"Yes."

He blinked, wobbled slightly, and tried to focus. "Taken him?"

"We tried to follow but could not."

"What? This is not possible. Not possible. Not even conceivable." He paced in small circles, tapping his forehead with his palms.

"Just now. I saw . . ." Sniffs and snot interfered with her message. ". . . the boy. Tuhj almost killed him." Tears had cut clean paths through caked-on dirt.

"Calm yourself, girl." He knelt down, embraced her, and calmed her.

"Your brave son tried to stop Tuhj from killing more of us. The thunderous flyer was so angry over Luahti's death. He swung his tail. He kicked stones and screamed. He threw some into the air."

After a few seconds of weeping, she lifted her head from his chest and bellowed, "He even ate Zor Mnakti. Ate him. Right in front of us." Burying her head in his chest and robes, she cried and wailed.

"What drove you to this, my friend? Or who?" Quaatsa asked his missing rogue.

*   *   *

As his master, mistress, and the new girl prepared to leave the *kiva*, Sqatweh bounded up the stairs in two easy leaps, crashing into the midday sunshine, wagging his tail and sniffing adventure. The fresh air and light bathed him inside and out, reviving him.

Dogs are not meant to be down in holes, he told himself. *All you can smell is dirt—it's like being blind.*

Smells broke across his nose like waves on the ocean, some from nearby sources, some from far away: the sweat of children, a piece of dried meat being meticulously chewed by an old woman, campfires smoldering with grease and charcoal from the previous night, a small herd of antelope browsing for a rare winter's morsel of greens. Each smell brought its own memories, images, and meanings—a treasure trove of information in each whiff.

Sqatweh looked around. There wasn't any obvious danger even though most of the people in the courtyard had scattered, scared off by the monstrous noise earlier.

Some freakish thunder cloud, I guess, he mused aloud.

A handful of children were playing with a ball about halfway across the courtyard. He went to introduce himself, tail raised and wagging cordially as he trotted.

They saw him coming and picked up the ball.

He sat, slapping his tail against the dirt. *Bummer,* he yipped. *I could catch that.*

Glancing back toward the *kiva,* he saw that no one else had emerged yet, and so he turned back to the children. Despite his disappointment, he put his tail up again and approached more slowly.

One of them squatted down and put a hand out.

Any food? he whined, lowering his head and peering out from beneath eyebrow ridges.

The children talked amongst themselves, seeming to understand, but no handout came. Instead, three scrawny dogs ran out from one of the ground-level apartments and came straight at him, barking and growling, tails down, teeth bared.

You're kidding, he barked at them, putting his tail straight behind him in a neutral position. *I'm just looking for a handout, not a fight.*

The local gang snarled and growled more ferociously. One of them barked back: *Get lost, outsider. These are our people, and this is our land, and it is our food.*

He studied them as they started to close in on him, two coming straight on while the third flanked him. They had attitude, but clearly no discipline or training. They were all smaller than he—the smallest merely bite-sized. *Together, you're only half my size,* Sqatweh barked. *One of you is going to get hurt.*

The bullies didn't back down.

Sqatweh looked at the children and glanced back at the *kiva.* Churl had just emerged and was squinting in the sunlight. *Fine, I'll go,* he barked, taking the harder path of peace.

Putting his tail down, he slowly turned to walk away. *Lousy neighborhood,* he whined. His stomach growled loudly. *I know.*

The bullies took his withdrawal as weakness, and when he turned, they charged.

At the sound of their noisy attack, he wheeled around to face them, ears folded and fangs bared. A dirty-white dog leaped onto his back, latching fiercely onto one of his ears. Meanwhile, a tiny, brown mutt sunk teeth into his right foreleg, and the third dog, the largest, slid under his belly, taking Sqatweh's hind legs out from under him. Suddenly, he was on the ground, belly-up.

Dirty tricks, he complained.

A gang member growled, *This is how we do it around here, outsider.*

Let me show you how we do it with jaguars and crocodiles. He easily stood up and shook them loose.

Predictably, they all rushed him again at once. He spun around to meet the tiny, brown dog, scooping it up in his mouth, teeth poised to crush its neck, but instead, he tossed it several feet across the dirt. The largest dog went mad with rage and blindly started chomping at any nearby bit of fur. With lightning speed, Sqatweh shot out a foreleg and swatted the animal to the ground, holding it under a massive paw and slowly bringing his mouth around the dog's neck. The defeated dog lay still and whimpered.

Just as he started to release the lesser dog, he yelped alarmingly and leaped backward and to his right. He sat, curled his body sharply, and licked at the burning pain in his left side. Blood pulsed out heavily from between two ribs.

A young boy stood merely feet away, holding a flint knife covered in blood.

Sqatweh faced the boy to attack. He growled, but it came out more as a gurgle, and foamy blood squeezed through the knife wound. Charging weakly at the boy, he struggled to stay focused on his target. He managed to smash into the boy, knocking him to the ground and pinning him.

From across the courtyard, his master's voice came: "Sqatweh! Sqatweh!" There were sounds of running.

Pinned down by Sqatweh's jaws, the boy struggled against him. Though unharmed, the kid screamed with unadulterated panic, which brought back the three dogs, who retaliated ferociously. This was no longer a simple territorial dispute. With weakness quickly overtaking him, he fought to stand and move so that the other dogs couldn't land a fatal strike at his throat.

However, when he stood up, the boy gained room to wield his knife again, thrusting it repeatedly into Sqatweh's belly.

Sqatweh jumped away, strength failing, vision failing, breathing failing. Blood flowed copiously from his shredded abdomen. Spotting Churl, he took a few steps toward his master but fell over sideways. He sniffed the air.

The old woman was holding Churl back.

Sqatweh whimpered. The ruffians circled him.

Home, he whined. *Master? Can we go home now? Maybe see the forests and jungles again. Smell the small animals and chase them. Maybe hunt a jaguar. That would be nice.*

In his mind, a jungle path opened before him. Shady and dappled with sunlight. Green. Lush. Moist. Filled with sound. Filled with scent. He was free, running toward a kind-looking woman standing beside a peaceful jungle waterfall. She held a peaceful, rose-colored light between her hands.

*   *   *

Rooshth gripped Churl's sleeve tightly, holding him back from running to Sqatweh, who lay bleeding and dying on the other side of the courtyard. They had just emerged from the *kiva* when the three mutts savagely attacked. It had just been the usual canine land skirmish, and then that canyon boy intervened and stabbed him.

"We must go help him."

"See how still he lies?" They watched the boy crawl out from under Sqatweh's body and drop the knife. "We can do nothing now."

"Mother! You have to," he begged. "You must have some potion to heal him. I know you do."

"No. Nothing now. He is gone. You will see him in the afterlife."

"No!" He tried to wrench himself free, but she was too strong. "Do something. You do not care. You are horrible."

At that, the old woman slapped him, spinning him into the ground. "This will cause trouble," she said, pointing her finger at him and burning him with her stare. "They will make us leave." Paranoia colored her tone. "Now focus on the prize and quit sniveling over a stupid, dead dog."

Apparently unaware of the drama unfolding around her, Tenateh was a blank doll walking toward Klanl Hivaht's apartment. "We are almost there," she announced happily. "The ladder with the red paint," she said, pointing to a long, rickety-looking, wooden frame.

Images of Sqatweh flipped through Churl's head: a puppy playing, hunting game together, wrestling, and burying his face in the great, thick fur. "It is wrong to leave him there alone," he said. "Can we not at least bury him or—"

"Shut. Shut. Shut up! Ignorant, Pitiful Boy." Fear and anger mixed in her tone. "Do you not see the bigger picture? The true task?" She faced him, grabbed both his hands, and said, "We are nearly there. The goal of my life. The completion of yours. We can get another servant dog."

He stood, putting his hand to his cheek, and caressed the small, ever-reddening tiny handprint left by his mother. "Servant dog? He was my friend." Looking back to Sqatweh's body, he whispered, "Good-bye, my friend."

Tenateh and Rooshth left him there and marched on at a brisk pace. They arrived at the red ladder and quickly climbed it. Despite their age difference, there was no difference between the girl's and the old woman's agility. As they crossed the rooftop to Klanl's apartment, Jooh Niteh, Klanl's wife, came out to greet her sister with a kiss.

In the midst of the chaos now unfolding around him, the pent-up anger and frustration that had been smelting Churl's soul for years finally completed its work. He had changed: no longer a child with a loving mother, but rather an adult contending with a demented parent. He saw her now as she really was: damaged, broken, and hell-bent on destruction in pursuit of an imaginary end. The nature of his love for her was profoundly and forever different.

"I used to be offended when others called you mad, Mother," he said, watching the woman ascend the ladder. "They did not know you. I thought them blind. But now you shame me. You *are* mad. It was I who did not know you. I who was blind."

Finally arriving at the bottom of the red ladder, he gripped the rails and put his foot to the first rung but didn't ascend. He simply hung his head in despair.

"Tenateh," he said suddenly and sprinted up the ladder.

▼△▼△▼△▼△▼△▼△▼△▼△▼△▼

Ancient Words

DECEMBER 23, 1177, OUTSIDE CROOKED NOSE GREAT HOUSE (HUNGO PAVI)

Quaatsa watched Sheweh hunched on the ground beside Luahti's body. She looked stoic from a distance—the picture of clarity, focus, and calm. But when he walked up beside her, he could see her hands trembled slightly as she brushed fingertips along the stilled face of her flyer, and her eyes blinked rapidly, holding back oceans.

Had she lived, this *quetz'al* would have been their only real chance of finding Tuhj and rescuing Totahmaa. He studied the flyer's corpse for signs of her demise. Her body lay in a tragic state: pool of mud made from her own blood, wings torn to shreds, compound fractures jutting from a leg, and part of her chest cavity had collapsed inwardly. These injuries and the parallel scratches all along her body were consistent with nearby tracks across the ground. Farther up the crash pathway, the large boulder that smashed her rib cage protruded from the ground.

Quietly, he addressed Sheweh, "It seems unlikely that Tuhj could have done this. The two were so close."

She sniffed and said, "This wing wound and subsequent crash-landing suggest possible *quetz'al*-to-*quetz'al* aerial combat. Maybe they were playing and something went wrong."

"An accident?"

"Might explain Tuhj's emotional state."

"I think not," said Quaatsa. "They seldom engage in rough play—especially in the air."

Standing and pointing in the direction of Luahti's skid, she added, "She was brought down. I know it."

"I agree, but by who?"

Quaatsa shivered. Bringing down a grown, flying, well-trained *quetz'al* was no mean feat. Generally, the only chance one had involved a squad of at least ten well-trained archers and another ten warriors who could throw a spear with deadly accuracy.

Scanning the area, he noted at least eight trainers with various degrees of injury: three on their feet and five lying on the ground—all being attended by Sheweh's people. At least ten figures still lay on the ground, alone and motionless, the terrifying final moments frozen in grizzly pantomime.

"Where is Gohm?" he mumbled to himself, squinting toward the north past the Great House. "He has taken Totahmaa."

"Totahmaa's with Gohm?" Sheweh asked.

"No. Tuhj," he said. "The girl told me."

"Oh . . . Oh?"

"Will any of us survive this day?"

She squinted at him. "You're thinking of the Word from the gods? Of the End?"

"Could it be anything else? Two tails—from the south. And suddenly two strangers—from the south—show up. One ancient and wrinkled beyond anything. The other frail and pale."

The strange words that the lizard told him popped into his mind and out of his mouth: "Lonely Mother."

Sheweh looked puzzled. "What?"

"At *Ton'ah Tashteh* (Fajada Butte), the two-tailed lizard said that to me. I did not know what it meant at the time."

"So what is it?"

"The old woman's name," he said, shrugging his shoulders.

Glancing around at the wounded, dead, and dying, Quaatsa said, "I wish Gohm would hurry."

"I have sent for him with one of the warriors."

Quaatsa looked back toward the Great House again but still didn't see anything. "How about you? Do you see him yet?" (Her vision—thanks to her spirit gift—was far superior.)

She put a hand up to shield away the sun. "Yes, there he is. Some ministers are with him."

"Good. We need to quickly form a plan."

* * *

"Pull that ladder up. Now." Rooshth's patience was thin, and she spat staccato words at Tenateh, "Girl. Go. Now."

Tenateh finally broke away from hugging her sister and obeyed, getting help with the ladder from Churl.

The sister had come to the door barely dressed, looking unsure and a little annoyed at Rooshth, but after greeting Tenateh, she seemed to have made some decision. Donning a gracious smile, she pulled her clothes more tightly around herself and said some warm- and welcoming-sounding words.

Rooshth awkwardly returned the smile and asked, "Is this the house of Klanl?"

The sister leaned in closer, turned her hands palm up with a shrug, and said something.

"Klanl. Is this the house of Klanl, High Shaman?"

"Klan'nahl?" asked the woman.

"Oh, this is going to take too much time," Rooshth said. She turned to Tenateh, who had just finished pulling up the ladder with Churl. "Girl? Tenateh."

"Yes."

"Tenateh, is this your sister?"

Still dopey, the younger girl smiled. "Yes. Her name is Jooh. Is she not pretty? She has a handsome husband; they will make beautiful babies." Then she directed a coy smile at Churl. "I would like to have babies someday."

Rooshth rolled her eyes and huffed, "Too much with the drug." She grabbed the girl by a shoulder and shook her slightly. "Tell your sister that we have come for the sacred tablet."

"We have?" Tenateh tilted her head sideways.

"Yes. Tell her."

"She will not give it to us."

Rooshth lunged forward and seized Tenateh by the throat, eyes wide with rage. "Tell her, or I will kill you right now," she said through clamped teeth.

However, under the influence of the powerful drugs, she seemed unmoved by the violence.

Incensed, Rooshth began to shake her by the throat violently. Tenateh coughed, flailed, and shook like a cornhusk doll.

A sudden shove sideways caused her to lose her grip on Tenateh. She turned to glare at the offender, Jooh, who stood there, yelling angrily and pointing at her sibling. Growling, she shoved Tenateh out of the way with both hands, sending her reeling backward to the deck. Then she spun around and slashed at Jooh's throat with long, sharp fingernails.

Jooh stepped back, clutching her neck. Blood trickled down across a collarbone. After looking at her blood-covered hand, she started yelling toward the courtyard and making a commotion.

"Shut! Shut! Shut!" Rooshth screamed. "You are going to ruin everything!"

Without warning, she pulled out her obsidian knife and sliced at Jooh. The surprise slash drew a jagged, crimson line across the woman's cheek. Jooh nimbly avoided the next few swings, but then Rooshth dealt Jooh a surprise kick to the left shin. A stomp to the left foot followed, and there was a loud snap as both women's feet punched through the roof. Rooshth pulled her foot away quickly, but Jooh's fell through, and her left leg sunk up to her left thigh while her right leg splayed out behind her.

Jooh bent forward trying to press herself up and out of the hole using her hands, but Rooshth brought the knife down hard into a kidney. The younger woman screamed in surprise and agony, arching, writhing, and clutching madly at her back.

In seconds, Jooh bled out.

Tenateh stood up from the roof deck and gave her fallen sister a puzzled look. When the lifeless body of Jooh twitched, she giggled. "You make me laugh, sis."

Rooshth faced Churl and said, "Stay out here and watch for trouble. It will be coming soon, and I have to work quickly."

"What?" he asked, seeming like he, too, was in a drug-induced stupor.

"Stupid boy. Stay here." She pointed violently to the rooftop deck, gesticulating with the bloody, black knife. "Trouble will be coming. Warn me when it arrives."

Grumbling, she turned to Tenateh and asked, "Why did he not help? He should have been better. Does he not know what is at stake? Pitiful Boy."

Tenateh shrugged.

Grabbing the drugged girl, Rooshth pulled her toward Klanl's apartment. "If I hadn't have been there myself," she said, loud enough for Churl to hear, "I would swear that boy came from some other womb."

She stormed into Klanl's apartment, Tenateh in tow, and scanned it quickly. "Where would he hide anything in this desolate, empty place?" she asked.

The farther north she traveled, the more simplistic and pragmatically people lived. Klanl and Jooh's apartment was a prime example: no furniture; everything on the floor; no decorations, trinkets, or icons; no murals—walls completely blank. Rugs, both woven and of tanned hides, covered most of the floor. A bed pallet of fur skins and blankets lay in the corner, waiting patiently for an occupant that would never return. The small cooking hearth in the center of the room, kindling ready, added homeliness and warmth to the Spartan space. Two *kachina* dolls near the doorway suggested that a newlywed couple lived here.

A few wicker storage jars stood in a corner. Rooshth quickly searched them but found no hidden power buried among the dried corn and beans. Neither did she find anything hidden under the bed pallet.

"Do you want me to help you find something?" offered Tenateh, semiconscious.

Rooshth wheeled on her heels and smiled, saying, "Yes. Yes, I do. Maybe you still have some use."

"Okay. What are you looking for?" She smiled, half of her mouth apparently finding it easier than the other half.

"*Shat'kuh Mongehweh.*"

"Oh, right. The sacred tablet."

"Yes."

The young girl put her hands on her hips and shook her head. "You will never find it. It is *very* well hidden."

"I think you are right, child." Rooshth let a sweetness edge into her voice. "Do you know where it is?"

"No."

Rage replaced sweetness. "What? You said you knew where the tablet was!"

"No. I said it was here."

Rooshth growled and tugged at her own hair. Then forcing herself to breathe slowly, she asked, "Well, then where is it?"

"I do not know. Did you know I already told you that?"

Rooshth cringed, on the verge of exploding. "Child," she started, forcing calm again, "how will we get the tablet if you do not know where it is?"

The girl looked right at her with a scrunched-up face, as if to suggest that Rooshth was entirely silly. "I will *find* it."

"But you said that it cannot be found."

Tenateh wagged a finger. "No." There was more face scrunching. "I said *you* could not find it. I, being of The People, will find it with ease."

Rooshth simmered.

"Did you notice beneath you?" asked Tenateh. The girl bent down and pulled back an edge of the rug to reveal the floor underneath. "See, we are on the second floor. This is not dirt under the floor coverings." A tight, uniform weave of thatch and thin branches formed a strong layer between them and the apartment below. This woven floor rested on thick, rough-hewn support timbers.

"Continue," Rooshth said through smiling, clenched teeth.

"Now, let us think . . ." Tenateh surveyed the room, a puzzled look on her face. "It seems that it would be a very bad idea to place a fire directly on a wood and thatch floor."

Rooshth studied the cooking hearth. It was a large flat stone with small stones set around it in the shape of a rectangle. At one end of the rectangle, a stick had been tightly fitted into place for use as a spit or hook. Underneath the stones, several thick leather blankets protected the underlying thatch from heat and stray embers.

"Ah. Now look at this," she said gleefully, pulling back the protective leather blankets. "See?"

The foundation stone of the hearth sat on little stone risers so that there was a space between it and thatch below.

"Hmm . . ." said Tenateh, starting to reach underneath the hearthstone. "I wonder what we might find—"

Diving to the floor, Rooshth knocked Tenateh out of the way. She felt around under the stone, and her fingers found something so smooth it was slippery. Unable to grip it, she pushed it to the opposite side of the hearth with her fingertips, scrambled around, and retrieved the hidden object from under the leather.

"There you go," stated Tenateh proudly.

Rooshth stared long and hard at Tenateh and then slapped her without warning, sending the girl spinning to the other side of the apartment.

After a long, relaxing sigh, Rooshth smiled and said, "Much better."

She held the stone tablet at arm's length and examined the source of power carefully, running her fingers delicately over the surface. Experienced eyes absorbed every nuance and marking. The pink-and-white-swirled stone resembled pipe stone, polished smooth and carved intricately. Checkered, blocky figures arranged in a tight grid covered one side of the stone, and the other side had images of people, gods, and flying reptiles.

Tenateh was struggling to her feet. Rooshth walked up to her and smiled again. "Great news. I know this writing," she said. "It is the language of the ancient pyramid builders of my home."

□ ■ □ ■ □ ■ □ ■ □ ■ □

Hostage

JUNE 20, 1938, OUTSIDE CHETRO KETTLE, CHACO CANYON

The glowing red light dancing in the night sky was an irresistible beacon. It poured up into the darkness from one of the local ruins, easily seen from the T57 that cruised south through the canyon on the eve of the summer solstice.

"Hmm . . . a secret ceremony? How could I resist?" Blackwood asked himself. He slowed the car, killed his headlights, and quietly rolled up to within about fifty yards of the Chetro Ketl. With panther-like stealth, he deftly bounded over boulders and rock walls through the ruins to investigate.

The voices of two women yelling and cursing came from the room with the reddish glow. Things sounded violent, and one kept yelling at somebody named "Boy" to do something with a stone.

He slowed, proceeding even more cautiously. Eventually, he crouched at the door of the noisy, little room and peered in via a small signal mirror kept in his cigarette case. Inside, an eight-foot-tall, naked woman, beautiful, with smooth bronze skin, flaming hair, and burning white hands advanced on a retreating Frankie Yellowtail. There was no sign of a second woman. Frankie held up some kind of stone before him like a shield or lucky charm, apparently hopeful that it would ward off the fearsome giantess threatening to bear down upon him.

She said, "Frankie! You can't believe that witch. You love *me*. Remember?"

"No!" the boy cried, crouching deeper under the cover of his stone.

"Say my name, Frankie."

"No. G-Go away."

"Please, Frankie." Her voice was sultry and charming. "I love it when you say my name."

Blackwood breathed, "Who is she? What is your name?" Her raw sexuality tugged at him with velvet-steel cords. "I'd say your name if I knew it." His jaw went slack as he watched her naked body moving.

"Say her name, Frankie."

The weary-looking defender stared into the woman's eyes, opened and closed his mouth—a sheep before slaughter.

"Go on . . ." she urged.

"Go on . . ." Blackwood urged, but watching the boy sob and shake in terror snapped him out of the hypnotic infatuation.

Steeling his resolve, he quickly stepped through the door. A strange "whoosh-thump" sound came from his left, opposite of the boy. The tiny Dutch woman, Ruth, suddenly stood there, clutching a giant stone ax nearly as large as herself and poised to strike.

"Like I thought," he whispered, "Dutch my exquisite arse."

The giantess failed to note either of the new arrivals, until the blonde axe-wielder directed a well-placed taunt in some unrecognizable language, which brought the flaming-haired nude around to face the insult. Instantly, Ruth swung the axe, cutting deep into the giant, like striking into the heartwood of a great sequoia. The impact spun the giantess around, nearly slicing her in half and sending her to the ground, twisted into some inhuman shape. Incredibly however, she managed to literally pull herself together in a way that defied description, and though wobbly, she got to her feet and directed an inhuman bellowing sound at the tiny axe-wielder, rattling Blackwood's chest and skull. The nude frosted this surreal, little cake by pivoting, stepping forward, and simply vanishing.

Frankie's voice interrupted Ruth's celebration: "Mr. B-Blackwood!"

Blackwood ran toward the boy despite the dangerous giant slayer and her fearsome, stone-aged weapon merely feet away.

"Oh no, you not!" screamed the woman, also running full bore at Frankie, unfortunately arriving first. She grabbed the boy by an arm and turned to face him with the intimidating weapon. Then she and the boy simply vanished with another "whooshing-thumping" sound.

He stood there for a long while, dust motes whirling and descending around him like tiny, chaotic parachutists trying to avoid the ground, a physical metaphor for his present mental condition. After several years of working for the Foundation, investigating and locating various occult artifacts, the talented charlatans and magicians he had seen were innumerable. However, he had never come face-to-face with any *real* witchcraft, sorcery, wizardry, shamanism, or dark magic.

Stunned, he mused aloud, "Real people, one can fight—kill if necessary. But demons and magic? How do you track someone who can vanish into thin air? How do you fight beings without blood?"

Functioning only semiconsciously, he turned around slowly and made his way back to the car, stumbling several times. He sat down, adrenaline shakes coming on, and fought off the dry heaves. Leaning back, closing his eyes, and breathing slowly, he started the motor with quivering fingers.

The roadster's ambiance washed over him, a soothing blanket of familiarity: the engine's purr, the subtle vibration through the car seat, the fine wood of the dashboard, the supple leather. Mental re-grounding followed physical: gas pedal, brake, clutch, shift lever, pistons, rings, oxygen, fuel, combustion, Otto cycle—everything predictable and explainable, as it should be.

After a few minutes, the nausea passed and trembling decreased.

"A cigarette would be exquisite," he bemoaned to the night. The pouch of chewing tobacco and cigarette papers laying in the passenger seat on his left mocked him. He studied them carefully, picked up the pouch, and opened it. Raising it to his nose, he gingerly sniffed it.

"No, no, no," he said, setting the chaw aside. From his glove box he pulled a little, metal flask. "Ah, bourbon, soother of souls, bracer of courage! Come thou and restore me with thy kiss." The liquor went down smooth and warm. The trembling eased into calm.

Throwing the pouch and papers out of the window with finality and annoyance, he put the T57 in gear and pulled out, heading north. The motor joyfully revved, kicking rocks backward and lifting his spirit as he gained distance from the supernatural.

His brain clicked into action, and he began processing aloud. "A trick? Some elaborate illusion?" He brushed his hand through his hair, aiding the wind in sweeping away mental debris. "Seems unlikely. No one knows I'm here. Why such trouble for a stranger? And how would they know where I would be?"

Tapping his fingers on the steering wheel, he concluded, "No, something more treacherous at play, I'm afraid." He smiled. "A mystery. Who knew vacations could be so fun?"

The filing cabinet in his mind marked "Hoax" was fat and well-documented, filled with memories of séances, mystics, magicians, charlatans, fakes, frauds, and escape artists. In fact, one entire "filing drawer" was labeled "Houdini." Blackwood had been a part of Houdini's staff in the 1920s when the escape artist collaborated with *Scientific American* to debunk various spiritualists around the country. The prestigious organization had issued an outstanding reward to any spiritualist who could demonstrate authentic contact with the "other side." Exciting times, they had been filled with intrigue and undercover work. As a young man in his late twenties, he was a knight on a quest—a crusader in the war for truth.

Blackwood's Eastern European mentor had been multitalented, and like all great magicians, the man possessed an almost supernatural insight into how people perceived their needs and desires. Houdini could play a crowd like a fiddle, and he could certainly see when another artist was doing the fiddling. "Motivation," he would say. "Motivation is the key to everything with people. When you do a trick, everyone wants to believe—even the skeptics secretly want to be proved wrong. And the believers . . . the True Believers . . . they are like tiny, fragile birds in your hand: you can caress them, stroke them, sing to them, and make them happy beyond their wildest dreams. Or you can crush them. It is a power awesome and weighty."

Blackwood pondered while the car purred, moving man and machine north through the canyon on the old gravel road. The bright, starlit night inspired him to turn out his headlights and slow down. The cool night air, the drone of the tires on the gravel, and the peaceful, silvery darkness composed a Zen-like narrative that finished restoring him.

Three people had vanished into thin air before his eyes—and one of those had been cleaved in half. He'd seen every trick in the book, but never this one. "Must be some rational explanation," he said. "After all, this is the age of Einstein and the triumph of reason over superstitious tyranny."

Squinting suddenly at something in the road ahead, he flipped his headlights back on. Two Natives walked toward him down the middle of the road.

He stomped on the brakes, bringing the T57 to a sliding stop. Gravel and dust flew forward into the faces of the pedestrians.

The two Natives shielded their eyes and faces from the light and the debris. Crimson and white war paint adorned their faces. There was a boy carrying a knife, bow, quiver, and spear; he was stripped from the waist up, and his chest showed a strange six-fingered tattoo. An older man wore a cape and had large, orange and yellow feathers tucked into braids wrapped around his head, making it look as if he had wild hair, full of fire. He carried a large wooden flute and bore the same six-fingered tattoo on his bare chest.

The boy jumped ahead of the older man and brandished his spear, which was almost seven feet long and wielded a nasty-looking flint tip. He held the weapon firm: right hand near the center of the weapon, left hand near the butt and locked against his hip. His confidence and form suggested extensive training and combat experience. His face alone could whither an enemy.

In the car, Blackwood grabbed the top of the windshield where the canvas top would attach and stood up in the driver's seat, head and shoulders above the glass. "Turq?" he called out. "Is that you?"

The boy relaxed slightly, tilted his head, pasted a suspicious look on his face, and replied, "Is that you, Mr. Black?"

"Blackwood. Yes," he said, relieved to see tension drain from the boy.

"Blackwood, what are . . ."

At that moment, thunder exploded on the road between the car and the two Natives.

Dust and dirt flew everywhere, surrounding the yellow roadster in a cloud that forced Blackwood to tightly shut his eyes and shield himself. Small pebbles clinked against glass and chipped paint. After a second or two, he tested the air, barely opening his watering eyes. Quickly, he blinked them back into proper function.

Two gigantic eyeballs stared at him hungrily from the night.

"Jesus-Harry-Houdini-Loving-Christ, help me," he said to himself quietly.

*   *   *

Lying on his side, Frankie Yellowtail lifted his head and looked around. He was alone on a flat rock surface. It was foggy. Quiet. Hunger and thirst gnawed at him on the inside. Hard stone dug into his ribs on the outside.

"Oh dear," he said, easing himself into a sitting position. He strained to see or hear anything, but the silence overwhelmed everything. Cupping his hands around his mouth, he shouted into the gray, "Hello? Hello-o!" His words vanished into the mist of the anechoic environment: no reverb, no reflection, no measure of transmission whatsoever. Neither sound nor light penetrated the eerie mist.

He wrapped his arms around his body, giving himself a hug.

Standing, he looked around again. "Which way? This way," he said, randomly picking a direction and slowly walking forward.

The fog pestered his vision. Blinking spastically, he waved his arms before his face in a repeating cycle of failed attempts to wipe it away. His attention alternated from his feet to the fog in front of him, which grew even thicker. After a few steps, his feet disappeared. After a few more, his knees.

Fear, which had thus far only been lurking, suddenly banged ferociously on the windows of his soul.

In just a few more steps, he could no longer see his hands.

Glass panes shattered as fear burst through.

Frankie started whimpering. "Hello? Help me, please," he called out into the fog, voice quaking and weak. Blinking and shuffling gingerly, he said, "I sh-should go b-back." His head jerked around, tossing his gaze from blank gray to blank gray. "Which w-way?" he asked the mist.

For lack of an answer, Frankie sat down on the rocky surface in the mist and hugged himself tightly, slowly rocking back and forth. He thought about his mother, but that made him sad. He thought about the naked giantess and the tiny Dutch lady, but that made him afraid. So he thought about the Babe, imagining the scene at Yankee Stadium during the ballplayer's prime: the roar of the crowd and the smell of roasted peanuts and popcorn filled him.

His stomach growled, but he smiled and said, "Hush, you."

He looked around the famous stadium in his head, and rain began to fall there. The boys of summer kept playing on—despite an increasingly wet and muddy field. The soggy ball pitched erratically, striking out Yankee after Yankee. The whole lineup had been exhausted, but now Babe Ruth was up to save the day. The homerun king pointed his bat into the stands, and the crowd screamed with the hope of witnessing history.

Frankie bounced with glee. The Bambino had pointed right at him. "I wish T w-were here," he said, punching his right hand into his ball glove, securing a pocket for the catch of his life.

The first pitch came: Ball! The second pitch: Strike! Then, ball! Then, strike! And, ball! The stadium filled with the cacophony of spectators: fans cheering encouragement, opponents yelling hexes. The famous batter hushed the crowd and winked at Frankie, who giggled. The pitch came, chugging toward Babe Ruth in slow motion. He swung and connected with the ball, which suddenly exploded like a giant water balloon, flooding the field, sending Yankees and visitors alike scurrying away from the deluge as it tried to sweep them up in its path.

The dugouts filled with water. The field filled with water. Bleachers bounded the newly formed lake, and The Great One treaded water somewhere over the pitcher's mound, struggling to stay afloat among the windswept whitecaps and heavy raindrops dancing across the gray surface.

"Bambino! Over here!" Frankie yelled. "Over here!"

The Babe looked his way and started swimming toward him, even as the water rose higher and higher, making the distance between himself and the boy grow.

"Come on, Babe!" His hero was struggling, coughing, and spitting up water as his strokes slowed. "You can do it! Come on!" Frankie longed to help Babe, but he himself couldn't swim. Panic wrapped cold tentacles around his soul as he suddenly noticed water in his seat. He had to turn away from his hero and run up bleachers to escape the rising deluge.

The rows went by: F, G, H, I . . . Pretty soon he was up to TT, panting and struggling. Each time he climbed a level, the water climbed a little bit farther, faster. Pretty soon, he was in the water— up to his chest—trying to keep climbing. The icy water made his breathing spastic and sapped his strength. One last time, he turned to look for the Babe, but the water quickly rose to his neck, forcing him to keep climbing. When he reached ZZZ, the water reached chin level, and there was nowhere left to go.

In just a few seconds, he had to stretch up onto tiptoes, face pointed skyward in order to get a breath. He waved his hands around in the water for stability, but his balance failed. The slip from the bleacher sent him plunging under the frigid flood. Below the surface, the murky gray hid everything; his own hands were invisible to him even as they should have been right before his eyes. Finally, his breath burst from his lungs, and water started to fill his mouth and sinus cavities. He choked and gagged and fought violently against the power of the water but was losing.

Then, he awoke with a start, gasping and coughing. The stadium gone. The Babe gone. The fog remained but had lifted somewhat, and it was raining.

He had slumped over on his side again, and while sleeping, water had gotten into his nose, stinging and burning. Shivering cold, he sat up to find himself sitting in two inches of flowing water, as if he were now in the middle of a wide brook.

Something small bumped into his backside. Reaching behind him, his fingers found something smooth and round. When he brought it around, he was staring at a baseball.

Turning the ball in his hands, he inspected the patriotic red, white, and blue of stitching, fresh hide, and ink. A single blemish where some bat had connected long ago marred the pristine ball's surface. Opposite of the bat mark, a barely discernible scrawl wished him warmly, "To Frankie, my Big Man. Hang in there. Ixtab said you might need this." It was signed, "Love, Mother."

Pressing the ball into a cheek, he hung his head and sobbed uncontrollably while rain and tears dripped from the end of his nose.

▼△▼△▼△▼△▼△▼△▼△▼△▼△▼

Between Strangers

DECEMBER 23, 1177, SOUTH OF CHACO CANYON A FEW MILES

Quaatsa gave Sheweh and Gohm some instructions and then left them there to carry out their duties. He surveyed the bodies of those slain by his *quetz'al*. His face was drawn, exhausted.

Rogue flyers tended to go south, so he did too. He ran for miles, passing *Zatu Nashtehweh St'ah*, a largely abandoned Great House that had once been a layover for pilgrims and travelers making their way into the canyon. A handful of children outside the crumbling structure divided their attention between watching him run past and watching clouds glide past. A small girl waved, and he returned her friendliness.

He thought of the great unknown that was now upon them. Over and over again, Quaatsa had reviewed and analyzed his conversation with the gods. "How could The People be no more? Not The People?" he'd asked himself. "Where will they go? We go?"

Running up onto a small rise, he stopped to catch his breath and scan the skies. The terrain here was open, providing excellent visibility in all directions. "He must be down here somewhere," he said.

Reaching for his *tzetoh*, the bagpipe-flute slung over his shoulder, Quaatsa pulled it out and inflated the large airbag, made from the bladder of a bison. Once the reservoir was filled and re-slung across his back, he blew into the mouthpiece and squeezed the bladder. Covering the three finger holes, the first note resonated with the fundamental frequency of the five-foot pipe—a long, low pitch with breathy

163

overtones. Thanks to the airbag, the surprisingly loud tone could be held for several seconds.

Quaatsa re-inflated the bladder and played three notes: low-high-low. It was the lyric they used to call the flyers back to their masters. Twice more he repeated the three-note signal and scanned the skies, hoping to see Tuhj appear.

The tones echoed from a distant cliff. "Where are you, Tuhj?" he asked. If the flyer was in the area, he would hear the call of the *tzetoh*.

His thoughts drifted to his wife, Kwi Dreh. She would now, as per his instructions, be packing food, supplies, and the other two children. Then she would head here to *Zatu Nashtehweh St'ah*, where he— and hopefully, Totahmaa—would rendezvous with her. The remote Great House seemed a safer place to be for her and the children when whatever-was-coming came. And whatever *it* was, he needed her to be there, to be with him in the end.

Thirteen summers they had been together. Many men his age had, by now, had two or more wives, either due to death or the choice to have multiple partners—he had only her. Until he met her, he had never considered marriage or a family; his single-minded devotion to duty would not share his mental or emotional energies. As a Shat'kuhat, he had had many assistants, some young men, some young women, and none ever attracted his attention—though several had desired it. Kwi, who had also been one of his assistants, was similarly devoted to her work. In her tasks, she worked harder and longer than others had, waking long before he did, retiring long after he did. It was her diligence and dedication that ultimately brought her to his attention.

As the two of them were traveling north together one day, he was admiring her great commitment, yet also concerned that she was missing out on a wholeness of life and the opportunity to experience a new level of what things could be. "Women should have families," he'd told her. "One cannot really comprehend the fullness of life until one has brought new life into the world. Watched it grow. Watched it learn."

"And men?" she'd said.

That brought him up short, betrayed by his own line of reasoning. In his young assistant, he saw himself reflected anew. The people thought him a wise and gifted leader, but what did he really know about life? He personally didn't have the intimate knowledge of watching a child grow and learn. Hypocrisy descended in his heart, a wet blanket across his pride. He remembered thinking to himself, *What do I not know that I do not know I do not know?*

It was as if he had always been walking east and west but now had discovered north and south. In that moment, he became *shoshteweh kina shoshteh*—that is, "between strangers." The phrase described someone experiencing profound transformation. The old version of the person was now a stranger to them, yet the person they were becoming was also a stranger. It could be a terrifying experience, a tumultuous freefall between releasing the known of the past and embracing an unknown future. It was a grand gamble with one's life.

He generally counseled such folks to embrace the unknown of the future. "After all," he said, "the glories, comforts, and fears of the past are like a dream; one cannot always distinguish the real from the imagined. The future, too, is a dream, with its own glories, comforts, and fears. So, what is there to lose? All that really exists is the present moment. Past and future alike are merely dream states. Trade one non-reality for another and see what happens."

The impact of his own logic had made him momentarily weak, and he stumbled. Kwi, walking beside him, noticed and reached to help. Of course they had touched inadvertently or collegially before, but this time it was different. When she gasped his shoulder and wrapped her arm around him, it was not the formal touch of an assistant; it was the caress of a soul-mate. With their faces merely inches apart, he stared into her eyes, saw her soul, and suddenly knew her across eternity and infinity.

"Can you see my soul?" he had asked.

She nodded and smiled.

They took the leap together, embracing the stranger of their future self while they embraced the present stranger before them. Each, in their hearts, was *shoshteweh kina shoshteh* no more.

And yet now, thirteen summers later, three children later, with one lost, a mad *quetz'al* on the loose, alone in the desert, and his love packing for the end of the world, he was again "between strangers." His own advice failed: he would not be trading one dream for another, but a dream for a nightmare.

"Keep going," he told himself with a sigh. Signaling again with his flute, he scanned the skies, repeating this routine every few minutes. Old eyes tricked him several times, making a distant vulture or eagle resemble his flyer.

Late afternoon came, and with it a setting sun, making it virtually impossible for him to spot the animal—even if it might be only a stone's throw away. (*Quetz'al* were treacherous devils to see during twilight.) He thought of meeting up with Kwi and having to tell her of his failure. "It would hurt less to be sliced with my own knife from spleen to liver."

He blew the flute again and started re-inflating the bladder, but his breath became shallow, rapid, and labored. Pulse raced. Skin went clammy. Sweaty palms went to his throat as he gasped. Falling to his knees, the world went gray around the edges. As the air around him seemed to vanish, he slumped to the ground on his side, crushing his flute, crushing his hope.

*   *   *

High atop *Ton'ah Tashteh* (Fajada Butte), Tuhj held his captive close to his body as a cold wind blew across the open desert and howled around the natural monument. Sheltered beneath one of his wings, Totahmaa would stay relatively warm.

He had carried the boy out into the desert, wandered randomly for a few hours, and then stealthily returned to the canyon. Flying close to the cliffs that were south of the canyon, his camouflage made him disappear against their rocky faces. Then, swooping low, he raced across the open terrain at breakneck speed while staying within a few yards of the ground. Out of sight on the backside of the butte, he finally alighted on the small, flat expanse at its pinnacle.

Hunched down and camouflaged, no one would see him. In fact, he had watched his master go home (near the butte) and then leave the canyon. Several times, Quaatsa had looked straight at him, never seeing.

Now Quaatsa's flute signaled in the distance, calling to him. He lifted his head and looked toward the sound in the distance, a longing in his eyes.

But Tuhj knew the human word "rogue."

Even though the trainers thought they hid from the *quetz'al* their dealings with "rogues," some of them knew. Tuhj knew. He had seen it with his own eyes once: the treacherous trap, the swiftness and severity of the strike, the butcher and distribution of the body for meat, the attempt to stage the scene as if it had been ravaged by wolves and vultures.

The stakes were high right now.

The boy stirred, still unconscious, probably in pain.

Tuhj felt remorse for hurting his master's own, but the boy's presence provided some security that the crimson and white warriors wouldn't strike—if they somehow found him. The trick would be to get the boy back to his father without getting killed. Once the boy was delivered, he would return to the plentiful hunting grounds far to the north and east. His eyes smiled as he thought about the fact that the Natives on the plains dwelled in teepees, which provided no protection against flying teeth and claws.

A plan formed in his head.

With the plummeting temperatures of a winter night imminent, he acted. Scooping up the boy, he dove off the butte and then ascended to incredible heights. Right away, he spotted his master on a small rise in the open desert, completely alone. Then he dove low, skimming the surface of the earth once again, staying out of the man's sight.

The boy shivered, and Tuhj held him closer.

Suddenly, in the distance, Quaatsa clutched at his own throat and dropped to his knees. Then he simply slumped over sideways, a lifeless bundle. The flute, the virtual life-link between master and *quetz'al*, was destroyed.

Tuhj cried, *Master! Master!* But his singsong words fell on unconscious ears.

He accelerated, but as he got closer and closer to Quaatsa, he began to have trouble breathing. The air grew thin, flying became difficult, and he was losing what little altitude he had. Staying airborne took all his effort and concentration, and he accidentally dropped the boy, who fell about six feet and tumbled across the desert floor in snow and dirt.

Finally, flying became impossible, and the tops of his feet scraped soil. He gasped at the air, coughed and blinked as his vision shrank away, and a rushing sound filled his ears.

He was on a collision course with his master. *In my death, so too yours, my master. So sorry . . .*

*   *   *

Wake, Quaatsa!

And he did: flat on his back, lying in a field, surrounded by strange grass and wildflowers that continuously changed colors from yellows and oranges to purples and blues. The sky above him reflected the bizarre artistry of the ground beneath it: blues and greens, with swirls of yellow dancing here and there—the occasional white puff punctuating the canvas.

He jumped up, looked around, and asked, "Is this heaven?"

You call it that.

You were just here.

Do you not remember?

(Each sentence had a different voice.)

"I remember. Why am I here? Have I taken The Journey?"

No.

"Then . . ."

Go to the Ahteh Shat'kuh *near you.*

He walked over to where three of the In-Between Spirits had taken on mostly human forms—strange, misty green-and-gold figures. They hovered over something in the grass. As he approached, they scooted away to reveal Totahmaa lying in the grass, unconscious. The boy's body was bruised and broken.

"Is he dead?"

No. But it was close.

"Will he live?"

Yes. But they must work more. At that, the *Ahteh* nudged their way in between Quaatsa and the boy, resuming their healing work.

Look there.

Quaatsa turned around. The giant flying rogue lay unconscious on the grass, breath slowing moving in and out of the great chest. He pulled his knife and approached the sleeping creature.

You will not need that.

We cannot let you hurt him.

He has a valuable role to play.

He has much for which to atone.
"Why did he do it?"
The witch killed his friends.
He was angry.
The part of him which he normally so admirably controlled was unleashed.
You know they hate humans?
"I have suspected this. Why?"
You are our favorite.
We gave you more gifts.
One of the finest being dominion over them.
"But they love their masters, do they not?"
You are one to be obeyed, revered.
Protected.
Served.
Feared.
"Why do they obey if they do not love?"
Quaatsa. One with such innocence.
Such ignorance sometimes.
Would that we could take you around the world and show you how seldom obedience from love actually occurs.
Most obedience is coerced.
"Forced service. Why would anyone do that?"
Many reasons.
"So the gods force the *quetz'al* to serve their masters?"
In a manner.
Through the Shat'kuh Mongehweh, *the* Ahteh Shat'kuh *confuse the newborn quetz'al.*
The hatchling supposes that you are its parent.
A mother.
A father.
This is why no other quetz'al *can be near during a hatching.*
And why the master must be there at the exact moment of the hatching.
Quaatsa pondered this.
Without this confusion, the young hatchling would eat you.
The quetz'al *would serve you as you serve the antelope of the fields.*
The man wrinkled his eyebrows, confused.

Serve you . . .

. . . to each other.

In fact, they would kill you all just as you would kill a fly.

Swiftly.

Effortlessly.

Thoughtlessly.

They find you quite tasty.

"I have had the displeasure of noticing that on occasion. Why do this? Why have them serve us?"

It is the end of their time. Your quetz'al *are all that remain in the whole of the world.*

Quaatsa turned up his palms and asked the clouds, "They do not cover the whole of the Earth? Am I so small that I know so little of the world?"

They numbered in the thousands of thousands, once upon a time.

Every corner of the earth.

Nowhere else do such magnificent creatures exist now.

An evil came upon Mother Earth from beyond, and the world changed. A great dark and cold set in.

Many died.

The world in which the quetz'al *flourished and dominated was no more.*

Their prey—gone.

Slowly, ever so slowly, their numbers dwindled, until they only existed in small pockets where food was sufficient.

In most places, they devoured everything in sight, ultimately starving themselves and everything and everyone else.

In other pockets, humans felt threatened and destroyed them.

"And we are the last pocket?"

Correct.

"Why?"

The People were different.

You have kept them in check and loved them.

In so doing, you have extended their life well beyond their allotted time.

"But they do not understand that?"

And neither did you until this moment.

He nodded. "Of course. What will become of them?"

Many will die tonight.

You, yourself, have commanded it.

He turned pale, grabbing his stomach. "I gave that task to Gohm."

The rest will travel northeast and northwest, searching for good hunting.

A strange sound caught his ears, and he turned his head different ways to try to identify the source but couldn't find it.

The Ahteh Shat'kuh tell us that your boy is healed.

Quaatsa quickly went to his son and knelt down. Still unconscious, the boy now appeared to be resting peacefully—bruises gone, bones in all the right places.

"Thank you. Thank you so much." He wept openly.

Stay your gratitude.

He, like your quetz'al, *has an important role to play in the future.*

We must tell you of your mission.

He listened intently while the gods spoke of things that made no sense.

In time, these events will be clear. For now, just remember our words.

"This will take a long time."

Yes.

"I am an old man. What you say might take many lifetimes."

Yes.

"Then how . . ."

Coyote Spirit, with its wisdom and knowledge, will pass to you when Gohm takes The Journey tonight.

When Sheweh also takes The Journey tonight, we will give Eagle Spirit to your son.

"But why must Gohm and Sheweh die?" He took a defiant posture. "They have done nothing."

The question went unanswered.

Additionally, you, your son, and your quetz'al *will be as we:* nohktesheh z'teh nohktesheh. ("Change brings no change.")

A six-fingered hand materialized out of the air in front of Quaatsa. It had a golden thumb on either side of four red fingers. The hand pressed its palm flat against his chest and began to vibrate and hum softly, and then suddenly a loud, electric crackle came from it. A blue-and-white dancing aura spread from the center of Quaatsa's chest and moved out to cover his entire body.

He screamed.

* * *

He dreamed of a world shaken apart, some violent force rocking everything he knew and loved out of balance. He was between strangers, and the world was collapsing around him. Bricks fell. Cliffs crumbled. People died. *Quetz'al* terrorized The People, devouring them and killing for fun.

Then Quaatsa awoke sometime after midnight.

Kwi was shaking him. "Are you okay?" she asked.

He scanned the little room at *Zatu Nashtehweh St'ah*. Confusion smeared dream and reality as he tried to distinguish which was which.

"You were having a nightmare."

"I was?"

"Yes. It was scaring the children."

"Oh. Sorry."

At the other end of the tiny apartment, his two youngest, Chiyoo and Seech, huddled in a corner. Chiyoo, eleven summers, held her baby brother, who was not yet two summers. They looked disheveled and distressed but relieved that Daddy wasn't going mad.

"You kept going on and on about finding the *Shat'kuh Mongehweh*, searching time and space."

"Oh. Was I?"

Sitting upright quickly, panic and distress gripped his face. "Totahmaa?" he asked her, fear in his eyes.

Kwi pointed to a pallet behind him.

He spun around, relieved to see his oldest sleeping soundly and deeply. Bending over the boy to inspect him more closely, he spied a charcoal smudge on Totahmaa's chest just barely peeking out from under the fur blanket. Pulling back the cover revealed a black burn mark in the shape of the six-fingered left/right hand of the gods. Tearing open his tunic, the same mark appeared on Quaatsa's own chest.

"Kwi, my love."

"Yes."

"We have more to talk about."

□ ▪ □ ▪ □ ▪ □ ▪ □ ▪ □

The Dream

JUNE 21, 1938, OUTSIDE
NATASHA YELLOWTAIL'S
CABIN, CHACO CANYON

Vince Nesci, Kenneth McKinney, and Natasha Yellowtail stood in front of her cabin scanning the darkness for signs of Frankie.

"How far you think he get without light?" Vince asked melodically.

"I don't know, but he goddamn went somewhere, Vince. Sorry, ma'am." Kenneth said.

"I think we wait *fino a domani*—until tomorrow, Kenneth."

"No!" said Natasha.

Kenneth swung his flashlight back and forth across the horizon again for the umpteenth time, its faint yellow beam sucked dry as it tried to penetrate the darkness outside the Yellowtail cabin. He rubbed his eyes and strained to peer into the night.

"What's that?" he said suddenly.

"Where?" Natasha asked, standing anxiously beside him, her own flashlight desperately waving into emptiness.

"There," Kenneth said, pointing. "I saw something moving." He stretched his arm forward with his flashlight pointing toward the unknown thing in the darkness, willing whatever-it-was to be illuminated. "Well, I thought . . . Must be tired. I'm starting to see phantoms."

Natasha and Vince swung their lights around in the direction Kenneth indicated. By chance, all three flashlight beams converged on the same spot, and two tiny, yellow-green orbs glowed to life in the night.

"*Gatto?*" Vince asked. "No. Coyote." Disgust and annoyance dripped through his Italian accent.

The two men cursed under their breath in frustration; they had been fruitlessly wandering around the homestead for hours with no sign of the missing boy. Even a check of the nearby ruins where he often sought refuge proved to be in vain.

"Is like—poof—he vanish into thin air," said Vince.

"This is so unlike him," Kenneth sighed.

"Coyote!" Natasha called into the darkness. "Coyote, have you taken my boy?"

In the darkness, the eerily luminous eyes tilted sideways, an expression of curiosity shared with its domesticated cousins.

"Natasha," started Kenneth. "That's just superstition."

"Is it? Just superstition? That is what you whites always say, thinking we are dumb and ignorant. Maybe you are just dumb and ignorant of matters you do not understand." A pointing finger and large arm motions punctuated her lecture. "Where is he? Where is my Big Man? How do you know that this is a coyote and not *Coyote?*" (She referred to a trickster spirit disguised in the form of an animal.)

"You whites?" Kenneth mumbled, a little hot. He stooped down and picked up a golf-ball-sized stone. Standing, he said, "Well, here," and pulled his arm back to throw.

"No!" Natasha pleaded, but it was too late: Kenneth pitched the stone hard and fast at the four-legged night-visitor.

The glowing eyes jerked sideways as the rock struck, but instead of yelping and scurrying away in fear, it snarled and shuffled laterally to them—more reminiscent of a regroup than a retreat. Their meager flashlight beams failed to follow the coyote.

"No wolves here, *si?*"

"I don't think so," Kenneth answered.

"What now?" Natasha asked. "What now about my Big Man? If that was Trickster," she hit Kenneth hard in the shoulder, "then you have doomed him." She hit him again, breaking down into an emotional wreck.

The large man turned toward her, held her shoulders firm, and said, "We'll have to look again at first light. You get some rest, and Vince and I will wait up in case we hear anything."

"*Buona idea*. You rest. We watch and wait, *si*," the Italian added.

She collapsed into Kenneth's chest, sobbing. He embraced her weary body, holding her close, almost intimately. When her knees buckled, he gently caught her up and carried her inside the cabin.

* * *

Ruth stood back on two feet, wiped dirt from her hands, and rubbed her hip, which still stung from the impact of the small stone. "Some consideration will have to go into your punishment, Mr. Kenneth Mac-Kin-eh-ee," she mused aloud.

From behind a patch of scrub, she retrieved her stash of clothes and supplies and immediately donned her panties. The bra was left there. She said, "Why hide one's most potent weapons? Nipples can turn the heads of infants and the heads of state." No obvious stains or smudges from her fight with Ixtab stood out when she inspected the skirt, so she whipped it in the air to smooth out some wrinkles and then wriggled into it, taking care with the tender bruise on her hip. The blouse was similarly inspected, smoothed, slipped on, buttoned.

She smoothed her hair and then shook her head, repeating this sequence twice more in order to get exactly the right version of disheveled attractiveness. A pea-sized object flew out of her hair and struck the ground with a snap the second time she shook. She knelt down to inspect. A beetle was rocking itself back onto its feet. "Probably lucky it was not a tick," she said.

From her large leather pouch on the ground, she pulled a long, fine silk scarf and wrapped it around her waist. Then she retrieved a tiny, woven basket with a lid and scanned the ground. It took a few minutes, but she found a night tarantula pretty easily. The creature protested furiously, waving its legs and arching its back, but nonetheless was unable to reach the offending fingers with its fangs. She dropped it in the little container and closed the lid. The basket went back into the pouch, and the pouch was slung across her back.

"Showtime," she said, striding toward the Yellowtails' tiny cabin with a spring in her step. She quietly giggled like a little girl.

*   *   *

Licking the long edge of the cigarette paper, Kenneth watched his sleeping companion while he finished rolling his smoke. Match struck, a long breath carried calm and stimulation deep inside his lungs. He held the smoke, tilted his head back, and exhaled up into the night sky, sighing a little.

Vince was wrapped in an old wool *serape*, lying across the flat bed of McKinney's Ford truck, snores fighting their way out of his face. His sleep sounds were erratic, without rhythm, and Kenneth gave him an annoyed look before setting off on a walk around the cabin. Casting his flashlight's beam about, it proved barely visible under the bright moon and stars, so he switched it off and jammed it down inside a jacket pocket with a huff. "No wonder I can't sell any of the damn things," he said, taking another draw off his cigarette.

The casual walk around the Yellowtails' place brought him back around to the truck just as his cigarette was expiring. He deftly held the nub, extracted the last of its life, and then flicked it out into the darkness. The paper wad hit the ground, making a sound louder than it should have.

It had suddenly become unnaturally quiet. The rhythms of human travel—stealthy human travel—whispered out from the nervous darkness.

Kenneth froze, pulled the flashlight from his pocket, and held it far in front of him with his left arm extended in the direction of the footsteps. His right hand slid down to retrieve the Colt belted around his waist.

"Frankie?" he whisper-called. "Frankie, is that you?" Then to his sleeping companion: "Hey! Mr. Italiano. Get your ass up. Somebody's out there."

Vince snapped alert, throwing back the *serape* and simultaneously brandishing his own gun, an Italian Walther PPK. (He and McKinney went back and forth about the manliness of Vince's gun. Kenneth insisted that it was for sissies, while Nesci usually countered that it was not the size of the gun that counted, but the skill of the shooter—at which point the conversation generally devolved.)

"What? What? Is Frankie, *si*?"

"Frankie?" Kenny called again.

"Frankie?" Vince added.

The footsteps were closer now, attempts at stealth gone. Despite their flashlights, neither could spot the intruder.

"Who's there?" Vince called.

Kenneth pulled the hammer on his revolver and threatened, "We shoot in five seconds. Who are you?"

Suddenly the screen door slammed shut on the cabin, and Natasha was on Kenneth, tugging on his gun arm.

"No," she demanded. "He might be hurt or confused."

A dread-induced cold sweat broke across Kenneth's forehead. "I hadn't thought of that. Damn." He quickly lowered his weapon, a slight tremor in his hand suddenly.

"Frankie? Is that you, my Big Man? Come on in here. I need a hug." Natasha waited a few desperate seconds, but no reply came. "Frankie, I really need a big hug."

From the darkness came a voice: "Ah-low?" Feminine. Apprehensive.

Kenneth raised his gun, hammer pulled again. "Hello? Who's there? Who's there, dammit."

"Ah-low. Mr. Mac-Kin-eh-ee?"

"Ruth?"

"Yes, sir. It's me. Ruth." Suddenly, she was totally visible, as if she had just stepped out from behind a shadow.

She looked pale and worried, hair disheveled, clothes mussed, as if she had run a great distance or endured some fight to reach them. "I have dream. Frankie lost. Is boy here? Is all right?" Her large, bright green eyes projected sympathy yet somehow remained adorable and enchanting with just a hint of sexual energy.

Natasha broke down, sobbing and wailing, and ran back into her cabin. Kenneth watched her go, shoulders drooping, head dropping. He sighed.

Vince turned to Ruth and asked, "How you know something wrong?" Suspicion colored his tone.

"I have dream," she replied, sounding irritated, subtly suggesting that he listen more carefully. Then she explained: "I have the psychic. I see things—sometimes they good, sometimes bad." She gazed into the distance and said, "Sometimes things I should see. Sometimes things

I not should see." A tear peeled away and rolled down her left cheek, a tiny droplet escaping an apparent lake of pain.

"Tell us about your dream, Ruth," Kenneth said.

Vince looked at him askance, a combination of annoyance and incredulity on his face. Kenneth shot back an "it-can't-hurt" look.

"I tell. I tell," she said. Then she pointed to the cabin. "I need sit. Tea? I very thirsty."

"Okay," Kenneth said. As the three walked up to the porch, he called to Natasha, "Natasha? May we come in?"

There was only silence, and Kenneth motioned for the other two to wait while he stepped inside alone. "Natasha?" Sobs were coming from the bedroom in the cabin, and he cautiously moved that way. "Natasha?"

She sat up on the bed, face swollen and red with emotion, jet-black hair matted to her face by tears. "What?"

"Ruth said she had a dream about Frankie."

"Yes, I heard."

"I want her to tell us about it." He looked down, hesitating a moment, and then blurting out, "She says she's psychic. Maybe she can help."

For several seconds, Natasha sat there without moving, unresponsive. Then, like a cat springing, she leaped from the bed, pushed past Kenneth, and dashed outside.

Kenneth recovered his balance and chased her out onto the porch where she was pleading with Ruth. "What do you know? Tell me what you know. I must find him. He is in terrible danger—I can feel it."

"I tell. You may be right. Maybe danger. I tell," Ruth said, stretching her hand out to catch hold of Natasha. "However I can, I help. I help, dear."

"Let's go inside," suggested Vince, motioning toward the cabin. "I'll make the tea."

*   *   *

Ruth scanned the place as they moved into the little cabin. When she say the religious and spiritual adorning the kitchen, she smiled.

Natasha quickly sat at the small table, despondent and emotionally wrecked. Kenneth sat next to her, exhibiting a more-than-just-neighborly interest in her welfare.

"You two are . . ." Ruth cast her mind for the right words, "the sweethearts?"

The two quickly set a larger space between them. Natasha turned away with a slight blush, and Kenneth said, "Only friends."

Winking at Kenneth, Ruth said conspiratorially, "Well, maybe someday not 'only friends.'"

The Italian had gone to the stove with a kettle full of water and was struggling to figure out how the thing worked. Finally, he selected a couple of tiny hunks of split log from the bucket beside the stove and shoved them in the fuel box, fanning and blowing on them, trying to coax enough life from the previous coals to get a new fire going. Ruth studied him carefully.

"Tell us about your dream, Ruth," said Kenneth.

"Please," Natasha begged, stretching her arms across the small table, palms up, inviting her to join them. Ruth sat down across from the boy's mother and briefly squeezed the offered hands.

"Yes. I tell." She loathed English. It was so difficult. "So many unnatural and dirty sounds," she would say. Speaking the white man's tongue was an exercise in being judged: people always had to pause to consider if the speaker might be stupid or incompetent. She secretly wondered if Caucasians had intentionally made their language difficult just so that they could intimidate other races.

"Dream vague," Ruth began. "Almost more . . . how you say . . . emotion than vision. Not much to see at all. I get fog and the sound of Frankie's voice calling for help."

Natasha's façade of strength cracked as fresh, silent tears ran down her cheeks. Ruth paused to look closely into Natasha's face.

"I am fine," Natasha lied. "Please continue."

Ruth took one of Natasha's hands in both hers and gripped it firmly. "I also feel earlier tonight he in great distress. Some great fight over him—a struggle to get him. I hear him yell, 'Mr. Blackwood!'" The best lies have a kernel of truth in them.

Natasha sniffed back tears, and Kenneth reached for her free hand and squeezed it. The gesture was allowed to linger.

"Blackwood?" Natasha asked.

"Hey, Vince," Kenneth said over his shoulder. "Isn't that the guy with the fancy car?"

"*Si*, that's him. He here to observe dances tomorrow—I mean, today." It was well into the morning hours now.

"Oh, the yellow car?" Natasha asked.

"*Si*." Nesci turned back to fanning the fragile flames within the fuel box, looking satisfied with his progress.

Natasha pulled both hands free and said, "Frankie was telling me all about him tonight at dinner. The boys were quite taken with him. He drove them around the canyon."

"You should see his car," Nesci said. "Is *molto beuno*. And *Italiano!*" His face beamed with pride and admiration.

"Why would someone with such a car have it out here in the damn desert? Sorry, ladies."

"Good question, Kenneth," Vince said.

"Do you think that this Mr. Blackwood could have taken Frankie?" asked Natasha.

The Italian scratched his head. "I no think so. He seem decent-enough fellow when I talk to him."

"But the worm eats the inside of the apple," Ruth offered, sounding generically wise enough to pass for profound insight.

They all nodded in thoughtful agreement. "True, true," someone said.

Kenneth leaned forward, eager. "Did you dream anything else?"

"No. I sorry," she said. Sitting peacefully, she watched them all carefully—and waited.

Kenneth stood up from the table first and started pacing the little room. Natasha folded her arms on the table and put her head down, silently sobbing—most emotion drained, replaced by hollow pain.

"Vince, did he tell you where he was staying?"

"No. He want to stay in camp, but we no have empty bunk." He poked at the fire and closed the door to the fuel box. "I think he sleep in car. I know I would. Oh, Ettore," he called out to the famous Italian auto designer, "your Bugattis are a little heaven on earth."

Kenneth scooted his chair back from the table and threw his arms in the air. "How will we find Blackwood to talk to him?" Exasperation and the late hour were taking their toll.

"Kenneth, I maybe have idea. Let me ask you outside." Vince motioned to the front porch. "I need cigarette."

"Okay. Me too."

Ruth went to check on the hot water for tea, which also happened to be closer to the front door where she could hear the men. They lit up, discussing the possibility of Blackwood as a culprit. There was some dispute over whether or not they could trust her. "Phase two," she said to herself.

Sitting again at the table, she gently stroked the back of Natasha's head and whispered cryptically, "There may be way to learn more. See more."

The boy's mother looked up, eyes red and messy. "How? Anything."

"You have some shirt or pants that belong to boy?"

"Of course."

"Get. And I try something."

"What?"

"Is hard explain. Get. I try," Ruth urged. "Is longshot. Risky. But I try for you." She touched Natasha's arm gently. "For boy."

"Okay." The desperate mother disappeared into the bedroom.

"He good boy," Ruth called to Natasha. "Such a good boy."

In a moment, Natasha reappeared, flannel shirt bundled up between her hands. She sniffed it and was visibly filled with the presence of her son the way only a mother can be. "Here."

Ruth carefully spread the shirt across the tabletop, smoothing it gently. Then she reached down into her bag and pulled out the tiny basket with its eight-legged passenger. She pulled the lid off of the basket and slammed it upside-down in the middle of the shirt, startling Natasha and trapping the tarantula beneath it.

"You trust me, Natasha?"

"Yes." She bore the same warmly crooked smile as Frankie.

"Finger here. Hold down."

Natasha did as instructed, keeping her index finger pressed down on top of the basket.

Reaching back into the bag, Ruth pulled out an ancient leather pouch with equally ancient stains all over it. From the pouch, she lightly sprinkled something like finely ground cayenne pepper all over the shirt. She traded that pouch for another and sprinkled something that appeared to be a mixture of ground rosemary and pine needles; it had a smell that was both fresh and pungent. Ruth returned the second pouch and brought out one final item.

"What's that?" Natasha asked, fear creeping into her voice.

"This?" She motioned to the black obsidian knife. "It old friend. You never see such?"

"No."

"It much power. You want touch it?"

"No."

Smiling, Ruth gently covered Natasha's hand that secured the little basket. "Knife only ceremonial. See?" She held it for Natasha's examination: razor-sharp divots in the jet-black, glassy stone caught the candlelight, and the leather-wrapped hilt looked soft and conditioned from centuries of human contact. "It only old ceremonial knife. But big magic!" She beamed and tried to make a reassuring smile. "Do good with magic. You still trust?"

"Yes," she answered, glancing down, embarrassed.

"Is good." She smiled again, radiating calm and assurance. "Now, when I say so, lift small basket straight into air. Be very fast." She imitated the motion that she wanted, then she looked intently into Natasha's eyes. "You understand?" (Given even a moment's opportunity, the angry tarantula would be coming after one of them.) "You must lift quickly."

"I will," Natasha replied, body language and face indicating that she would be a trustworthy team player. She sat up a little straighter and nodded, prepared for action.

Ruth rolled up the sleeves of her blouse and then grabbed the obsidian dagger with a firm right hand in an ice-pick grip. Shaking her head back and forth, she chanted, *"Ishtoo ishtoo. Kotaw'wiki-eh."* At first quietly, but then louder and louder. The melody of the chant cycled through in a cadence that mismatched the syllables, creating the impression of two different songs or chants at once. The violence of her head shaking increased with the tempo and intensity of the chanting. As it went on, her eyes began to roll back up into her head.

Just as her volume reached nearly a raw scream, the two men burst back into the cabin. At that moment, Rooshth stopped and shouted, "Now!"

Natasha obediently jerked the small basket up into the air.

Blinded by the sudden light exposure, the tarantula hunched down, confused as to which way to run, but mad-as-hell and ready to lash out at anything. Ruth quickly struck the confused creature with the open palm of her left hand, making a crunching-splatting sound as bits of goo and blood sprayed across Frankie's shirt. Its hairy legs splayed out underneath her palm. A Jackson Pollack of tarantula guts spread from the flannel to Natasha's blouse.

Natasha reeled at the sight, shaking her hands in the air and alternately looking from the mess on Frankie's shirt to the mess on her own blouse. Rapid and shallow in-breaths suggested the onset of a major panic attack. The men ran to her.

"Ishtoo Ishtoo! Kotaw'wiki-Ehhhhh!" Rooshth screamed, and then she held her breath, quickly stood up—keeping her left hand on the smashed arachnid—and held the knife high overhead. With a quick and violent motion, she drove the dagger through the back of her own left hand, through the remains of the tarantula, and deep into the wooden table.

Natasha screamed.

▼△▼△▼△▼△▼△▼△▼△▼△▼△▼

Far Sight

JUNE 21, 1938, INSIDE NATASHA YELLOWTAIL'S CABIN, CHACO CANYON

Kenneth McKinney heard Ruth chanting louder and louder, getting more and more wild with her incantations. He and Vince rushed in the door from the porch as the woman drove the obsidian blade through the back of her hand, nearly to the handle of the dagger. Blood poured freely from the wound, pulsing out with each heartbeat, painting the black glass knife and flowing across the back of her hand and down her fingers. Her life essence mingled with the tarantula's and soaked into Frankie's flannel that was stretched across the tabletop. A crimson splotch spread from her hands to cover the entire shirt.

Ruth breathed in shallow puffs, facing down unimaginable pain. Face sallow and sweat covering her forehead, she reached into her bag to withdraw a black candle, which she then rolled around in the gruesome liquid that covered the shirt. "Match," she said, barely a whisper.

Suddenly seeming calm and coherent, Natasha jumped from her chair to retrieve some kitchen matches.

"Natasha?" Kenneth asked, but she just ignored him. "Vince . . ." he whispered, but even the practical-minded, even-keeled mason was entranced by the drama.

Natasha lit the candle for Ruth, who then held it between two fingers of her left hand—even as it was pinned to the table with the knife.

"Make dark," Ruth breathed, nodding to the two hurricane lamps illuminating the small cabin. Vince turned one out, and Kenneth extinguished the other.

The small candle produced an unusual flame: almost three inches long and a rosy-pink color. In its warm light, Ruth's left arm appeared suspended in air, rather than lying flat on a tabletop. It was as if someone had cut a hole into the top of the table in the shape of the bloody flannel shirt.

Hunched around the table, they all peered down into another world—or maybe somewhere else in this world, as if they were high in the air, looking down through a window in the floor of an airplane. Vague shapes resembling the tops of clouds could be seen. The "airplane view" descended into the clouds, and the sounds of rain and wind came through the tabletop portal. A thick fog obscured their visibility until suddenly a small break in the mist revealed a human figure curled up on a large, flat expanse of rock. It was raining gently, and the figure lay in several inches of water, shivering and saying, "Bambino! Over here!"

Natasha jumped up, screaming, "Frankie! Frankie! I'm here. It's Mother. Where are you, Big Man?" The boy couldn't hear her and went on with his strange dream, legs pumping and arms flailing about. "Frankie . . ." She dissolved, weeping, and Kenneth put an arm around her.

Down "below," Frankie sat up abruptly, choking on water, and the boy's mother reached for her son, putting a hand through the portal.

"No," Ruth whispered. "Not safe."

"Please, Natasha . . ." Kenneth said, gently tugging her arm, which was cold and wet when she pulled it out.

Natasha's watery eyes trained on Kenneth. "We must help him."

"Ruth," Kenneth said. Looking pale and weak, she acknowledged him. "Ruth, where is the boy?"

"In the In-Between."

"What does that mean?" he asked.

"There is this world," she started, her voice thin while her head woozily motioned around the cabin. "There is heaven, where the gods live." She looked up toward but beyond the ceiling. "Your boy is In-Between. Not heaven. Not here."

"Is that hell?" Natasha asked. "Is my Frankie in hell?" The intensity of her voice raised to near panic.

"No," Vince said soothingly. "She no say that."

"That's right. Look," Kenneth said, pointing to the boy. "He's all right. Just alone and afraid."

"So afraid." Natasha cupped one hand to her chest and extended the other toward her son.

The boy was holding something in his hands and then pressed it into his cheek. "What is that?" Vince asked.

"A baseball," Kenneth said, confused. He looked to Ruth for an explanation, but she gave no sign of understanding. Instead, the expression on her face was a mixture of aggravation and distress.

"How do we get him back?" asked Natasha. "Can we go get him?"

"No," Ruth said quietly.

"Then how?"

"We find who put him there."

"So, the boy was taken?" Vince asked.

"Yes. Somebody took boy, Miss Nah-tah-sha."

Kenneth pointed down toward the portal. "It's changing."

The "airplane view" rose quickly away from the boy, darkened, and then descended on a view of the canyon, illuminated by the silvery moonlight. A gravel road with a lone car traveling on it could be seen "below." After "descending" a little farther, the unmistakable shape of Mr. Blackwood's T57 Bugatti was obvious, heading north, but without headlights on. Suddenly, the car turned on its lights and slid to a stop. Two figures walking in the middle of the road were illuminated by the yellow beams. The "view" descended more, and they could identify the two walkers.

"Turq," Natasha said quietly.

"And Zed," Vince added.

"Are they wearing paint?" Natasha asked.

Now the "view" clearly showed the painted faces of Turq and Zed. The boy was bearing weapons and looking ferocious. The father's strange headdress and cape were equally unnerving.

"Is that flute?" asked Vince.

Kenneth answered, "I think it is."

"He is *Kokopelli*," Natasha said.

Vince tilted his head sideways. "Who?"

"The wild-haired flute player of legend," Kenneth explained. "Another damn superstition. I've seen petroglyphs of him, and there are stories."

"Is he a god?" Vince asked.

Natasha glared at Kenneth and then said. "No. Not god. Not angel. He just is . . . a sort of traveler."

From Vince: "What this mean?"

Natasha continued, "Sometimes he brings good luck and can be helpful. Many people see his image as a symbol of good luck. But sometimes he brings destruction."

"What's the difference?" Kenneth asked.

Natasha turned her palms up and shrugged. "Who knows?"

"But why is Zed dressed that way?" Vince asked.

Kenneth leaned over the table more for a closer look. "Good question. Maybe something for the solstice?"

In the portal, Blackwood started to talk with Turq, but suddenly, the sound of thunder exploded through their viewing portal with enough force to rattle the dishes and windows of the cabin. A cloud of dust and debris erupted in front of the yellow roadster, blinding Blackwood and forcing the two Natives to retreat from the car. In the midst of the cloud appeared a large winged animal reminiscent of a medieval dragon with a long neck. The creature reared its head back and stared menacingly at Blackwood and the T57.

In the cabin, they gasped almost in unison, and Natasha whispered, "*El Diablo.*"

Vince jumped back from the table, crossing himself and exclaiming, "*Sí. Sí.* It the Devil."

"Yes," Ruth said calmly. "Two Natives and Blackwood have taken boy. They serve the Devil."

Kenneth caught her studying their faces closely.

"Look," said Natasha. Within the portal, the winged creature yelled and spat toward Blackwood. Turq ran to stroke its tail while Zed ran and stood in front of the creature, waving his hands and talking to it.

"See," said Ruth, "he commune with Devil."

Vince crossed himself again.

Turq ran to his father, and the two embraced, fear and despair clearly marking the boy.

Ruth said, "The boy there—he so innocent and afraid for his friend."

Zed pulled two pieces of stone from a hidden pouch and showed them to Blackwood.

Ruth gasped. "See stones?" She pointed excitedly with her free hand. "They magic. Big magic used to kidnap boy to In-Between."

Natasha asked the obvious question: "If we had the stones, could we get Frankie back?"

Ruth grimaced, deep in thought and pain. Finally, she said, "Yes, I think possible. I could do this."

"Well then," Kenneth said, "we'll just have to get those stones."

Vince nodded his head. "*Si*. Get stones. Get boy."

Ruth looked up at them and with a deadly serious tone said, "They will come here. We will be ready."

Natasha looked at Kenneth, hope and uncertainty blending in her eyes.

*   *   *

With cautious optimism, Quaatsa Mukaama and his son headed north along the road, in the middle of the night, about a mile and a half from the Yellowtails' cabin. Tuhj flew above them, somewhere in the night, undoubtedly thrilled.

As they walked, he reflected on his life. He had been a leader of many hands over seven centuries ago. Now he had taken the name Z'teh-nohktesheh Moonhawk, essentially meaning "no change," of the Moonhawk clan. Most people, however, knew him by the nickname that Vince Nesci had given him: Zed.

The glory days of The People were gone. They had built the great structures in the canyon—great religious and spiritual *kivas* and the fantastic apartment dwellings that at one time housed more than thirty thousand people. Families thrived. There was commerce and prosperity. The gods smiled, and they all enjoyed full bellies and quiet nights. What's more, the gods had even given The People the *Shat'kuh Mongehweh*, a tablet of power that taught them how to commune directly with the gods, perform powerful magic, and control the great flying creatures, the *quetz'al*. The flyers were their hunters, their army, and their identity.

Until the day the witch came to town.

She sensed the Chacoan's powerful magic and wanted it for her own. Her very arrival sent some of the *quetz'al* into rebellion—including his own personal flyer, the giant alpha male, Tuhj. Somehow she learned of their sacred tablet and tried to steal it for her own. Her efforts were ultimately in vain, and the tablet was broken into three pieces, hidden in time and space, guarded by a vengeful goddess.

In the ensuing chaos of the witch's arrival, Tuhj committed unprecedented atrocities. The gods punished him severely, forcing him to be their hand of justice, dealing death to *quetz'al* who had formerly trusted him with their life. Tuhj had spent the last few centuries hunting down and killing all of the other rebellious, vicious creatures. His mission of assassination had taken him all over North America. The last rebel *quetz'al* had been terrorizing people in southern Arizona a few decades ago, eating cattle and horses and generally being a nuisance; Tuhj dispatched the vermin with ease.

Now Tuhj was alone. No mission. No real life. Just waiting to take The Journey.

With nothing to do, Tuhj had become bored, tending to make a nuisance of himself—the last thirty years had tried Zed's patience. The creature could sense that their collective mission to restore the sacred tablet was nearing its end, and he grew impatient.

The gods foresaw that the witch would become more powerful and seek again to have the tablet for herself. To stop Rooshth, the gods cursed Zed and his son with immortality, appointing them to collect the tablet pieces before she could. They had acquired the first piece of tablet from a *Conquistador* several centuries ago, saving him from the wrath of the witch and leaving her hurt and injured, with a white-hot vengeance. The second piece they had only acquired a couple of decades ago from a bad man who sought to sell it, ending his life of pillaging the honor and memory of The People. Now, both he and his son had sensed that Frankie Yellowtail had just discovered the third and final piece. How the dimwitted, weak boy had outwitted or overpowered the guardian, Ixtab, was anybody's guess, but somehow he had done it.

Zed's plan now was simple: go to Frankie's cabin, get the tablet piece, unite it with the other two pieces, and then go on to be with their family and ancestors in the next life.

He sighed—a deep, emotion-expelling breath. In their ancient tongue, he said, "Immortality is a burden, son."

Turq looked up, puzzled.

"One sees too much, buries too many, endures too much loneliness."

The boy nodded.

"May the gods grant this burden be ending."

"Yes, Father."

The sounds of a distant automobile drifted through the night, and Zed grimaced. "Automobiles will never catch on. Who could stand to just sit in a box for so long?"

Turq asked, "Have you never ridden in a car?"

"No. If I should need to go fast, I will take a horse."

"Or Tuhj."

"Ooh," he replied, rolling his eyes. "That would be suicidal."

"I have done it before, and I know you have too." His son playfully pointed an accusing finger.

"Only reluctantly." He looked up, scanning the skies, and then bent down to quietly say, "That flyer is reckless. He once did a power dive to show off while I straddled his neck. I could have killed him."

Turq laughed. "He has never done that to me."

"He still likes you."

Turq laughed again.

The People had built beautiful roads for people to *walk*—the only form of human transport at that time. When the sacred dogs came along, it seemed natural and obvious for a horse and rider to go around, yielding to those on foot. Zed and Turq still had not gotten used to the idea that cars didn't simply go around, so hearing—but not seeing—a car behind them didn't cause alarm. When they were suddenly illuminated by bright, yellow light, they turned around to see an automobile bearing down on them and sliding to a stop. The old Native raised his hand to his face to shield his eyes from the blinding light and the flying debris. Once the vehicle stopped, Turq jumped in front of him, assuming a defensive position with his spear.

The driver called to Turq from the car, identifying himself as Mr. Blackwood. Turq seemed to know him.

Just a moment later, both Natives heard a very faint rustling sound overhead, like a flag blowing in the wind. They looked up warily and stepped away from the car.

Tuhj landed dramatically between the Ancient Ones and the auto, popping his wings, deafening them all with his thunderous landing, and blinding them with dust and debris.

The flyer reared back, breathing hard and coughing up a massive wad of First Spit from deep within his throat. After a moment, he hurled it at Blackwood's vehicle, nailing the hood and covering it with something that was a cross between phlegm and jelly. The car bounced up and down from the force of the impact. Then Tuhj reared back to send the ignition spit—Second Spit, which was secreted by a different set of glands near the front of his mouth.

"No, Tuhj. No!" Zed yelled. At the same time, Turq jumped forward to grab Tuhj's tail. The *quetz'al* spat anyway, but the startle skewed his aim, sending the Second Spit wide to the right of the car.

Both Natives were relieved to see that Blackwood and his car were not turning into a smoldering pile of ash.

Zed ran around to place himself between Blackwood and Tuhj, who was preparing another load of Second Spit. He put his arms up, waving in the air to get Tuhj's attention. "Hey, hey! Tuhj, no!"

Tuhj protested, explaining in his singsong way the inherent dangers of the automobile and how it was his duty to destroy them all.

"No. That is not your duty," said Zed flatly.

The creature looked away for a moment and then turned back, explaining that the car was about to maliciously crush them and how it was his duty to destroy any threat to his master.

"Well, that is true, but the danger had passed by the time you got down here."

Tuhj snorted and turned away, huffing.

"Yeah, you were late," Turq said pointedly. Then he went around to the driver's side door to Blackwood and switched to English: "Are you all right?"

"Yes, it would seem that I'm unscathed." Glancing down at the slime covering the hood of his car, he said, "The same cannot be said of my car." He sniffed the air, crinkling his nose at the acrid odor of the mucus. "What is that?"

"The spit, the *quetz'al*, or the man?" Turq asked. "Well, that," he said, pointing to the mucus, "is First Spit. It comes from one of these." He pointed to Tuhj. "It's called a *quetz'al*, and he is the only one of his kind left in all the world. His name is Tuhj. And that is my father, Quaatsa Mukaama, known as Zed."

"Hello," Quaatsa said to the driver.

"Hello. C. J. Blackwood. A pleasure, sir," he said, giving the older Native a slight bow. To Turq, he asked, "Why is it called First Spit?"

"Because it comes before Second Spit." Turq smiled broadly.

"*Second* Spit?"

"Yes, it comes after—"

"Son! Mr. Blackwood, this is quite awkward. The First Spit will not hurt your automobile. It will wash away in the rain. If the Second Spit had struck, then, sadly, you and your car would have been consumed by fire in just a few moments."

"Oh." Blackwood kept switching his gaze from the mucus to the creature. "So, your large pet here—I'm assuming that it's yours—is a dragon?"

"What do you mean?" asked Zed.

"A dragon. Flies through the air, breathes fire, fights knights in shining armor, terrorizes small villages."

In their native tongue, Zed asked his son, "Do you have any idea what this man is speaking about?"

"No. I must ask Frankie if he knows what a dragon is." Returning to English, Turq then said to Blackwood, "We do not know what a dragon is."

"Creatures from legends. They lived in China and Europe a long time ago. Basically, this." He gestured toward Tuhj with both hands.

"Tuhj has traveled very far," Zed said, "but he has not been beyond this continent—at least I do not think so. I will ask him." He turned to the flyer and spoke in its singsong tongue: "Tuhj, you know of the Great Water to the east and the Great Water to the west, yes?"

He did.

"Have you flown across either of the Great Waters?"

The creature leaned back on its tail, sitting like a tripod, and laughed without bothering to answer, making a sound something like a trombone glissando, up and down.

Back to Blackwood, Zed said, "No. He thinks the idea of traveling across either of the Great Waters is ludicrous. In fact, he laughed." And was still laughing.

"He laughed? The dragon has a sense of humor?"

"Sadly, not a very good one," Turq answered in all seriousness. "But then again, he is not human."

"Quite obvious. So, gentlemen, what brings you out for a walk in the dark in the middle of the night with war paint and a pet dragon?"

Zed turned it around: "Why were you driving down the road in the middle of the night without your headlamps on?"

"Fair enough. Clearing my head. Why the war paint? Is this for the solstice?"

"White men call it war paint. But it is a spirit mask—protects us from evil spirits when we go to war or we go to celebrate. We walk now to Frankie Yellowtail's cabin," answered Turq. "He's found the last—"

Clearing his throat loudly, Zed gave his son a stern look.

"Found the last what?"

"Just child games, Mr. Blackwood," Zed said. "The boys like to play all kinds of imaginative games."

Blackwood looked unconvinced. "Painted faces for child games? Besides, I don't think you'll find Frankie at his home."

"Why not?" Turq asked, a protective edge to his voice.

"I think that he may have been kidnapped. I don't understand what happened."

Turq gripped his spear aggressively. "What? Who took Frankie?"

"Explain what you saw, Mr. Blackwood," Zed said, placing a calming hand on the boy's shoulder. In their native tongue, he whispered to Turq, "Has to be Rooshth Va Manahken. Only one with the motive and power."

The boy's jaw set, eyes burning as he nodded slowly.

Blackwood told his story. "I was drawn to an eerie red light glowing in the night sky. Upon investigating, I witnessed some violent altercation between two women. One was . . ." He paused and cleared his throat. "One was about eight feet tall and completely nude. The other was that tiny woman from the store, Weatherby's Mercantile. The tiny woman had a stone ax and cut the large woman in half. Then the large woman got up and disappeared. I then tried to rescue Frankie, who had a chunk of stone with him, but the tiny woman grabbed him and disappeared."

"Ixtab?" Turq asked his father, switching to the ancient language.

Zed shrugged. "Maybe. Why would they fight?"

"Where did they go?" Turq demanded of Blackwood, in English.

Blackwood swept his hands apart and made a whoosh sound. "They just vanished. They didn't 'go' anywhere."

"A stone?" asked Zed. "You said that the boy had a stone."

"Yes, about this big," said Blackwood, indicating its size with his hands.

In their native tongue, Totahmaa said, "Father, this is terrible. She has taken Frankie to the In-Between. How will we get him? We cannot go there. Can she kill him there?" Anger, fear, and sadness were quickly whipping his soul into a tempest. His face flushed, and tears welled up in his eyes.

Quaatsa addressed his son in English: "Totahmaa, your friend needs his friend, Turq. Be calm. We will find a way."

"But how?" the boy asked, switching back to their language.

"We will find a way," his father repeated in English. "Focus, use English." He opened his arms for the boy to come, and his son did. "So old, yet so young. Too much burden, my son."

While they embraced, Blackwood moved to get out of the car. As soon the door pushed outward slightly, Tuhj let out a descending cascade tone, the meaning of which was quite clear to all. The driver chose to stay in the car.

Father and son turned to face Blackwood.

"Mr. Blackwood, we must deal with this, and I must ask you to tell no one about seeing Tuhj in this way. Many would come seeking him for a trophy."

"I understand; you have my word. Please, let me help you find Frankie. I tried and failed to rescue him once. I feel a debt to him."

"What can you do to help?" the older Native asked.

Blackwood stood in the car looking awkward yet somehow confident. "What kind of help do you need?"

"All right. You are clever. We will need a plan. From what you witnessed, it seems that the witch has taken the boy into the In-Between, which is a place where none of us can go." They explained the In-Between to Blackwood.

"So what does she want?" Blackwood asked.

Zed held his hands palm up and shrugged. "She's just a witch that does evil things, Mr. Blackwood. Who knows if she wants anything?"

Blackwood tried getting out his car again but only rekindled the ire of Tuhj. He sighed, standing in the car with his hands on his hips and trying to avoid hitting the steering wheel. "You must be honest with me. Kidnappers do what they do in order to gain something. Whoever they take is only a token as valuable as the intended trade."

Turq blurted out, "She wants the rest of the *Shat'kuh Mongehweh*." Then he looked at his father, prepared for a backlash, but none came.

"Does that have something to do with the stone the boy had?"

Zed reached into a pouch kept beneath his long robe and pulled out two chunks of stone. "There are three pieces, remnants of a single sacred table. Here are two, and she apparently has acquired the third from Frankie. These are what she wants."

"May I see them?"

"No. They are sacred."

The driver looked disappointed. "Very well then. She has Frankie as her leverage, and we have the two . . . stone pieces." Blackwood stroked his chin and neck absentmindedly, saying, "We'll have to wait for her to contact us with her demands. Then we can form a true plan. Kidnapping negotiations can be tricky, and I expect this one will be trickier than most."

"Good," said Zed. "I have experienced much—gained much wisdom. But I have never dealt with a kidnapping before." Casting Turq a conspiratorial glance, he continued, "I have handled numerous raids, where one tribe or nation captures women or children or horses, but such is not done for trade—they steal for keeps. Totahmaa and I are grateful for your help."

The newly formed rescue team smiled all around, and then Turq said, "We need to tell Frankie's mother."

▼△▼△▼△▼△▼△▼△▼△▼△▼

Chaac

DECEMBER 23, 1177, INSIDE KLANL HIVAHT'S APARTMENT

Rooshth had difficulty holding the tablet; a subtle vibration, combined with a slippery-smooth polish, made it like trying to hold a chunk of wet ice. Cradling the magic power in her arms, her jittery hands caressed the carved figures. She glowed with anticipation like a small child admiring a big gift.

Deftly and quickly, she read the inscriptions on both sides. "This is your basic spirit incantation," she announced to whoever might be listening. Looking up briefly to speak again, she realized that she was alone in the little room. (Churl and Tenateh were just outside the door trying to retrieve Jooh's body from the hole in the roof where it was lodged.)

"So, there are," her finger slid zigzag down the tablet, "these intermediate spirits that do the bidding of the gods." More zigzagging. "Or whoever knows how to summon them—like me," she said with a sly smile.

Glancing around the room, she announced, "Let us give it a little test."

The words on the tablet flowed naturally from her tongue. She pointed at the hearth, and the tablet gave a little popping sound while a small, green mist momentarily appeared in the hearth. Then the small cooking structure exploded into flames, taking half the thick, leather protective mat with it and charring the ceiling.

Giddy, she cackled loudly.

Churl came running in. "What happened? Are you well?"

"I am beyond well. I have never been as well as I am right now." She pointed to the hearth and the low fire now burning within it. "Watch!"

Pointing again at the hearth and repeating the words, the slight green shimmer—with a few black swirls this time—surrounded it, and then it again exploded with fire. Part of the mat caught fire this time, and smoke started filling the small apartment.

"Mother!" said Churl, stomping out one of the nascent sputtering flames.

"Is this power not amazing?"

"The apartment is on fire."

"Relax." Waving her arm around and calling the spirits—now more black than green—snow began to swirl around the apartment and rapidly accumulate on various surfaces. Much of it melted as it extinguished various sputtering fires. Inebriated by her newfound power source, she laughed drunkenly. "Do you see?"

"See what?" asked Churl. "Snow? A crazy woman drunk on power she does not understand?"

"Oh, you are *so* slow-witted. Still you do not understand. I can now heal you. Let us do it now."

"Maybe you should get more experience," he said, turning for the door.

She grabbed a shoulder and spun him around to face her. Putting a finger in his face, she said, "Nonsense. This is so easy." She tapped the stone with the same finger. "I just tell the spirits what I want them to do, and they do it."

The snow stopped, and a voice came from outside: "No."

Tenateh, still drugged, still wobbly, stood in the doorway of the apartment. "It does not work that way," the girl continued.

"Of course it does, child. Did you not see . . ."

"A simple trick that requires no skill."

"Simple? Yes. I just think it, and it happens. How could anything be simpler?"

Tenateh got her scolding face on again. "Any fool can scare a dog with a whip and get it to run away. Getting the dog to come back with dinner is totally different."

"Explain, child."

"The tablet is something like a whip or stick. The spirits must trust you, like the dog. Otherwise, you will get uncertain results."

"How do I get them to trust me?"

"I do not know that part."

"Absurd!" Rooshth said, focusing back on Churl. "Enough. Let us begin. Now. Come over here, Pitiful Boy."

"Mother, I do not think—"

"I know. You never think. *That* is your problem. Now come over here and lie down and be silent so I can concentrate."

"Woman, this is dangerous," Tenateh said.

Rooshth paused, looked coldly into the girl's eyes, and then kicked her in the stomach with enough force to knock the girl out of the apartment. Tenateh fell backward onto her sister's body, clutching her stomach, unable to snatch a breath.

"Now," the old woman said, turning back toward Churl, "you will be still and let me concentrate." Her eyes had just focused on her son when the end of a small log struck her in the face, dislocating her jaw with a crunching sound. Dropping the tablet, she reeled and brought her hands to her face.

"Wha . . . ?" she mumbled through a crooked jaw.

The other end of the log was in Churl's right hand. He pointed the crude weapon at her, eyeing down it at her. "Mother, this madness will end now."

Keeping her eyes on him, she bent down and grabbed the sacred tablet. She opened and closed her mouth gingerly, and with a couple of pops, the joint slipped back into place, making her wince. Cradling her face with a hand, her jaw delicately worked up and down.

Several parallel jagged scratches had started to bleed. She rubbed slippery, red fingertips together. Glancing down at them and then pointing them at him, she said, "You hit me. Made me bleed." Then, after a moment of staring each other down, she asked, "Madness? What madness?"

"You heard me." He paused. "My whole life I have followed you. North we went, pursuing your dream. In all my life, you never asked me what I wanted."

"But you are a child. You have no idea what you want."

"I can do more than you think," he shot back. "I am stronger than you think. Do you know what I want?"

She eyed him and waited.

"Do you? Do you?"

"I can guess what you *think* you want."

"What I think I want? Oh please, Mother. Do tell me what I think I want."

Staring deeply into his eyes and stepping gingerly toward him, she said, "I know. I do." Her voice was melodic and gentle. "You want what every strong, young man wants. A beautiful wife. Many children. Strong sons. Good hunting. A peaceful village, with friends and plentiful food. These are everyone's dreams, my son."

He relaxed his grip on the log, and she touched his left arm reassuringly.

"We must find you a beautiful wife. Do you like her?" she asked, gesturing behind her toward Tenateh but never taking her eyes off of Churl. "She is nice: pretty, ample breasts, good birthing hips. I am sure she would make a fine wife for my strong, smart son. Then we will settle down, and the two of you can raise a big family. We will find a peaceful place with good hunting." She gave him a weak smile. "It will be everything you want."

She broadened her smile to radiate motherly tenderness and care. When he relaxed a bit more, she grasped his wrist, standing very close to him.

"What about you?" he asked.

The question caught her off-guard, making her retreat slightly and remove her hand from him. "Why? What about me?" she asked. "Do you have room in your dream for your old mother?"

"I do have a place for you in my dream." Exhaling deeply, he lowered the crude weapon to his side.

Tilting her head sideways, she smiled, stroked his upper arm gently, and said, "Tell me, my son."

"I want you to be with others who will admire and appreciate everything that you have done. For you to truly be among kindred spirits."

"You really do admire me, after all," she said, glowing. "What do you have in mind?"

"The Underworld."

"What?"

She barely had time to bring her arms up to block her face as Churl hefted the log overhead and brought it down on her, breaking a bone in her forearm with a cracking sound. Her face contorted in shock and pain. She tried to cradle her broken arm and duck away, but Churl had raised the weapon with two hands and was swinging down at her again. Ducking and dodging, she evaded most of his blows as he chased her around and around the apartment. Several times, she tried to flee through the apartment door, but he always blocked her exit.

After a few seconds, their deadly game of cat and mouse left her breathing in great heaves.

"Son, please . . ." she appealed, lifting her hands toward him.

But his rage was deaf, and he swung furiously, striking her outstretched arms. Fingers buckled and broke under the force of the impact, and she squealed. Instinctively, she pulled her hands back to her body and retreated, breathing in sporadic, shallow gulps. He followed her into a corner and brought the weapon down on her again and again—a wild-eyed madman on a mission. She slumped down, crouching low, trying to make herself a small target. Crossing her arms over her head, she absorbed blow after blow, rough wood tearing skin. Blood ran past her elbows toward her shoulders.

Finally, he was tiring, but so was she. One of his blows smashed her arms down, and the blunt weapon made contact with her head. The cranial strike made her ears ring, and her vision went double for a few moments. Then voices caught her attention—distant, child-like voices. She looked around and found nothing, but the voices persisted. They were whispering, "Over here. We can help you. You don't have to die."

She scanned the room again, which was difficult with Churl trying to cave in her skull. There, on the other side of the room, black mist paced—back and forth. The strange formation seemed inviting, friendly—trustworthy.

"Head injury," she whispered, shaking her head and blinking.

"Over here. Yes. Here. Let us help you. We can save you."

Her head suffered another blow, and her vision blinked out momentarily while the sound of rushing waters filled her ears.

"What do you want?" she cried.

"I want to kill you!" Churl screamed. "I thought you would have figured that out by now. I am trying to make it perfectly clear." He stood over her, panting.

"We want to help you," the voices whispered.

"How can you help?" she asked, starting to collapse physically and emotionally.

"Help you? You," Churl started, while raising his weapon, "will be," he punctuated this with a particularly forceful blow, "with others," another near-lethal blow followed, "who can," and another, "appreciate your . . ." Still another blow.

"Say the words," came the whisper.

Rooshth was at her end, barely able to focus. Terrified for her life. Physically racked with pain and trauma. Barely functional. Ripped apart inside by the magnitude of her son's betrayal. Still, something in her sharp, old mind clicked into place.

"The words . . ." she said.

She managed to just utter the incantation, two thoughts paramount in her mind: *hold him* and *save me*.

Churl swung the log with all his might for a massive final strike. It would have been a fatal blow—her strength gone completely, her guard down. However, as the weapon swung, the black mist jetted from across the room and grabbed Churl by the throat and the weapon hand, picking him up off the ground. He kicked his dangling feet, looking for purchase, and clawed at the mist with his free hand. The mist swung him around, pinned him against the wall. With a dull clunk, the blood-spattered log dropped to the floor.

Some of the mist flew in tight circles around Rooshth's body. Contusions and abrasions vanished. Bones moved back into position, fused. Her energy surged, and she quickly jumped to her feet, watching her son struggle with the black mist, held fast against the wall and struggling to breathe.

She approached her trapped son, accusing finger jabbing at the air. "I should punish you for this—crush you. Thought you could kill me and get away?" Then her countenance changed. Putting hands on her hips, she slowly shook her head and pleaded, "Do you not see now?"

Head close to the ceiling, he cast his eyes down to look on her, answering with choking, coughing sounds.

"See the power of the magic. I will transform you into something great and powerful! Together, we can return and rule all of the lands. You asked about my dream. That is my dream for you. People will worship us. They will fear us. They will love us. They will carve our names and glorious legacy into their pyramids so that all people forever will know us." She raised her arms in victorious fists.

Churl struggled to speak. "Mother . . ."

"Do you see now?"

The mists loosened their grip slightly. He managed to say, "Yes. I see more clearly than ever."

"Good," she said, genuinely pleased. "Finally. Why are you so stubborn?"

"I blame my upbringing," he said.

She ignored his jab. "Now, I shall—"

"I do not want it," he choked.

"What? You said . . ."

"What I see more clearly than ever is that you belong with the lost spirits of the Underworld. If this thing ever releases me, I will kill you."

Her face flushed anew, and her eyes burned white-hot. After a moment, she cooled slightly and said, "I can make any woman love you."

His eyes bulged slightly as he struggled against mists that had tightened their hold. "No . . ." he coughed.

"We can go anywhere. Explore. Or settle."

He shook his head.

"You will be big, strong, and powerful. I will make you like a god."

She started reciting the words, and he screamed, "No!"

As she finished the incantation, the black mist swarmed over his body, leaving him barely visible. Rooshth looked on with anticipation of her glorious new creation. "Now," she began, "you will be what you should have been. What you can be. What I want you to be. I have sacrificed so much for you."

As if through a thick cloud of gnats or flies, brief glimpses of the mist's work could be seen. Churl's muscles were growing, bulging visibly under his tunic. The white complexion of his skin darkened. A strong jaw, noble nose, and manly brow were forming on his otherwise weak-looking face.

Rooshth stood on the balls of her feet, straining to see. "Ah. This is going to be good. He will be wonderful. He will be a god to behold," she said, bouncing up and down on her toes and clapping. The transformation took longer than expected, however, and her excitement waned. Once again, this quest was trying her patience.

Putting her hands to her head, she sighed and looked down. Churl's feet were on the floor. They were no longer small and white, but huge and dark, with bluish patterns across the top and long, sharp curling toenails like claws. Then she looked up to his face. It was at the ceiling, neck bent sideways. The center of his face pushed outward, nose and jaw growing and stretching, taking on the image of a distant but familiar memory.

The black mist vanished, and her enthusiasm turned to horror. "No, no, no, no, no!" she said, her voice rising in pitch and intensity.

"What has happened?" came a voice behind her. Tenateh walked through the door, clutching her stomach. "What have you done?"

"Shut up, child. I need to think."

Standing before her, Churl, her son, the Pitiful Boy, was now fully transformed into the image of Chaac, the Mayan Rain God. He was huge, filling the apartment and barely able to stand even when hunched over. His muscles bulged and rippled, revealing fantastic strength and power. Dark blue reptilian scales accented his golden skin, forming armor across his arms, thighs, feet, chest, and back. A long tapir-like nose and mouth extended from his face, with viper-like fangs jutting from an over-extended upper jaw. His long tongue whipped in and out of his mouth like a snake sampling the air. In his right hand, he grasped a brilliant gold scepter studded with ivory-like alligator teeth and bearing a huge obsidian ax blade.

Churl-Chaac looked himself over and then stared long and hard at his mother.

Tenateh lunged at the old woman, pushing her down and out of the way. Then she stood before the hulking man-god and wept.

*   *   *

In the courtyard below, a dog was dead.

Klanl Hivaht knelt by the deceased animal, taking in the situation: a large, powerful dog, clearly bred for war, had been killed by a child with a small knife. He looked from the dog, to the boy, to the other children, to the other dogs, and back to the boy. Shaking his head, he looked to the gate of the Great House, as if some answers might walk through at any moment.

Suddenly, one of the Elite warriors ran up to him from a group of nearby children. "High Shaman Klanl, those children say the visitors ascended to your apartment. They had Tenateh with them, and they have heard fighting and screaming."

"Jooh was up there," Klanl said and began running, the messenger following close behind.

Several other Elites joined in. When they reached the long, straight side of the Great House's D shape, where his apartment was on the second level, they found that the red ladder had been pulled up—a defensive move.

Klanl belted out, "Get a ladder! Quickly." Toward the apartment, he called, "Jooh! Jooh! Can you hear me? Are you there?" After a moment of silence, he barked at the warriors, "Hurry!"

Two warriors returned with a ladder and propped it against the structure. His foot was on the bottom rung before they had stabilized it against the structure. He quickly ascended to the second level.

Jooh lay motionless near a gaping hole in the roof, covered in blood.

"Jooh!" He ran to his wife and knelt beside her, shaking violently. The warriors came up the ladder on his heels and then turned away respectfully while their leader dealt with the immediate horror. His wife's young body bore the marks of her violent end. Pain contorted her lifeless, pale face. Bruises had stopped emerging, and scratches stopped bleeding without having scabbed. Underneath her body, a growing pool of blood released a crimson trickle that wound back to the hole in the roof and dripped into the apartment below. Bits of flesh and blood ringed the jagged edges of the hole. After she died, someone had moved her into her current position: flat on her back, arms at her sides, hair neatly bundled under her head. Klanl rolled her body over, revealing the fatal knife strike through a kidney.

Klanl and the warriors studied the body quietly and somberly, all knowing that a violent death often made The Journey more difficult. Those dying Out of Nature often sought revenge. The desire for vengeance made moving on difficult. The shaman always had to pray extra hard to guide those souls who determined to stay behind. Sometimes, in fact, the prayers failed, and the angry spirits wandered the desert, running amok as a whirlwind or occupying the body of an animal—vultures, scorpions, and spiders being the favorites. Eventually, the soul would simply get bored, or the animal it occupied would die. Most of these souls would eventually take The Journey, joining their ancestors and loved ones.

Some souls, however, were so angry, so hate-filled at the moment of their death, that they never took The Journey. These ultimately became part of the *Ahteh Shat'tohl*, the black mists, rogue spirits bent on destruction and mayhem.

One of the warriors put a hand on Klanl's shoulder. "She has a good soul, High Shaman. She will take The Journey, and you will see her again."

Klanl kept his head down and nodded, tears dropping to the deck.

"Klanl," another warrior called. "Your apartment."

"Yes?" he asked, sniffing back powerful emotions.

"You should see it. I . . ." His voice faltered as he struggled to find the words. He gave up. "I do not know how to say it."

Klanl rose and turned toward the door of the apartment, where two of Sheweh's Elites cowered. He scowled at them as he bolted past, entering the apartment, an angry man on a mission. Little things caught his attention first: scorch marks on the rug and ceiling; a pile of melting snow in a corner; water soaking almost everything; pots and benches turned over; the old pilgrim-woman with the wild silver-white hair picking herself up off the floor; his assistant, Tenateh, weeping and standing in front of . . .

"What?" He froze.

Churl, in the form of the Rain God, Chaac, sat hunched on the other side of the apartment. His head was part man, part animal, part snake. He was covered with strange markings and colors. Slowly, he turned his head to look at Klanl with emotionless yet penetrating eyes.

A squeak popped out of Klanl's throat, and he quickly and shakily backed out the door.

"Is it real? Perhaps it is a trick," one of the warriors suggested hopefully.

Klanl looked at his trembling hands. "I do not know."

From the same warrior: "How did it get inside? The door is too small."

"Perhaps it is just a trick of magic. You," Klanl said, pointing to another of the warriors.

The man lifted his eyebrows in surprise.

"Yes," Klanl said. "Throw your spear. Let us see if it bleeds."

"At that?"

"Yes." Klanl and one of the other warriors positioned themselves in front of a window opening to watch.

Reluctantly, the chosen warrior slinked closer to the apartment door and quickly peeked inside several times, trying to be stealthy, trying to gather courage. After mumbling a prayer and rubbing his elbows, he sprung into the doorway and hurled his spear.

The weapon flew true.

The man-god raised a hand, as if catching a ball, and the flint spearhead cut right through it, puncturing completely. Looking curiously at his hand with the weapon lodged in it, Churl-Chaac touched his ax to the business end of the spear, and in a brief flash of light, the shaft disintegrated into a fine powder of charcoal. The punctured hand bled, but the man-god wasn't concerned.

Klanl and the warrior squatted down below the window. The High Shaman said, "This is going to be a problem." He aimed his voice at the window and called, "Tenateh?"

She answered, but Klanl could not understand the language she was using.

"What?" he asked.

Desperate and unintelligible words streamed from the apartment.

"Is it safe for us to come in?"

There was no reply but sobs.

"Ready your spears," Klanl commanded. "If it makes a move toward me or the girl, throw both spears immediately. You might delay it long enough for me to get her out alive."

The warriors positioned themselves on either side of the doorway, weapons ready.

He crept into the apartment, focused on the girl. Slowly, he moved to her side, never taking his eyes from Churl-Chaac. (The man-god, too, never took its eyes off of the High Shaman.) Klanl put his arm around her and whispered, "Back out slowly. Then we can get you out of here."

The girl looked at him, shocked.

"Come now. We can get you to safety. Away from this monster."

With irritation in her voice, she spoke again to him in a strange language.

"Please, Tenateh. I do not want to lose you, Sister-of-My-Wife." He started to gently pull her backward toward the door, but she jerked loose.

Tenateh's sudden movement startled Churl-Chaac, and the man-god stepped toward them. Two spears flew and struck him in the chest. He roared and recoiled from the impact, but the weapons ricocheted off his natural armor, leaving scratches but drawing minimal blood. One spear fell harmlessly to the floor, shaft split and spearhead shattered, and the other spun wildly through the air, nearly striking the wrinkly, old woman.

Churl-Chaac stepped closer, grasping at Tenateh, but the floor of the apartment collapsed.

□ ■ □ ■ □ ■ □ ■ □ ■ □

The Trap

June 21, 1938, Canyon Road Near the Yellowtail Cabin, Chaco Canyon

C. J. Blackwood drove north, Zed in the passenger's seat on his left, and Turq back in the rumble seat. The night sky was bright, and the constellations had shifted subtly since he first nearly ran over his two passengers.

"There! That is it," shouted Turq from the rear, standing and pointing to a faint light from a small cabin in the distance.

The driver pulled the car off the road to a stop.

"Why do you stop here?" Zed asked.

"This witch, is she clever?" Blackwood asked.

"Yes."

Blackwood rubbed his chin and stroked his neck. "I'm concerned about how she'll contact us."

"What do you mean?" Turq asked.

"If she is clever, and you two have a long-standing feud with her, then she knows that she can't contact us directly."

Zed nodded. "That is true."

"So, how will she contact us about Frankie?" Turq asked.

"An emissary," answered the boy's father.

"Indeed. Kidnappers generally like to use an emissary in order to keep their distance," said Blackwood. "But who? She's basically a stranger to the canyon. Who does she know?"

"Kenneth," Zed answered.

"Who?"

Turq chimed in eagerly: "McKinney. Kenneth McKinney. He owns the little store where she started working."

"Weatherby's? Anyone else?"

Zed shook his head. "Not that I know of."

"Me neither," Turq added.

"So it's reasonable to assume that she will try to contact us through this Kenneth McKinney." He tapped his fingers on the steering wheel, considering something. "Okay. When we arrive at the Yellowtails' cabin, you two should tell the boy's mother that Frankie is missing, since she doesn't know me. I'll wait outside until you signal. Be ready for her to respond with denial or anger."

"Of course," Zed acknowledged.

Then with surprising agility, the fifty-something-year-old Native bounded out of the car—without using the door.

"What are you doing?" Blackwood asked.

"Just a little reconnaissance." Then Zed attached his large wooden flute he'd carried to a leathery bag that had been hidden under his cape. A smaller flute was already attached to it; this second flute went to Zed's lips. The bag was inflated, giving Zed the look of a hunchback with crazy, fiery hair. Transformed into the flute player, *Kokopelli*, he played a series of long, low notes that carried far across the canyon, echoing from distant cliffs seconds later.

"A bagpipe?" Blackwood mused under his breath. "What's he doing?" he whispered to Turq.

"He's calling Tuhj."

*　*　*

Low, woody, and distant tones entered the cabin from the night, surprising the four anxious occupants of the Yellowtail cabin. Natasha ran to the window and peered outside, both hopeful and dreadful.

"They soon come," Ruth said. The woman's white-and-cream design silk scarf wrapped her self-inflicted knife wound and had already turned crimson. Little pain showed on her face, and Natasha noticed that she handled the knife-wounded hand as if it were merely thorn-stuck.

Kenneth tilted his head slightly and asked, "You said they're coming?"

"They soon come. Yes."

"How you know this?" Vince asked.

"Flute used in magic. They prepare," Ruth explained. They all nodded, approving the logic.

Kenneth rushed to the screen door and pressed his face to the metal mesh, hands cupped around his eyes. "We should take them by surprise," he said, pulling his revolver and checking the rounds in the cylinder.

"*Sì*," the Italian said, maneuvering to a window.

"Could be some time still," Ruth said.

"What?" Kenneth asked.

"Flute ceremonial. Mean they *prepare* now," she explained, hinting that they pay closer attention.

"But you say 'they soon come,'" Vince pointed out.

"Yes: today, not tomorrow," explained Natasha.

"Oh." The Italian rolled his eyes.

Natasha continued, "For us—especially someone like Zed and Turq who are so isolated—time is fluid. Time serves men, not vice versa. So we wait until they arrive. Then what?"

"I hide in little room there. You," Ruth pointed to the men, "use guns, make show tablet pieces. Then grab."

Natasha furrowed her brow. "Why are you going to hide?"

"The boy—Turq?—he cause trouble if see me."

"Right." Natasha nodded. "Frankie told me about how Turq had caused trouble yesterday." Then she looked down at the bloody flannel and mess on the table. "I will clean this up."

Vince jumped up and announced—somewhat too jovially, "I will pour tea."

Kenneth returned to the door, and Ruth packed her belongings back into her bag.

Natasha gathered the flannel from the table and tried to pick it up delicately, but it was soaked in blood and threatened to drip everywhere. She turned to the kitchen sink and grabbed a large metal bucket filled with food scraps and waste. Then she carefully and quickly grabbed the shirt by its edges and dropped it into the bucket. A towel was used to sponge up the remaining blood. Finally, she used a rag and some water to finish cleaning the tabletop and then washed her hands at the sink.

Drying her hands on her apron, she turned to grab the bucket and haul it outside, but stopped as Ruth unwrapped her hand. "Want me to take that ruined scarf?"

"No. I wash." She held the messy silk close, protectively.

Picking up the bucket, the sight of the bloody mixture of food scraps, waste water, and flies flipped some internal switch, and Natasha had to bolt from the cabin. With one hand clamped on the bucket and the other clamped over her mouth, she ran behind the cabin toward the outhouse. Halfway there, she dropped the bucket and vomited violently. The first heave emptied her stomach, but several gut-wrenching, unproductive waves followed.

"I cannot lose him. I cannot," she said to the night, wiping the mess from her mouth with her apron. Tears flowed once again, and her body tried to heave out more emotional pain, but she fought it back, breathing shallowly and covering her mouth with her apron. In a minute or so, she turned to go back to the cabin, leaving the bucket where it lay.

Kenneth and Vince had followed her into the night and were stepping up to comfort and support her—now that the vomiting was over. Ruth also followed but at some distance; she kept nervously glancing up at the stars.

"Come back inside, Miss Natasha," Vince said. "Tea is ready now. You have tea. Feel better."

Kenneth approached Natasha and put a hand on her shoulder. "You okay? Feeling better?"

"Yes, a little. A rest and some tea sound good."

Except for Ruth, who seemed to be in an inconspicuous hurry, they walked slowly around to the front of the cabin. By the time the three got back to the porch, Ruth was already inside and seated in a chair that she had pulled over to the stove.

* * *

"Tuhj? You're calling Tuhj?" asked Blackwood. "I've got mixed feelings about that. On the one hand, he is a rare animal—far beyond anything J. J. Audubon could have dreamed of—and definitely worth a second look. Yet, on the other hand, he just recently tried to exterminate me with extreme prejudice."

Zed resumed the tones on his flute.

Blackwood leaned against the side of his car and crossed his arms. "Okay. How long will it take for him to get here?"

Turq leaned on the rear of the car, looking into the sky. "Who knows? He comes when he comes."

"He seemed well-trained earlier. Why not come right away—when called?"

Turq started laughing. "Well-trained? It used to be like that. Then he got tired."

"Tired?"

"Yes, tired and cranky," the boy said, shaking his head.

"Just recently?"

Turq's face scrunched up in concentration. "Sometime maybe two or two and a half centuries ago. Hard to say exactly."

"You mean years—two or two and a half years ago," Blackwood said. "Do you know what a century is?"

"No," said Turq, voice dripping sarcasm. "I remember that there were a lot of Spanish missionaries through here at the time, and the Mexicans were selling our people as slaves. Right, Father?"

Zed stopped playing the flute and nodded.

Blackwood laughed politely. "Ha ha. So, how old is Tuhj?"

The boy stood up, away from the car, and put his fists on his hips. "I am not joking, Mr. Blackwood. Tuhj is more than seven hundred years old."

"Pardon me?"

"Why?"

"Why what?"

"You said, 'Pardon me.' Why do you need to be pardoned?"

"I meant for you to repeat yourself. I thought you said that your animal was more than seven hundred years old."

"I did say that," the boy replied humorlessly.

"That is impossible."

"He is very old—*and* gets quite cranky." Turq turned away from him indignantly.

"How do you know he is that old?"

Speaking over his shoulder, the boy said matter-of-factly, "Tuhj is only ten summers older than I am."

"Come on. You're pulling my leg."

Zed smiled and said to Blackwood, "See what I have been dealing with? For a very long time."

Blackwood considered his long-held, "common sense" notions that had been overturned tonight: dragons existed, witches with real magic existed, people could vanish into thin air, demon-goddesses cut in half could pull themselves together, and there seemed to exist some reality—maybe multiple ones—beyond this world.

"Okay, so maybe," Blackwood said.

"Okay, what?" the boy asked.

"That's good to know. Good to know that Tuhj is old and cranky."

"Very."

They waited in tense silence for a while, scanning the skies for any sign of the flyer. Blackwood grew impatient but used the time to study his "young" companion carefully: his face was youthful under paint, and his body that of a growing boy, yet his eyes betrayed a depth that few old men possessed. "Turq, do you know who Peter Pan is?" he asked.

"No. Peter who?"

"A boy who had eternal youth."

"Poor bastard," said Turq, turning away.

Blackwood tilted his head sideways and asked, "What is it like to be a boy for so long?"

"Mr. Blackwood," interrupted Zed, "what is it like to be full grown yet still so young?"

"Touché," said Blackwood.

They all leaned back against the car, quietly watching the stars slowly turning. Eventually, the sky began brightening in the east. Blackwood pointed and said, "Look, the sun will be rising soon. That may make it easier." Unfortunately, neither Native took the conversational bait.

"So Tuhj has become a bit cranky in his old age?" asked Blackwood, smiling jovially and trying to get a conversation going.

Zed shrugged. "He has just become cranky. No particular reason. Maybe lonely, but the *quetz'al* are not very social really."

"A general characteristic around here," Blackwood mumbled.

"Except when they mate," added Turq.

"Right, son. They can bond for life." Zed turned away to scan the skies some more, and the nascent conversation stumbled. Silence descended once again on the trio.

Finally, as a dull red-orange glow started climbing over the horizon, Zed and Turq both looked straight up overhead and then to the west. Blackwood stared intently into the fading constellations, trying to follow their gaze and straining to hear whatever they had heard. Unfortunately, no shadow movement caught his eye, and no whispering flutter fell to his ear.

Then Turq pointed behind Blackwood.

A puff of warm air blew the locks of Blackwood's hair and raised goose-flesh on the back of his neck. He turned around slowly.

Tuhj stood there, staring down with those huge eyes again. In the dawn twilight, the flyer's appearance was even more menacing. Its head and neck were almost pelican- or stork-like: a long neck finished with a smallish head and pointy beak—except that Tuhj had a large crest on top of his head. His body was short in proportion to the ten-foot-long neck. A powerful-looking chest sprouted wings from oversized shoulder sockets. The thin wing-skin stretched across a frame of fine bones that resembled a giant hand. Stocky, leathery lizard legs held its body weight securely, while ending in dangerous-looking, clawed toes. The tail had a razor-sharp paddle on the end.

Blackwood was mesmerized. "I feel something like a toad before a vulture. Will it let me . . ." he said, slowly stepping toward it with one hand outstretched.

"No, he will not, Mr. Blackwood," Turq said, stepping in front and lowering the driver's hand with his own. "That is not safe—if you enjoy having two arms."

Zed stepped from behind the car and spoke to Tuhj in the *quetz'al* Song, making strange vocalizations consisting of complex vowel sounds, a great deal of pitch variation, and few consonants. The flyer turned its head sideways toward the cabin and then back to the old Native, who made just a few more "comments" and then went quiet.

Tuhj replied with more singsong vocalizations and then sprung high into the air.

As Tuhj flew up into the sky, Blackwood said, "He's not a dragon. Dragons supposedly have four legs, while he has only two." He looked away in thought and then back to the flyer, saying, "He's a pterosaur. They must have survived here in North America all these millennia."

"What?" Zed turned to him.

"Fantastic creature. That's all. Where's he going?"

"Look out," replied Zed. "And to create a distraction if necessary."

"Okay. Let's go?" he asked.

"Yes," Turq said, climbing into the T57's rumble seat.

"Yes," said Zed, climbing over the passenger door into his seat.

Blackwood made a show of opening his door, sitting down, and then closing the door after himself.

In a few minutes, they arrived at the Yellowtail cabin. Blackwood stayed in the car and watched as the two Natives walked solemnly up to the cabin, waving at figures standing in the doorway.

Turq called out: "Miss Yellowtail? Miss Yellowtail, it is Turq. I need to talk to you about Frankie."

Reaching into his pocket, Blackwood pulled out his cigarette case, shook it slightly, and looked disappointed. "I know what I'd conjure up if I had magic," he told the dashboard. His mind thought about different possible negotiation scenarios and their outcomes. In the best one, the witch chose a poor meeting point, arrived with the boy, and they easily overpowered her to rescue the hostage. In several others, the boy either died or did not get rescued. In the worst scenario, the witch got to some other players and somehow convinced them to do her "dirty" work.

Just then, a man came from behind the cabin, brandishing a small pistol.

"Walther PPK?" Blackwood mused. "Girly. But not a bad weapon."

The man standing in the doorway—tall, rugged-looking type— pulled his revolver and motioned for the two Natives to enter.

Blackwood quickly lay across the passenger seat, out of sight. Then he sighed. "Not off to a great start."

* * *

About an hour earlier, Natasha re-entered the cabin and saw Ruth sitting next to the stove. "Are you all right?" she asked.

Rubbing her shoulders, Ruth said, "I have some chill."

"Do you need a blanket?"

"No. By stove is good. Good heat."

Natasha had exactly four teacups in the cupboard. Vince grabbed them and poured the tea.

"I apologize. I have no sugar," Natasha said. "There is some milk in the ice box that needs to be used."

"I get milk. You know we Italians prefer the *espresso*. Strong and black. With the tea, I like cream." Vince retrieved the glass milk bottle and put a few drops in his tea. "Anyone else?" He smiled invitingly.

"Not me," Kenneth said.

"None for me, thank you, Vince," Natasha said.

"Some for me is good. Just little," Ruth answered, holding up a thumb and index finger. Vince obliged her.

The four of them sat in silence, absorbing the warmth of the tea in the waning hours of the cool summer night. Caffeine started its work, but the late hour was difficult to overcome. All were sleep-deprived and worried. None braved conversation.

Natasha watched Ruth expectantly glancing from the black of her tea to the black outside. Short, wavy hair sprang back and forth with the woman's nervous head motions. Sitting in the wooden chair, she was almost child-sized. Were it not for a woman's features, she might have been confused with a ten-year-old. She had a certain prettiness, with her golden skin, green eyes, and shiny, white hair—though not features that most would consider "beautiful."

Ruth drank her tea like a novice afraid of getting burned. The tiny woman held the cup in her right hand, and the saucer rested in the palm of her left hand, which seemed perfectly fine: blood gone, no swelling, and barely a mark from the knife that had completely penetrated it earlier.

Natasha studied the deep gouge in the tabletop left by the obsidian dagger, fingering the damage for confirmation. Her gaze switched back to Ruth's wounded hand again, but Ruth put the saucer down on the table and folded her left hand underneath her right arm near her elbow, casually holding her cup in her right hand. The women locked eyes, and a curtain of social awkwardness fell between them—a curtain embroidered with danger.

Clearing her throat, Natasha forced an appropriately pleasant-looking smile and said, "Your hand seems to be doing very well. That makes me glad. I would be remiss if you had suffered permanent harm when trying to help us."

"I fast healer. Use strong medicine while you were outside still." Smiling, Ruth reached out to touch Natasha's arm with her left hand. "I happy to help." Her eyes looked kind and sweet, but there was a storm behind them.

A surreptitious glance at the hand on her arm revealed that there was now no mark at all—no trace of the knife wound. She quickly looked away, and both women stared awkwardly into their teacups.

"Like your tea?" Natasha asked.

"Yes, thank you."

Vince, who had been half-dozing in a chair, snorted awake and stood up. "I will take care of bucket." He shook his head and wiped his face with both hands, trying to brush away the drowsiness.

As Vince headed to the door, Kenneth said, "Good idea, Vince. That thing will attract coyotes and all kinds of damn vermin. Pardon my French, ladies."

"Thank you, Vince."

"Is no problem, Ms. Yellowtail." He quickly walked out the door into the night on his mission.

A few minutes later, the sound of a car coming down the road brought an alertness that the caffeine could not. They looked at one another with collective questions: Is this them? Is this it?

"Let's turn out the lights," Kenneth said.

"No," commanded Ruth, with sudden authority. "Need make look innocent. They suspect nothing."

Kenneth's face took on an I-should-have-thought-of-that look. "Right."

Pointing toward the little bedroom, Ruth said, "I go hide." Natasha nodded, and Ruth quietly grabbed her stuff and slipped into the bedroom, closing the door.

As soon as the bedroom door clicked shut, Natasha jumped up to join Kenneth at the front door. In barely a whisper, she asked, "Did you see her hand?"

"What?"

"Her hand. Where the dagger had been."

"What about it?"

"Did you see it?" she pressed.

"No," he said absently. "I'm sure it's a bloody mess."

"But it is not."

"What?"

"Not a mark. Completely healed."

"That doesn't make any sense, Natasha. How could . . ."

The lights of the car turned toward the cabin.

"This must be them," he said.

The car slowed and stopped when it got within about fifty feet of the front porch.

Kenneth's mouth hung open. "Wow."

"It is just a car, Kenneth."

"No, Natasha. *That* is a just a truck." He pointed toward his Ford, which the T57 was parking beside. "But that is not just a car."

She huffed, irritated. "Who cares? We must get those two pieces of stone."

"Right," Kenneth said.

Zed and Turq got out of the car, appearing just as they had when seen inside the little magic portal: one in war paint, and the other dressed as *Kokopelli*. Natasha's left hand covered her mouth while her right hand wrapped around her waist. She made a little squeaking sound.

The two Natives waved, their countenance as that of messengers bearing a great load. Natasha and Kenneth returned their greeting.

"Something is wrong," said Natasha.

"Are you ready?" asked Kenneth.

"Where's Vince?" She looked out into the night for the man and then to the new arrivals. "I do not think . . . they could not have—"

"Miss Yellowtail? Miss Yellowtail," said Turq. "We need to talk about Frankie."

□ ■ □ ■ □ ■ □ ■ □ ■ □

Sprung

JUNE 21, 1938, YELLOWTAIL
CABIN, CHACO CANYON

It was hard to tell who hated whom worse. Tuhj hated her for killing the love of his life, Luahti, and Rooshth hated him for having ripped her arm off once—a wound that took centuries of pain to heal and regrow. The thought of taking her arm again would have made him smile, except that *quetz'al* do not have lips.

Earlier in the night, Tuhj spied on her as she spied on the little cabin disguised as a coyote. He watched her dress, enter the cabin, follow the sick woman out, and hastily return. At that point, he returned to his master, who had called earlier with the *tzetoh*. Now, he sat some distance away from the cabin, peering in the windows and trying to get a sense of what was happening inside. He dared not get too close; somehow the witch seemed to be able to smell him or sense his presence another way.

The witch went into the bedroom of the little cabin as Zed and Turq arrived. She waved her arm in a peculiar way, and the shimmering, curtain-like portal opened that allowed her to pass into the In-Between. Stepping through, she abandoned the clueless occupants of the cabin. After centuries of practice, she seemed to move into and out of that world with ease.

His master had summoned him to instruct him to watch her, which he had already been doing, so he hadn't paid very close attention, which turned out to be unfortunate. He was unsure whether or not he had been given additional instructions. Since a near-fatal crash caused by the witch a few centuries ago, his hearing was fading. Calls from the master's flute were clear enough, but when the master spoke to him, most of the words were lost, garbled, and muted. Understanding Master's Song now took all of his concentration, and he was becoming more and more detached from Master and the boy.

He waited for a while, but the witch didn't return. Bored, unsure what to do, and feeling like his mission was accomplished, he launched straight into the air, ascending high into the sky with just a few wing strokes. The canyon was starting to come alive: people began stirring, animals began their routines, and flowers greeted the morning light. In the distance, the great circle in the ground that was the ruins of the Birthing Chamber could be seen. Several half-costumed individuals had already gathered there to begin preparations to dance.

Curiosity drew him toward the readying dancers. As he gained height, approaching a soaring altitude, his skin changed from dark gray to light gray with splotches of white. Anyone catching a glimpse of him with their peripheral vision would mistake his winged shape for that of a tiny, wispy cloud.

*   *   *

Turq sat in a chair at the table in the Yellowtail cabin—ironically, the same one that he had occupied yesterday as a guest. Now, men he had known for years held him and his father prisoner at gunpoint.

Kenneth McKinney said, "We know you've got Frankie."

"We do not," Zed calmly said.

Turq burst out, "Why would we do such a thing?"

"Quiet, my son. We do not have Frankie. The witch has taken him to the In-Between."

"Ruth used her psychic powers to show us Frankie," Natasha said. Uncertainty dulled the accusing edge in her voice.

Turq turned to face her, asking, "Is he okay?"

"He seems to be," Natasha said. "What do you want with him? What does Mr. Blackwood want?"

"We do not have the boy," Zed said. "We came here to tell you that the witch has him."

"Sure," said Kenneth.

Vince Nesci stood by the door, keeping an eye out for Blackwood. He said, "Hmm . . . Let's have look inside your bag."

Turq stiffened.

"If you like," said Zed.

His father's compliance was alarming, and Turq started to protest, but a scolding glance from his father hushed him.

Zed started to untie his wrap, saying, "It is under my cape, which I will need to remove."

"Do it slowly," Kenneth said, holding his gun a little firmer and shifting his weight.

His father stood, removed his cape, and carefully draped it over the chair in which he had been sitting. The flute and its bladder were unslung from one shoulder, and finally a satchel was unslung from the other shoulder.

Turq gingerly touched the feathers in the cape as they rustled in motion, eyeing them fondly. (He and his father had trapped the eagles and hawks together.)

Abandoning his post, Vince grabbed the leather satchel tersely. The Italian's eyes bore the hate of betrayal as he stared into Turq's eyes accusingly.

"Sit," said Kenneth to Zed, harshly.

The satchel was set down on the table roughly. Vince flipped open the leather flap, rifled through the contents, and quickly found the two fragments of the *Shat'kuh Mongeweh* at the bottom. "What are these?" he demanded.

His father put on a naïve face. "Simple artifacts from the last of our people."

"Simple artifacts? No written language exists for Anasazi. Try again?" said the Italian, veins standing out in his neck.

"You are right, my friend," Zed said apologetically. "This is the only example of the ancient language, and we guard it most closely."

"We need these, Zed," Kenneth said.

"Why?"

"To save my son," blurted out Natasha Yellowtail. She dissolved into tears and ran into the bedroom.

Watching the two white men examine the pieces of the sacred stone tablet made Turq simmer. "Mr. Nesci," he said, "please be careful."

Something softened in the Italian's eyes, and he held the stones more gently.

"Thank you," Zed said.

"*Si.*"

Kenneth called toward the cabin's bedroom. "Ruth! Ruth, come out. We found the stones you wanted."

Natasha came out of the bedroom, confused. "She is not there."

"She left?" Kenneth asked. "How? When? Dammit."

Folding thick arms across his chest, Vince said, "We need to get Blackwood in here."

"Yes," Kenneth said, going to the door and peering out carefully. He yelled out at the yellow roadster. "Blackwood! Mr. Blackwood, get in here!"

Vince asked the big man, "Is he coming?"

"It's hard to see."

"You want go out there?" Vince asked.

Kenneth glared at the Italian, cocking his head sideways, and answered, "You think I'm nuts? He may have a whole damn arsenal out there."

"Do you see Ruth?" Natasha asked.

"No," said Kenneth, double-checking.

Vince stepped to the bedroom door and peered in. "Where she go?"

A faint foomp-swoosh sound filled the cabin. Turq turned toward the sound in time to see Ruth appear suddenly on the opposite side of the table from the bedroom. She crossed the space as Vince turned around and said, "Surprise. I here." Then she violently struck him on the side of the neck with her forearm, the impact/press motion cutting off blood to his brain. After a brief wobble, he collapsed, unconscious.

"And thank you," she added, picking up the two pieces of stone and smiling.

Fury burned in Turq's eyes, and he balled his fists watching Rooshth holding and fondling the sacred fragments. She gloated and danced a little jig. In one of the ancient tongues, she sang, "Now I have the pieces all. The tablet long destroyed be whole. My son I raise. He sing my praise. And we shall reign eternal." Then she danced a little more.

Zed spoke to her in English. "That cannot be done."

She smirked and said, "I find way."

"There is no way. Your son is dead. At your own hand. Gone forever."

She exploded at them in the ancient tongue again: "No. No. No. I have found a way. I have consulted the priests of the south who worship your precious *quetz'al*, and I have consulted the priests of my people even farther to the south. Demons and gods and goddesses far and wide." She leaned in toward Zed and, using English, said quietly—and frightfully calmly, "Trick is . . . Life for life."

Natasha started breathing heavily. "What does that mean? Life for life?" She looked desperately to the men and then back to the witch. "Where is Frankie? You said that if you had the stones that you would get Frankie."

The witch smiled wryly and said, "And I will—I always keep my word. But for me. Not for you." She backed away from the table and waved her arm in a strange way. "My boy live!" she said jubilantly. "You boy die," she said in a whisper through pouty lips.

* * *

Blackwood wrapped the shoulder strap of his Mosin-Nagant 1891/30 sniper rifle around his forearm, slowly stretched himself across the hood of his T57 roadster, and leaned in to peer through the scope. His head automatically slipped into the perfect position, his target just floating in front of his vision. The luminescent reticle for low-light shooting cast an ominous crosshair.

His breathing slowed, calming him and tuning him to the rhythm of his heartbeat. Reality vanished as the image became his new reality, and a familiar intimacy between him and his target descended.

"Whoa," he said to himself.

Ruth had just knocked Vince cold with a single blow and was in a dangerous-looking argument with Zed. Things had quickly tilted in her favor: the witch still had the boy hidden in some mysterious other world, and now she had all three stone pieces.

"Do something," Blackwood said. "Don't let her escape."

Zed and Turq just sat there.

"Apparently, all talk," he sighed.

He watched the woman back away from the table and wave an arm. Suddenly, strange stray light appeared in his optics—something that gave the impression of a faint curtain of light next to the woman. Canting left and right slightly, he scrutinized the image, but the "curtain" was fixed in the room. Pulling his eye away from the scope, the aberration disappeared. He returned to the optics, and the strange image returned.

The tension in the little cabin escalated.

"Up to me," Blackwood said. He could only see Ruth from the waist up. "The good Lord gave you two elbows. I'm taking one." It would be a delicate shot, but at this range—with this weapon and her tiny frame—she could easily bleed out with any gunshot wound, taking with her any hope of getting Frankie back.

He held his breath. Time slowed.

Crosshairs followed the witch's right elbow. Blackwood's pulse tapped in his veins: whoosh-whoosh-whoosh.

The witch raised her hands over her head to dance.

Whoosh-whoosh-squeeze.

The weapon kicked, sound cracking into the distant dawn. The bullet grazed one of the mutton bars, and the entire window imploded, glass shards following the projectile's trajectory.

He re-sighted his target. The witch was angrily clutching her ear while blood poured down her right arm and chest.

"Hmm. A quarter-of-an-inch more, and the Yellowtail cabin would have gotten painted with a fresh coat of witch brain," he said.

Suddenly, the shape of Turq flew across his field of view, and there was a gunshot from inside the cabin. Ruth disappeared, and he saw Zed and Kenneth scrambling across the room together.

Blackwood set the sniper rifle in the driver's seat, grabbed his machine pistol, and ran up to the porch. He burst through the door, weapon scanning the room. Turq and the witch were wrestling on the floor. Vince, not far from them, was still unconscious. Zed and Kenneth were bent over Natasha on the floor.

Pistol in his right hand, Blackwood yanked the table away with his left, tipping it over and giving him a clear line of sight on Kenneth. "Drop it!" he yelled.

The big man dropped his gun like it was poison. His eyes were gushing, hands shaking. "I shot her. I shot her."

"I will help her. You help Totahmaa," the Native said to Blackwood in a calm tone that defied disobedience.

"Who?"

"The boy."

Blackwood assessed the struggle between the boy and the woman: it was even, though both fought for possession of the stones, rather than control of the contest. The witch's ear had been blown to pieces, ragged flesh dangled from her head, and the bleeding wound liberally lubricated the wood floor. "Stop!" he shouted, but neither responded. "Stop, or I'll shoot!"

Still, the two kept at it, so he approached them cautiously, eschewing their dangerously flailing legs. Suddenly, Ruth threw a stone fragment toward the middle of the room, and it simply vanished.

"I think she has some kind of portal open to the In-Between," Blackwood said.

"What?" Kenneth asked.

Zed looked up briefly, Natasha's blood all over his hands. He tersely said, "Stay away."

Then the second piece of stone went through the portal and vanished. The witch crawled toward the location of the invisible doorway, dragging a tenaciously clinging Turq. Blackwood maneuvered to cut off her escape, and he tried to stomp on her hands as she army-crawled across the slippery floor. Each time he struck, she jerked her hands to the side and avoided his heels. Finally, he tricked her and crushed one of her hands, trapping her—or so he hoped. Unfortunately, she grabbed the ankle of the offending leg and managed to throw him backward. It was as if a tiger had laid ahold of a ragdoll and tossed it.

With a "foomp" sound, Blackwood's world vanished. He was no longer in the cabin, but surrounded by and falling through the thick fog of the In-Between. Breathing was shallow and unproductive, leading to nausea and dizziness. Panic and fear—so generally foreign to him—clamped hard again to his soul for the second time in just a few hours. He wasn't a fan.

An immeasurable amount of time passed. Whether seconds, minutes, or hours, it was impossible to tell, but suddenly, a hand appearing in the fog broke the visual and chronological symmetry. Thrashing about and groping aimlessly, the gnarled ancient thing managed to clamp claw-like, thick, yellow fingernails around his right arm. The powerful grip flexed bones in his forearm, threatening to break them. Blood vessels ruptured beneath the skin as pain radiated up and down his arm, contorting his face in pain.

A moment later, a second hand appeared, quickly lashed out, and grabbed his shirt collar. A face followed: it was the witch—but not young and beautiful. Her skin was drawn and tight, a form-fitted, leathery mask partially covering a hideous skeleton face. A two-inch tear in her forehead revealed yellow-white bone underneath. The bright green eyes were dark—almost lifeless, sunk into deep sockets with blood vessels swollen, crisscrossing corneas like crimson spider webs. Her white, scaly scalp was bald save a few stray patches of dirty, yellow hair stained with mildew. The right ear was gone, the bleeding wound spraying floating droplets into the free space of this freefall environment.

"You!" she spat. Her ancient and putrid breath burned his nostrils and brought fresh waves of nausea. "Later. Later. Later for you I deal."

Then with a great jerk on both his shirt and his arm, which made a popping sound, she threw him out of the In-Between. There was motion, light, and then a crashing sound as he smashed against the upended kitchen table back in the Yellowtail cabin. Rolling to his side and crouching in a fetal position, he vomited and spat. Gulping at the air, his usual color returned to his face in a few seconds.

Once his equilibrium was restored—and the vomiting had passed—Turq and Zed bent over to examine him.

"Mr. Blackwood?" The boy placed a hand gently on his shoulder.

Blackwood blinked and said, "I think I'm okay." Attempting to roll to his side and stand suggested otherwise, however.

Zed held up a hand, palm outward, saying, "Do not get up so fast."

"What was it like?" Turq asked. Then: "Did you see Frankie?"

"What?" Blackwood said. "No. No, I didn't see your friend."

Turq looked disappointed.

Blackwood continued: "I'm sorry. It was . . . disorienting. There was a thick, wet fog. I was suffocating—even though I could breathe. I was falling. But not. It was like drowning." He looked from boy to man, confusion on his face. "There was no ground. No ground! How could there be no ground?"

"Calm yourself, Mr. Blackwood," said Zed, quietly. "Do not speak so much right now."

"Frankie was surrounded by fog," Kenneth said from across the room, where he still knelt beside Natasha.

Excruciating pain drilled into his brain, threatening his consciousness as he tried again to sit up. His right arm was powerless. After freezing for a moment, he switched his weight to his left arm. "I think my arm is broken," he panted, looking at his right arm.

The old Native approached the injured limb and looked thoughtful. "Here . . ." Gingerly, Zed touched up and down his arm, as if scanning or measuring something invisible. Bruising and swelling in the shape of talons were rapidly occurring at the site where the witch had grabbed his arm. His "medic" mumbled ancient chants and then stroked his arm with a red-tipped, yellow feather while chanting some more.

Surprised, Blackwood said, "My arm's gone numb."

"Be quiet, Mr. Blackwood," Turq said.

"Not broken. Badly damaged though." Zed frowned. "Your elbow is dislocated."

"Dislocated?"

"The bones are not fitting together right."

"I understand what it means. It will go back together," Blackwood said. "I'll just tough it out until it snaps back into place."

"No." Zed made motions with his arms and explained, "One bone here. One here. Like this. Should be here, like this."

Blackwood's own medical knowledge was limited to two areas: first, fixing minor injuries, and second, causing major injuries. This was a major injury to be fixed, and it was out of his league. "Can you do anything?"

"Yes. You want me to fix it?"

"Please do."

"Uh . . . Mr. Blackwood, I'm not so sure—" Kenneth was cut off by Zed's sudden motion.

The Native grabbed both the upper and lower parts of his arm with a firm grip, violently folding it, straightening it out, and then re-folding it rapidly.

There was a loud popping sound, and his world winked into blackness.

▼△▼△▼△▼△▼△▼△▼△▼△▼△▼

Stone Relief

December 23, 1177, In and Around Crooked Nose Great House

The sounds of chaos raging above gave the occupants of the first-floor apartment sufficient cause to flee in terror. They were long gone by the time a young woman, an older man, and an eight-foot-tall blue giant fell through the ceiling.

Rooshth jumped back as the floor gave way, barely escaping the fall and watching with shock as the others in Klanl Hivaht's apartment plunged below. Tenateh landed near the hearth, badly bruised but intact. The High Shaman was less fortunate and lay sprawled across the hearth on his back. His left leg twitched, and blood poured from the back of his head.

Churl-Chaac had landed on his feet, head and shoulders poking up through the hole in the floor. He reached for Rooshth, and she just had time to snatch the tablet at her feet. His iron grip locked around her waist, squeezing the wind out of her as he pulled her down to the first-level apartment. "I can fix this," she squeaked.

Unable to fit through the apartment doorway, the blue giant made his own exit. Chunks of rock, debris, and mortar exploded into the evening light of the courtyard as he kicked through the stone wall of the Great House. Children, dogs, and other curiosity seekers scattered like blowing seeds when he stepped through the new opening. He threw her over his shoulder and started to carry her toward the gate of the Great House, but then turned south, running across the courtyard and directly at the apartments built into the curved wall of the Great House's D shape. His speed was incredible, and he bounded easily over the apartments and the structure's wall.

He landed near some warriors that were attending a bunch of wounded and dead. They paused to stare and watch the great bluish man-thing. Other warriors had been on guard and started calling a shrill alarm as they gathered together in a defensive formation. Then the newly formed phalanx charged, their whistling and hooting echoing loudly throughout the canyon. Churl-Chaac cut a path parallel to the face of the Great House and then headed north through the canyon.

Slung over his shoulder, Rooshth bounced and shook, tightly gripping the stone tablet to her chest. Despite the uncomfortable jarring, she still felt intoxicated. "My son is the Rain God!" she said. "I will win you back, and we will be truly be unstoppable. We will rule the world!"

The two made quick progress up the canyon as shadows started spreading across the canyon floor. They passed numerous Great Houses and other buildings, as well as crowds of people carrying traveling bundles—some even had loaded travois strapped to scrawny dogs. She had the impression of witnessing a mass exodus.

Above the organized chaos of human flight, a *quetz'al* flew up and down the canyon, bellowing an alarm. "Come down here, you foul thing, and I will show you something to be alarmed about," Rooshth said, shaking her fist at them from her upside-down vantage.

Churl-Chaac hurtled an obstacle, jarring Rooshth's body and knocking the wind out of her again. Once she caught her breath, she told him, "You are a monster now. No one will want to be near you."

The cadence of his running slowed slightly.

"Just like always: I alone love you. You need me. I need you."

His running sped up.

"The girl was alive, you know. You abandoned her."

His running slowed.

"We could go back for her. Maybe she could forgive you."

He stopped.

"Yes. Let us go back. Get her. Grab her. She might still love you."

He slowly turned back toward the south.

"Yes," she said soothingly. "Think about it."

Distant movement in the fading light caught her eye as she looked north. People were advancing on them—lots of people. In a tight formation. With purpose. By twisting her body around and straining to lift her head, she was able to see them better. Armed with bows, arrows, spears, and knives, they were led by a crazy-looking woman screaming commands.

Some of the archers had already planted and released a volley.

Rooshth looked up in the air, just in time to see a cloud of arrows disappearing from out of the sunlight above into the shadow of the canyon, an invisible death about to rain on them. "Churl!" she screamed. "Run! Run! Run now!"

Like all human beings, instead of running, Churl-Chaac turned around.

At that exact moment, nearly twenty arrows peppered him from head to toe. They hit armor and flesh, most of them harmlessly scratching him and bouncing away. One arrow, however, buried itself into his left cheek. Screaming, he reeled backward, dropping both her and his axe. He clutched at his face, pulled at the arrow, and with a loud roar, dislodged the flint arrowhead from cheekbone.

She hadn't escaped injury either; one arrow lodged shallowly in her right hamstring, and another went through-and-through her left calf, arrowhead on one side and fletching on the other. She screamed and tried to flail around in a panic, but every movement was excruciating. By arching her back, she was just able to reach the arrow in her hamstring. Huffing and grunting three times, she jerked it free on the third time. Touching the other arrow brought paralyzing pain, so she left it alone.

A second volley of arrows arched at them. Her son dove to cover her. On hands and knees, his giant form shielded her tiny body. Most of the arrows missed them or simply bounced off the armor on his back, but one struck home in the bottom of his right foot.

Under the cover of her massive son, she shook violently with rage, screaming in frustration and pounding a fist against the ground. Then twisting her torso around to face her son, she reached up and touched his massive chest, amazed. Responding to her touch, he looked down into her face, blood flowing from the gaping wound in his face. Instead of loving eyes adoring a mother, only hate-filled orbs looked down on her.

The crazy-sounding woman screamed some commands.

Warriors flanked left and right to form a circle around her and Churl-Chaac. Archers planted and drew bows while those with spears took various aggressive stances. They were obviously well-trained, disciplined, and battle-hardened. Their leader crossed into the circle of warriors and bent down to peer at Rooshth underneath her son. Then the woman stood, pointed an authoritative finger at Churl-Chaac, and commanded him to do something. (It appeared that she thought Rooshth was a hostage.)

"Let me up, fool," Rooshth barked, but her son didn't. So she wiggled and scooted free, getting to her feet with great effort. The arrow sticking through her calf made her wobbly, and she hobbled mostly on one foot, each step nearly bringing her to tears. Despite her physical condition, she stood proud, bowed slightly to Sheweh, and then bent over to grab the *Shat'kuh Mongeweh*.

This triggered something in the commander, who began pointing furiously at Rooshth and yelling commands. The warriors locked their spears against their hips, points set forward menacingly, deadly. They slowly shrank the circle, one step at a time.

Churl-Chaac picked up his ax and stood, crushing the arrow in his foot.

The commander shouted, and the warriors stopped. Then she tried to talk to Rooshth, signing with her hands. Outlining the shape of the sacred stone, she then laid her hands out flat, as if accepting a gift.

Rooshth shook her head, crazy silver-white hair dancing. "You must be a bigger fool than my son if you think—"

The leader of the warriors angrily repeated the gesture, stomping her foot for emphasis.

Holding the stone up, Rooshth waved it back and forth, yelling, "Come get it, primitive canyon whore."

The "whore" barked at an underling, who then quickly turned his spear around with a snap and handed her the butt end. She took it and made thrusting motions toward Rooshth, each one bringing the flint spearhead gradually closer. After half a dozen or so "stabs," she repeated the hand gesture of asking for the stone.

Rooshth set her jaw and ground her teeth. "Oh, I understand. But it is not going to happen." Growling, she bent down, face wincing and twitching, and broke the arrow sticking from her calf and pulled it out. Despite the pain, she locked eyes with the warrior woman the whole time. Standing upright and defiant, she tossed away the arrow fragments with a huff.

Then she started to recite the incantation.

Yelling orders, the commander thrust a spear at her while the warriors charged Churl-Chaac. She turned away, easily deflecting the woman's strike.

Just at that moment, her son swung his ax in a big, full circle, and a great squall of wind and rain emanated from it. The torrent shoved the warriors back, sending them staggering for balance. Several dropped their weapons, trying to shield their eyes.

Rooshth jumped up and down, feeling suddenly giddy.

Then Churl-Chaac lifted the ax straight up over his head, shouting angry, vile words that Rooshth herself couldn't recognize. The air crackled, and the ground shook violently while a brilliant flash blinded them all and knocked them back to the ground. It took a few seconds for her to recover her sight, but when she did, many of the warriors lay dead, their skin black and scorched. Two were curled up in the dirt, clutching burns and wailing.

Her son raised his ax again. Another blinding flash and explosive sound filled the air as lightning shot from the ax again, scorching the ground in a great, long zigzag that ran from him to one of the Great Houses nearby. The flash from this second bolt lit up the darkening canyon, revealing more warriors lying motionless on the ground, and still more near-fatally injured. In the distance, sections of a Great House could be seen to have collapsed during the first lightning strike.

Rooshth clapped and bounced, her eyes moist with maternal pride.

The remaining warriors bunched up, regrouping in an attack formation. One of them commanded the obviously suicidal charge, and they attacked in unison, bravery shorn up with battle cries of shrill yips and trills.

As Churl-Chaac raised his weapon a third time, Rooshth suddenly had the feeling of something missing. "Where did that foul canyon whore—"

She turned to face the sound of rushing footsteps. The warrior woman lunged at her, driving the spear through her rib cage, out the other side, and into her blue giant.

Mother and son were tightly pinned together by the spear. As Churl-Chaac struggled, Rooshth shook and spun, each movement excruciating. She gripped the shaft of the spear for dear life, trying to minimize her own motion.

The commander pulled a flint dagger from her belt and lunged at the pair. Churl-Chaac spun to his left, dodging the attack and also dislodging the spearhead that bound him to his mother. He stumbled, dropping the axe. Rooshth fell away to the right, cringing on the ground where she landed, barely able to move. Her breaths came in shallow spurts and gurgles.

The handful of charging warriors pounced on the blue giant, bringing him to the ground and stabbing at him with their knives. Churl-Chaac's blood made him slippery, and the warriors could not hold him down. Rising to his feet, he easily shook them off. Two warriors were killed when he spun around with a stiff arm the size of a tree branch. The remaining warriors recovered their spears and started thrusting at him. One or two strikes landed, but nothing sufficient to slow him.

Getting to her feet, Rooshth helplessly watched as the warrior woman grabbed a spear and swung it by the butt end, slicing her blue behemoth across the back of a knee with the flint spearhead. Taut ligaments and tendons popped like cut bow strings, and her son fell to one knee, screaming in pain, his roar shaking the ground.

The warriors jumped her son again and began to gain the upper hand. One or two deep thrusts had hit their mark, and his strength was fading.

She saw the stone tablet lying on the ground a few feet away and despaired; the short distance might as well be miles and miles away. She touched the spear jutting from her chest and gingerly probed the entry wound. The weapon had gone through the lower lobe of her left lung, missing vital organs and major blood vessels. Instead of dying immediately, death would come slowly and excruciatingly as she drowned in her own blood, conscious until her final breath.

"Or not," she spat angrily, staring at the *Shat'kuh Mongeweh* lying just out of her reach.

An involuntarily scream came out of her mouth as she scooted across the ground in the fetal position. Every movement brought nearly overwhelming pain. Twice she almost fainted. Finally, the tablet was within reach. She paused to breathe, but the sounds of her son's struggle urged her forward, and despite her body's protests, she stretched out her arms and grabbed the stone. Gasping and gurgling, she began to recite the words.

The black mists again returned to her, numbering more and more with each word of the incantation. They swarmed her, and she begged them not to die, to be whole. Carefully, she grasped the bloody shaft and pulled the spear through her chest while she recited. Pull, scream, a word, pant, pull, scream, another word, more panting, and so it went. When the shaft was free, she said, "Churl . . ."

Blood poured from the spear wounds. She was weak, faint, nauseous, and cold—barely able to finish the incantation. Curled up in a ball, tears streaming from her eyes, the contrast between her silver-white hair and the crimson of her own blood caught her attention. She stroked her hair, saying, "So pretty." Closing her eyes, she said, "A little rest, I think."

Then, within her, there was a loud snapping and popping sound.

Rooshth's eyes sprung open wide. Arching her back, she screamed as fire burst through her chest and engulfed her. Yellow and orange flames covered her body, burning her—yet not consuming her. Just as suddenly, it all stopped.

With the sounds of the ongoing battle crashing down around her, Rooshth sat up, mobile, energized and healed.

Churl-Chaac was still embroiled in his life-or-death struggle. All but two warriors were dead or dying. They circled him, staggering and exhausted but still intent. As he got up from all fours, they made feeble jabs at him, which he easily blocked and evaded.

Maddeningly, the warrior woman grabbed another spear and charged Rooshth, who simply ducked and kicked from below, sending her rolling and tumbling sideways. The warrior rolled to her back and kicked her legs, expertly kipping into a fighting stance between Churl-Chaac and Rooshth. Suddenly, murderous determination flared in her eyes, and she spun and leaped, driving her spear at the blue giant.

"No!" Rooshth screamed, thrusting the tablet out toward him. "Preserve him forever!"

Without even reciting the incantation, the black mist appeared, swarming Churl-Chaac and the commander. It buzzed and hummed but had arrived too late; the warrior's deadly thrust went true. The giant raised up on tiptoes as the spearhead found its mark deep in his heart. After a strangely whimper-like scream, he fell to the ground in a crumpled heap with the warrior woman lying across him. The mist continued its swirling magic around the pair.

"No, no, no, no, no!" Rooshth cried. "He must stay forever!"

The canyon fell strangely silent for a moment as the black mist evaporated.

Sheweh's body lay fallen across Churl-Chaac, still grasping her spear. The wooden shaft stood almost vertically: butt end pointing to the darkening sky, business end buried deep into the blue giant's chest cavity. Neither figure moved.

Rooshth broke the silence with a yell that rose from deep within the core of her being. The surviving warriors also screamed as they fled in panic.

The warrior and the Rain God had been turned to stone.

□ ■ □ ■ □ ■ □ ■ □ ■ □

Resurrection

JUNE 21, 1938, SEVERAL MILES SOUTH OF YELLOWTAIL CABIN, CHACO CANYON

For the second time in his centuries-long life, Zed rode in an automobile. "I do not think these will catch on," he said to C. J. Blackwood.

"What you think of Italian craftsmanship, Zed?" Vince asked from the rumble seat.

"It is everything to be expected."

"Indeed. Indeed," the Italian proudly said, not catching the subtle slight.

Zed studied Blackwood's recently dislocated elbow: it was swollen and red. With his right hand resting palm up in his lap, the man drove the T57 with his knees and left arm, still managing to shift quickly and smoothly. Fortunately, the mostly straight, little gravel road seemed easy to navigate, though it was plagued with wicked washboards and the occasional cantaloupe-sized chunk of rock.

"Only couple more miles, Mr. Blackwood," Vince said.

Zed thought of Natasha, resting comfortably back at the cabin. Had his son been a moment slower at jumping the witch, Kenneth would have shot him, instead of her. Under their curse of Eternal Life, the two of them healed extraordinarily quickly. Turq would have merely winced and kept going. As it was, Zed had to spend precious time and energy digging the bullet out of Natasha's arm and then stitching and bandaging her. He looked down at his hands and rubbed off more dried blood.

Kenneth and Turq were in the Ford, leading the way. The truck slowed and stopped in the middle of the road. Blackwood stopped the car as doors flew open on both sides of the truck. Its occupants jumped out and jogged back to the roadster.

"I will go up to see if she is already there," Turq said.

Blackwood started to protest, but Zed held up a hand. "Believe me, Blackwood. He is the best choice. Fast, clever, and well-trained."

Turq gave a not-in-front-of-my-friends look that preteens and teens have been giving parents ever since there were preteens and teens. Zed sighed, having seen this look more times than the average parent. "Go, my son."

His boy ran perpendicular to the road several hundred yards and then cut south, moving parallel to it. In just a few seconds, he was barely discernible among the backdrop of the wild scrub and dirt.

"Oh my . . ." Blackwood said.

"I knew he was athletic, but this beats the hell out of all," said Kenneth.

Vince scratched his head. "Holy Mother! How such a thing possible?"

"I've nearly given up on what I consider to be possible or impossible in the last twenty-four hours," Blackwood said.

"Sounds wise," said Vince.

Somewhat distant and with a small smile, Zed said, "He has certain . . . gifts."

Kenneth cleared his throat and asked, "So, Rain God Rock is really named after a real Rain God?"

Zed climbed over the passenger door and hopped out of the car. "Yes and no," he said, twisting his feet in the dirt and pounding it with his toes. "Her son was deformed and weak; the witch used the power of the *Shat'kuh Mongehweh* to try to make him stronger. Unfortunately, she could not control the evil spirits that sought to hijack the power of the sacred tablet for their own amusement. These *Ahteh Shat'tohl* appear as black mists and turn one's words inside-out, twisting them. They transformed her son into a real-life likeness of the Rain God of the south—complete with thunder axe, which you," he pointed to Blackwood, "saw her wield against the demon-goddess, Ixtab."

"Okay," Blackwood said. "Magic gone wrong. Boy transformed."

"As a god, he must have been spectacular—everything she would want in a perfect man," Kenneth said.

"*Sí.*"

"You're thinking about Greek gods, gentlemen," Blackwood said soberly.

Zed nodded. "True. The Mayan Rain God has the face of a wild tapir, blue skin with scales, and stands over eight feet tall. An impressive figure and terrifying warrior but less than desirable for one's child," he explained.

Vince scanned an imaginary, giant warrior standing next to him. "*Mama mia.*"

Blackwood lifted an eyebrow quizzically. "He died at the little outcrop named for him?"

"Not exactly."

The men looked confused.

"Not *at* the outcrop. He *is* the outcrop. Rooshth tried to save him when Sheweh Du'hat, my friend, landed a fatal blow with her spear."

Kenneth said solemnly, "He must have been a brave and skilled warrior to take down such a fierce, god-like enemy."

"Yes, *she* was," he said, memories pulling him somewhere else for a moment.

Vince gently put a hand on Zed's shoulder and asked, "She was the boy's mother? Your wife?"

The ridiculous notion made Zed burst out laughing. "No, just a dear friend. Turq's mother died in the winter before her forty-third summer. She lived old and lived well." Then he continued his story: "Somehow—though only the witch knows—both her son and Sheweh (my friend) were turned to stone. I have long thought that probably the *Ahteh Shat'tohl* tricked her once again—but with fatal results."

"Can't she use the tablet to change him back into flesh?" Kenneth asked.

"Yes, but he would just be that: animated flesh. She thinks that she can use the Vital Force that binds Frankie's soul to his body in order to then bind her son's soul back his body."

Blackwood tilted his head to the side. "Will that work?"

Zed shook his head. "It will not work. Her son's soul would have to be close. And the boy would need to want to re-inhabit a fleshly body. Both these necessary conditions are unlikely. Her son's soul is far away in a much better place, and I am sure it is peaceful and happy. Why come back?"

"Will the tablet have power while it's broken?" Blackwood asked.

"No."

"So, she have to reunite pieces first," Vince said.

"Will there be some time when she's vulnerable? As she puts the pieces together?" Blackwood asked.

"She will be distracted, yes. However, she cannot make the tablet whole again. Only the power of our gods can that. When we get the pieces, I believe the gods will do such a thing and take Totahmaa and me to our ancestors. The tablet reunites, then we reunite." Looking toward the horizon, he said, "Where is that boy?"

*　　*　　*

Tuhj flew in lazy circles, gaining and losing altitude alternately. The sun warmed his skin, and the cool, high-altitude air chilled it.

His favorite pastime for the past few decades had been "people spying:" making imaginary reconnaissance missions for himself and carrying out fake attacks. If he was alone and far from observation, he would even do low-altitude runs and dives involving spitting (and flaming) different targets. Once, he flamed an outhouse, taking great pleasure in seeing the occupant run for his life, surprised, with pants dragging around his ankles. Luckily, only Turq had learned about the burned outhouse, and he had kept it private from Zed—though more than a few rides and errands were required to buy the boy's silence.

The canyon filled with people as it did with sunshine. The populace reflected anticipation of the day: bright, eager, promising, hopeful. They arrived on foot—both human and equine—and they arrived in cars and trucks, the stench of which fouled his nose with an acrid, numbing odor. Soaring higher, to escape the exhaust, the menagerie of human color mingled below: dark and darker, light and lighter, white and whiter. Many wore elaborate costumes of animals, shamans, or human-sized *kachinas*. One was dressed as *Kokopelli*—the legendary figure based on his master.

The flyer looked back toward the Yellowtail cabin. Master would want to know if the witch had emerged from the In-Between, and what she was up to, so he reluctantly circled back toward the little two-room home. The truck and the car were gone.

Oops, he sang.

Tuhj scanned paved roads, dirt roads, and gravel paths. In a just few seconds, he spotted Zed a few miles farther south of the cabin, standing with some people near both vehicles, and Turq was running toward them. As the boy arrived at the men, a large dust devil a short ways off caught Tuhj's eye. Generally, such common sights disinterested the centuries-long desert dweller, but this one was different: it had erupted at dawn, and it didn't wander with the wind.

Kachina? he pondered aloud, thinking the whirlwind might be a dangerous desert spirit.

He flew over to investigate.

Not Kachina. Worse.

*　　*　　*

Sitting inside swirling walls of dust, Frankie Yellowtail looked around, disoriented and confused. Flying debris obscured his view of the terrain outside the whirlwind. There was a large, gray boulder inside the tornado-like enclosure.

"What h-happened to the fog and r-rain?" Frankie asked nobody. He remembered dreaming about the Babe and awakening in several inches of water. There had been the strange arrival of a baseball. He closed his eyes and pressed his fists against the sides of his head, grinding them against his temples, trying to squeeze memory out of his brain. A quiet groan escaped his lips as more recollections dribbled out. "Stone. Pretty, blonde woman. Giant, naked woman. Fighting. Mr. Blackwood."

His eyes popped open, wide with anxiety, and his gaze tossed left and right while he scrambled backward, crablike, until bumping up against the boulder. Touching and examining the large, gray stone in the dust-red light, he said, "This is R-rain God Rock." He passed both hands across a larger portion of the surface and looked at the outcrop sideways. "S-something's different."

Then he smiled. "I'm back in the c-canyon!" Bringing the mysterious baseball out of his pocket and cradling it gently with both hands, he explained the situation to it: "We are b-back in the canyon. That's g-good. We should w-wait here until M-mother or Turq finds us. N-now don't b-be afraid, okay?"

The ball was "okay" with this, and Frankie gave it a reassuring pat.

"Who you talk to?" came a woman's voice.

Startled, Frankie wheeled around, hiding the ball behind his back. Ruth stood there, still pretty but somehow worn and plainer—a little ragged around the edges.

"N-no one. J-just me."

She held three chunks of stone in her right arm and a stone ax in the other. She walked around the rock, approached him, and set the stone fragments on the ground. "I need your help, Frankie," she said calmly.

"O-Oh?"

"Yes. You remember I save life?"

"You d-did?"

"Yes." She nodded. "Evil she-giant try kill you, but I stop her with axe." She held the ancient weapon up as evidence. "Whoosh!" she said, re-enacting the slice that nearly cleaved the goddess in two.

"R-right." He actually couldn't remember, but she seemed so sure that he thought she must be right.

She set the ax down, business end on the ground, butt leaning against the rock. Patting the outcrop gently, she said, "I need introduce you someone."

"Oh?"

"This," she said, stroking the rock, "this my son. Name is Chur Keleh. Means 'beautiful one' in language of my people."

Frankie examined the rock carefully, with new eyes. The whirlwind apparently had scrubbed away thick layers of red New Mexico dirt. Now an ancient, weathered statue carved from smooth, gray stone seemed obvious. There were arms, a chest, legs, and some kind of animal head. "How did he g-get turned into r-rock? He's l-like a statue."

"No matter. I love him and want him back."

He ran his hands along the shape, confirming what his eyes told him. On the back side, he encountered another shape: a smaller human—a statue on the statue. "What is this?"

"Oh, she kill him."

Jerking his hands back and pressing them to his body, he asked, "How? He's stone."

Her face twisted up in anger. "He not stone when run through with spear. After. Then make stone. Both."

"Why did she kill him?"

"Evil woman. She hate son because," she paused, stifling tears, "because he different. She hate him because he different." Turning away from him, she wiped a tear from her cheek.

Frankie stood straighter, taller, and felt his face go red. "Other children m-make fun of me," he said. "They s-say I talk f-funny. They like to trick me and b-be mean." He shook his head. "But no one ever killed me. That was evil."

She pouted at him. "You help me?"

"Y-yes," he said, putting fists on his hips, eager to be the hero.

"See stones?"

"Yes."

"They need put together, as one large tablet," she said.

"How w-will you do that?"

"I need like glue."

"Elmer's g-glue?"

"No," she answered. "Frankie's glue."

"I d-don't have any glue," he said, shaking his head.

"Yes. You have glue," she said, as if she just had the most brilliant idea in the world. "If we glue stone back together, I can bring boy back—make flesh. You and he be friends. Make play and fun."

"Me and Churl and T," he said, mind buzzing with possibilities. "We could be The Three Stooges of the Canyon."

Ruth smiled broadly. "Could be."

"H-how do I have the g-glue?"

"Now, I tell. You promise be brave?"

He kneaded his hands and took a half-step away from her. "How b-brave?"

"Brave like you friend Native boy."

"Turq?" He looked at the ground and said, "I d-don't know." Then, looking back to her, he said earnestly, "T's the bravest person I know." And he meant it.

"He always protect you?"

"Yes."

"He brave to help you?"

"Y-yes."

She stiffened her back and stood a little taller.

Frankie did the same.

"Now, you be brave," she said. "Help Churl. Make Totahmaa proud how brave you can be," she said.

"Who?"

"I mean Turq. Make Turq proud."

He kneaded his hands more aggressively as his mental and emotional gears turned and ground against each other. "Yes," he announced. "I w-will be b-brave. As brave as T."

"Good," she said, smiling and patting him on the head. "Stand up. Hold out hands."

He did as he was told. Suddenly, she thrust an obsidian knife into his right hand, maneuvered to his side, enclosed the knife-holding hand with her own right hand, and grabbed his left arm above the wrist.

"Hey!" he protested, fighting against her grip. She was much stronger than she looked.

"Be brave, boy!" she yelled. Then with one deft move, she forced his right hand to slash his left wrist, cutting delicate blue veins.

He went into panic-induced spasms. Mouth agape and unable to breathe, he looked at the slash across his wrist. Blood pulsed from the wound and pooled inside his palm. Crimson life flowed down his fingers in rivulets, dribbling to the ground. He collapsed against her, knees buckled, feeling dizzy and nauseous.

"Good, boy!" she said, holding him up. "You were brave! More brave than your friend."

His head cleared for a moment, and he said, "You're j-just like them. You're mean. You're a b-b-bully."

"Oh," she said, "do not worry about that." She beamed at him proudly, saying, "I much worse than bully."

"You p-probably hurt your own boy—turned Ch-Churl to stone yourself."

She shook him violently and then released his right arm and twisted him around and down to the ground with his left arm. "Release knife. Now grab stone," she commanded, pointing to a nearby piece.

He obeyed. As he held the piece, she dribbled his blood along the edges—as if applying glue from his gash.

"Drop. Get next."

"Glue" was applied to the next piece.

When the third piece was finally done, she released him. His right hand immediately went to the deep wound on his left wrist. He stumbled away from her, feeling faint and sick again.

Ruth crouched in the dirt, bent over the three pieces. Suddenly shouting harsh-sounding words in a strange language, she stood and spun around to face him, a piece of stone in each hand. Walking slowly toward him, she pressed the two pieces together and then pulled them apart repeatedly. "You 'glue' not work. Must get 'glue' straight from heart, boy! More potent there."

He retreated, fell, and scooted across the dirt. On the ground, he felt vulnerable and weak. The blinding, spinning wall of dust hemmed him in from behind.

Despite her size, she crossed the space to him in just a few steps. As she towered over him, she said, "We try again. Harder this time." Then she struck him in the side of the head with one of the tablet pieces, and the world went black.

Dark Savior

June 21, 1938, Rain God Rock, Chaco Canyon

C. J. Blackwood opened the trunk of the T57 and lifted a floor panel, revealing an arsenal.

Vince Nesci whistled. Kenneth McKinney pushed his hat back and rested a boot on the bumper, getting a closer look. Turq, who had returned a few minutes prior, craned his neck to look in the trunk as he stood alongside the car.

Zed smirked, saying, "Those will not help against the witch."

"Perhaps not," said Blackwood. "I suspect that we will need your powerful magic in order to subdue her, but if she is successful in raising her son, then we will need everything available to take down an eight-foot-tall warrior-god with a magic axe."

The two other Caucasians nodded at his wisdom and made their choice: the Italian took a shotgun with a small box of shells, and Kenneth chose the same rifle that had earlier taken the witch's ear.

"That's bolt action, Kenneth. Would you prefer something else?"

"No," Kenneth answered. "This one looks damn lucky. Besides, I've got a real sidearm as a backup."

Vince looked up from inspecting his choice and gave Kenneth a look, mumbling, "Right. Someday . . ."

Kenneth smiled.

"Zed, would you like a weapon?" Blackwood asked.

"I am already armed," the Native answered enigmatically.

"What about me?" asked Turq.

"Have you ever used a gun?" Blackwood asked.

"No."

"Now's not a good time to learn," Kenneth said.

"How hard can it be?" came the protest. "Just point that end and pull the trigger."

"In principle," Kenneth answered. "In practice, there's a little more to it."

"Really? Such as?" asked the boy.

"Well," Kenneth started, "these things have a kick."

"Kick? What's a kick?" Turq asked defiantly, as if Kenneth were making things up. "It has no legs. How can it kick?"

Zed interjected, "Totahmaa. This is not the time. You are master of your weapons. Merely think it, and spear or arrow goes where you will."

Turq crossed his arms and cast his eyes down, silently fuming.

"Besides," Blackwood said, placing a hand on the boy's shoulder, "you may need to help your father with the magic."

The boy shot him a cold look and shrugged off the hand.

Blackwood cleared his throat and turned to the rest of the group. "Obviously, we should approach this whirlwind with caution. Perhaps, since the witch is using it to hide, she can't see out of it very well. I think we should be able to drive all the way up to the Rock without detection."

"She has ways of knowing without seeing," the older Native said.

"We'll have to risk it. Hopefully, she'll be distracted with her own activities."

*　　*　　*

Tuhj gained altitude and prepared for an attack dive that would bring centuries of waiting to a conclusion.

The dust devil below him appeared as a mere dot—the two people inside even smaller. Rolling onto his back, Tuhj flipped tail-up and began his dive. Air rushed past his face, filling his nose with cold air. Secondary eyelids protected his vision from small particles and wind-chafing. With wings folded, his tail was his rudder.

The random noise of the turbulence formed a bubble of around him, rendering his hearing useless. His peripheral vision, however, became enhanced at these extreme speeds. The world became an infinite horizon spanning the circle of the earth. The sky was clear, and the morning sun quickly shortened the shadows in the canyon below.

In seconds, the shape of the boy lying across the boulder was clear. The witch had tied him up and was waving a dagger over his naked chest. Despite her wild chanting and screaming, the boy lay still, apparently oblivious to her evil incantations and his plight.

Tuhj stretched out his body, becoming longer and skinnier to reduce his wind profile even further. His wings twitched, prepared to pop open.

The witch raised her obsidian weapon high above the child, standing on tiptoes for maximum speed and force of impact. Just at that moment, Frankie became alert, terror carved into his face as he made a fruitless struggle against his bonds.

Thunder detonated as Tuhj's wing membranes vibrated with earth-shattering magnitude. Turbulence from the breaking action ripped the dust-devil apart, leaving all three of them engulfed in a cloud of blinding dust. Tuhj alone could see—thanks to his nictitating membranes. He gently grabbed the boy with a claw and lowered him from the rock, placing him opposite the witch. Then he grabbed her by the left leg—in a very ungentle manner—and leaped into the air.

She was wily and almost escaped his grasp once, so Tuhj adjusted his grip, squeezing hard. At this point, most victims would have passed out from the pain or died from internal hemorrhaging. The woman screamed and pushed and railed against his grip, and at one point, she bit hard into his talons, causing him more amusement than anything else. As he gained altitude, he grabbed one of her arms with his free talon, and then he pulled his legs in opposite directions, trying to rip her in half.

What would have easily killed larger prey was only making her angrier.

Annoyed, he released her.

She fell and tumbled through the air while he cruelly dove below her. He came up and collided with her. The impact cast her upward, increasing the violence of her tumble. Circling her as she plummeted again, he swatted her with talons and tail alternately, batting her up and letting her fall. Despite the ferocity of the midair beating, whenever they locked eyes, she pierced him with a single-minded hate.

You will fear me, he sang. *I will break your soul, and I will break your body.*

Again, he went under her and rose to swat her with his tail, but this time she grabbed it. Tuhj shook his tail, spun, and flipped, but nothing would shake her off.

Her weight compromised his steering, and the new center of mass made his flight unstable, creating dangerous navigation problems with the ground only seconds away. A few powerful strokes bought him several hundred feet of extra altitude (and time). Reaching between his legs, he tried to grab her with his beak. She was just within reach, but the tumbling and turbulence made it impossible for him to get a decent lock on her. Twice, he almost snagged her but had to let go in order to restore altitude.

Very well, witch. So be it, he sang.

Folding his wings, he accelerated toward the ground once again. The earth approached more rapidly than usual due to the higher terminal velocity brought on by extra weight of the witch. Suddenly, his eyes went wide, and he glanced back to the tip of his right wing.

The tips of his wings extended beyond his tail, and when he folded up for the dive, the witch switched from tail to wing.

With her knife, she stabbed and slashed at his flight webbing.

* * *

A few minutes earlier, Turq and the men stood around Blackwood's car. They all startled at Tuhj's thunder and watched the whirlwind explode into nothingness.

"Frankie! Frankie!" Turq said, running toward Rain God Rock. In moments, he arrived. "Are you okay?"

Frankie was terrified, in shock, and in pain. His feet were tied with thin leather cords, and his wrists were bound with a bloody silk scarf.

"She c-cut me, Turq. She i-is evil."

"More evil than you can imagine, my friend," he said, hugging him tightly.

"Untie me, T."

Turq cut through the bindings and said, "Let me see where she cut you." After a quick inspection, he called back to his father, "Father? Father, Frankie's been cut."

Zed ran to them and bent down to examine Frankie's wrist. "The bleeding has mostly stopped. That is good." He smiled at Frankie, saying, "She kept you alive by binding your wrists so tight. She is evil but not too smart. Lucky you." Turq and his father exchanged a knowing look: she had wanted him alive in order to remove his still-beating heart.

"Yes. L-lucky me," Frankie echoed.

"Does it hurt much, Frankie?" Zed asked.

"Yes. It h-hurts a lot. I w-want to go see Mother."

Zed wrapped the injured wrist back in the scarf and said, "Frankie, hold this very tight for a while. Understand?"

"I understand. Can I s-see Mother?"

Then his father felt up and down Frankie's arm with his fingers, squeezing here and there. "Better?"

"Y-yes. Thanks."

The three white men ran up to the Rock.

"Frankie! You okay, boy?" Vince asked, shotgun hanging down at his side.

"Y-yes, sir. I w-want to see Mother!"

Kenneth scanned the horizon, saying, "Soon, Frankie. We need to wait just a minute. Where did the woman go?"

Blackwood pointed up into the sky. "Uhm. There."

Turq looked up to see Tuhj beating and tossing the witch around like a shuttlecock in a sadistic badminton match, battering her mercilessly.

"No one could live through that," Kenneth said.

"She will," Zed said, disgust edging his voice.

"What in God's name is that?" Vince asked.

"It's a d-dragon. He c-came down from heaven to rescue m-me. Right, T?"

Turq smiled. "Close enough, Frankie."

"His name," said Blackwood, "is Tuhj."

"Oh," the Italian said, like he'd been missing something.

Turq's father gathered the three pieces of stone and cleaned them carefully, removing all traces of Frankie's blood, while the others watched the lopsided battle above.

One of the men gasped and pointed.

His father stood and shook his head, saying, "Oh no."

The witch clung to Tuhj's tail, who had started a power dive, obviously thinking that he could shake her loose by popping his wings. However, she had switched her hold, latching onto one of his wings.

"What's she doing?" Vince asked.

"She is destroying that wing," his father answered solemnly. "This will kill him."

Tuhj began spinning, and suddenly the witch released her grip, tumbling free toward the earth. Both were dropping fast.

"Come on!" Turq cried to the flyer. Their *quetz'al* had only moments to pull out into a glide path. With luck, he might have some chance of surviving.

But Tuhj continued to spin, out of control.

"No, no, no, no!" yelled Turq, starting to run toward the impact point, but his father held him back.

"What's h-happening?" Frankie asked.

"Damn dragon's gonna crash," Kenneth said.

"Oh dear," Frankie said with sincerity. "I was h-hoping to m-meet him. I've n-never met a dragon before. T, have you ever met a dragon?"

Turq didn't answer. He stared, frozen in horror and despair as Tuhj quit struggling, body limp, wings whipping chaotically in turbulence.

The witch hit the ground first, her body bouncing several feet into the air. Moments later, Tuhj did not bounce but crumbled like an egg striking the kitchen floor. His body cavity split open, and bones were pulverized under the force of the impact.

Blackwood, Kenneth, and Vince started walking toward the fallen body of the witch.

Turq balled his fists and looked at his father, who suddenly looked like a weary, old man with tears streaming down his face.

Breaking away from his father's grasp, Turq grabbed his spear and ran to the fallen *quetz'al*. Grasping their longtime family friend around the massive head, his own tears flowed in great rivers and sobs. He ran his hands over the cracks and splinters in Tuhj's beak while memories flooded his mind and emotions ran wild; grief and anger battled for dominance. Turning to eye the witch, who lay mostly still on the ground about fifty yards away, anger gained the upper hand and became rage. He yelled, "Why should evil live while good dies?"

Screaming a blood-curdling war cry, Turq ran full-speed at the unconscious woman, pushing the white men out of the way. Somewhere behind him, his father's voice called, but the words couldn't penetrate his blood-lust. When he reached Ruth, he raised his spear high over his head and drove the sharp flint tip down into her chest with all his might. It punctured her sternum, broke ribs across her back, and lodged in the soft ground underneath her.

The woman's eyes popped open, and she grabbed the spear with two hands. She struggled against the weapon and cursed at him in an ancient language, vehement hatred gushing from her lips like a flooding arroyo.

"Get out of the way!" Vince called.

"We can't get a clean shot," said Blackwood.

Turq ignored them and pushed the spear deeper into the ground, pinning the witch firmly. After pulling his dagger, he knelt down next to her head, tilting it to the side, and bracing it against the ground with his knee.

"You," he said in a language they once shared, "will now go to join your son in the emptiness beyond this world. I hope you wander in desolation, searching for but never finding him. He will flee your evil presence forever."

Her eyes went wild, and she screamed as he brought the knife to her neck. Then suddenly, she became quiet and limp, giving him pause.

"I have been here before, boy," she said with a curious smile.

Suddenly wary, he looked down.

She had gripped the shaft of the spear and jerked it free from her body. The bloody stone point hovered inches above the gaping wound in her chest.

Immediately, he went to slash her throat, but she jabbed the tip of the spear into his foot before he could cut her.

Turq dropped the knife and pulled the spearhead out. Rolling to his side, he grasped his ankle and screamed. A greenish-black color was spreading around the wound slowly and running up the veins of his leg. Blisters formed on his skin over the tainted veins.

The witch stood and grimaced at the men with guns. They unloaded on her, only managing to stoke her wrath further. She waved her arms in circles out to her side, spun around, and "threw" a gust of dust, dirt, ice, and snow at them. The burst of debris hit the men, sending them sprawling backward. Then she kicked at the ground as if she were kicking rocks, and stones of all sizes flew up to pelt them. They scrambled behind Rain God Rock for shelter.

Turq's body was going rigid, yet it trembled violently. He panted, making guttural sounds when he exhaled. Ruth strode toward him, malice in her eyes. Turq met her gaze with equal force.

She said, "Look like your body not like my blood. Look like much pain." Examining his foot, she added, "Especially there." Then she pounded the wound with the butt-end of the spear.

Spinning around like a little ballerina, she presented herself, saying, "Look. I fine." Her wounds had closed up and nearly disappeared.

Standing at the top of his head, she swung the spear and struck him in the face with the butt end of the spear like she was playing golf.

Turq felt something like an electric shock, a synaptic stutter as his vision blurred and went double. He felt for a moment like he was floating, and a strong impulse to sleep seemed to press on his brain from the inside. What he could see of the canyon and the witch was as if he were looking down the wrong end of a telescope; everything was small and distant. Just when he was about to surrender to the sleep, a sharp jab under his jaw roused him back to full consciousness.

"Wake up, fool," the witch hissed. She was standing over him, pressing the flint spearhead up underneath his jaw, near his throat. "Not done. We need play together, boy. Besides, I still need resurrect my beautiful son. I no see why your heart not do."

Bending down, she grabbed him by the hair and started dragging him toward some ruins a few hundred yards away.

"Father," he squeaked.

* * *

Frankie had been sitting very still, holding his wounded wrist as Zed had instructed. He sat just around the side of Rain God Rock from the men who had retreated there moments ago. They were busy trying to watch the witch, and so they missed the small "tink" sound behind them. Frankie heard it and looked. There, lying in the dirt, was Ruth's obsidian knife. He crawled to it and tucked it into his pants.

As he crept back to the Rock, the baseball started vibrating and jiggling in his pants pocket. He stood up and retrieved it. Holding it in his hands, he asked, "What d-do you want, ball?"

"Go help T."

"What?"

"T is in trouble."

"Why are y-you talking?"

"T needs help."

"H-how can this be?"

"Witch. Danger. Help your friend. Be a hero."

"But I d-don't understand . . ." He turned the ball over in his hands, examining it anew. "Y-your voice sounds f-familiar . . ."

Then the ball said, "Say my name, Frankie."

Frankie thrust the ball away from his body at arm's length, trying to stay away from *her*. Then he heard his lips betray him: "Ixtab," he said faintly.

"Again," came the whisper.

"Ixtab."

"Go, Frankie. Help your friend."

"Okay," he said, starting to run, faster and faster and faster, still holding the ball straight out in front of him. Unable to control his speed and unable to stop, he was hurt, afraid, and exhausted. Being clumsy and weak, he normally had no speed and no stamina, but today, he ran like an antelope. "Stop," he pleaded, but it was impossible; he was driven, compelled—thrust forward by Ixtab's will.

As Frankie approached Ruth, she had just beat his friend with a spear and was dragging him across the desert toward some ruins.

"Throw me," said the ball.

Huffing and puffing, he said, "W-what?"

"Throw me. To the witch."

"I c-can't throw that far," Frankie said, but the voice repeated itself, sounding very insistent and very impatient.

He stopped, set his feet the way that baseball pitchers do, closed his eyes, and threw the ball with all his might. When he opened his eyes, he saw the ball strike Ruth in the back of the head and explode in a great burst of water, drenching her and T both.

Ruth turned around. The look in her eyes passed sentence on him: "You're next."

She started towing Turq again but failed to notice that the water soaking into the ground made very strange mud: a rosy-orange color that seemed to glow even in the midmorning sun. A column of the unnatural mud rose from the ground and took the shape of a woman—a very tall, very naked woman. Mud became bronzed flesh with burning-white hair and fiery hands.

Ixtab directed a scream at Ruth.

The witch dropped Turq and slowly turned toward the source of the voice. A primal terror had sculpted Ruth's face into a mask of dread. Her hands went up into a defensive posture, and she slowly retreated, taking small steps.

Frankie said, "Oh dear. That's n-not good."

▽△▽△▽△▽△▽△▽△▽△▽

Pulling the Thorn

DECEMBER 23, 1177, ACROSS CHACO CANYON FROM CROOKED NOSE GREAT HOUSE

Chaco canyon was carved by the slow but unstoppable action of a small river. Tributaries drained into it, feeding it as it made its way toward wherever life intended. These tributaries washed significant sections of the nearby high-country down into the canyon, providing a fertile and irrigable plain for planting. Over time, the washouts grew, some of them becoming so large that they formed mini-canyons, spurring off from the mainline of the canyon. A few of these canyon spurs were secluded.

One such spur, across from *Zatu Nashtehweh Tza Bu'vah* (Crooked Nose Great House), was a veritable fortress within the canyon—a relatively narrow entrance on the canyon side, with three looming cliffs ringing it. Here is where The People penned the *quetz'al*, keeping them in one location. The space was suitable for training them using various whistles and flutes, like the bagpipe-styled *tzetoh quetz'iteh*. The bodies of freshly killed doves, which they domesticated and raised in coops, dually served as bait and reward during training.

At one time, pilgrims regularly visited the canyon, paying elaborate gifts to The People in exchange for a *quetz'al* taking their prayers directly to the gods. Now, not only did the visitors (and their trade goods) rarely come, but many of The People were actually afraid of the flyers and felt like the animals kept away good trading partners. Economically, the animals drained precious resources these days; managing them was expensive and time-consuming, drawing energy away from food production during these increasingly resource-scarce and drought-ridden days.

Quaatsa and Sheweh believed that Tuhj's open and violent rebellion would provoke other *quetz'al* into a massive revolt, threatening the very existence of The People. Gohm Thlahk had reluctantly agreed with them.

The Chacoans couldn't be responsible for unleashing ferocious animals into a world unprepared to cope with them. In times past, Mother Earth flourished enough to provide the flyers with everything they needed. Now, however, Mother struggled, and the animals could destroy themselves through their unchecked consumption of every living thing in sight. They would spread, find a new place to nest and feed, decimate that environment, and move on—a destructive cycle that would repeat until Mother Earth was barren.

Not all lives were equal; there was an order to Life, and the *quetz'al* now threatened that order. Left to their own devices, rogue flyers would quickly destroy everyone and everything around them. Under the control of The People—thanks to the *Shat'kuh Mongehweh*—their marauding, terrorizing days had come to an end. Lately, however, the return of such treacherous times was only a breath away.

The age of the *quetz'al* must end.

While Rooshth and Churl-Chaac battled for their lives, Gohm entered the *quetz'al* pen, prepared for the worst task of his life.

He watched the animals nervously grouping together, suspiciously eyeing him and those with him. Absentmindedly, he mumbled, "It could very well be that, come dawn tomorrow, no one will remain to control them."

One of his two assistants overheard. "What do you mean?"

"Oh," he said, waving the question away, "nothing. Just rambling about nonsense."

He and each assistant carried a clay pot decorated with the elaborate black-and-white geometrical images characteristic of canyon pottery. Nachtu'veh Quianteh, the lead trainer in charge of *quetz'al* care and feeding, as well as two of his own assistants joined Gohm. To the animals, Nachtu'veh's presence suggested feeding time, and when he arrived with a net full of cooing and squawking doves, the sleepy flyers became immediately alert and attentive.

"Okay," Nachtu'veh said, eyeing the hungry *quetz'al* lumbering toward them. "How do you want to do this?"

"Each animal will need to eat at least two doves," Gohm said. "Dip each dove into the jar, getting it thoroughly wet, and then toss it to the animal. We will need to spread out to reach all of them."

One of the assistant trainers started wailing, tears cutting channels across his dirt-caked face—like the Chaco River itself. The other was quietly fighting back sobs, attempting to be stoic, like the two older men. Gohm's own assistants quaked. Despite the emotional turmoil upon them all, the four younger men seemed resolute to their task.

Gohm, Nachtu'veh, and the younger men were *nin'sheh todoh*, that is, "pulling the thorn." The phrase was literally applied to having stepped on a barbed thorn: having it in was bad, pulling it out was worse, having it out was best. It was the putting down of one's family pet. It was exiling a dangerous blood relative. It was the killing of one's first antelope: exchanging the beauty and grace of one life for the nourishment and survival of another.

"Still your mind, close your heart, and do what must be done quickly," Gohm told the younger men. "You will have time later to grieve and consider the magnitude of what we do now."

To the flyers, Gohm proclaimed, "*Quetz'al*! You have honored us with your lives of devotion, commitment, and protection. We need you now to commit one last act of protection for us. We pray your mercy and trust as we ask you to protect Mother Earth from your own nature." With that, he reached his hand out to Nachtu'veh, who gave him a dove. The bait was swished around in a pot, slowly removed, and then tossed toward the outside of the gathering herd. A single tear slipped from his eye.

"Let's go," he commanded. "Let us pull the thorn. Remember: the poison does not distinguish between *quetz'al* and man. Do not splash it into your face."

The men acknowledged his warning and spread out, repeating Gohm's action over and over again. Just as they had dosed nearly every animal, a bright flash filled the sky, and the sound of thunder pounded through the canyon, startling man and beast alike.

Gohm automatically looked up. Beautiful, bright stars budded in the purple-mauve sky. "Strange," he whispered.

Nachtu'veh called to him, "What was that?" They had all stopped in their tracks, similarly scanning the skies.

"I do not know. Come. We should finish."

Quetz'al, despite their enormous size and power, feared thunderstorms. Nothing is more treacherous than lightning, hail, and wind-driven, pounding rain when one's primary mode of transportation is flying. Fear flirted with panic, scattering the creatures to look for cover near the cliffs and call out to each other in their swooping vocalizations.

The two men's groups split, each taking a different side of the spur. Nachtu'veh, on the north side of the canyon, urged his assistants to hurry after the six or so animals they hadn't yet dosed. On Gohm's side, all animals had been fed.

"We have some left," noted one of Gohm's assistants. "What do we do with it?"

Gohm thought for a second and then answered, "Double up the dose."

They started going back and giving the animals more. One of the greedy flyers came up to Gohm for a fifth dove, lowering her head and shaking it gently back and forth—their way of begging for attention or a treat. An assistant started to toss it another, but Gohm intervened.

"No. See her eyes? She has had enough." The animal's pupils were dilated, and she wobbled on her feet.

A moment later, the female beggar dropped to the ground and started twitching, her thin *quetz'al* eyelids quickly turning blue.

After another lightning flash and thunderclap, Gohm looked across the pen toward Nachtu'veh's team. A few of the animals continued to head even farther back into the canyon spur, seeking safety from the cloudless thunderstorm. "Nachtu'veh? Did you see some of the *quetz'al* going there up the spur?"

There was no reply, and he started to walk toward the men but realized that it was pointless; the three were taking turns drinking from a pot.

* * *

Like the other *quetz'al*, Naskiteh had been surprised to see the human Nachtu'veh come into their nest—especially in the early evening. The trainer had several other humans with him, including his master, Gohm, dressed in long robes. The timing of the visit, along with the presence of the master, suggested that this wasn't just a feeding call.

The master somberly spoke something apparently meaningful to the other humans. Then he took one of the treats, shoved it into a black and white jar, and gave it to Klisk'toh, who always barged her way to the front of the group, flapping her wings, cooing and shaking her head.

Greedy. Undignified, young brat, he sang quietly to himself.

The jars were the same ones used to give the flyers medicine. Naskiteh had been given medicine three times. The first was when he had been poisoned by eating a dying antelope (who had probably poisoned herself eating some toxic scrub). Another time, they made him sleep in order to mend a nasty wound from a training accident. The last time, several *quetz'al* were getting sick for no apparent reason, and the humans gave everyone medicine.

Inhaling deeply, he tried to smell today's medicine. *Hmm,* he sang. *Nothing.* It looked like none of the other flyers could detect anything either.

While Naskiteh watched Klisk'toh and all the other *quetz'al* who had been given medicine, lightning flashed across the sky, blinding him. A brief moment later, thunder pounded through the nest, echoing, rumbling, and crushing his hearing. He started moving toward the back of the spur where the cliffs could provide more shelter. Nearly blind and essentially deaf, he staggered and stumbled, making a chaotic retreat.

He felt his way to a spot at the base of a cliff face, and his hearing finally started to return. The singsong cacophony ringing through the pen announced that the herd was still together in the nest, and no one had been hurt. Friends called for friends, adults called for juveniles, and juveniles called for adults.

As his vision slowly recovered, Naskiteh searched around for Klisk'toh, eventually spotting her on the opposite side of the canyon. She was already going back for more medicine, looking a little wobbly on her feet. *Too much med-iz-uhn, Greedy One,* he sang, shaking his head.

Another blinding flash and pummeling thunder burst scattered the *quetz'al* again, but he stayed put, fighting his urge to run and flee. Before his vision returned, the faint sound of juveniles crying caught the attention of his recovering ears.

Slow step by slow step, he felt the ground with his claws and inched toward their desperate, escalating wails. As his vision improved, he was able to make out their shapes and move a little more quickly to them.

Singing calmly and gently, he tried to ease their fears: *Little ones, it is only a distant storm. This lightning will not hurt. It is far away.*

One of them moaned, *Wise one, my belly hurts.*

What do you mean?

I feel sick. I ate three.

Another one chimed in, *I dared her. I'm sorry, I didn't think—*

Three? asked Naskiteh. *That's quite a lot of med-iz-uhn.*

My head aches, and I feel dizzy, sang a third juvenile.

He tilted his head in a comforting way and sang, *This is only to make us sleep and feel better tomorrow. Tomorrow when the sun rises, how much better . . .*

Just as his eyes became fully functional again, the youngest of the children fell over, unconscious, taking rapid, shallow breaths, and quickly turning blue. Blood trickled from its nose. Then he noticed that all the juveniles were bleeding from their nostrils.

The humans can help, Naskiteh sang. *Nachtu'veh will know what to do.* Quickly spotting the trainer, he hopped-skipped-half-flew over to him. He called out, but the trainer ignored him and was drinking medicine from the pot himself.

Crying, Nachtu'veh finally pulled the jar from his lips and locked eyes with Naskiteh. After a moment, the trainer dropped the jar, which shattered upon impact, splashing liquid everywhere. Blood ran from his nose. Pivoting on one leg, he dropped to the ground unconscious, shaking violently. Foam oozed from his mouth. One assistant trainer repeated the motion exactly, but the second started vomiting blood and coughing while trying to run, but he, too, quickly succumbed.

Looking back to the juveniles with some panic in his eyes, Naskiteh gasped. Two more were on the ground, not breathing. He turned toward the master, Gohm, who was walking in his direction with the two younger assistants.

Master! Naskiteh sang out, turning to face Gohm. *Something is wrong with the med-iz-uhn.*

There was a rigid and determined expression on the humans' faces that gave him pause.

What is going on? he wondered aloud. *Do they know that it is bad? Why would they give dangerous med-iz-uhn?* An anxiety akin to heartbreak oozed within him.

Suddenly, something rumbled his chest violently, and a noise like the sound of a boulder falling on a large pile of dried bones burst from within Naskiteh's chest. He collapsed to the ground, disoriented and confused. *Couldn't be thunder again,* he tried to sing, but there was no sound in the air; his tongue flapped uselessly.

Struggling to get to his feet, he sang, *My chest,* but again, no words came out. He looked around, confused. All the *quetz'al* were on the ground now: those that weren't dead or dying rose slowly, having apparently been thrown down, like him, by the mysterious, explosive rumbling within their own chests.

As sound returned, another flyer, named Yak'ehtaa, staggered up to Naskiteh. There was pain in his eyes as he sang, *I have some fire inside me. Feels like something broke.*

Me too, sang Naskiteh.

They did this on purpose, you know.

What?

Bad med-iz-uhn. His song burned with accusation and hate. Yak'ehtaa was one of several larger, young males who hated The People.

But they care for us, sang Naskiteh.

Like slaves. The younger male tossed his head around the pen and sang, *Look: our friends and family die all around us at the hands of the humans.*

But why? That makes no sense. Still, there have been rumors that the humans grow tired of us . . . Naskiteh surveyed the death and shook his head. *No. There must have been something wrong with the med-iz-uhn.*

No, sang Yak'ehtaa. *It worked just as they planned.*

A man in a long, flowing cape was getting up off the ground and clutching at his chest. Two other humans near him seemed fine as they attended him.

Who is that? sang Naskiteh. He blinked his eyes and shook his head, trying to stimulate some distant-feeling memory to surface. *I should know who that is.*

Someone important, probably, sang Yak'ehtaa. *But who cares. Stupid humans.*

True, sang the older flyer. *I do not know why I should even care.*

Naskiteh cast his gaze back to the clutch of juveniles, all of whom lay still on the ground now. He went back to them and nudged them one at a time with his beak, but none responded.

The three humans advanced with the medicine.

Naskiteh glared at them and called to Yak'ehtaa, *They did do it. You are right.*

Faces he had known his whole life lay scattered, frozen in torment, victims of mass murder. Families, partners, and children lay huddled together in macabre sculptures of devotion and comfort. The few survivors, like him and Yak'ehtaa, surveyed the scene, looking shocked and confused.

Then with an almost audible sound, he felt something within him click into place. It was a puzzle piece fitting into his heart that he didn't know he had. It was earthy, wild, violent, and dangerous.

And he liked it.

Humans, he sang with disgust.

Murderers, sang Yak'ehtaa.

Murderers, he echoed.

Another flyer called out, *Kill.*

Naskiteh rose up on his feet, flapped his wings twice, and jumped forty or fifty feet into the air, an overwhelming feeling of power and sense of revenge completely filling him. In a moment, he was airborne. Around him, other *quetz'al* had done the same. They were all calling out in a very un-singsong voice, mourning, angry, and vengeful. Occasionally one would bellow a bone-shattering scream.

Kill. Kill. Kill, sang Naskiteh.

They all started chanting and calling it in unison, circling higher and working themselves into a fever. When the moment seemed right, Naskiteh initiated an attack on the three humans, folding his wings and diving like a flint spearhead cutting through air. The men began to run, but it was too late. He popped open his wings, a thunderous proclamation of his rage, his power, his might, his vengeance.

The caped man stopped running and turned around just as Naskiteh's outstretched talons grabbed him by the arms, ripping one off during impact. Screaming, the man dangled from Naskiteh's foot until he was flung into the side of a cliff with a satisfying crunch.

He circled back to finish off the other two men, but other flyers had followed his attack line and pounced. Little was left of the human bodies by the time he finished his circle.

Calling his army of revenge into formation, the remaining dozen or so *quetz'al* fell into position behind him. The flying phalanx left the pen and climbed higher and higher above the canyon. The Great Houses lay before them like so much free candy.

Hundreds of helpless humans were running south, to escape the canyon.

Some of them made it.

▼△▼△▼△▼△▼△▼△▼△▼△▼△▼

Shattered

DECEMBER 23, 1177, SOMEWHERE IN THE MIDDLE OF CHACO CANYON

Rooshth threw her body across the gray stone shape that had only moments ago been her son, locked in battle with the leader of the canyon warriors. Howls, moans, and wails came in waves as anger and sadness alternated, one following the other in a spiral of increasing intensity. Within a few minutes, physical exhaustion took over, and she simply lay still, sobbing quietly.

She tried to stand, but crackling sounds, like dried eggshells being crushed, gave her pause. There was a charred coating covering her skin, as if she had been burned. She probed the thin, fragile layer, but everywhere she touched—no matter how softly—dandruff-like black crust flaked away, revealing beautiful new skin: smooth, lightly tanned, and tight across firm muscles.

Still unsure about what has happening, Rooshth got to her feet with surprising speed, strength, and agility. Vigorously brushing the crusty layer away, tiny, dark flakes fell like black snow all around. Her arms, legs, stomach, neck—everything was as tight and strong as when Churl had been born. Her hands went to her face, and more black snow fell, taking with it her old revolting, wrinkly, and leathery facade. Grabbing a lock of hair, she pulled it around hopefully but frowned; the hair was thick, lush, and smooth as it had once been, but it retained its silver-white color.

Hearing footsteps approach her from behind, Rooshth turned around to look.

Tenateh stood there uncomfortably, breathless and winded but alive. The girl had lost the magic of the tongue, so Rooshth could only read her body language and emotions, which communicated plenty. Despite blood running down her left leg from somewhere up near her hip, a bruised left knee with a nasty gash revealing tendons, and what appeared to be a broken left wrist, the girl had hefted one of the warrior's spears over her head.

Rooshth almost didn't care. For a moment, death sounded warm and inviting, like a long, restful sleep.

Stepping forward suddenly, Tenateh suddenly hurled the weapon.

Her survival instinct roused, and Rooshth twisted sideways and swatted at the missile. She avoided becoming stomach-spleen shish-kabob, but the sharp flint still managed to carve a deep gash, slicing her left side as it passed her.

Tenateh fled, and Rooshth spat curses after her as the cut started burning.

Knowing it would need attention, she pulled aside her tunic and dared herself to examine the gruesome wound. The dim evening light revealed smooth, beautiful skin, unbroken and unharmed. Only a trace amount of blood outlined the site of the laceration.

It took a moment for the full meaning of the sight to sink in. She ran her hand back and forth across the place where organs should be peeking through skin. Then she explored the rest of her body. "So strong. Beautiful. Immortal."

Then she turned and fell across the statue of her fallen son, a guttural scream erupting from her soul as she pounded the stone with her fists. "Why, why, why? He could have beautiful. Strong. A god among men."

She scanned the ground. "Curse that tablet." The offending stone lay near her feet. "Damn it to the darkest corners of hell."

She kicked it, feeling some small measure of revenge as it skidded across the dirt. When it came to a stop, she chased it down and kicked it again. "You tricked me," she told the tablet.

Scanning the nearby ground, her eyes fell on the great Rain God's axe. Though nearly as large as herself, she managed to hoist it overhead and swing it down with all her might on the betrayer. Sparks and tiny bolts of lightning flew in every direction, and the deafening clang made her ears ring painfully.

She inspected the contemptuous object, but no damage could be seen.

Enraged, she re-hoisted the weapon and swung again, sending yet another shower of sparks and lightning, leaving her ears ringing even more painfully.

Still, there was no damage.

Bellowing every curse she knew in all the languages and dialects that she knew left her feeling slightly better. Over and over again, she struck the stone with the axe, yet it remained unscathed. She even created special *ad hoc* curses, but no amount of physical, emotional, or verbal abuse could harm the sacred tablet.

"Ah . . ." She smiled, shaking her finger at the tablet.

Slowly, she whispered the tablet's incantation as she raised the weapon again. The black mist reappeared, swarming both stone and weapon. As she finished the words, she brought the ax down with every ounce that her renewed strength could muster. Upon impact, a bright light filled her vision and threw her back ten feet or more. The world went silent as she landed hard upon her back.

She stumbled to her feet, elated but winded, and searched for the tablet. It was right where she had struck it, appearing unharmed. Jumping up and down and swinging her arms violently, she invented more curses.

Uttering one more curse, she kicked the stone as hard as she could.

Three equal-sized pieces went sliding across the ground separately.

This development, though the best one yet, was less than satisfactory; she wanted the thing gone—destroyed—or at the very least, unrecognizable. Had the tablet been a man, she would have beaten him until his identity was permanently hidden behind blood, bruises, and bashed bones. In a fit of anger, she hurled the three pieces in random directions one at a time, cursing them as she did so: "Go to hell! And may Ixtab devour anyone who comes looking for you!"

* * *

Half in the mortal world and half in the In-Between, Ixtab watched the angry woman pitching a fit. Since the boy was an infant, the goddess had been watching Rooshth wreck both her and the child's life. The woman had nothing, had achieved nothing. Such would be the boy's inheritance—had he lived, and she died, that is.

The goddess smiled and said quietly, "Very well, mortal. Should be fun. Your blind ambition and unrestrained behavior amuse me. But I'm not going to have any fun unless someone can find your silly tablet pieces. How could anyone find them in hell? I'm sure the Moon God won't mind if the pieces come out for a visit."

Crossing her arms over bare breasts, she said, "Looks like we'll be intersecting paths for quite some time. I fear, however, that I am going to have to restrain you one of these days."

A piece of stone tablet flew past her, escorted by a black cloud of very confused Lost Souls. They seemed to recognize her deity. Stopping, they argued amongst themselves and finally asked her for directions.

"Hell, ladies? Why, yes, I can help you with that."

*　*　*

For the fifth time, Quaatsa woke in the night. The third and fourth times had been to the sounds of loud commotion out in the courtyard of *Zatu Nashtehweh St'ah*, the lonely Great House to which they had fled. The second time had been to his nightmares; he had awoken the younger children with his screaming. The first time, it had been the popping silence.

The loud crunching-popping sound from deep within his chest awoke him instantly. His eyes popped open, and he lay there clutching his chest, otherwise paralyzed. Then a palpable silence descended on the land like an acoustic fog, lasting only moments.

The gods' words were coming true: the witch had managed to destroy the sacred tablet, creating the *Shat'kuh Mongehweh Ildah Gn'oh* (the "sacred tablet hidden in thirds"). They said she would hide its pieces in time and space, and he had to believe that this had just happened.

With the tablet destroyed, so would be The People—as the gods had also foretold. In fact, the diaspora had already begun; all night long, people were coming into this remote Great House, terrified and weary. Some carried their dead, telling of the *quetz'al* savagery and how the flyers had gorged themselves on human flesh. Their tales were horrific. Though valiant and sacrificial, Sheweh's Elites had not been able to protect The People.

This, the fifth time Quaatsa woke, it was to early morning light.

The sun began to rise, bringing morning to mourning in the courtyard: families huddled together, searched for loved ones, cried aloud for the dead and dying. His own family huddled in the tiny apartment, except for his wife, Kwi. "Probably attending someone or fetching water," he surmised aloud.

"A little more rest," he whispered, lying back down. However, just as he closed his eyes, Kwi returned.

"Look who I found," she said, presenting Tenateh hobbling in the little doorway.

He sat up in bed and pulled the blanket around himself like a tight robe. He went to her, and they hugged. She started crying, unleashing torrents. In a minute or so, she passed out, falling into him. He and Kwi carried her gently to their bedroll.

The noise woke the older children.

"Father!" they each cried, jumping up and mauling him with hugs and kisses. Relief and reorientation showed on their faces. Now that Dad was up and well, he would make everything normal again.

While they made small talk and teased each other, Kwi gave some dried bison to everyone to chew on while she ground some grain in the apartment's grinding bowl. (She had left the apartment to replace the missing kernel-crushing roller stone when she ran into Tenateh.) Kwi paused her grinding to tell Totahmaa, "Boy, fetch wood and start a fire so I can feed us."

Totahmaa had been telling Quaatsa of the white-haired woman, of getting bowled over by a *quetzal* and surviving, and of staring down Tuhj to calm him. When his mother interrupted his moment of glory with chores, the preteen rolled his shoulders forward, his eyes backward, and looked up at the ceiling. He huffed, "Mother . . ."

Quaatsa said, "Go now, my son. Our *shosh'nehti.*"

Totahmaa turned to his father, beaming at being called "young warrior." He sprung up and dashed out the door with a sense of mission and surprising speed and agility.

Kwi smiled and said, "Go help your brother, Chiyoo."

273

The girl jumped up, kissed her father on the cheek, and eagerly sped out into the morning light.

Quaatsa knelt on the floor next to his wife, helping her grind the corn. They had always made a great team. Together, they were a right and left hand, achieving *itam koyaqatsi* ("we harmonize Life"). They worked in silence, enjoying this rare moment of exquisite aloneness.

The children eventually returned with two small armloads of dried twigs and sticks—not enough fuel to keep anyone warm on this cool winter morning, but it would be enough to cook a few corn and bean cakes. They stacked the wood in the small cooking hearth with practiced hands.

"Father, it's ready," Totahmaa announced.

"No, not yet."

The boy studied the carefully arranged pile, made a few adjustments, and said, "Now?"

"No."

Again, there was carefully scrutiny of the hearth, this time by both Totahmaa and his sister. She offered a few suggestions, but he ignored them, making his own corrections.

"Now?"

"Something is missing."

"What?" The boy stared so intently at the pile of sticks and kindling it should have ignited spontaneously. "The smaller kindling is on the inside, with sticks getting larger on the outside of the stack. I even left a small opening where you can light the kindling."

"Ah, yes. That is what is missing."

"I do not . . ."

Quaatsa smiled. "The fire."

The boy was confused.

"I say any *shosh'nehti* in this house capable of staring down a *quetz'al* is capable of starting a fire."

The boy's eyes grew large, and he beamed again. "Can I?"

"Go ahead."

Totahmaa dashed to one of his mother's supply satchels. He retrieved a thin, flat piece of wood about the size of his forearm and then took out the long, slender fire drill and put its business end into one of several notches in the flat wood. Underneath the notched wood (the first piece), he placed a second flat piece of wood. Then the proud, young warrior began twisting the drill back and forth in his hands, using a palm-to-palm rubbing motion and sliding them down the shaft. He had seen this done his whole life, of course, but it wasn't as easy as it looked; it took some care to spin the drill, press down, and keep it in the small notch all at the same time. It was taking several attempts.

"Not so hard and fast yet," Quaatsa said. "Wait until you see some smoke."

"Okay," said the boy, getting back to business.

After a minute or so of successful spinning, the tiniest trickle of smoke began to rise from the notch.

"Now, go very hard and fast!"

The boy responded by doubling his concentration, spinning the drill, and pushing down hard on the shaft. In another minute, a steady stream of smoke rose from the notch.

"Now, tap the board to knock your coal out."

The boy took his weight off the notched board, lifting his knees just enough to pull the two pieces up. With a small tap, a single glowing ember the size of a dried corn kernel fell out and was caught by the second board.

"Blow gently."

Unfortunately, Totahmaa's first breath sent the tiny ember flying off the catch board and into his sister's lap.

She screamed, stood, and hopped up and down while wiping her lap.

"Hey!" the boy yelled.

"You tried to burn me."

"No, I did not."

"You did."

"Did not."

Quaatsa interjected, "Where is the fire coal now?"

The two children searched the floor and finally found it: a cool black lump sitting in the dirt.

"Oops," Quaatsa said. "You must start over."

The boy gave his sister a dark and vexed look. Then he refocused, replaced the two boards under his knees, and started again. In a short time, he produced a replacement coal and barely blew on it. He grabbed the little bird's-nest-looking bundle of kindling and let the tiny ember slide off the catch board into the "nest." After a minute or so of more barely blowing, a small bundle of flames burst to life in his hands.

"Look!"

"That is great," Quaatsa said, genuinely proud.

"Mom? See? I did it. I made fire."

"Good work, son," she said.

Suddenly, the boy yelped and dropped the bundle of fire into the stones and sticks awaiting it.

"Lesson one: blow gently on the young ember," said Quaatsa. "Lesson two: one's hands make a terrible hearth."

They all laughed, and the commotion roused Tenateh from her sleep.

Quaatsa mixed a bean paste with the freshly ground corn meal, and his wife went to the girl and asked, "How are you?"

"I hurt."

"Where."

"Everywhere. *Ep no'hmi ep ni'hmi.*" (Inside and out.)

"We have a fire now, and we are making breakfast," Kwi said. "Would you like some bison?"

"Yes. I should not be hungry, but I am."

Kwi handed her a small strip of the dried meat, saying, "You should be hungry. It is morning, and you had a very busy night." The young girl took the meat gratefully and chewed heartily.

Quaatsa slid over next to Tenateh and asked, "Were you there? Did you see what happened?"

The girl froze, chewed once or twice, but then seemed to have lost her interest in eating.

"I was there." She recounted the story: falling through the apartment floor, finding the old woman mourning, the stone bodies of Churl and Sheweh, trying to kill the woman, and the woman's destruction of the *Shat'kuh Mongehweh.*

"Three pieces?" he asked.

"Yes, *Shat'kuh Mongehweh Ildah Gn'oh.*" Her mouth smacked dryly as she talked.

"Here," said Kwi, offering some water from a dried squash ladle. "Totahmaa, take your sister and fetch more water."

Quaatsa placed the cooking stone over the fire and continued to work the corn and bean mash for the cakes while Kwi went to nurse the just-awakened baby. "What happened to the pieces?" he asked.

"She threw them in different directions."

"The People, too," Quaatsa said with a sigh. "Shattered and scattered into time and space."

"Yes. How will we find the pieces?"

"That is my task."

Tenateh looked puzzled.

He explained, "The gods told me of this. She has cursed it so that they are hidden until a full moon. We have time to plan and wait. When the moon is coming full, I will wait in the canyon and search all night."

"You have to wait? And search in the dark?"

"Yes."

"But such a task may take many such moons. Many summers even!" She looked concerned.

"Yes."

"I will help you."

He flattened out a ball of corn-bean mash and placed it onto the now hot cooking rock. Shaking his head, he coolly said, "No. It is my task, given to me by the gods."

"You need someone to help you."

"Totahmaa will help. He also has this task." Watching the slowly baking corn cake, he inquired, "Now tell me, after the witch destroyed the table, what happened?"

The girl took a breath and another sip of water from the ladle. "The *quetzal* went rogue," she said. Screwing up her face, she looked to the ceiling, pondering, searching for a better word. "No, not rogue. They were wild—like foaming coyotes with the crazy sickness: tearing at everything, sparing nothing, striking for no reason. The People were evacuating, which was wise. If they had been in their apartments . . ."

He flipped the corn cake and sighed. "What did the flyers do?"

"A few struck at people from the air, in the manner of hunting or war, while others flung themselves into the Great Houses, smashing walls and collapsing them. Many people were crushed. They say that Sheweh's surviving Elites killed one or two."

Another sip of water. "They spat fire everywhere—it was bright like day in the middle of the night. The whole of the canyon was ablaze and stank of blood and death. The screams were deafening. And the *quetz'al*'s constantly thundering wing-pops—it was maddening. Some people got so confused that they ran back into the canyon. Death was certain for them."

She cast her eyes to the floor and added, "So many Lost Souls." Then she looked to Quaatsa, saying, "I could see them. Nearly as terrified as the living."

Quaatsa exhaled deeply as he pulled one cake off the cooking rock and gave it to Chiyoo. He put on another to cook and asked, "What stopped them? The flyers, I mean. Many people seemed to survive despite the severity of the attack."

"Nothing stopped them. They got full."

Through a break in the leather cover hanging in the doorway, he could see The New People: homeless, hurting, hungry, and helpless. The weight of the future collapsed on him, and for the first time in his life, he didn't know what to do.

□ ■ □ ■ □ ■ □ ■ □ ■ □

Reunion

JUNE 21, 1938, NEAR RAIN GOD ROCK, CHACO CANYON

C. J. Blackwood, Vince Nesci, and Kenneth McKinney crouched behind Rain God Rock, taking turns at peeking out from behind it. Blackwood recognized the goddess, who had just formed out of the mud and was threatening Ruth.

"What the hell?" asked Kenneth.

"It's *Diablo*," the Vince whispered, taking off his hat and ducking behind the bolder. He knelt down, crossed himself, and began praying the Rosary.

"That's a woman. I swear, you think every damn strange thing's the gawd damn devil," said Kenneth.

Ruth had dropped the boy and tried to retreat, but in a few bounds, Ixtab had her caught up by the throat. The witch's feet flailed about, kicks falling hopelessly short of landing any strikes against her enormous assailant. After a few seconds, she went limp.

"She just pass out?" asked Kenneth.

"That would seem to be the case," said Blackwood.

All three men abruptly looked at the ground, each other, and then the surrounding countryside. The earth under their feet had begun shaking violently. Blackwood held on to Rain God Rock for stability but quickly scrambled away from it when it started humming and radiating heat.

He noticed that the earth wasn't the only thing shaking; Vince shook, sweat, and breathed in short, quick puffs. "Kenneth," he said, "take him back to your truck."

Kenneth seemed happy to have a manhood-preserving excuse to evacuate and quickly escorted his Italian friend away from the scene.

The violent quaking suddenly stopped but was followed by the sound of a hundred stones shattering at once. The noise knocked Blackwood to the ground.

The Rock emitted a groaning sound and stood up, unfolding itself into the enormous stone image of the Mayan Rain God. A human-sized chunk of stone that had been attached to it crumbled, and the animated stone deity casually brushed it away while turning its inhuman head left and right, surveying the area.

Casting fiery eyes on Blackwood, the newly formed golem bellowed a vile roar. Then it sauntered toward him slowly and ominously, a terrifying parody of a Western movie gunfight. The ground rumbled, complained, and strained under each step. When it was within two strides of him, it abruptly stopped, wheeled around, and started marching toward the witch and the goddess.

Collapsing backward on the ground, he sucked in great gulps of air and stared into the blue sky. "Well," he huffed, "that was interesting."

* * *

Ixtab held Ruth off the ground, eye-to-eye with her. "Hmm . . ." she said. "Haven't we been here before? Save your strength—or not. After all, you'll have plenty of time to rest." Smiling, she reiterated, "Plenty of time."

She relished in the terror that she saw in Ruth's eyes. The woman tugged and pulled at her grip, feeble arms quivering with the strain.

The skin around Ruth's neck slowly charred from the heat of divine hands, and tendrils of smoke rose around the witch's grimacing face. "Oh, dear," she said, wrinkling her nose. "You are starting to smell foul. I enjoy the aroma of roasting pig or goat. I do love burnt goat. But burnt human flesh just stinks—unless it's a human heart, of course. I am a goddess, after all; we have certain . . . weaknesses."

A thump-rumbling sound caught her ears, and Ixtab quickly glanced to her rear. "Do you hear that? Here, let me turn you so you can see." She pivoted slightly to allow Ruth a view of the rock creature hurrying clumsily toward them, its footfalls sending seismic pulses across the desert floor.

"Do you know who that is? You should recognize him."

Ruth started to pass out again, but Ixtab slapped her back to awareness. "No, no. You need to pay attention."

In seconds, the golem stood beside them, stone child staring at fleshy mother.

With flair and pomp, Ixtab said, "Rooshth, I present Churl, your son. I thought the two of you should be reunited. Isn't that what you wanted? I am going to let the two of you be together forever."

The stone figure went around behind Ruth, wrapping an arm around her face. With his other arm, he easily peeled her grip from Ixtab's arm and pulled her body tight against his torso, pinning her arms against her chest.

Ixtab released her grip and watched Ruth kick the creature futilely with her heels.

Smiling warmly, she said, "Aw, how sweet: mother and son together again." Then she frowned and canted her head sideways. "But it's not fitting for a mother to try to beat her son so." Wiggling her fingers at the creature's feet, it picked up a leg and wrapped it around its prisoner's legs, completely immobilizing Ruth.

"Better," said Ixtab, putting hands on hips and shifting her weight to one leg. She sighed contentedly and then wagged a finger at Ruth. "I always knew that someday I would have to restrain you. Now, have we learned our lesson? Do not meddle in the affairs of a goddess, okay?"

Ruth struggled to breathe.

"I'll take that as a yes," conceded Ixtab. "What next? Let's see."

Ixtab surveyed the area. On the ground behind the stone creature, paralyzed, lay a local Native boy. Standing behind her, looking sheepish and scared, was Frankie Yellowtail. "We have unfinished business, young man," she said to Frankie, a craving hunger twisting her face.

Turning back to Ruth, she said coldly, "Okay. Bye-bye now." With that, the features of the golem started to melt, losing identity as arm or leg or face. Rock flowed across skin, covering and crushing. Popping sounds came from shoulders and other joints as they dislocated under the pressure. In seconds, the creature had become the woman's coffin, completely encasing her.

Ixtab walked up to the stone column with its prisoner and pushed it over, sending it to the ground with an earth-shaking thud. "Oh, dear," she added. "Hope that wasn't too uncomfortable."

"Now," Ixtab said, "who first?" She wandered toward the paralyzed boy but hesitated and turned back to Frankie, saying, "I will save you for last. Say my name, Frankie." She waited, hand cupped around her ear until he whispered it faintly. "Good."

"Let's take a look at you. Ah, you are the young warrior Totahmaa Mukaama," she said to Turq. "So eager to fight The Great Witch, Rooshth. Foolish. But brave."

The boy lay still in the dirt, apparently paralyzed to some degree. She straddled him and examined the mark burned into his chest, her oversized fingers tracing the handprint with four fingers and a thumb on each side. "Oh. I know this symbol. You have the mark of your gods. How special." Kneeling in the dirt beside him, she leaned in close and smelled his face, letting her hair fall around his head and brushing the skin of his chest with her nipples. "Not yet a man." She sighed. "But you have been a boy for so long. Will you ever be a man?"

Looking deeply into his eyes, she suddenly pulled away, shocked. "You want to hurt *me*? Ha. I am not the one who cursed you with eternal life. *Your* gods did that, not me." She studied him harder and said, "And you would reject it. Amazing! You despise that which so many around you covet."

Smiling, she sat up and declared, "This is your lucky day. I have to follow certain . . . rules." A huff of disgust escaped her lips as she rolled her eyes. "According to such that I must abide by, you are too young. Furthermore, you have the poison of that witch's blood flowing through your veins. No telling what it's doing to your soul, and the thought of it turns my stomach. I expect to collect a delicious, clean soul from you someday."

Tossing long, black hair behind her with a flick of her head, she pointed a finger at him and said, "Since I am having such a good day, I shall do you an enormous favor." Bending over him again, she placed the finger on his chest and started tracing out circles around the handprint-mark. Around and around and around she went, her finger glowing hot, burning its path into his chest. The boy was immobilized, unable to cry out, but his abdomen twitched up and down in spasms as tears flowed from his eyes. The branding took several minutes.

Finally, she stopped, stood, and said benevolently, "Dear boy, you will now become a man. It will take some time, but mature, you will. Age you will not. I have drawn on you the circle of your life. So long as it is there, you live. Keep a close eye on it."

She patted her tummy and asked him, "Are you hungry? I am starved. It has been a very busy day, and I haven't eaten in a while."

Starting to stride away toward Frankie, she suddenly turned back to Turq and said, "By the way, my gift has certain . . . strings attached to it. You will be hearing from me again, so don't wander too far away."

* * *

Zed managed to get to Frankie before the goddess did. The frightened boy tried to hug him and pull on him, urging them to run from the approaching goddess. The old Native tried to comfort him. "Stay behind me. Keep me between you and her."

"I'll t-try," he said.

"Be brave, okay?"

"Again? That d-did not work out so well l-last time."

"What? Trust me, Frankie."

"Yes, sir."

"Good. Then do as I say."

On this day of High Sun, Mother Earth resonated with the power of the gods—a perfect day to restore the *Shat'kuh Mongehweh*. Magic would flow quickly and easily between heaven and Earth.

Sitting on the floor of the desert, Zed held the bottom portion of the sacred tablet between his knees and then held a single eagle feather toward the sky. Like an antenna, the sacred plumage channeled the gods' will and power through his body. With his free hand, he gently placed the middle piece of stone in position against the lower one. There was no sound, no flash of light—nothing to betray the fact that the two pieces mended; the fine crack between bottom and middle simply vanished.

Holding the two mended stone parts with his knees still and the feather aloft again, he brought the top piece down and started to slip it into its position, but a shadow passed over him. Ixtab was diving over him to get at Frankie, and one of her knees knocked him in the forehead, sending him tumbling backward. The top fragment fell to the ground, and he dropped the feather.

The goddess lay prone on Frankie's body, smothering him and extracting his soul while the boy screamed and wailed.

Zed sprang up and ran after the tossing and floating feather. As he angrily chased the plume in the mad breeze, his son crawled toward him using his arms, legs dragging behind. Whether a favorable wind, the will of the gods, or dumb luck, somehow the feather went straight to Turq, who caught it.

"Here," the boy said, extending his arm with great effort.

After grabbing the feather from his son, Zed sat down by the tablet pieces and breathed slowly. He exuded a surreal calmness despite the external chaos. His body-hairs stood on end as the magic surged through his body this time, electrifying him. Slowly and carefully, he put the final piece in position. Again, no flashy external sign, just the simple extinction of the hair's-width gap separating the final pieces.

Frankie went quiet and motionless.

Zed stood and shouted at Ixtab, "You must stop!"

Surprisingly, the goddess actually stopped. She got to her feet, covered in sweat, saliva, and dust, and wiped her mouth clean with an arm. Approaching Zed cautiously, she asked, "Do you know who I am?"

"Yes."

"Then say my name."

"That is not necessary," he replied firmly, trying to stand a little taller. "Your work is done here. Look," he said, holding up the restored tablet. "There is nothing for you to guard, nothing to protect. No need to feed on this boy's soul. Move on, away from this place."

She laughed. "Is that writing on that tablet?"

"Yes," he said. "It does not concern you."

Shaking her head, she said, "I think it does. I recognize that script. It is the language of the Witch Rooshth. How did it come to you?"

"A gift from our gods."

She looked away in thought and then turned back sourly. "Then your gods must know me."

"Indeed they do. I have been warned."

"Did they tell you what my name is?"

"I already answered that."

"But I don't believe you, Quaatsa," she said, shrinking herself to the size of a petite mortal. She walked toward him, a dangerous sexual predator homing in on prey. "Prove it to me. Say my name for me. I'd really like that."

He backed away. It was hard to tell which was tighter: his grip on the tablet or his lips pressed together to keep himself from talking.

"I think," she said, giving him a seductive smile, "that you do want to say my name."

"No!" he cried, trying to look away when she licked her lips and puckered at him. Desire for her seemed to be burning his very soul.

"Yes, you do. Go on . . ." Her voice was sweet and easy. She sashayed, rocking her hips with each step toward him. Her hair swung back and forth across her chest, alternately revealing and hiding nipples.

He froze and opened his mouth, a lamb before the slaughter, but then from behind her came a feeble voice saying, "Ixtab."

Frankie was on his feet, wobbling toward them.

"Frankie, no!" Zed exclaimed, feeling somehow released from the goddess's powerful seduction.

Ixtab turned to the boy, saying, "Frankie, my dear. Say my name again."

"Ixtab," he said. "Ixtab.

The goddess tossed Zed a gloating look.

He looked around desperately for help. His son, normally his right-hand in difficult matters, had passed out and lay face-first in the dirt, arm still outstretched where he'd given him the feather. Blackwood lay face-up in the dirt near where the stone creature had first animated. The other two Caucasians were cowering in Kenneth's truck.

A confused expression took shape on Ixtab's face. "Frankie?"

Suddenly the boy sprang forward, displaying uncharacteristic speed and agility. Ixtab turned to flee, but in her mortal form, she was smaller and slower than he. He pounced on her from behind, landing both of them in the dirt, Ixtab face-first. Straddling her, he seized her neck with one hand and pushed on her head with the other. The goddess's face was turned sideways, pressed down into soft earth.

"Oh, Frankie," she said managed to say, still sounding seductive. "Say my name again."

"Frankie!" Zed called to the boy, anguished. "Do not say her name. It gives her power over you."

Then the boy surprised them both, lifting the goddess's head and shoulders out of the dirt by a clump of her gorgeous hair and saying, "Not . . . any . . . more!" Then he slammed her head down in the dirt repeatedly. "You hurt my friend. You hurt me. You tried to hurt Mr. Moonhawk. Did you hurt Mother? Did you?"

"Frankie," Zed said, "you will only enrage her."

"Irrelevant," said Frankie.

"But . . ." started Zed.

The goddess no longer struggled; she appeared to be getting weaker.

"Observe, Mr. Moonhawk." He held up her face, her eyes fluttering closed and rolling around without focus. "See how pretty? She is the flame in a land where men are moths. Our admiration feeds her, but our rage sequesters her power. I discerned such when I fought her the first time, yet my own resolve was insufficient at that time." Pressing her face down hard back into the ground, he said, "However, I am quite resolute now. I have taken back my soul—and part of hers, too."

"You must not. Give it back," pleaded Zed.

"No. A spark of her divinity now infuses my flesh, my soul, my mind. I shall no more be weak of body nor slow of mind." With that, he jumped up in one smooth motion, looking pleased. He flexed the arm that until minutes ago had been decrepit and only mildly functional; it was in perfect condition.

The goddess lay on the ground, diminutive, drained, and harmless.

"Goddess," Zed addressed her. "You need to go. Go away from here. Return to the land of your people. There is nothing for you here."

It took a minute or so for the goddess to get to her feet, but she eventually stood, staring at the two of them for some time. Some decision went on behind her eyes, and then she said through tight lips, "You know, your boy is mine." Then she stepped forward, spun to her left, and vanished.

A lump formed in his throat.

Departure

JUNE 22, 1938, YELLOWTAIL CABIN, CHACO CANYON

Kenneth McKinney, Natasha Yellowtail, and Zed all watched Turq as he lay on the little bed in Natasha's bedroom, looking frail while he shook, shivered, and sweat. Wet rags applied to his forehead cooled his fever but did little to stem the toxin of the witch's blood. Between episodes of unconsciousness, they urged him to take fluids.

Kenneth stood. "At least let me fetch the doc," he said, frustrated.

Zed looked up from where he sat cross-legged on the foot of the bed and replied, "No. No doctor can help this. The blood of the witch has poisoned him. If there were medicine to help, do you think I would deny my own son?" Kenneth noted an uncharacteristic edge in the Native's voice.

"Can he fight the poison himself?" Natasha asked from the head of the bed, her bandaged, bullet-wounded arm healing nicely.

"Yes. The fact that he still fights is a good sign," said the boy's father.

Kenneth heard his Ford truck pull up, driver- and passenger-side doors open and close, and then footsteps sprinting up the porch steps. A moment later, Vince, Frankie, and Blackwood crowded into the tiny room, reeking of smoke and diesel fuel.

"Is done," said the Italian.

"Thank you, Vince," said Zed. "Though not a proper death ceremony for a *quetz'al*, Tuhj's spirit will be at peace knowing that coyotes and vultures will not feast on his flesh."

"*Si.* You are welcome. He was quite large. It required much diesel fuel, but no scavengers—four- or two-legged—will be bother him." Pointing a thick, calloused finger at Turq, he asked, "How about boy?"

Kenneth answered, "Like this most of the day, though he seems to be settling some. We managed to get him to drink a few sips of tea."

"Good," Vince said. "That's good, *si?*"

"Yes," answered the old Native.

"What now, Zed?" Kenneth asked.

Looking weary, the boy's father took a breath and sighed slowly. After a long pause, he said, "Now? Go home."

"What you mean?" asked the Italian.

"Our mission, given to us by the gods, was to recover this tablet. If the witch had collected all the pieces, she would do incredible damage and harm."

Kenneth shook his head. "But you said that she could not restore the tablet. And so she could not use its magic."

"Yes. But she did not know that," Zed said frankly. "She would have continued to search in vain for a solution, committing more evil and murder toward her futile end. The older she got, the more powerful she would become." Pointedly, he added, "And you know how powerful she was. Who knows? She might have actually become more powerful than the tablet itself."

"Okay," said Kenneth, "so now you'll go 'home?' I thought you two were from the canyon?"

"Yes, of course," he replied. "But now we merely live here."

Kenneth asked, "How many years since you had a home?"

"I have lost count. It becomes difficult after so long." His eyes went up and to his right, sorting memories. "I remember it was winter. I had gotten a Word from the gods. We went to convene with them, and they warned us. The witch arrived the next day . . . I think. People scattered. *Quetz'al* fled. Conquistadores came and went. Missions came and went. Whites came." He looked at them with a twinkle in his eye and said, "I do not want to be here when you leave."

"Where will you go?" asked Natasha.

"To our ancestors. We will go to be with the boy's mother, brothers, and sister."

"How?" asked Vince.

"The gods will take us," he said, smiling. Suddenly his right hand was twitching, and the strange dot-shaped scars across the back of it pulsed with gold-and-green color.

"What is the meaning of this unusual manifestation?" blurted out Frankie.

They all eyed him suspiciously.

"What?" he asked. "A legitimate question."

Vince leaned toward Natasha and quietly said, "He is doing this all morning. Talking strange."

Zed smiled at Frankie and said, "That means it is time."

Frankie looked back and forth from his mother to Turq to Zed. "Time? You have to depart? Now? Why the expedited timetable?"

"Yes. We go when called," the old Native said, wearing a measured smile.

"And Turq?" Frankie wrung his hands while raising an eyebrow.

"Yes, Frankie. He must come with me."

"Well, that is not a desirable outcome. He may stay here with me and Mother." Frankie pointed angrily at the cabin floor with his finger and said, "He will stay, and you may leave by yourself, Mr. Moonhawk."

The adults all looked down, at a loss for words in the awkward space of the moment.

Blackwood found some first: "Frankie, are you happy here at your home?"

"Yes, of course."

"What are things that make you happy about it?"

"A warm, soft bed," he said, scratching his chin. "Cakes made from cornmeal, slightly overcooked on the outside while being slightly undercooked on the inside. Tender beans made into twice-cooked *frijoles*." A proud smile grew across his face, and he added, "Mother's are the most exquisite."

"Your friend wants what you have," said Blackwood. "To be with *his* mother. Eat *her* delicious food. Sleep in his own warm bed."

"No," said the boy flatly, folding his arms across his chest. "He can stay with me. Right here."

Natasha sighed. "Frankie . . ."

"We must get to the Birthing Chamber," said Zed, clutching the back of his hand.

"The what?" asked Kenneth.

"You know it as *Casa Rinconada*. There is something like a road to heaven there. The tablet will guide us so the gods can take us home." Zed was making a horizontal circle with his hands and then lifted his right hand up and down.

"How we get boy there? Boy more asleep than awake," said Vince.

"The truck," answered Kenneth. "Let's put him in the back of the truck. With Blackwood's car, we can all get there."

"Good," said Blackwood, standing up and walking outside.

"Grab him up by the corners of the blanket," suggested Zed, unfolding himself and stepping out of the little room. Kenneth and Vince folded Turq into his blanket like a taco and carried him out of the room. Frankie and Natasha followed.

Kenneth stood next to the truck, holding his end and waiting for Blackwood to hop onto the flat bed, but Frankie got up first, leaping up in one great bound. Together, they gingerly set Turq on the wooden planks of the bed.

Vince jumped up and sat next to the boy, saying, "I ride here. Keep boy steady."

"I shall do the same," said Frankie.

"No, Frankie," said his mother. "You should stay here."

"Why?"

They all went rigid at the uncharacteristic belligerent tone of Frankie's question, but the collective tension dissipated with Natasha's quick thinking: "My arm hurts again, Big Man. I need you to help me put a fresh bandage on it."

"Then we can go?"

"We will try, okay? Right now I need you," she pleaded, looking deep into his eyes.

"Very well," he reluctantly agreed. "But let's try to hurry."

"Sure," she said noncommittally, casting the men a knowing look. "Say, Big Man. You are talking kind of funny today. Do you feel okay?" She touched the arm that had been crippled.

"I do not talk funny," Frankie said, pulling away from his mother's contact. "I do feel different today, Mother. I feel good. I feel smart. Strong."

The men waited for mother and son to enter the cabin, and then Zed literally hopped into Mr. Blackwood's T57. Kenneth climbed into the driver's seat of his truck, and they all pulled out, slowly heading for *Casa Rinconada*.

* * *

Half an hour later and five miles from the cabin, Zed, sitting in the passenger's seat, said, "Blackwood?"

"Yes?"

"Why a car? I can walk faster than this." A smirk of disgust curled his lips briefly.

"Me too. But if we go faster, the truck will bounce a great deal."

"I see. Trucks are useful for carrying big loads or many people. I still do not see the point of a car," he said matter-of-factly.

Blackwood considered something and then asked, "At this speed, how long will it take to get to where we are going?"

"At least an hour. I could get there faster on a horse."

"Yes, you've made your point," said Blackwood.

The T57 pulled up alongside the truck, and Blackwood called to Kenneth, "We're going to take a side trip. We'll meet you there in about an hour." The cowboy merchant acknowledged the message with a two-finger wave.

Gently passing the Ford, Blackwood slowly opened a space between the two vehicles.

"This is better. My horse can do this," said Zed, scratching the back of his right hand.

"How about this?" said Blackwood, smiling and winking as he threw the car into second gear, revved the engine, and popped the clutch. Tires spun, shooting dirt and gravel backward. Acceleration pressed the men back into their leather upholstery.

A turbulent wind picked up Zed's long, dark hair and danced with it. He felt elated, despite tightly gripping the seat cushion beneath him.

Blackwood beamed. "Well, what do you think now?"

"Good."

"Just good?"

"No. Very good."

"So, you understand now?"

"Indeed, Blackwood. Indeed."

The car cruised up and down the canyon, the two men quietly sharing the meditative tangent. Zed's muscles loosened as the fresh air washed over his body, bringing a mental and semispiritual cleansing of the past two days' trials. His body began to relax for the first time in a very long time. Foreboding and uncertainty had taken a toll on his psyche and his soul.

After some time, Blackwood broke the silence. "Say, Zed?"

"Yes?"

"Do you have a cigarette?"

"No, my friend. Sorry."

"Damn. Well, we better get you to your destination now," said Blackwood.

"Yes."

Casa Rinconada lay before them, a crumbling circular wall mostly buried in earth. Excavation of the sight had begun but proceeded randomly and sporadically. Archaeological teams had uncovered most of the floor, including the very place where so many ascensions to heaven had occurred centuries before.

Holding the tablet tightly, Zed carefully descended the ruined stairs leading down to the stone-paved floor of the ancient Birthing Chamber. Pointing to a little rise in the floor, he called up to Blackwood, "There is where Tuhj hatched."

Back up at ground level, Blackwood's face appeared over the ancient stone wall. "Oh?"

"The moment I looked into his eyes, there was a connection. We were bonded. I called to him in *quetz'al* song, and he burst out of his shell and waddled to me." He pointed to another spot on the floor, saying, "I stood over there and held him for a long time. Then he got hungry." Zed shook his head. "Tuhj was always hungry."

Blackwood said, "That is extraordinary."

"I wish I could have been with him when he took The Journey—to have seen the light go out as his soul departed."

"It was an honorable death."

"As he would have wanted. He—as we all do—dreaded old age. Becoming weak. Dependent."

Blackwood's head disappeared behind the wall, and Zed heard him say, "Down there. Watch out on the stairs. They're pretty decrepit."

Moments later, Blackwood followed Kenneth and Vince as they carried Turq down the old steps in the blanket-sling. They laid him carefully on the ground, avoiding any rocks or chunks of debris.

Fever finally broken, Turq was semiconscious, glancing around at the men, the sky, and the Birthing Chamber.

"Son," he said.

His boy rolled his head toward him and smiled. In the faintest whisper, he asked, "We go now? See Mother?"

"Yes." The marks on Zed's hand shimmered more brightly, and he held it up for his son to see.

Turq smiled peacefully.

"It is time," Zed announced, holding the sacred tablet tightly to his chest with his left hand. "Please," he asked the men, "prop him up in my arms so that I may carry him into the afterlife."

Turq tried to stand on his own but wobbled and started to collapse. Kenneth grabbed him under the shoulders and hoisted him up to Zed, who grabbed him firmly around the waist with his right arm. Kenneth wrapped the boy's arms around his father's neck.

Green-and-gold mist started swirling around father and son, and the two began to rise slowly. The three other men quickly stepped away.

"Thank you, gentlemen," Zed said.

They nodded.

The *Shat'kuh Mongehweh* hummed in his arm, and he closed his eyes. Turq was small and easy for Zed to carry, but as they rose, some invisible force tugged on the boy. Opening his eyes, he looked down, puzzled.

As he searched for some possible entanglement, a deep, resonant, and thunderous voice said, "Not yet."

The ground below him liquefied, and a large, naked woman rose from within it, saying, "He is mine. I have paid for him, and you cannot take him. This is the deal I made with him."

"What?"

"The boy's life belongs to me," Ixtab said coldly. "Do not try to take him away."

Suddenly, Turq started screaming as the branded circle on his chest glowed red and sizzled. As they rose higher, his agony became more intense.

Ixtab stood with hands on hips, saying matter-of-factly, "He will not survive if you try to take him from this world."

When they kept rising, her countenance changed. Pointing at him angrily, she yelled, "My slave. My property. I will burn his body and soul with the flame of my hate if you keep going. Mercilessly, without conscience, he will be utterly and excruciatingly destroyed. There will be nothing left to take into your afterlife."

Her threat was real: the burning ring on the boy's chest grew, getting deeper and wider. Turq's breath came in rapid, short bursts, emitting puffs of smoke as he exhaled. His arms and legs convulsed for a few moments, and then he went stiff, wrenched and twisted with pain, saliva foaming at his mouth.

"I am sorry, my son," Zed said. He opened his mouth, slowly releasing a moan that built in volume until it exploded out into the desert. Veins bulged in his neck and forehead. Agony twisted his face.

Then, he dropped his boy.

Kachinas

JUNE 22, 1938, CASA RINCONADA, CHACO CANYON

Vince Nesci, Kenneth McKinney, and C. J. Blackwood watched in alarm as the ascending father-son pair struggled against something unseen.

"What's wrong?" Blackwood called up.

No response came.

"Do you hear that?" he asked the other two.

"What?" asked Vince.

"I hear a woman's voice talking."

Kenneth shook his head. "I don't hear—"

Zed wailed loudly and then abruptly dropped his son.

Blackwood dove and landed under the boy, half-catching him and absorbing most of the boy's impact with his own body.

He looked up from the ground and saw Zed accelerating, ascending farther and farther into the sky, eventually becoming just a dot against bright blue. The sound of his agony rose and vanished with him. Finally, there was nothing.

"Blackwood?" said Turq. His eyes were rolling around in his head, coherence barely within his grasp. Smoke wafted from the charred circular brand across the boy's chest, like a strange loop of burnt bacon.

"Yes?"

"You can let go of me now." Smoke came from the boy's mouth as he spoke. Focus slowly seemed to return to his eyes as he took in the scene around him.

Realizing that he still held the boy in a tight hug, Blackwood released him, saying, "Sorry."

"Is this the Birthing Chamber?"

"Yes," answered Kenneth.

"And my father?"

Vince and Kenneth studied their feet.

Blackwood pointed up. "He's gone, Turq."

The boy looked up briefly and then looked at the ground. He seemed to mentally change gears several times, starting twice to say something but then remaining silent. Finally, he said, "Thanks for catching me."

"Of course. Are you injured?" Blackwood asked.

"No." The boy's chest seemed to have finished smoldering, and he gingerly fingered black flesh encircling the god's hand mark.

"Does it hurt?" asked Vince.

"A little. I have had worse."

The three men glanced at one another. Blackwood wondered aloud, "What could be worse than having your chest burned inside out?"

"Damn," said Kenneth. "What happened? Was it the witch?"

"Ixtab, the goddess."

"Oh," said the Italian. "She no goddess. Is she-devil."

"What'd she do?" asked Kenneth.

The boy looked down at his chest and traced the circle with his finger. "This," Turq said.

"What is it?" he asked.

"A black circle. When she made the mark, she said that I would grow up eventually," the boy answered. Sitting up and looking distant, he added, "Earlier, she said I was her property."

"Her property?" repeated Vince. "What does that mean?"

"Like a slave?" asked Kenneth.

"I do not know," said Turq. "She also said that when the circle faded, I would die." He stood up and brushed dirt and dust off of himself.

"Well, despite some smoke damage, you look like you're okay, T," said Kenneth.

Feeling his chest and head with his hands, the boy responded, "Yes. I am. Whatever Ixtab did to me must have purged the witch's toxins from my body." He hopped up from the ground, jumped around, and swung his arms. "I do feel better. I feel great."

All three men smiled and congratulated him, but Vince asked, "What about your father? How will you get to him? Will he come back for you?"

Turq looked up into the air and then down at the ground, trying to hide his face. "Ixtab said that I could not leave. As we went higher and higher, she burned me inside and out, threatening to roast my soul. Father had to release me to save me."

"So you're stuck here?" asked Kenneth.

A tear peeled away from the boy's eye, which he quickly wiped with the back of his hand.

"Let's get you back to the cabin," said Kenneth.

"Good idea," said Vince.

Turq fidgeted, looking uncomfortable.

"What's wrong?" Blackwood asked.

"Speak up, boy," said Vince—a little too commandingly.

"I do not think I should return," said the boy.

"But why not?" asked Kenneth. "It's your home. You can live with me or the Yellowtails. Or with someone else if you like."

Sighing, Turq said, "I am over seven hundred summers. If the goddess speaks truth, I will become a man. That might happen normally—in the next few years. But what if it takes longer?" He addressed them with surprising clarity, sounding like a wise, old man rather than a squirrelly twelve-year-old. Continuing his explanation, he said, "And once I am a man, Ixtab said that I would not grow old."

Blackwood connected the dots. "You are worried about staying here—having to explain?"

"Yes. And I have spent most of my life seeing my friends and family die around me while I carry on. I cannot continue to do that."

"What you want to do?" asked Vince.

"I think I should leave. Travel. Wander alone across the earth."

The Italian said, "How lonely. Anyway, how you do this? No one let boy travel alone. You need food, money."

Blackwood stroked his chin and rubbed his neck, surprised by what he was thinking. "Perhaps I can help." He felt like the words had popped out before they could be properly vetted.

"What do you mean?" asked Kenneth.

"I could use the company—as well as an extra pair of hands," he said, not sure he could believe what he was hearing.

"Doing what?"

"Oh . . . different things."

Turq considered the offer.

"Of course," began Blackwood, "I'd have to get the permission of my employers, but I think I can persuade them."

"Who you work for?" asked Vince.

"Let's just say I work for a nonprofit foundation."

The other two men were skeptical to the notion of Turq running off under the care of a near-stranger. They were trying to brainstorm other options.

Turq had lost interest in the conversation.

"I need a cigarette," said Blackwood, twitching his fingers restlessly. Suddenly, he blurted out, "Can you teach me how to roll cigarettes?"

The conversation between Vince and Kenneth abruptly stopped. They both looked at him, confused.

Kenneth asked, "Can who teach you to roll?"

"The boy," said Blackwood, staring hard at Turq.

"As long as you have the right leaf," answered Turq.

"Okay," Blackwood said, holding out his hand to shake on the new partnership.

The boy eyed him, shocked and confused.

"If you are willing, of course," Blackwood amended, half-withdrawing the offered hand.

"Well . . ."

"I do very specialized work, and I could use an intrepid assistant for covert ops," Blackwood said. "You would have to earn your keep. Learn quickly. Be diligent."

"I guess . . ."

Blackwood leaned forward and rested his hands on his knees, eye-to-eye with the boy. Pointedly, with a man-to-man tone, he said, "You must be sure. I cannot afford risk. Will you come work for me? Travel with me?"

Turq rubbed his elbows, stood tall, and with his hands on his hips, said, "When do we leave, Boss?"

They shook hands. Each smiling.

Blackwood wondered what he'd just done.

*   *   *

The long, mostly straight road heading south across Arizona made it easy for the yellow roadster to exceed ninety mph. The wind in their hair exhilarated the two new partners.

Turq held his hand outside the car window, letting it ride up and down on the gusts like a porpoise riding the bow wake of a yacht. Absently, he said, "I think Father was wrong about automobiles. He would have liked this."

Three comic books sat on his lap, along with a few packs of baseball cards—all courtesy of Kenneth. One rag he already knew: a Dick Tracy story that Frankie Yellowtail had read to him several times. The other two were new—at least as "new" as things got in the canyon: a three-month-old Doctor Occult story and a two-month-old Slam Bradley. He and Frankie used to argue about which comics were best. Turq preferred Doctor Occult and its magical bent, but Frankie liked the tough guys and the "coppers."

Blackwood said, "I can teach you how to read."

"Great," he said, displaying a mastery of preteen sarcasm.

"It will be . . . we'll use the comics."

He perked up slightly. "Sounds more promising than the Bible-and-cane method used by the traveling priests. They tried to teach us all Spanish a couple of hundred years ago. '*Leer esto o te quemarás en el infierno.*' What a disaster."

Blackwood laughed. "Sounds like you learned something."

"Not from them."

"Well, we'll have to discuss the Spanish Inquisition one of these days. Turq?"

"Yes?"

"Do you know anything about *kachinas*?"

"Sure. Why?"

"At Casa Grande, we'll be looking for some. I need to be able discern if they are fake or real." He scanned the horizon as he drove.

"Do you see one now?" asked Turq, searching the horizon.

"What? No. Why do you ask?"

"Well, you are looking around like you saw something."

"Oh. No, I'm merely enjoying the scenery. It's so different than what I'm used to. So dry. Rocky." He paused for a moment and then added, "A poetic, barren beauty."

"Well, this should be an easy task."

"Really?"

"Sure. A real *kachina* is terrifying. You'll need fresh underpants afterwards for sure."

Blackwood furrowed his brow. "How could a doll be so scary?"

"A doll?"

"Yes. I said we are going after some *kachinas*."

"Oh . . ." Turq said. "A child's toy? A doll?"

"Of course. What other *kachinas* could there be?"

"Well, first there are the toys—the dolls. Then there are the dancers wearing costumes. Finally," he turned in the passenger's seat to face Blackwood and in a low, serious voice said, "there are the real things: the spirit *kachinas*. Ghosts that play coyote and terrorize people. Scary stuff."

Suddenly, Blackwood was pointing behind him excitedly. "Is that one there? Coming across the desert. Look!"

Alarmed, Turq whirled around in the direction of Blackwood's finger, saying, "It is important to quickly get its color—different types of *kachinas* have different colors, which is important for assessing the threat." His eyes flipped all over the horizon, almost in a panic. "Where is it? What color was—"

Blackwood was laughing loudly.

"Oh, hardy-har-har," said Turq, sitting straight in the passenger's seat and folding his arms across his chest. "You would not be joking if there was a real one."

"I'm sure."

Turq tried to sulk but kept half-smiling.

Smiling, Blackwood said, "I got you good."

Turning his head and lifting an eyebrow, Turq said, "You *will* pay for that, you know."

"I know," said Blackwood. "Say, roll me a cigarette?"

"Sure. I will do two."

"Two?"

"One for you. One for me."

"Aren't you a little young?"

Turq laughed.

"I see your point," Blackwood said. "Why not? Roll a couple of fat ones for us."

The boy expertly produced two fat cigarettes in no time.

Taking his first drag off the cigarette, Turq futilely combed down his now-close-cropped hair with the fingers of his free hand, grooming losing to the breeze. He rubbed his scalp and the back of his shaved neck.

"Feel strange?" Blackwood asked.

"What?" the boy asked.

"Your hair."

"Yes. Sort of naked."

"Ever had it cut?"

"Oh," he said. "No. We canyon folk not understand how cut hair. Lucky hair grow slow. Only twenty-four inches after seven centuries." He rolled his eyes.

"I probably deserved that. Nice work with the Tonto voice."

"Thank you. Of course my hair's been cut before, just not ever this short," he said. "To us, long hair is good. Strong." He pumped his fist. "The mark of vitality. The sign of a great warrior."

"Attractive?" asked Blackwood, taking a drag from his cigarette, one hand on the steering wheel.

"Attractive? Attractive to what? Lice?"

"Girls."

He blushed and turned away. "I suppose, but who cares? Frankie was into girls, but I just do not get the fascination."

Laughing, Blackwood said, "You will. We're going to have to fight to keep the girls off of you in a few years."

Annoyed and blushing more, he tried to explain. "Girls are . . . are . . ."

"What?"

"I do not know how to say it in English."

"Right . . ." said Blackwood, taking his turn at sarcasm. "Most white boys your age would say that girls are gross."

"Gross?"

"Extremely undesirable—to be avoided at all possible costs."

Turq screwed up his face in a hyper-pensive manner, giving the notion proper intellectual consideration while he drew a deep breath through his cigarette. "Yes," he said conclusively, exhaling smoke. "Definitely gross."

"Clothes fit good?"

"Yes," he answered. "White boys like their clothes tight though."

Smiling, Blackwood said, "You'll adjust."

After a few minutes of riding in silence, Blackwood finished his cigarette in one deep breath. Flicking the stub out into the desert, he said, "Hmm . . ."

"What?"

"I know that your name couldn't have always been Turquoise Moonhawk."

The boy finished his cigarette, cast the stub out into the desert, and shook his head, saying, "Nope. It was a good name. Strong. Nothing like Tom or Keith or James. So weak. And how are those even interesting at all?" He snickered and repeated, "James."

"What? James isn't a boring name," said Blackwood. "So, give it up. What is your original name?"

"My full name is Totahmaa Kwi Mukaama—a proud name that sounds good."

"Certainly a mouthful," Blackwood said. "What was your father's full name?"

"Quaatsa Mukaama. They do have a nice rhythm and ring to them. Do they not?"

"What do they mean?"

He laughed a little. "Well, our name Mukaama means something like 'time hunter.' It refers to my father's old task of reading the seasons and reading the signs and Words from the gods."

"Interesting."

"Quaatsa means something like 'strong voice.' Apparently, he was a very loud infant."

Blackwood laughed. "Okay. So how about Totahmaa?"

"It . . . uh," the boy stuttered. His eyes were going misty. "I have forgotten," he lied.

"That's all right," said Blackwood. "I have no idea what my name means. The meaning of most white names is irrelevant or forgotten. In fact, most people don't even care."

Turq tried to quickly and discreetly wipe his eyes with his forearms.

Blackwood caught the motion. "You okay?"

"Sure. Just . . . some dust in my eyes." After pretending to blink something away, the boy asked, "What is your full name? Does it have ring, rhythm, and meaning?"

"My full name?" he asked. "It definitely has ring and rhythm."

"No meaning?"

"Okay. You can decide for yourself. My full name is Connal James. Connal James Blackwood. My friends usually call me C. J."

Turq smiled—his first real smile in the two days since they had left Chaco Canyon. It felt good, but guilty at the same time.

"You said, 'James,'" he answered, starting to laugh, giving up guilt.

Blackwood's mouth hung agape. "Yes. What? Why is that funny?"

"*Jay-mehz*! It means 'rabbit poop.'"

Shaking his head and laughing, Blackwood said, "Well, I guess it *does* have meaning."

About the Author

Sean M. Cordry holds a PhD in physical acoustics and has taught physics at a variety of colleges for nearly twenty years, where he has earned a reputation for being enthusiastic and creative. In addition to teaching, he holds the rank of third-degree black belt in tae kwon do; he and his wife own a successful martial arts school in beautiful East Tennessee. He is a student of Zen, and despite a degenerative muscular disease (myositis), he tries to stay in shape. One of his many talents is the ability to see and make connections between seemingly unrelated events—a talent that shines in this, his first, novel.